BLUE BLINDFOLD

LARISSA SELF

ISBN 978-1-68517-012-7 (paperback)
ISBN 978-1-68517-013-4 (digital)

Christian Faith Publishing, Inc.
832 Park Avenue
Meadville, PA 16335
www.christianfaithpublishing.com

Cover Design: Keith Silvas

Printed in the United States of America

For Dr. Doug Bennett, founder of Magdalene Hope,
thank you for the amazing work you do.

AUTHOR'S NOTES

Human trafficking is an epidemic that has spread across the globe at an unprecedented rate. While doing the research for this book, I was astounded by the amount of money being made at the expense of our children: $150 billion a year, and the overhead cost and risk for the traffickers is zero. They take our women and children at random. While our hearts break, our children are being abused, their self-worth destroyed, and at times are killed. Though the characters in this book are fiction, I based the storyline on modern-day heroes who fight every day to stop traffickers. There is an amazing group of people that have made it their life's mission to fight against such atrocities, Magdalene Hope (magdalenehope.org), V4CR (Vets for Child Rescue, vets4childrescue.org), and Rebecca Bender (rebeccabender.org) are three such notable organizations.

The Lord has made them the covenant for the weak and oppressed: "I am the LORD. I have called you for a righteous purpose, and I will hold you by your hand. I will watch over you, and I will appoint you to be a covenant for the people and a light to the nations, in order to open blind eyes to bring out prisoners from the dungeon, and those sitting in darkness from the prison house" (Isaiah 42:6–7 CSB). I hope you'll check them out and give them your support as it's our children who are at risk. *Help stop slavery— end human trafficking.*

—Larissa Self

A word from one on the front line:

Human trafficking is the second fast-est-growing crime in America. By the time you read this book, it may rank number one. This needs to stop. Please become a voice for the voiceless and help put an end to this growing epidemic. You have the power to stop traffickers from exploiting those most vulnerable. Whether it's by making people aware, assisting victims to freedom, giving jobs to survivors, donating to organization on the frontline, supporting NGOs (non-governmental organizations) who run safe houses, writing articles, or books to highlight this injustice as my friend Larissa Self has done. God did not create us to be bought and sold as products off a shelf. He created us in His image, to love and care for one another.

Dr. Doug Bennett, DDiv.
Founder of Magdalene Hope

If you or someone you know is being trafficked, you can call in an anonymous tip for immediate help to The National Human Trafficking Hotline in the United States: 1(888)373-7888.

ACKNOWLEDGMENTS

Our world is filled with so many broken souls, but none more prevalent than those trafficked. May God's mighty hand shield you and protect you. *"So do not fear, for I am with you; do not be dismayed, for I am your God. I will strengthen you and help you; I will hold you up with my righteous hand"* (Isaiah 41:10 NIV).

My love and thanks to Jesus Christ, my Lord and Savior, who gives all life meaning. Thank you for opening my eyes.

To my husband David, who has supported my endeavors from the beginning. You're the best husband a woman could ask for; I love you dearly. To my children, Deysi and her husband, Glen; Lindsey; Kato and her husband, Conner; and Daniel, I love each of you so much and thank God for you every day.

To my mother, Ann, for all her support and love.

Thank you, Sandy Armstrong, for editing all my manuscripts thus far. For your honesty and friendship over the years. There are no words to express what a tremendous blessing you have been in my life.

I have been incredibly blessed, and my life enriched because of these women: Sheri Bryant, Tami Foshee, Shannon Lassetter, Margaret Schulz, Carrie Prestage, Brandi Pyle, and Susan Rolfsen—you ladies are beyond amazing! You have made this writing journey fun. Thank you for your support, encouragement, and suggestion. I couldn't have done it without you.

To Jenny Estes and Gay Chambers, what can I say, I was terrified to join a critique group, but you made it fun. Your guidance and suggestions have helped me to be a better writer. I value our friendship and thank God for bringing us together.

Coffee Girls…you ladies keep me sane. I loved meeting you for our early morning coffees, and even now, though I've moved, you still include me via FaceTime. I love and miss you dearly, Annette Cotterell, Tami Foshee, and Shannon Lassetter.

Keith Silvas, my web guy (I love the fact I have one) and the amazing cover artist to this book series, thank you for all that you've done for me. It has been such an honor to work with you, read your book, listen to your amazing podcast, and share your art. Can't wait to see the next cover to this series. You can find Keith at www.keithsilvas.com.

Finally, to the man of the hour, Dr. Doug Bennett, thank you for doing what you do to help women get off the streets and into a better life. You, sir, are a rare breed. May the Lord bless you in all that you do. My life has been enhanced from simply knowing you. God bless.

CHAPTER 1

We, as a society, can no longer think of slavery as something from our past. We may have changed its name to Human Trafficking, but make no mistake, slavery is alive and well, and is a global money-making business. The statistics are astounding. The International Labor Organization and the US Department of Labor agree, there are about 40 million victims of human trafficking worldwide, and 75% of those are women and young girls. Human trafficking is a $150 billion a year business that does not discriminate. Though Asia is the most lucrative for human traffickers, Europe comes in at a close second…this, I'm afraid, includes Ireland. The Anti-Human Trafficking Unit, along with the Anti-Human Trafficking Task Force, will work in conjunction with the Garda Síochána to eradicate all such practices from Ireland.

—Kate Walsh, Director of AHTU
Blue Blindfold Campaign, 2016
Dublin, Ireland

Present Day

Clay's body slammed hard against the side of the trunk when the car skidded to a stop. He heard men's voices but couldn't distinguish between them. When the trunk's lid popped open, he saw his assailants, Craig and Allister, and a third man he didn't recognize.

"Aye, lads, dump 'im here and let's be off," Allister ordered. "Gallagher has another job for us in the mornin', and we've three hours ta get back ta Dublin. And the boss isn't ta know about this. Are we clear?"

"Yeah," Craig answered. "Anyway, the Yank won't be a bother to us anymore."

Fwoosh! blew from Clay's mouth when Craig's boot plowed into his gut.

Positive another kick was coming, Clay curled into a ball. Instead, he heard the car doors slam shut. Rocks and dirt from the road pelted his face as it sped off. He lifted his arm to shield his eyes from the debris but wasn't fast enough. Coughing up blood and dirt sent a sharp pain through his midsection, forcing him to roll onto his back, where he stayed.

Great, now what? Clay thought as he sank into the soft grass, easing some of his discomfort.

The physical abuse he had just endured left him exhausted, both tangibly and mentally. Unable to do anything, Clay looked straight up into the night sky. "Wow," he whispered. The vast starry dome above him momentarily took his mind off his quandary.

Stargazing from his home in California looked nothing like this. Pollution, along with Fresno's city lights, prevented the starlit sky from being experienced the way he was experiencing it now. In awe of its beauty, another "wow" passed through his lips.

As mesmerizing as the stars were, he needed to get up. With what strength he had left, he pushed off with one hand, forcing his body to roll over onto his side. His mind screamed, *Augh!* Not able to handle the pain, he collapsed onto his back.

"Ah, geez. A broken rib. Maybe two."

The constant pounding in Clay's head made it impossible for him to relax. The cold breeze and damp grass beneath him only added to his misery and caused his teeth to chatter. Then a stupid thought came to mind—an old saying: "beneath a blanket of stars." A chuckle rumbled in his throat at the ridiculous thought that stars looked like a blanket. They supplied no warmth at all. *Great! I'm going to freeze to death.*

Unable to move, he pleaded, "I need a small favor, God. I'm no help to Kayla like this. If you wouldn't mind sending a little help this way"—*cough!*—"I would be forever in your debt." *Cough, cough!*

Despite the cold, Clay was grateful Allister and his thugs had thrown him on the side of the road, out of harm's way. As he lay motionless, his eyes fluttered in a slow rhythmic gesture, until he could no longer stay awake. "Dying in my sleep might be a good thing," he mumbled just before he passed out.

*   *   *   *   *

Something or someone tugged on Clay's arm, trying to do what, he wasn't sure. He just wanted to sleep. A man's raspy voice and broken English confused him. *What's he saying?* The words finally broke through Clay's groggy mind, but opening his eyes and mouth was a challenge. His cracked, dried lips had fused together and wouldn't allow him to speak. A hard yank on his right arm, caused his eyes and mouth to fly wide open with a screeching, "Yeow-ouch! Ah, geez. Easy, buddy. I think my ribs are broken."

A slight and significantly older gentleman still held his arm, saying, "Eh, sorry about that, laddie. You're near frozen. Come on then, let's get ya up."

The man's small stature was no match for Clay's weight and size. While the man pulled on his right arm, Clay pushed off with his left. "Whoa," he said while holding on to the man for stability. "Give me a second. Everything's spinning."

"Oh, aye. No rush. I'm Ian."

"Uh, I'm Clay Warner."

"It's good ta meet ya, Clay."

"Believe me, the pleasure's all mine. I didn't think anyone would find me and I'd just rot here. Thanks for stopping."

"Ah, no, laddie. I travel this road ta town near every mornin'. You'd be hard ta miss."

Scanning his surroundings while holding his left arm over his ribs, Clay saw nothing but countryside. "Huh. Who knew?"

Physically, Clay's body emulated how he felt—terrible. His damp, sandy blond hair stuck to his swollen face with crusted blood and dirt around his swollen lips. He wiped his hand across his mouth, hoping to clean some of it off but only made it worse. With no saliva to spit, he dug his finger inside his mouth and pulled out a tiny pebble and dropped it on the ground.

Ian scratched the top of his head. Clay was sure he had questions and half expected the first one to be "How d'you end up here?" Instead it was, "Have ya ever experienced the wrath of an Irish woman, laddie? Never ya mind, boy, ya will soon enough. The wife awaits, and she'll be none too pleased ta see the mess yer in."

Only one side of Clay's mouth curled up. "So does she attack verbally or physically?"

"Aye, ya sound as if ya've met her before." Ian laughed. "Come on. Let's get ya ta the car."

Still woozy, Clay stumbled over to Ian's old Fiat. He laughed under his breath at the trouble he had gotten himself into. He was alive and, at the moment, feeling parts of his body he had never felt before. He held on to the side of the car and groaned while he waited for Ian to open the door. Before he got in, Ian removed a bag from the front seat then leaned it back and helped Clay in.

"Easy does it. You okay, boy? Yer a bit big for the car, but home is just up the road."

"Yeah, I'm great, thanks."

Once settled, Clay took in a deep breath. Intense pain shot across his midsection, and he grabbed his side. *Ah, geez, that hurt.* He inhaled with more caution the next time and forced his mind off his pain by taking a mental inventory of his belongings. The only possessions he had with him in Ireland were a credit card, a backpack (that he no longer had, thanks to Allister and his henchmen), and his wallet.

He had taken every precaution when preparing for this trip. Knowing he needed to travel light, he only took what would fit in his backpack. Clay had packed five T-shirts, two pairs of jeans, and socks and underwear. He traveled in his cargo pants because of the extra pockets. At the last minute, he decided not to take his travel kit. Whatever he needed; Clay knew he could buy once he arrived in Ireland.

Having gone to the bank prior to leaving California, Clay had ordered a thousand dollars' worth of euros, so he'd have some cash on hand. Worried that his credit card might get lost or stolen, he put a limit of three thousand dollars on it. He found that amusing. *I'm the one who got stolen and lost.*

He had roughly fifteen hundred dollars left on the card after buying his airline ticket. With that and the cash he carried, he knew he had enough money for a few nights in a hotel. Another smile crept across his face when he remembered the cash. He had stashed most of it in the bottom of his shoe that still pressed against his foot, and he muttered a thankful, *whew.*

"You'll not die today, boy," Ian said as he got in the driver's side and started the engine. "Just a bit of road between us and home."

Ian patted Clay's leg right before he felt the car lurch forward. Pain shot through him again, but this time, he held back the urge to cry out. Being scrunched up in the front seat of the compact car was uncomfortable, but he refused to complain. Especially when Ian had been kind enough to stop and help.

The car bounced and swerved down the narrow dirt road as it dipped and shot up like a rollercoaster. Clay couldn't see anything until the car suddenly topped the hill and dropped again, heading down a slight incline. A gray stone house stood out in the open with a dilapidated wooden chicken coop next to it. Several chickens ran around freely but had enough sense to hop out of the way when Ian pulled up in front of the house and parked.

"I'll help ya if ya've a mind to wait," Ian said before he exited the car. He scurried around to the other side and offered his hand. As Clay struggled to get out, Ian yelled, "Oi, Mary, we've a visitor!" Then to his guest, in a more subdued tone, he offered, "Here ya go, laddie. That's it, easy does it. Mary!"

The front door opened, and an older woman, small in both height and size, stood with her hands on her hips, scowling. "What's all the ruckus about? I've no time for this, Ian!"

"We've a visitor."

"Oh my!" Mary gasped. "What's happened, Ian? Did ya run the lad over with yer car?"

"Auch, no. He's been beaten and dumped on the side of the road is all."

"Is all?"

"I'm sorry, ma'am. I asked too many questions about my sister, and these guys took offense to it. Next thing I know, I'm in the alley behind a bar, having the living daylights beat out of me." *Wait! My wallet.* Clay panicked for a split second and patted his front pockets. *Whew! They didn't take it.*

"Oh my."

"Yeah…sorry…um, listen, I don't want to be any trouble. Maybe I could use your phone?"

"You know someone here, do ya?" she asked.

"I don't know where *here* is," he answered with a slight grin. "But no, I'm in Ireland looking for my sister. She came here with some friends after her college graduation. Her friends came home. She didn't."

"We're 'bout thirty-five minutes north of Cork," Ian explained.

"Oh, I'm sorry for ya, boy," Mary said. "That's rotten, that is. Yer ma must be crazy with grief."

Leaning against the car, Clay managed, "Um, no, my parents died a few years ago in a car accident. It's just Kayla and me."

Ian's expression went from apathy to sympathy. "Oh, I'm sorry ta hear it, laddie."

Not meaning to tell his entire life story, he stayed focused on Kayla. "Thanks. This trip was a gift from my folks. They set the money aside for my sister before they died. They wanted to make her dream of coming to Ireland a reality. I thought nothing would happen to her here, but"—he let out a weary breath—"I guess I was wrong."

Watching the couple exchange looks, Clay realized he had done what he hadn't intended to do—made them feel sorry for him. He glanced at Mary and could see her eyes had moistened. Her husband put his arm around her and offered, "No need ta call anyone, laddie. You'll stay with me and the missus. Right, Mary?"

"Oh, aye," she agreed. "Inside with the both of ya. I've the kettle on. That should warm ya up."

"Right, in we go."

"Thanks, but I don't want to be a bother."

"Auch, no, laddie, no bother. Not a bother at all."

Having Ian help him inside the house was awkward. The older man, significantly shorter, struggled to get into a position that would be helpful. Once indoors, Clay used the wall to hold himself up, releasing his host from the responsibility.

Ian rushed down a short hall that led to a small sitting room. He picked up a few odds and ends then removed a newspaper from the chair nearest the fireplace and dropped it on the floor. "Sit here. The fire will thaw ya soon enough."

Clay felt terrible for all the fuss he was causing but did as Ian asked. He shuffled over to the worn chair and sat down. The heat radiating from the fireplace warmed him immediately, and he was grateful to be indoors and out of the cold. "This is great, thanks. And thanks again for stopping to help me."

"A good word never broke a tooth."

"I'm sorry, what?"

There was a soft chuckle in Ian's voice when he explained, "It's an Irish saying, 'Show others kindness and kindness is always returned.' Ya owe me no thanks."

Mary hurried into the room, set a tray down on a table next to Clay, and handed him a cup of hot tea. "Cream and sugar? A biscuit?"

"Eh, yeah, sure." Clay didn't have the heart to tell her he didn't like hot tea. He took a sip and nodded. "This is great. Thank you."

Mary's brows drew closer together with the slight tilt of her head. She wiped her hands on her apron and took a seat next to her husband. Each eyed him with concern. Clay hurt too much to squirm, so he did the only thing he could and smiled. Realizing the couple wanted more than his dazzling pearly whites, he asked, "Um, do you have a phone? If you don't mind, I have a number the bartender gave me to call if I got in a bind. I think this would fall under that category."

"Oh, aye, we do," Mary answered. "There's plenty of time for that, boy. Rest a wee bit, then ya might have a wash. Ya've a bit of a stench about ya."

Clay lifted his collar with his left hand and sniffed. He reeked of beer and something else, something he hoped wasn't what he thought it was. "Sorry, I don't drink, and I don't normally urinate on myself. The guys that attacked me must have doused me in both."

Her nose crinkled. "Oh, never ya mind. Go on, Ian, help the boy up. When yer settled, give me yer clothes and I'll wash 'em for ya."

"Mary, give him a minute ta rest."

"Actually, Ian, I think I would like to get cleaned up if you don't mind. The smell is getting to me. I'm sorry, Mary, I should have introduced myself, I'm Clay."

"Well, then, Clay it is."

"Do ya think ya can manage the stairs? Ya've a bit of a climb."

Ian stood and led Clay to the kitchen and pointed to the house phone. After the call, Ian took him upstairs. At the top of the staircase, was a large, open area with several closed doors lining its walls. Ian went to the door at the far end and opened it.

The spacious bathroom had a free-standing tub next to the window and had an old shower curtain that hung from the ceiling above it. The sink and toilet were next to one another, on the opposite side, giving anyone taking a shower plenty of room to get in and out. Towels hung on a rack that was easily accessible from the bathtub.

Ian examined the bathroom and gave his grunt of approval. "It's as it should be, laddie. Towels are clean, and I'll see if the missus has a spare toothbrush. Now strip down, boy, and I'll take yer clothes ta Mary." Ian waved his hand in an up and down motion, indicating he wanted all of Clay's clothes, and he intended to have them now.

As ordered, Clay lifted his shirt. When he did, pain shot across his right side, stopping him from completing the task. He blew air from his mouth, trying his best not to cry out. Ian must have seen his discomfort and gave him a hand. He gagged at the sight of Clay's battered, black and blue body.

"Where d'ya say the attack took place? Didn't ya say behind a pub? Yer back is sliced ta bits."

Clay turned his head, struggling to see what Ian was talking about. With pain lashing out at him, he groaned and faced forward again. "Yeah, in the bar's back alley." Then, remembering some events that had taken place the night before, he added, "I was on the ground for most of it. I think I might have landed on some broken glass when I went down."

"Aye, I'd say ya did. I canna see anythin'. My eyes aren't what they used ta be. Mary should have a look after ya've washed," Ian advised. "Yer a big lad, and I've no clothes ta fit ya. I've a friend about yer size. I'll give him a ring and see if he can spare a few things."

"Thanks, Ian. All my stuff was in my backpack, including my passport." At the mention of his passport, Clay's shoulders and head slumped. *Awe, man, that's not good.* That would be a problem he would have to solve later; for now, his only concern was his sister. Anything else he'd worry about later. All he wanted to do now was find Kayla.

Ian eyed the young American. "Not ta worry, ya've a life, and that's what's important. Yer sister has a chance because yer alive. Material things can be replaced, remember that, laddie." Without waiting for Clay to comment, Ian left the bathroom.

Transfixed on the closed door, Clay took in slow methodical breaths, hoping to control all the raw emotions he was feeling. Ian was right. He could replace everything he'd lost, but Kayla needed him alive. His plan so far wasn't working. Clay scoffed at himself. "What plan? I don't have one. I need help or I'm never going to find her."

Before he left California, he had convinced himself he could find his sister alone. Reality had given him a hard punch to the gut, literally. He needed help. Though grateful Ian had allowed him to call the number the bartender had given him, Clay still didn't know what to do.

The guy at the bar felt sorry for him and had insisted he call his buddy. Actually, the man had been adamant that whoever he left the message for could help. Clay hoped he was right. A computerized voice had answered his call, telling him to leave a message. Frustrated that he hadn't spoken to anyone, Clay prayed that he'd get a quick call back. Until then, he needed to focus on the task at hand.

Stepping into the tub, he twisted the faucet handle without thinking and a blast of ice-cold water shot out at him. His body recoiled. Pain pierced his side as he reached over and turned on the hot water. He tucked his body in at the far end of the bathtub until he felt the temperature change to warm. Satisfied, he stepped under the shower nozzle with his head tilted so he could wet his hair.

The water, oddly enough, felt good trickling down his battered body. He stood under it for quite some time before attempting to wash. With a small cloth he had covered in soap, Clay began the arduous task of cleaning everywhere he could reach without causing himself too much pain. When he rinsed, he took his time and let the water flow over his back and then gave the same time to his face and chest.

A knock on the door interrupted his lingering. He turned both handles off at the same time and grabbed a towel. "Yeah, give me a second."

"I've the clothes I promised ya. I've set 'em at the door. When yer done, Mary has food for ya."

"Thank you, Ian."

Clay stepped out of the shower and dried off. Wrapping the towel around his waist, he opened the door and found the clothes folded in a neat pile on the floor. He bent over to pick them up and quickly shot upright, crying out, "Augh!" Holding on to the door frame, he caught his breath. Then, putting a little more thought into it, he knelt down with his back straight, grabbed the clothes with his free hand, and stood. He released a loud puff of air when he did.

Not able to move right away, he held onto the door. "Ah, geez, that hurt." Then, backing into the bathroom, he closed the door, and set the clothes on the sink. "Okay, let see if I can get these on by myself."

With the exception of his socks and shoes, Clay got dressed. Those he would need help with. Before he went downstairs, he took a moment to examine his face in the mirror. A nasty cut over his left eyebrow needed stitches. Another deep gash next to his right ear could be problematic, but the tiny cuts on his chin he could take care of himself. His right eye had different shades of purple speckled throughout the red that encompassed it. He would have a nice shiner in another hour or so.

Checking the bathroom one last time, Clay grabbed his socks and shoes and headed downstairs. When he went into the kitchen, he found another man leaning against the counter, holding a hot cup of something. Hot tea, he guessed.

"Well, you're a right mess, aren't you? I'm Stewart, Ian's neighbor."

The two men shook hands. "Clay Warner."

"You're American?"

"Yeah. I'm from Fresno, California. I'm guessing I owe you my thanks for the clothes?"

"Aye, sorry they're a bit worn, but ripped jeans are in, are they not?"

Grateful just to have clean clothes, Clay answered, "To some they are. Thank you."

"You've a nasty gash over your eye. I'll take you around to Emer to get you tended to. Thanks, Mary, for the tea. Come on then."

The surprised expression on Clay's face made Ian chuckle. "Ya need a wee bit of help with the socks and shoes then, eh?"

"Yeah, sorry. I think I have a broken rib...maybe two."

Mary motioned for Clay to take a seat at the kitchen table. He did as she asked and said, "Thanks. I really appreciate your help."

"Not a bother at all, there ya go."

"So this Emer guy, is he the local doctor?" Clay asked.

Both men laughed out loud. Though Mary didn't share her thoughts outright, her eyes gave away the fact that she found his question to be funny too.

"Aye, boy, somethin' like that," Ian answered, walking out of the kitchen, chuckling.

*   *   *   *   *

Though the village seemed small, it was large enough to have two gas stations. The narrow main road through town had people walking or riding bikes to work. Stores were in the process of opening. Shopkeepers waved to friends as they passed by or stopped to have a quick chat before their day began.

Stewart drove all the way through town before he turned onto another narrow road with a cluster of houses on either side. None of them looked like a doctor's office. Stewart parked the car in front of a house at the far end of the road. There was an old bicycle with a basket hanging from its handlebars, leaning against the wall next to the front door. Inside the basket was a large raw fish wrapped in brown paper with its tail dangling over the side.

The men heard shouting when they got out of the vehicle. Clay and Stewart eyed one another, but before they could move toward the door, it flew open, and an older woman stormed outside in a huff. Not noticing either man, she spun around, bellowing, "Yer no match for Doc Doyle, Emer! No manners at all! Stupid, stupid, stupid!" The woman climbed onto her bike and peddled off, all the while yelling obscenities. The woman's age didn't hinder her speed, and she disappeared before either man realized.

Stewart's lips parted, forming a goofy grin. "Eh, yeah, the doc has a bit of a temper, but will fix you right up."

Clay hesitated for a moment before he followed Stewart toward the door. Neither was in a hurry to come face-to-face with whoever caused the last patient to leave in a fit of rage. Stewart casually walked in, but Clay was more cautious and peeked in first. The receptionist greeted them. Clay stepped inside and shut the door then wondered if he should have left it open just in case he needed to make a quick exit.

The young woman behind the desk asked them to take a seat. She was on the phone scheduling an appointment with another patient. When she hung up the receiver, she looked over at Stewart and Clay with welcoming eyes. The sudden shock of seeing Clay's battered face changed her pleasant expression to a serious one. She stood so fast that her chair spun around several times before she made it to the doctor's office. Once inside, she slammed the door shut, jarring Clay's nerves. Then, just as fast, the door flew open, and the young woman rushed into the waiting area, stepped to one side, and motioned for Clay to go in.

Clay glanced over at Stewart, who flashed another cheesy grin at him. "This one you do alone. Not to worry, you'll not die. Maybe a good tongue lashing, but nothing more."

"Hurry, would you! I've not got all day" came a female voice from inside the doctor's office.

"Go on, lad, she'll not kill you."

"You keep saying that. Now I'm worried."

Stewart laughed and gave a quick nod toward the doctor's examining room. Clay got up from his seat and, in two strides, was at the door. His body took up the entire door frame, and he had to duck his head so he wouldn't hit it when he stepped through. Seeing a woman with her back to him, he cleared his throat to let her know he was there.

"Well, come in! I've not got all day. What can I do for you?" the doctor asked before she turned around.

Instead of the cantankerous old man that Clay had expected, he found the doctor to be a beautiful, young woman. There was nothing grouchy about her at all. She was gorgeous. Taller than most Irish women, her skin was pale and smooth, and thick, dark brown hair cascaded to her shoulders. Her eyes were a stunning blue that jumped out at him.

Completely dumbfounded by her appearance, Clay stared at her for a moment before he blurted out, "You're not a guy." Fully aware of how stupid he sounded, he muttered, "Um…sorry…um…"

"Nothing gets by you, does it?"

"What? No…I'm sorry, I didn't mean any—"

"A fight, no less. Sit!"

The doctor's bad temper Steward had warned him about was flaring, and he stammered, "Uh…"

"Men and their oversized egos!"

"Eh, not exactly."

"You're going to tell me you weren't in a fight?"

"Well, no, I was, but—"

"Well, then you deserve this. Take a seat," the doctor ordered.

Growing more frustrated, he explained, "Um, I'm Clay Warner. I'm in Ireland searching for my sister. I went to the last place she had been seen. It was at a bar… I mean a pub, and these guys didn't like the questions I asked." With his right hand, he did a circular motion around his face. "And this is what I get for asking about her."

The doctor studied him for a few seconds as if deciding whether she should believe him. She said nothing when she reached for the needle. Then her expression softened. "This will hurt, but I like to offer my patients the choice of numbing. Some decline."

His lips formed a childlike grin as he sat down. "I'm a big baby, so please numb away."

"I'm Dr. Emer O'Farrell. I'm sorry about your sister. Do you know what happened?"

Clay's shoulders sank when he thought about the answer to her question. Then just as fast, shot upright from the pain, sucking in air as he did.

"You're hurt a little more than you're letting on, aren't you?" She put the syringe on the tray and wheeled it over to the examining table. "Please stand up and take off your clothes."

"But we've just met, Doc," he joked through clenched teeth.

"You think I've never heard that one before? Now get a move on. I've—"

"I know. You don't have all day. I got it."

Once he took off his shoes and stripped down to his boxers, Clay sat down on the examining table. Emer offered him some support when he lay down. Then she grasped a lever on the side of the table and raised the footrest to help support his long legs.

While Emer examined Clay, her fingers slid along his side, pressing ever so lightly. She seemed at times to caress his body more than examine it. Not sure if he should make a joke about it to her, he said nothing. Then seeing the doctor smile while her fingertips glided over his stomach made him feel uncomfortable. He opened his mouth to say something when she said, "You have very nice skin and wonderful muscles."

Clay wasn't sure who was more horrified by her comment, him or her. The stupid look he had had on his face earlier when he first saw her, was the same expression she now had. Then he felt her fingers press hard into his side. "Yeow-ouch!"

Her hands slipped off him and dropped. "Sorry."

Surprised by how forceful she was, he said through gritted teeth, "Do you always talk about your patients like that when you examine them?"

He could tell her blunder embarrassed her, but she resumed with the examination. She moved her fingers down the other side of his body and pressed hard against his ribs, causing him to wince.

"You misunderstood, you Yanks always do. You've two broken ribs. No more exercise for a few months."

"I didn't come to Ireland to exercise."

"No, I guess you haven't. Do you know what happened to your sister?"

"No. Only that she was at a bar... I mean a pub, with some friends. They went back to the hotel, and she didn't. She met some local guy who invited her to a party and went with him instead. When her friends couldn't find her, they filed a missing person's report with the police and then had to go home."

"I know what a bar is, so no need to correct yourself. How long ago?"

"Yeah, well, you would be the first. Everyone looks at me like I'm an idiot for not understanding Irish slang," he griped. Then, remembering her question, he answered, "She's been missing for ten days."

"You'll feel a bit of a prick, then you shouldn't feel anything." Emer had the needle in his skin, near his eye, before he could protest. He jerked when the needle went in. "You okay?"

"Geez. A little aggressive there, aren't you, Doc?"

"Don't know what you mean. Do I need to be gentle with you? You're a big boy. I'm sure you can handle a tiny prick."

"Well, even a small amount of compassion would be nice."

"You've come to the wrong place for that. But if it's a wee bit of compassion you need, if you feel anything, let me know, and I'll give you another prick to numb the area better."

"I think you'd enjoy it too much," he said, only half joking.

Her mouth curled on one side as she held up the needle, so he could see it. Clay swallowed and hoped he wouldn't need another shot. Emer pushed the needle through his skin without a second thought and stitched him up.

As soon as she finished with the wound over his left eye, she checked the cut near his right ear. "This doesn't need stitches. Just a good cleaning and tape should do." Once she had it cleaned and taped up, she asked him to sit up. She moved around the table to get a better look at his back. Clay could feel her fingers once again slide over his skin. This time, her touch was soothing.

"There are pieces of broken glass in your back. If it hurts when I pull the shards out, I can give you another prick to numb the area."

Clay grinned. He could tell from her voice she was teasing him. "No, just pull them out."

The first time the tweezers dug into Clay's skin, his body shuddered, and he wished he hadn't been so fast to wave off numbing the area first, but he let her continue without a break. It took several minutes before Emer had finished removing all the tiny fragments of glass from his back. "All done." Then something cold and wet touched his skin, making him flinch. "You can handle me digging the shards out, but not the iodine?"

"Sorry. I wasn't expecting it. It's cold."

"A few cuts need to be taped up. Almost done."

When she finished, Emer brought the tray with the pieces of glass and set it on the counter next to him. "Wow, that's a lot. All I could feel were my ribs. I didn't even notice my back. Thanks, Doc."

She ignored his comment. "I'm going to wrap your ribs, but there's nothing more I can do for them. You need to rest and let them—"

The door flew open with Stewart standing in the doorway. "Typical, Emer! You got the man down to his kex. Or should I say, my kex."

"Stewart! I'm not done with my examination. What's the matter with you, barging in here like you own the place?"

"You're taking too long. I've other things to do than wait around while you're in here faffin' about."

Clay wasn't sure if he should be embarrassed that Stewart had walked in on them or upset at him for cussing at the doctor. "I'm okay, Doc. I'll take it easy, no need to wrap my ribs. And what do you mean, faffin' about?"

Stewart laughed. "Wasting my time, and Emer has the art of that down to a science."

The young receptionist peeked around Stewart, grinning. Seeing her, Clay grabbed his jeans and slipped them on. Never taking her eyes off him, she said, "I'm sure those kex don't look the same on you as they do on 'im."

Once he got his pants zipped up and buttoned, Clay grabbed his shirt and pulled it over his head. But before he had his head through the hole, he asked, "Kex?"

Emer snapped at Clay when she answered. "Your boxers..." Then, waving her hand around in the air at him, she translated, "Your underwear!"

When his head popped through his shirt, there was a puzzled expression on Clay's face just before it registered what she meant. "Uh, wait. They're used?"

"You think I'm going to give you my new pair? Of course they're used!"

"Seriously, I could have gone the rest of my life not knowing that." Leaning on the examining table for support, Clay slipped on his shoes. "Um...sorry, Doc. Thanks for your time." He patted his pants' pockets for his wallet and found it wasn't there. He wiggled his foot around in his shoe and realized he didn't have his money either. He had accidentally left his wallet in his jeans that Mary was washing, and his money must have fallen out in the bathroom when he kicked off his shoes. Making eye contact with Emer, he stated the obvious. "I left my money at Ian's."

Stewart regarded Clay for a second and frowned. "Convenient."

"The two of you, get out!" Emer ordered.

"Hey, Doc, I'll get the money to you, I promise."

Emer was furious.

"She's not cranky because of the money. It's all the bargin' in when she's with a patient," the young receptionist explained. "She's not used to it like Doc Doyle was. He enjoyed it, ya see."

Emer glared at her. "How he worked in these conditions, I don't know! Now go on, the lot of you"—the doctor's arm swung out with her finger pointing at the door—"get out!"

Clay turned beet red and couldn't leave the examination room fast enough. Stewart didn't linger and followed him out. The receptionist kept her eyes on Clay and whispered as he passed, "Oh my, you're a big one, aren't ya?"

"Lily, would you mind?" Emer asked, still angry.

"Mind what?"

"Blasted! Get out and call a locksmith."

"Oh, right, sure," Lily said as she shut the door behind her.

CHAPTER 2

Clay left a message when he called the number the bartender had given him. The computerized voice explained that someone would return his call as soon as possible. After his visit with the doctor the day before, Clay returned to the farm and offered to help Ian with a few chores that required more than one pair of hands. It was during this time the call came in and Mary took a message. When he and Ian came in from doing their work, she shared everything the man said.

"The gentleman's voice sounded more American than Irish," she explained, "but I did hear a slight Irish accent. The fella said he would be in town at two tomorrow and would meet ya at Sean's pub."

When his assailants dumped in the middle of nowhere, Clay remembered thinking how lost and hopeless he had felt. With his mangled body sprawled on the side of the road, there had been little else for him to do but feel sorry for himself. But he remembered thinking, *God, I know you don't think much of me, but when I'm dead, please let someone find my sister? Don't let her die.* Now, sitting at a table in another bar, very much alive, he couldn't help but think God had his hand in all of this.

He looked up when the pub's door opened and Emer walked in. Clay watched as she made her way through the tables over to the bar. She took a seat on a barstool and set her purse on the counter. The bartender looked her way and asked, "Ya needin' the usual?"

"Yes, that would be great. Thanks, Sean."

She glanced around the room at the other patrons when her eyes locked onto Clay's. Instead of ignoring him, she smiled, turned to the bartender, and asked, "I'll take mine over there, Sean, if you don't mind?"

"It's no bother. I'll bring it to ya when it's ready."

Slipping off the stool, Emer grabbed her purse and made her way over to Clay. When she arrived at his table, she asked, "Do you mind?"

Having watched her from the moment she walked in, Clay stood and offered the seat across from him. "No. Please."

"Can I buy you a drink?" she asked, eyeing his glass of water.

Her comment brightened his mood. He had left her office without paying and knew she must think him destitute. "No, I'm good, but thank you. I stopped by your office this morning and paid my bill. I gave the money to Lily."

"Oh, I didn't know. She didn't tell me you stopped by."

"She asked me on a date."

"She what?"

"Yeah, she enjoyed seeing me in Stewart's...kex. Said she wouldn't mind seeing me in them again."

"What an imbecile! I can't believe it."

"It seems to run in your office."

That made her blush. "Sorry about that. It wasn't very professional of me. You're not like the men I've met here. You surprised me is all."

Clay chuckled. "It's okay. I was expecting a cranky old man when I walked into your office. Because of your first name, I just assumed you were a guy. And the way Stewart and Ian talked about you led me to believe you were. You're quite beautiful yourself."

She smiled with a slight laugh. "Emer's short for Emerson. My mother and father have always called me Emer." Then scoffing, she added, "The people of this town treat me like I'm a cranky old man. I hate this place!"

"Then why do you stay?"

"I needed a job, and because of my youth and my mouth, I couldn't get one anywhere else. Dr. Doyle retired and needed an immediate replacement. I took it sight unseen. I'm from Dublin, where no one knows your business, or at least if they do, they don't care. Here, everyone wants to meddle in your life. When I first arrived, every unmarried man lined up outside my office ready to strip down to his kex. Several neglected to tell me they didn't wear any."

This time, Clay laughed, clutching his ribs when he did. "I bet they didn't. How old are you?"

"I'm twenty-eight. I'm a bit of a genius. I finished my studies in five years, unlike my peers that took eight, and I'm honest." She paused for a few seconds before she continued, "Which at times makes me seem not very compassionate."

"At times?" That seemed to amuse Clay. "You know there are ways to be honest and compassionate at the same time."

"Sorry, I'm not one to hold your hand and tell you you're dying because of the lifestyle you live."

"The woman that ran out of your office yesterday—is she someone that's not living her life the way she should?"

"Who? Oh, you mean ol' lady Murphy? Ah, well, she's an alcoholic and eats only fish. She's killing herself, and she wants me to give her a prescription when all she needs is to change her diet."

"At least she exercises. Peddling up and down some of these hills would be a good workout," Clay attested.

"Yes, there's that." Then, changing the subject, she added, "And you're sitting in a pub having a glass of water. I'm surprised Sean hasn't kicked you out."

A goofy grin cut across Clay's face. "Well, you said everyone here knows your business. There's not a soul in this town that doesn't know who I am and the reason I'm here. When I arrived this morning, people called out my name and wished me luck today. I'm guessing Irish luck."

"There's no such thing. Why'd they wish you luck?"

"You haven't heard…well, you would be the only one that hasn't. I'm meeting a guy here that's going to help me find my sister. He'll be here at two."

"It's a quarter of one, I'd say you're early."

"Ian brought me in this morning. I had to take care of a few errands. One being to pay you for the office visit yesterday and another to buy a new phone."

"So where were ya lookin' for yer sister?" Emer asked with a slight change in her dialect.

"In Dublin. She and her friends spent ten days traveling around to all the tourist places in Ireland. They were going to spend their last three days in Dublin—doing what, I'm not sure. The itinerary she gave me had them scheduled to fly home out of the Dublin Airport, but Kayla never made her flight."

"Whoever you upset, they couldn't have dumped you in a better spot. We're almost three hours from Dublin. In the middle of nowhere. They wanted you lost."

"God had other plans for me, I guess, and sent Ian to my rescue."

Clay saw her expression change from one of indifference to curiosity. "Yer not one of those ravin' Christian loons, are ya? If that's the case, why didn't yer god take better care of yer sister?"

"You know you slur your 'yers' and drop the ending of some words when you get passionate about things?"

"I do not!"

"You do! And what's wrong with having a little faith? There's no harm in it. I'm not on a street corner preaching the Word of God to anyone. I'm just living my life the best that I can. If you don't believe, that's your business. I choose to believe. But you're right, I don't understand why my sister did what she did or why God allowed her to go missing. Bad things happen to good people all the time."

"And what if you find her dead? How does that solidify your faith?"

Her words cut deep. He had already considered that, but hearing her say it inflicted a pain he couldn't hide. "I don't expect you to understand. But in a nutshell, my sister hasn't gone to church for some time, not since she started college. She got sucked into all the parties going on around campus. She assured me that she wasn't doing drugs, but I knew she was drinking. You see, Doc, she made her choice, and it seems those choices got her mixed up with some very bad people. I'm not sure if she's dead, but if she is, I'll find her, take her home, and bury her next to my parents. My growing part in all of this will be the journey I take to that end. Be it a good ending or a horrible one."

Emer sat back in her chair and stared at him. When she finally spoke, it was in a near whisper, "I'm sorry, I meant nothin' by it."

He gave her a weak smile.

"Listen, I get the partying at school. While at university, I got invited…well, for a short time anyway, to parties, but because I was always studying, I declined. That's why I finished my studies early and my…well, I can't say we were friends, but they didn't finish school on time or even at all."

Clay understood the thrill of being out on your own. It was just the carelessness that came with it he didn't get. Going to a party with a stranger in a country that's unfamiliar is dangerous no matter how you spin it, and Kayla should have known better.

"Yes, but that was at school," Clay argued. "Here, she should have shown more restraint. Everything about what she did was unsafe. She had to have known and just chose not to care."

"Even at university there were creepy boys that I would've never gone anyplace with, but yes, in a foreign country, I wouldn't have gone anywhere with a stranger." Emer shifted in her seat and asked, "Anyway, you said the person you called can help. How?"

"The bartender gave me a number just before I got the crap beat out of me. He remembered seeing my sister and felt bad for her. He explained, if she got involved with the people he thinks she did, I'd rather she was dead. That these people would sell her to the highest bidder."

"Human trafficking? Here…in Ireland?" Emer asked, stunned.

"Yeah. Apparently, it's a problem here. The police confirmed that. Girls go missing all the time, most are runaways. An officer told me there are traffickers in Europe that pay a high price for blond, blue-eyed girls. The police are sure networks exist all over Ireland that they haven't found yet and if traffickers have Kayla, they're convinced she's no longer in the country."

"I'm verra sorry for ya, I canna imagine your pain." Clay grinned at her, and she smiled back. "Okay, I have to work hard not to speak my old neighborhood dialect. I can't help but revert back to it every now and then."

"It's cute."

"Cute? No, it's not. I've worked hard for my credentials, and I've worked even harder to rid myself of my old neighborhood dialect. Sometimes I regress."

Sean set a plate of food down in front of Emer and announced, "The chips are fresh, go easy so not to burn yerself. Clay, yer sure I canna get ya a wee bit of food?"

"Thanks, but I'm good. Mary has taken it upon herself to feed me."

"Oh, aye, she's a grand cook. Cheers." Sean left, leaving Clay and Emer alone once again.

She inhaled the aroma from her food before she took a bite. Sean was right, the fries were hot. She burned her tongue on one and dropped it back on her plate.

Clay chuckled. "I hear there's a terrific doctor in town with an excellent bedside manner that can help with that burnt tongue of yours."

"Yeah?" Emer gave him a silly smirk and added, "I hear she's quite charming and smart too."

Laughing, Clay grabbed his side and cringed, but still managed to say, "Yeah, she does have a charming snootiness about her."

Emer didn't take offense; instead, she found it amusing. The rest of their conversation was about the town and the people that lived there. Clay sat and listened mostly, only asking a few questions now and then. For the first time since he had arrived in Ireland, he honestly felt relaxed. Whether it was because of the beautiful woman that sat across from him or the light conversation, his bruised body and his sister's whereabouts weren't eating away at him. It disappointed him when Emer had to go, but he understood. When the doctor walked out of the pub, he looked at his watch. It was a quarter of two. He slouched in his chair and crossed his arms. "I guess it's back to worrying."

*   *   *   *   *

At exactly two o'clock, a man came into the pub. He was average height, slim, wearing worn blue jeans, and a dress shirt with its tail hanging out from under his thick sweater. His brown hair was short and clean-cut. He wore a red Angels baseball cap flipped around backward and Oakley sunglasses, looking like he had just walked off an airplane from California. Clay remembered Mary mentioning the guy spoke with an American accent.

He watched the man take off his sunglasses and survey the pub. When he caught sight of Clay, he lifted his chin, acknowledging he saw him and made his way over to the table. Clay stood and shook the hand being offered.

"Oi, Clay?"

"Yeah. I'm sorry, I didn't get your name."

"Oh, right, I'm Eddie." Then zeroing in on the barkeep, he yelled, "A pint please."

"On its way," Sean returned.

Eddie pulled a chair out and took a seat. He tucked his sunglasses into the collar of his dress shirt. Noticing the glass of water in front of Clay, he asked, "How long have ya been nursin' that?"

Sean set down a glass of beer. Before he left, Eddie leaned back in his chair, lifting two legs off the floor, and asked, "Bring the man a pint, would ya?"

"He's not a drinker. He's one of those Bible thumpers," Sean explained.

"And ya let him sit here with water? That's a real shame, that is."

"I like 'im, he's a good man. You needin' anythin' else?"

"Nah. Here, keep the change." Eddie paid for his drink and let the chair come down with all four legs on the floor. "Sorry, I didn't know. We could've met at the local church."

"Honestly, I would have met you anywhere, even in a strip club if I had to. I need some help to find my sister. She's been missing for eleven days, and when I asked around about her, I got a major whoopin'." Clay placed a hand gently on his ribs. Without pause, he continued, "Now the bartender said you could help. So my question to you is, can you?"

"I take it you've gone to the local garda, and they've informed you there's not much that can be done for her?"

Clay was getting agitated with Eddie and didn't like that he answered his question with one of his own. Instead of giving him the obvious answer, Clay asked, "Are you from Ireland or the US?"

"Born and raised in Chicago, but I've lived here for the last fifteen years. I travel mostly hunting for young lasses, much like your sister. I'm still searchin' for my mine, ya see. I haven't found her yet, but I've found a few others and brought them home. I work for several organizations whose mission is to find missin' girls. But if your sister's a beauty, then the police are correct, she's no longer in Ireland. Eleven days may as well be eleven years. But I'll help ya find her… if I can."

Eddie's honesty felt like a hard punch to Clay's gut. He was becoming more frightened for Kayla. Expressing his fears wouldn't help, so instead, he asked, "Is the bartender an informant?"

"No, he's more a buddy. He and I became fast friends when I started lookin' for my sister. He's not blind to the crazies that drink at his pub, and he hears all kinds of stuff. Stuff that has helped me find a few missin' girls."

"Crazies? Like the ones that didn't like me asking questions?"

"Aye, and they're diggin' in their heels at that pub. All kinds of stories are comin' outta there. Stories that will help us. Though you'll need to come back to Dublin with me. We'll not find your sister here."

"I need to let Ian and Mary know what I'm doing. They've been good to me, and I don't want them to worry."

"Great! Point me in the direction, and I'll take ya there. Then we'll be off." Eddie stood up, slugged down the rest of his beer, walked over to the bar, set his glass down, and then motioned for Clay to do the same.

When Clay set his glass on the counter, he told Sean, "Thanks for letting me hang out here today."

"No problem. Best o' luck to ya. Hope ya find yer sister."

Nodding at Sean his thanks, Clay followed Eddie out. As he stepped through the door, he felt like his luck was about to change. Or at least he hoped it was.

*   *   *   *   *

The scenery from southern Ireland to its east coast was spectacular. It was nothing like southern California, where tumbleweeds and desert laid claim to most of its terrain. Lush green fields covered the countryside in every direction. Clay understood the attraction that Californians had, wanting to vacation here.

His first drive through the country had been in the trunk of a car. He still wasn't sure how they had squeezed him in, but now, riding in the comfort of Eddie's Land Rover, he had plenty of leg room and an amazing view.

Before he left with Eddie, Clay had gone by to say goodbye to Emer and thanked her for her help. She, of course, showed no interest but wished him luck just before she slammed the door shut—yelling once again for a locksmith.

Lily's cheerfulness was infectious. She leaned toward him and whispered, "She's a wee temper, but no bother. Come back home to us. We've a date, remember?"

Clay chuckled. "Promise to go easy on the doc—she's out of her element here."

"There's no fun in that now, is there? She's a toy to be played with and a bit of amusement I quite enjoy."

Heading for the door, he joked, "You're terrible. One day it's going to come back and bite you in your tail end. Take it easy, Lily."

"A minor diversion in Emer's mundane life will nae kill her, or me. Keep in touch, would ya?"

With the promise to do so, Clay waved and closed the door behind him. He liked Lily. She had a great sense of humor, and he almost felt bad for Emer. Then he thought better of it and decided Lily was exactly what the doctor needed to keep her grounded.

His next stop was a different story. When Clay arrived at the farm to say goodbye, Mary cried and Ian choked up but managed to say, "All the best ta ya, laddie. We'll miss ya and be prayin' for yer sister's safe return."

"Thanks. Listen, I owe you my life. I'll never forget what either of you did for me. When this is all over, I would like to come back to see you. That's if it's okay?"

"Oh my, Clay. You've a place here ta rest yer head, always. No need ta ask."

Mary motioned with her hands for Clay to come and give her a hug. He was happy to oblige. Clay shook hands with Ian and promised to call with any news, good or bad. They were grateful for that and waved as he drove off.

Sitting in the front passenger's seat, Clay listened to Eddie's accent switch from Irish to American as if he couldn't decide what nationality he was. Despite Eddie's inability to stick with one accent, Clay felt somewhat hopeful. Not a lot, but just enough to keep his spirit up.

Eddie gave a small lecture on Ireland's history as they drove the three hours to Dublin. It wasn't until they were an hour outside the city that the conversation moved to human trafficking.

"It's bad enough that Ireland has been raped and pillaged from the Vikings, Norman invasion, and Great Britain, not to mention all the rebellions against the English rule, but now it's pillagin' from its coffers women and sellin' them off to the highest bidder, all in the name of money. It's nothin' personal, ya know, just business dealings for the snakes doin' the sellin'."

"Well, it's very personal for me."

"Aye, it is. But ya have to know, to them, it's just business. Ireland hasn't taken the dealings of traffickin' serious enough. It's only been in the last six years that the lawmakers have made such atrocities illegal here. America's not any better. Congress only thought to add laws to its books in 2001, and traffickin' humans has been around far longer."

"I didn't know. Honestly, I'm only hearing about it now because of Kayla."

"My enlightenment was fifteen years ago with the abduction of my sister. A few years back, I had some retired Marines come askin' for my help. They had a lead on a girl and thought I could lend them a hand. In return, they promised to assist me in my endeavor to find my sister. Of course, I offered my help. We found four girls that month, includin' the one they were lookin' for in Istanbul. The traffickers had sold the girls to a wealthy man, but one of his daughters didn't like it and called the American embassy. By the time the call came in, it took us twenty-five hours to get the girls on a plane and send them home. Not a bad day's work."

Clay tried to swallow back the lump that had formed in his throat. When he spoke, his voice was hoarse. "I think the world just got a lot bigger. How are we going to find her?"

Eddie glanced over and saw the worry on Clay's face. "Aye, it is. We were lucky that day. But with a wee bit of luck and a whole lot of grace from the good Lord above, we'll find your sister."

"Do you believe in God, or are you trying to pacify me?"

Never taking his eyes off the road, Eddie answered, "I'm a believer that there are things out of my control, things that I can't explain. So I give credit where credit's due. The things these eyes of mine have seen, no man should ever have to see, nor should any woman have to live through. I've faith that God will one day bring my sister home, yet I believe it won't be me that does it. I'm God's tool to use at His pleasure and it's an honor to be the one He employs to transport others back to their families. Ya see, I've no family to worry about. My wife's my job and my kids are all the girls I find."

Eddie took a quick glance over at Clay and gave him a brief smile before he continued. "I've enough on my plate, ya see. No need to add to it. So yes, in answer to your question, I believe in the almighty Savior, Jesus Christ. He's brought us together for a reason. I've no doubt we'll get your sister back. But to be honest with ya, she'll not be the young woman she once was—that is, if those that took your sister have sold her. She'll have had the life sucked right outta her. They do it quick, you see. So the girls don't put up too much of a fight. You need to understand, it'll not be easy for ya to see, but she'll be alive and God has a good method of healin'."

Another imaginary mass formed in Clay's throat, causing the muscles in his neck to move up and down trying to unblock it. Peering out his window, he fought hard to work his fears down. He'd figured Kayla was dead in a gutter somewhere, and the police would find her body soon. He wasn't sure which would be better, finding her dead, or alive and horribly abused. He was angry at his sister for putting him through this. Then just as quick, he realized he was feeling sorry for himself. He also had a moment's lapse in his faith, wishing it had been one of the other girls that had gone missing and not Kayla. Shame washed over him, and he prayed a silent prayer, apologizing to God for even thinking such a horrible thing.

He had seen one or two movies on the subject of human trafficking, but they were just for entertainment. If the filmmakers hoped to open people's eyes to the horrible problem of human trafficking, they failed miserably. The main character always seemed to have unique skills that would help lead him to his daughter and would help save her from her abductors. In Clay's reality, he had no skills whatsoever and had already gotten beat up and squished inside the trunk of a car. Why they hadn't killed him, he didn't know. He hoped that would be their biggest mistake.

Clay asked, "How do we start?"

"The American Marines I told ya about? Well, one's come to Dublin lookin' for another young girl that was on holiday here in Ireland. She's been missin' for several months, and he's a lead that brought him back to me. And now to you. His name's Billy—he's a black dude, very smart, and very talented with his hands. When I got your call, he was with me. His thinkin' is, if we find your sister, we might find the other girl."

"Talented with his hands?"

"Oh, aye! The bloke can snap a man's neck with no effort at all."

Clay's eyes widened. Eddie saw it and grinned. Clay glanced out the window, thinking, *I'm no Liam Neeson, but God might have just given me some skills, inadvertently of course, but skills nonetheless.*

*   *   *   *   *

The sun had gone down by the time Eddie pulled over and parked the Land Rover. He explained they had a long walk ahead of them—one that couldn't be helped. Traveling on foot helped to loosen Clay's legs, and though his guide didn't seem in a hurry, both men traversed the streets with purpose. Neither spoke as Eddie led them through a seedy part of Dublin. A putrid smell hit Clay's nostrils, making him want to gag. Every corner turned, the stench followed.

The moisture in the air added to the chilly temperature, but Clay did his best to ignore it, as well as his broken ribs. Adrenaline had kicked in, making him very focused. Every step he took, was a step taking him closer to Kayla.

When they came around the last corner, it was as if a light switch had flipped on. The dark, dreary neighborhood he and Eddie had just traveled burst open to a city that was very much alive and moving. Buses and cars filled the streets, with pedestrians occupying the sidewalks. It took Clay by surprise, but his escort didn't seem phased by the sudden change in their surroundings. Clay followed him across the busy road to an old granite building, but instead of going inside, Eddie took him to the side of the structure and down some steps. Clay recognized the place right away. It was the last place Kayla had been seen.

Each concrete step they took down to the landing was painted black with a yellow stripe in the center, giving some guidance as to where they should place their feet. At the bottom of the stairs was a large window and an open door that allowed the foul odor of alcohol to filter outside. A single lamp hung over the entrance, illuminating everything in its proximity.

A young woman and two men stood outside smoking cigarettes and chatting. They ignored the two Americans as they walked past and went inside. The bar was enormous and at full capacity. It took up the entire basement of the building above. The lighting was dull, and with the walls painted dark burgundy, it made it near impossible to see the faces of its patrons. Eddie and Clay had to squeeze past people to get to the back of the room. Clay's size and bruised face caught the attention of those closest to him, but let him pass without comments.

The chatter and laughter drowned out the music that played through the speakers. Because of it, the noise level inside made it hard to hear anyone. Eddie led Clay to the far corner near a hallway with a sign that read "The Jacks." They stopped in front of a small round table where a black man sat with his back to the wall. He stood when he saw his friend. Eddie leaned over the table and shouted, "This is the bloke I told ya about. As requested, he's here to meet ya."

Offering them a seat, the man extended his hand to Clay, who shook it and yelled, "I'm Clay, you must be Billy?"

"Yeah, I am. Sorry to be meeting you under these circumstances, but I think we can help each other."

"I hope that's the case. Why are we here?"

Billy pointed at someone behind Clay. When he turned to see who it was, he nearly jumped out of his seat. One of the four men that had beat him was chatting with friends. Eddie grabbed Clay by the shoulder, preventing him from getting up.

"I take it he's one of the blokes that didn't like ya askin' after your sister?" Eddie inquired.

"Yeah, he is. How did you find him so fast?"

"He's a moron. The kind of moron I like. The punk can't keep his mouth shut. He bragged to some people that he'll be coming into some major money soon. All he needs is a few more girls," Billy answered.

Baffled, Clay asked, "Why don't you call the police or something?"

"The cops, or garda as they're called here, are no help. Not all are skimmin' and turnin' a blind eye to the problem, but we don't know which ones are, so it's best to keep the police outta it for now," Eddie explained.

"Then what are we going to do?"

"As all heavy drinkers do, he'll have to take a leak soon," Billy answered. "The jacks are down that long corridor, which also leads to a back door and an open alley."

Clay knew the alley well. "I'm sorry, my Irish isn't that great. You said leak, so I'm guessing jacks are the restrooms?"

"Aye. Billy checked the place out earlier. His name's Derrick, a local Dubliner. His ma's a whore by choice, so it's no surprise the bloke thinks there's nothin' wrong with him stealin' a few girls for a buck or two."

"Come on. He's moving." Billy pushed his chair out hard when he stood, smacking it into the wall behind him. He told Clay to cut in front of Derrick and keep moving toward the back door. Billy fell in right behind the young Dubliner with Eddie following. The hall was tight with people making their way back to the bar. When they reached the men's restroom, Billy shoved Derrick hard in the back, forcing him to keep moving forward.

"Oi! What the—" Derrick's drunken reflexes made him slow, so when Clay opened the back door, the next push from Billy forced Derrick's face into its edge, nearly knocking him out.

Billy and Eddie grabbed Derrick from either side and hauled him out and up a set of steps. Derrick groaned, brought his hand up to his nose, and felt blood.

"Yer mad as a box of frogs. Leave off, will ya! Let me go or you'll regret it!" Derrick yelled.

In one fluid motion, Billy flung Derrick around, slammed him up against the wall, and punched him hard in the gut. The young man puked and relieved himself at the same time.

"The big man's gone and wet himself." Eddie laughed. "Not so tough without your mates, are ya? I can understand your frustration, not being able to do much about the circumstances you now find yourself in."

Still hunched over, Derrick glared at Eddie. He had one hand on his stomach with the other one on the wall, keeping him steady. He spat on the ground and stood upright.

Still grinning, Eddie pointed at Clay and asked, "Do ya remember my friend here? You and your goons beat him and left him for dead."

Seeing Clay again enraged Derrick. "Oh, aye, I do. Stupid Yank! Yer worse than leeches, stickin' around where yer not wanted!"

"You know something about my sister, and I want her back." Clay's calm demeanor was rapidly being replaced with anger.

Derrick laughed. "You'll not see her again, ya moran! She's gone. Sold ta be the whore that she is!"

Furious, Clay fought to stop himself from lunging at the guy. Billy didn't. He swung his arm with a balled-up fist and hit Derrick in the stomach again, knocking the wind out of him.

"Now, Derrick, my man, stop faffin' about. Where's the lass? Where d'ya have her holed up? Tossin' ya over the docks will be my pleasure if you're of no use to us. One less slacker, I say. Now out with it!"

Clay didn't know what Eddie meant, but he hoped Derrick understood and, more importantly, believed him.

"She's gone with the rest of 'em. Sorry, it's nothin' personal." Derrick spit again.

"Are you kidding? She's my sister!" Clay moved closer and drilled his finger into Derrick's chest. Fear shot across the young man's face, and he tried to back up, but the wall prevented him from going anywhere. With their faces only inches from each other, Clay added, "It's very personal to me. Now, where is she?"

Leaning in to Derrick's ear, Eddie whispered something that frightened him. His eyes bulged as he shook his head. "No! Please, ya wouldn't do it!"

"I've nothing to lose if I do. You, however, will have more to worry about than just the taste of vomit still lingerin' in your mouth. So go on, give the man the information he's askin' for or you'll be dead by mornin'."

"I'll be dead either way!"

"Nah! Only if ya don't give us what we want."

Scared that Eddie would keep his promise, Derrick blurted out, "The *Crystalline*. It sails at the end of the week. And if ya go ta the garda, they'll turn their backs on ya because there's big money for 'em not seein'."

Billy leaned closer to Derrick and said, "That's okay, we're not going to the police, not when we have the best that Ireland has to offer. You've heard of the ARW…Fianoglach (Fi-a-no-glock)?"

That shut the young Dubliner up.

Eddie's scowl lifted to a crooked grin. "Oh, there we go, that's got the man's nerves a flutterin'." Then, seeing Clay's puzzled expression, he explained, "The ARW is Ireland's toughest and can't be bought— the Army Ranger Wing. We've a couple retired ARW that can't wait to kill a few human traffickers. Givin' ya over to them will be a joy."

If Derrick wasn't happy to hear that bit of news, Clay was. A strange feeling washed over him, releasing him from a tremendous amount of anxiety he hadn't realized was weighing him down.

"Come on," Billy ordered. "The van's down the street a few blocks." Then his fist hit Derrick square in the jaw, knocking his head into the wall. Billy's action startled Clay as he watched Derrick's body crumble into a heap on the ground.

Eddie patted Clay's shoulder, saying, "Not to worry, my man. We canna have him yellin' on the way to the van. Now he's a drunk mate needin' our help to get him home."

Billy pulled him up and slung Derrick's left arm over his shoulder. Eddie took the other side, and the two began the laborious task of hauling him up the hill to the van. A group of men passed Clay and his friends, heckling Derrick when they saw he had wet his pants.

Eddie called out to the group, "He gets nervous when he's talkin' to the ladies—it's a real shame!"

There was a roar of laughter that faded the further away the two parties got from one another. The road quieted the more distance they put between themselves and the downtown area. A blue van came into view when the men turned the corner. Clay saw it and asked, "Is that it?"

"Yeah—here, take the keys and open the back for me."

Oddly enough, Clay wasn't nervous and rushed to open the back doors. He stepped aside so the two men could get Derrick inside. Billy crawled in first, hauling Derrick in with him. Eddie shut the back doors and held out his hand. Clay dropped the keys into his palm and followed Eddie to the driver's side, momentarily forgetting the passenger's seat was on left.

"Eh, sorry," Clay said before he jogged over to the other side and hopped in.

They drove thirty minutes north, along the east coast, to their next destination. Clay had no idea where he was. He had been lost since he'd arrived in Ireland. He didn't like the feeling of not knowing where he was, but seeing the Irish Sea gave him some comfort. The body of water was the only thing familiar to him. Not that it was the Pacific Ocean, which he was used to, but getting a glimpse of the sea's water every now and then set his mind at ease.

The van hit a pothole when Eddie turned off the main road onto a dirt one, jarring everyone inside. Clay grabbed his side in pain and held on to the door, trying to stop from being slung side to side.

Billy yelled, "Easy, buddy! Remember, I'm not strapped in back here."

"Sorry about that." Eddie stopped when he reached a gate. Turning to Clay, he asked, "Ya mind?"

Clay said nothing as he opened the door and jumped out. A wire loop was all that kept the gate closed. He lifted it over the top of the post and pushed it open all the way. Eddie drove through and stopped some distance, giving Clay room to close the gate. Within seconds, he was back in the van, and they were moving again.

Eddie pulled up to an old barn and parked. With no explanation given as to why they were there, Eddie jumped out and opened the back doors. Derrick was conscious, but Eddie still helped him out by grabbing one ankle and pulling. "Out with ya."

"Okay, okay, I'm comin'!"

"Does someone care to tell me where we are and what we're doing here?" Clay asked.

He waited for Billy or Eddie to answer, but before either could, a hand came down on his shoulder. A jolt of fear shot through him, and he spun around so fast the person who owned the hand stepped back. Clay had his fists balled up, ready to hit the guy.

"Easy does it. We're all friends here."

"Sorry, you scared me."

"The reaction I was goin' for," the man said, grinning.

Billy had Derrick's right hand pinned tight behind his back in a wrist lock to prevent him from fighting his way free. With a quick nod to his left, Billy started the introductions. "This is Clay. His sister's been missing close to two weeks. This piece of garbage is the one that took her, or at least he's been bragging that he did."

Offering his hand to Clay, the man said, "I'm Patrick. Sorry about your sister. Let's see if the lad's telling the truth. I've a wee torture chamber inside. This way, gents."

Patrick gave a nod toward the barn. Derrick squirmed and wiggled a little dance, trying to free himself from Billy's grip when he heard the words *torture chamber*. Clay could almost smell his fear. He watched Billy force the young man toward the barn door, when Derrick blurted out, "They use fishin' boats! They force the fishermen to do it, or they'll burn their boats. A fisherman opened 'is mouth ta some honest gardai and now they've got ta hang low for a bit. It's all true. Really! It's all I know."

Eyeing Derrick with the sides of his lips quirking upward, Patrick stated, "Aye, you're the real deal, aren't you, boy? I know the fisherman in question. He had a bit of a fire on his boat because of it. His wife said she'd rather lose their livelihood than go before God knowing what they've done."

With a questioning look, Clay asked, "What are the fishing boats used for?"

"The traffickers use them to transport their cargo to larger vessels that are waiting for them out at sea. The docks are crawling with AHTU, so they had to come up with another way to get the girls and boys on the ships without being seen. Ireland is full of fishermen trying to make a living. Some struggle and do the bidding of the traffickers for the money. Others are forced into it."

Even though he had half expected the answer he got, his own fear momentarily paralyzed him. The blood pumping through his veins seemed on fire. When he inhaled, he barely noticed the sharp pain in his side. He was more afraid for Kayla now than he had been since he'd known she was missing.

Clay forced the fear out of his mind, trying to gain control of his thought process. He took another deep breath and focused on the pain coming from his ribs. When he was sure he could speak, he asked in a rough voice, "What's AHTU?"

By the sympathetic look Patrick directed at him, Clay half expected the man to offer some reassurances, but instead of consoling him, Patrick simply answered his question. "Ireland's Anti-Human Trafficking Unit. It's a branch of the Department of Justice and Equality. The AHTTF is the Anti-Human Trafficking Task Force that falls under the AHTU. The titles alone explain what they do. You have to understand, Ireland is fast becoming the hub for human traffickers.

From here, they sell those being trafficked for commercial labor, sexual exploitation, or both. Massage parlors in Ireland are full of them."

"So if my sister didn't get shipped off somewhere, she's still in Ireland?"

"That would be the obvious assumption."

Droplets of rain hit Clay. He held out his hand and looked up into the night sky. Billy didn't need to be told to take Derrick inside the barn; he twisted the young man's arm and forced him to move toward the door. The rain came down in a steady flow. Clay followed them in while Patrick held the door open.

Why the rain made Clay think about his needing to shower, he couldn't fathom. He hadn't bathed since yesterday morning and remembered he didn't have any other clothes with him. Derrick and his friends had taken his backpack, which had everything he owned inside it. He would need to buy a few things before he started to smell but would have to worry about that later—now, he had more pressing things to deal with than his hygiene.

Once inside, Clay watched Billy handcuff Derrick to a secure chain cemented into the floor. Taking in his surroundings, it occurred to him that the word *barn* had disguised a more accurate definition of the place. It was a workshop, neatly arranged by someone who like order. It was lit up like daylight inside, which allowed Clay to see everything.

Scattered electronic components covered a large table to his left. In the back corner was a small cage that looked like an armory. Inside it had several different semiautomatic rifles and handguns arranged on its wall by make, model, and size. Neatly stacked boxes on the opposite side, filled the corner under the well-crafted stairs that led up to a loft. In the center of the room was a white board, along with a small table and chairs spread out around it.

Derrick's sudden outburst drew everyone's attention back to him. "Oi! Whatcha gonna do wit me? I told ya all I know. Honest, I did! I'm just a recruiter. When they need more girls, I get 'em. That's all!"

Clay had never, in all his thirty-one years, wanted to hit someone as badly as he did Derrick. His hands flexed repeatedly, ready to release his frustration all over the young man, when he felt a hand on his shoulder.

"He's not worth the energy," Patrick assured him. "Take a seat, and we'll get to the bottom of what he knows, and believe me, he knows more than he thinks he does."

Picking up a chair, Patrick placed it in front of Derrick and began the interrogation.

"Okay, I can see you're a man of wisdom, so I'm going to ask you a set of questions and you'll share all that wisdom of yours with me. Got it?"

The young man glanced at Billy, who stood next to Patrick with his arms folded and his biceps tensing, as if he couldn't wait to hit him again. "Yeah, sure. I'll tell ya what I know."

"Great. Just a wee curious as to why you picked Clay's sister?"

"Yeah, well…she said her ma and da died a couple of years ago. She said they left her the trip ta Ireland. Her girlfriends were ugly eejits, goin' on about this and that, and I could tell the girl was tirin' of 'em fast. I offered ta take her to a party that a friend was throwin'. My intentions were nothin' at first, just wanted ta show the girl a wee bit o' fun. But then rememberin' her parents were dead, I thought I could make a bit o' cash. My money was runnin' low, ya see."

"So you take her to a party…or was that a lie?" Patrick looked quizzically at Derrick.

"No, no! I took her ta the party. But my friend, the one that got me the job of findin' girls, liked what he saw and wanted ta know her story. I told 'im, and that was that. He dropped somethin' in her drink and took 'er. He gave me a wad o' cash for 'er. Says to bring him a couple more, and he'd gimme more money."

"Wait! You mentioned she was being shipped out on a boat. What was the name?" Clay asked, snapping his fingers, trying to remember.

"The *Crystalline*," Billy reminded him.

Clay stood on the other side of Patrick and pointed at Derrick. "You told us she shipped out with the rest of them! Were you lying?"

There was a spasm in Derrick's throat which made it hard for him to swallow, and he choked before he spoke. "I dunno…honest.

My friend really took ta 'er and was definitely gonna have some fun wit 'er first."

"What's your friend's name, Derrick?" Patrick asked.

His eyes went wide with fear. "Yer man here"—Derrick slung his head in Eddie's direction—"said I'm a dead man no matter what! So I've no need of sayin' anythin'."

Eddie's good humor showed on his face, and his laugh only added to it. "You've a life now, boy. I'll not tell if ya give us what we need. No one needs to know ya spoke with us."

"Exactly. You'll become our informant. It'll be our little secret," Patrick said in a reassuring voice.

Derrick just stared at Patrick. Clay couldn't decipher his demeanor because the fear that had been there a few seconds ago had disappeared, along with the anger the young man had displayed earlier. He had to wait, like the others, for his answer.

"Does it pay?"

Eddie laughed out loud while he clapped his hands. "Absolutely brilliant! You're not so bright yourself, are ya? You've a life to live if you work for us, boy."

"True, but I've bills like the rest of ya, and if I'm not cullin' out the girls for…" Derrick stopped just shy of saying his employer's name. "I have ta eat!"

"I'm sure the authorities will give you something for all your hard work," Patrick offered. "Now the name?"

Patrick's manner never changed. He stayed calm and his tone never wavered. Clay liked him. He was easy to like, and Clay thought that might be the reason Derrick was receptive to him. So it was no wonder that the next words out of their new informant's mouth were, "Brian and 'is son, Ronan."

The mention of the names made Patrick lean forward with an elbow on one knee. "Gallagher?"

For whatever reason, Patrick's mention of the last name made Derrick squirm once again. "Aye, ya know 'em then?"

Slowly rising to an upright position, Patrick glanced around the room at each of the faces staring back at him. "We've got a lot of work to do, gents. This one isn't going to be easy."

CHAPTER 3

The rain from the night before made the midmorning air damp and cold. Clay went outside to make a few phone calls while he waited for Billy and Eddie. He had been the first to shower and felt a lot better now that he was clean and wore fresh clothes. Patrick had given him a pair of black military cargo pants that were comfortable, along with a black long-sleeved T-shirt and a light jacket.

As he leaned against the outside wall of the workshop, Clay thought about the calls he needed to make, one being to his office back home. Warner Technologies was a growing company and Clay's baby. He had started the business in his parents' garage fresh out of high school, but it didn't take off until after he graduated from college.

It had been one piece of imaging equipment that he donated to the children's hospital in Madera to try out, which eventually propelled him and his new company into the fast-pace technology world. Since then, his company had modified his first creation into several new projects. Four major oil companies already had the equipment operational; two ocean mining companies were integrating it into their programing, and a wealthy financier bought it for a university archaeology dig. The technology would help these industries make their finds more precise and lessen the stress on the environment. Clay saw it as a win for everyone.

Warner Technologies was a multimillion-dollar company that employed ninety-three people. Clay knew each new project his company was working on was on target. He had handpicked each employee, all highly motivated individuals. Calling his office was simply a courtesy to let his secretary and business partner know what was going on at his end.

He looked at his watch and calculated the time difference in his head. No one would be at work because of the late hour, but he would leave a message for Marsha so she would have his new phone number. His secretary answered on the first ring. "Warner Technologies, this is Marsha. How may I help you?"

"Hey, Marsha. What are you doing at the office this late?"

"Hi, boss. I'm helping Dale with a report that he needs for his meeting tomorrow."

"Oh, right. I forgot about that."

"That's understandable—you have a lot on your mind."

"Yeah, I do. Um, listen, I just wanted to check in, but since you answered, how's everything going?"

"Terrific on this end. Has there been any news?"

"Yeah, there has. I'm with a former Marine and a couple of guys that are retired Army Ranger Wings. They're Ireland's version of the US Marines. They're all fighting against human trafficking now and are helping me find Kayla. Last night, we found the guy that took her. Patrick got him talking, and he told us who has her."

"Oh, my word, Clay! Human trafficking?"

"It's scary, but at least we know who has her."

Clay heard a sigh of relief and then, "When are you going to go get her?"

"You'd think it would be that simple, but there's more involved than just our going to pick her up."

"I'm sorry to hear that. What's next?"

He thought about that for a second. "That's a good question. I'm not sure. The guys I'm with have been working on a plan. So we'll see."

"Please don't worry about anything here. There hasn't been any hiccups and everyone is working hard to keep the projects on target. Everything's on schedule. You just concentrate on getting Kayla back."

"Thanks, Marsha. Tell everyone I really appreciate them taking on the extra workload. And can you do me a favor, please? Would you pay off my credit card?"

"Absolutely. I'll take care of it as soon as we hang up. Anything else?"

"Thanks, but that should do it. If you need me, this is my new phone number. Mine got stolen."

"Wow. I'm sorry about that. Do you want the heads of each department to have your new number?"

"Uh, no. If something comes up, have Dale take care of it. I'm not in the right frame of mind to deal with work related issues right now."

"Sure. I'll let Dale know. If there's anything that I can do from here to make it easier for you there, just call, day or night. I'm available."

"Will do. Thanks again, Marsha. Just knowing you and Dale are at the helm helps me tremendously. Take care and I'll call again in the next day or so."

"Clay, I'm praying for you and Kayla." Then Marsha reminded him, "Day or night, don't forget."

"Thanks. I won't, believe me. If I need you, I'll call. We'll talk soon." Clay hung up after he heard his secretary say goodbye.

He had the best employees, and because of them, he could rest easy and not worry about his business back home. Just hearing Marsha assure him of that reinforced what he already knew.

Taking in a satisfied breath, he thought about his next phone call. That call went to Ian and Mary, and as expected, Mary cried when he told them everything that he knew about Kayla. Ian relayed his gratitude for keeping them informed. Before he hung up, he asked for Emer's number. Ian only had the one to her office, and passed it on to Clay.

The third phone call he made, Lily picked up on the second ring. "Hello, Dr. O'Farrell's office. How may I help you?"

"Hey, Lily. How's it going?"

"Howya, Clay. I'm still waitin' for my date."

"Honestly, I wish I was there instead of here. Is the doc in?"

"Yeah, she is, but she's with a patient. I can interrupt if you think it's important."

"No!" His body jerked upright away from the wall. "No, no. That won't be necessary. I'll call her later."

"Sorry, Clay, her schedule's full today. Here, I'll give ya her mobile number, then ya can give her a ring after hours."

"If you're sure she won't mind?"

"Oh, aye, she'll be flippin' mad, but ya know I live for that temper of hers."

He laughed. "I bet you do. Have you found a locksmith?"

"Oh, aye, I did. Sent 'im to her flat instead. She was fumin' when she couldn't get in! Her patients and I had a great laugh."

"You're wicked to the core, Lily, but I like you. Go ahead and give me her number."

Clay had just put Emer's number in his phone when he saw Billy walking toward him, clean-shaven and wearing similar clothes. He wondered if something was up. If he read Billy's body language correctly, he seemed unconcerned and laid back.

"Hey. How d'you sleep last night?"

A casual conversation. "Great," Clay answered. "You?"

"Not bad for sleeping up in the loft. Patrick has a nice setup here."

"He does and apparently has boxes filled with black military clothes." Clay grinned.

"Yeah. I'm glad he does, though. After sitting in that pub last night, I reeked of cigarettes."

Clay couldn't agree more. "Does Patrick have a family? That's a big house for one man to live in alone."

Billy glanced over his shoulder at Patrick's house and then back at Clay. "Yeah, a wife and three girls. He's been married twenty-eight years to the same woman."

That surprised Clay. "I had no idea. Are they here?"

"No. Because of all the men coming and going here, he didn't want them around."

"I don't blame him. How long have you known Patrick?"

"Believe it or not, almost twenty years."

"You're kidding?"

"Nope. The US military does a lot of training with Ireland's military. They even have joint ops sometimes. He and I were team leaders and our teams trained and worked a lot together. Sometimes in the US, but more often than not, I came here. We became good friends over the course of ten years of working together."

"Hence your amazing hands."

"What?" Billy asked.

"It's nothing. Just something Eddie said before I met you. After you hit Derrick a few times, I thought you were a thug until I remembered you were in the military."

"Oh, yeah. I was trained by the best combat infantry in the world."

Clay didn't doubt that. He was grateful for the man's skills. "Listen. I wanted to thank you for what you're doing for my sister. I'm sure I would have gotten killed if I went looking for her by myself again. Honestly, I'm surprised Derrick and his friends didn't do it the first time."

"You're welcome. It's what I've dedicated my life to."

"Why?"

"Why have I dedicated my life to fight against human trafficking? For more reason than one, Eddie being one of them. I met him ten years ago when he was looking for his sister. He was torn up about it back then. I guess he still is, but now, he just lives each day the best he can, knowing she's gone. I hope one day to bring her home to him."

Clay couldn't imagine living his life without Kayla in it. It would kill him. How Eddie was still standing after all these years was amazing. "Did he ever have any leads on his sister's whereabouts?"

"Yeah, he did. Believe it or not, Eddie's good at this. He almost had her in the Ukraine, but he fell into the same dilemma you did. Outnumbered and in a foreign country with the authorities giving up before they even got started. He's pretty sure a wealthy man in northern Africa bought her, and after that, her trail went cold."

"Geez..." Clay didn't like hearing that. If Kayla wasn't found soon, he was afraid she wasn't going to be found. And once she hit the open waters of the Atlantic Ocean or Irish Sea, it would be over for her. They had to find her and do it soon.

A black Land Rover pulled up in front of Patrick's workshop. Four big Irishmen got out and waved at Clay and Billy, but instead of coming over to them, they headed toward the shop. Clay and Billy took that as a sign they should go in too. Once inside, Patrick introduced his team to Clay.

"I'd like you to meet Connor, Niall, Harry, and Gerard." Clay shook hands with each one as Patrick mentioned their names. Then, making sure he didn't forget anyone, Patrick asked, "You fellas remember Billy and Eddie?" The four men nodded that they did.

"Oi, I'm hungry. Do ya have any food around 'ere?"

"Oh, and this pathetic soul is Derrick, our informant."

Connor took a fruit bar from his coat pocket and threw it at the young man. It bounced off him onto the floor. Derrick reached for it but turned his nose up when he saw what it was. "This is rubbish! I need real food."

Motioning with his hand, Connor said, "Then I'll take it back. It's my favorite."

Derrick ripped open the bar and crammed it in his mouth. His childlike manner made everyone watching laugh; even Clay couldn't help but find his ridiculous behavior funny.

While shaking his head at Derrick, Patrick went over to the whiteboard that had maps and photos of Brian and Ronan Gallagher on it. "Okay, gents, let's get to it! Clay, if Derrick's telling us the truth, and Brian Gallagher has your sister, these men will be the ones to get her back."

There was a red circle on the map near a river that Patrick had highlighted yellow and now pointed to. "This is Brian Gallagher's place. He's turned it into a fortress with a small patch of foliage on this side, here. The river is a direct shot to the fishing ports. The girls, we're sure, never travel by road. It's too risky. They have so many boats coming and going that the authorities can no longer randomly search them. They have to know for sure which ones are carrying the girls. Gallagher has his moles in the AHTU and in the local law enforcement. No one's to know what we're doing, lads. Got it? It's just us."

Patrick rolled out a large piece of paper on a table, and the men gathered around. Derrick had sketched a drawing of Gallagher's property and promised he had been out to the place numerous times.

Ronan, Brian's son, had shown Derrick around, bragging outright about the ins and outs of everything that went on there.

While pointing to a small building illustrated on the map, Billy offered, "This is the location Derrick said Gallagher housed the women sometimes. They move them pretty fast because Gallagher doesn't like them staying on his property for too long. He never has more than two to four women at a time on the premises. It's too risky. Ronan explained to Derrick that the longest they've kept girls there was five days. The only reason they would keep them longer is if they were waiting on another shipment from the US or South America. I don't want to say we're in luck, but they happen to be waiting for a shipment. Or at least that's what Ronan told Derrick. My hope is they haven't moved Kayla because of it."

"Our man here"—Patrick pointed at Derrick—"will call Ronan later today to see if he can get an invite onto the property. He swears he and Ronan party together all the time." Then, eyeing Eddie, he stated, "You'll go with him and wiggle your way into Ronan's confidence."

"Not a problem," Eddie assured him.

"Good. While they're busy doing that, Connor, Niall, and Harry, you'll go on a recon mission, here." Patrick pointed to a spot on the map, near the river and on Gallagher's property.

"Where am I gonna be, boss?" Gerard asked.

"You'll be with me. I have a friend at the AHTU that I trust. We're going to pay her a visit. Billy, if you don't mind hanging tight here for a while and make sure our guest, Derrick, doesn't leave, I'd be in your debt."

"No problem. Your country, your gig. I'm here to help in any way I can. Besides, if Gallagher's waiting on a shipment from the US, then I have a few calls to make. I might get some intel on who's supplying him with the girls."

*   *   *   *   *

Patrick and Gerard left first and wouldn't return until later that evening. Connor, Niall, and Harry loaded up everything they needed for the next couple of days and left midafternoon. Derrick had done his part and set up the meeting at a club in Dublin with Ronan. He and Eddie were working out the details and would leave around eight in the evening. Billy had been on the phone for the better part of the day, digging up as much information as he could from his contacts back home. This left Clay with absolutely nothing to do but to roam Patrick's property.

Ireland was beautiful—there was no denying it. Patrick's land only enhanced that impression with its green landscape and fresh air. On either side of the road Clay walked, stone walls separated the fields. They were covered in green moss and had been battered over the years by Ireland's harsh weather. Horses and cows grazed in the pastures, unaware of the crazy world moving rapidly around them.

A trickling noise caught Clay's ear. He followed the sound and stepped off the path, down a small incline. When he found the source, he stopped to admire its beauty. He thought it odd that he could hear moving water, but when he looked at the stream, it seemed motionless. It took Clay's eyes a few seconds to adjust to the shadows and light before he could see it flow.

The tranquility of the moment was broken when he walked across the rocky beach to get closer to the water's edge. His feet crunched and ground the stones with each step he took. It wasn't until he knelt down by the stream that nature's harmony returned.

Clay reached for the water and let it trickle through his fingers. It was freezing cold, but that didn't bother him. The sensation he felt as the water swept past his hand mesmerized him. The stimulation gave his mind a moment of clarity, allowing him to focus on all that had happened since he'd arrived.

When he stood, he took in a deep breath. The crisp air even smelled good. Clay was falling in love with Ireland and her beauty but then remembered she also had a dark side—one he wished he hadn't met. Since this mess with his sister started, he hadn't prayed. Not once. And now, submerged in the tranquility of his surroundings, his grief had a crushing hold on him. Collapsing onto his knees, he bent over with his head resting on the small rocks and wept.

The physical pain he suffered because of his battered body was nothing compared to the mental anguish he now felt. For the first time since he'd received word that Kayla was missing, he let his emotions go. Whatever kept him from praying, be it his anger or his pride, had disappeared.

With his face down, a scripture came to mind. He let the holy words filter through his head and knew what he needed to do. He lifted his eyes toward the sky and then held out his arms and prayed an earnest prayer. He whispered the scriptures out loud from memory. "'Be strong, do not fear; your God will come, he will come with vengeance; with divine retribution he will come to save you'[1]... Please, Father God, forgive me because I do fear! Please, Lord, bring Kayla back to me." Clay's head dropped again as he wept.

He stayed in that position for some time. It wasn't until he heard footsteps coming up behind him that he rose to a kneeling position. With his back to whomever was there, he listened intently and heard the steps halt.

Even with the slight turn of his head, Clay couldn't see who was there. He fought to push back his grief, but it still had a chokehold on him. His voice struggled to get out, "It's okay, I'm done."

He rose to his feet and reversed his body's position until he saw Billy standing some distance back. "Sorry, man, I didn't mean to intrude."

"It's okay. I was bound to lose it at some point. Better here than out there." Clay wiped his eyes.

"Listen," Billy moved closer to Clay, "I know you think this is just another job for me, but it isn't. It's personal for me. Not like it is for you and Eddie, but nevertheless, I take every case personally."

"Why? You don't have any connection to Kayla other than me."

"That's true. However, toward the end of my military career, about twelve years ago, my commanding officer sent me and five other Marines to an embassy to help with security. It was a brief deployment, but during that time, the ambassador's daughter got abducted. She was fifteen, pretty, and she knew it. She met a local

---

[1]   Isaiah 35:4 (NIV).

guy she liked at school, and one day ditched her detail to be with him. That detail was me and another guy."

"Wow. I had no idea."

"Well, you wouldn't. I don't talk about it much. Anyway, we found her, but not before she'd been raped and her face sliced open in several places. She wasn't picture-perfect anymore...well, not in the eyes of the world anyway. Her parents didn't blame me because she had done this more than once. It didn't matter, though, because I blamed myself."

Not knowing what to say right away, Clay just stared at him. Then after a few moments of silence, he offered, "When my parents died and it was just me and Kayla left standing at their gravesite, I thought my world had ended. But now...well now, I know what it feels like to be totally alone. I need Kayla back. Dead or alive, I need her back."

Clay's eyes watered again, and he wiped them. Billy clasped his hand with Clay's in a tight grip and placed his other hand on Clay's shoulder. "I hear God likes it when we pray together."

The mention of God and prayer from Billy stunned Clay. He was grateful the man had faith in God and not just in himself and his friends. Both men bowed their heads, and Billy prayed. The only sounds, other than the words Billy spoke, were the leaves fluttering above, the sound of running water, and the birds singing. There was almost an eerie calm surrounding the two men as they prayed. When Billy closed the prayer with an amen, Clay opened his eyes, looked straight up, and said, "Forgiven."

Billy didn't ask what he meant by that. He released Clay's hand and shoulder at the same time and motioned with his head that they should head back to the workshop. Clay didn't object and followed him. Neither said anything until they had the building in view.

"I know I've already told you, but thank you for doing this for me. I thought I was the only one around here that had any investment in finding my sister. I don't know why, but I need you to know that you're forgiven and so am I. There's no way I could've stopped Kayla from doing what she did. She would've just told me to stay out of her business. Actually, she would have yelled at me that I'm not her boss or parent. I could have no more saved Kayla from herself than you could have saved that young teenager all those years ago. I mean, it's weird that I'm even saying this to you, but there's a strange sense of peace that has liberated me from all that guilt."

The muscles in Billy's face flexed. "I know you're right. I'd love to be free from this self-condemnation, and I keep hoping, with each child I return home, the guilt from that day would subside. But it's rooted in too deep. I hope one day to feel that same liberation that you're feeling now. Honestly, I think the guilt helps me concentrate on the job at hand. But who knows?"

Clay understood and said nothing more about it. He sensed there was something else on Billy's mind, and because of it, he stayed where he stood while waiting for his friend to find the words he needed to say. When he finally spoke, Clay could hear the sadness in his voice. "Your sister—Kayla—if she's in Ireland, she's still alive. My contact back home confirmed that a shipment of South American girls is heading this way. They couldn't stop it in time but were glad to know I'm here and can work on it at this end. Also, Gallagher's name popped up in their intel. The girls are on their way to him."

"This is good, isn't it? I mean, we should be able to find her, right?"

"I don't want to get your hopes up. Kayla may be alive, but she won't be the same. You need to understand that. She's been raped, beaten, and drugged. The young woman we find will only be a shell of who she was. You need to prepare for the worst. It's been twelve days now, twelve days of hell for her, with no end in sight."

That sucked the air right out of Clay. He could only nod his head that he understood. Billy put his hand on Clay's shoulder and directed him back to the workshop. But before they went in, Clay asked, "The ambassador's daughter, she has to be around twenty-seven now. Do you know if she's happy? I mean, living a normal life kind of happy?"

Billy stared at him for a few seconds, and during those moments of silence, he understood without hearing Billy's next words. "She never leaves the house because she's afraid of her own shadow."

The tightness in Clay's throat was back, along with the guilt. No, he refused to let it consume him. When he saw his sister again, and he knew he would, he would make it very clear to her, that though he wasn't her parent, he was her older brother. Overly protective at times, but she would have to learn how to deal with that.

*   *   *   *   *

"Kate, I would like you to meet Clay, Billy and Eddie. And this bit of garbage is Derrick. He's the informant I told you about. He'll get Eddie onto Brian Gallagher's property."

Kate Walsh was in her mid- to late forties, average height and slim, almost to the point of being too skinny. She was pretty and spoke with a soft Irish accent. Clay would never have pegged her as someone that would join the military or the Anti-Human Trafficking Unit (AHTU), but she was a twenty-year veteran and had been on the task force for the last six years. Kate had authored the first in-depth report on human trafficking within Ireland and the fishing industry for the Blue Blindfold Annual Report, a report that propelled her into the current role she now had, the director of the AHTU in Dublin.

"You're sure you can manage that, Derrick? Gallagher's not a man to entertain unfamiliar faces."

"No, but he'll listen to 'is son, and Ronan will listen ta me. Besides, I'll get 'im ossified, d'yaknowwhatImeanlike? And take 'im ta 'is da. Brian will be happy for the care I've given ta 'is blood."

Eddie shook his head. "You're a true Dubliner, are ya not? Canna speak to save your life." Then facing Kate, he assured her, "I'll get in, one way or another, I guarantee it. I'll have the boy eating out of my hand by the time he takes me to meet his da."

One eyebrow lifted as she eyed Eddie with uncertainty. "Let's hope so. Or this will end badly for many people, starting with you and Derrick."

With Kate's last words, Derrick's loftiness changed to an overwhelming fear. "If we had a girl ta take 'im, we'd have a shoo-in!"

"I have that covered. One of my agents will be your bait. She'll meet you at the club."

"Are ya dense, woman? None of yer agents are gonna pass! She'll be too old. Nothin' over twenty-five, and they have ta be spectacular, even at that! No bucket o' snot will fly with Gallagher. Ya need ta let me pick a girl, one I know he'll like."

"You're crazy if you think I'm going to let you abduct a young girl! My agent will pass—you'll see."

Derrick shook his head and asked, "Right, then, how we gonna know who she is?"

"Don't you worry yourself about that, she'll find you."

He still didn't agree with Kate and snapped, "Yer an eejit if ya think she'll work! I'll just get Ronan ossified 'til he canna stand and then take 'im home ta 'is da."

"Do as you please, but you'll be taking my agent with you when you go," Kate reiterated and then turned to face Patrick. "I'll go along with your plan, but this is the closest we've gotten to Gallagher. His clandestine methods make it difficult to pinpoint where he operates from. We've searched the property three times and found nothing, not even a strand of hair. Now that we have a good understanding of how Gallagher operates, we're sure the girls aren't on his property."

Eddie joined in the conversation by adding, "I've heard whispers of girls travelin' down the Liffey, as well as a few other rivers. If that's the case and we mess this up, the girls will get scattered, and we'll not find a one of them."

Patrick's foot rested on a stool. He dropped it, stood to his full height, and announced, "Then we get it right the first time. Okay, gents, you know the plan. My men should already be hiding on Gallagher's property, and they'll stay there until further notice. If something goes wrong, they'll be the ones to get you out. The guards will check you for weapons the second you step foot on the grounds. So you'll have to go in empty-handed."

"What will I be doing while all of this is going on?" Clay asked.

"Waiting here. Billy, you'll come with Kate and me. We have a few leads on that shipment of yours."

"Seriously! You want me to stay here? That's my sister. I think I should be there when you find her."

Kate shot an unsympathetic glare at Clay. "Your outburst is the very reason you're not going! You're too emotionally connected to this and are liable to get my agent or one of Patrick's men killed. Let us do our job, and with any luck, we'll get your sister back and a few others that might be with her."

If she didn't get it through Clay's head, Billy did. "Our talk earlier—don't forget what I told you. I'll find her and bring her to you, dead or alive."

Billy's "dead or alive" comment sent a chill down his spine. He hoped they would find Kayla alive, but remembering their earlier conversation, he understood what Billy meant. One way or another, Kayla would be returned to him.

"Okay, I'll stay. But don't leave me hanging! When you have her, call me."

With the promise that Billy would, the meeting ended and because of the late hour, those who needed to go, went their separate ways. Clay felt useless as he watched the last vehicle drive away. The guilt of not being the one to save Kayla was almost too much for him to bear, but he needed to let it go.

When the last taillight disappeared, Clay slipped his hand inside his cargo pants pocket and felt his phone. Right away, he thought of Emer. He pulled it out and scrolled through his short list of contacts. He had Billy's and Eddie's numbers, his office number in Fresno, Ian's and Mary's home number, and Emer's office and cell numbers. That was it. He paused for a split second before he pushed Emer's number. He wasn't sure why he wanted to talk to her, nor how well his call would be received. Remembering his conversation with Lily, Emer's receptionist, he whispered, "Why not? She'll be mad at Lily and that's what she lives for," and then he pressed "call."

It rang a few times before he heard a woman's voice say, "'ello?"

"There you go again, dropping letters to your words." A slight chuckle warmed Clay's voice. "Hello, how are you, Emer? It's me, Clay."

"I know who it is, you buffoon! How d'ya get my number?"

He laughed. "How do you think? I heard you finally got the locksmith to come out."

"I'll fire her one day! She thinks it's funny and—"

"Well, it is funny! Come on. Sending the locksmith to your apartment was clever, even for Lily."

"It was lashing like crazy. Not to mention, I was completely knackered when I got home! It wasn't funny."

"Lashing…knackered?" Clay asked.

Calming down, Emer let out an exasperated breath before she answered, "Raining and tired. You are aware they have Irish translation dictionaries for Americans? Honest. I've seen them. You should buy one."

Clay's voice gave away his smile. "Since we're on the topic of translations, what does *ossified* mean? I was guessing drunk."

"That's correct."

"And a bucket of snot?"

Emer laughed. "Who have you been talking to?"

"No talking on my part, just listening to the guy that helped beat me up, while he answered a few questions."

"Oh, Clay, that's great! Does he know where your sister is?"

That familiar lump was back and wedged in his throat. He did his best to rid himself of it before he answered. It didn't budge. "No, not yet. I mean, he really isn't sure if she's still where he left her. But the good news is, Eddie introduced me to an American Marine and some of Ireland's finest, Army Ranger Wings, all retired. They're now fighting against human trafficking here in Ireland. Everyone took off and left me here to twiddle my thumbs. Kate said—"

"Who's Kate?" Emer interrupted.

"She's the head of the Anti-Human Trafficking Unit in Dublin, or I should say she's the director."

"Oh." Emer sounded surprised by her title.

"Anyway, Kate's convinced I'd be a liability. She's probably right. Eddie and the others are good at their jobs, or so they say. I just hope they can find Kayla…preferably alive."

This time, Clay's voice gave away his sorrow, and he thought he heard Emer sniffle. He didn't mean to make her feel bad. "I'm sorry, I didn't—"

"An ugly person!" she blurted out.

"I'm sorry, what?"

"A bucket of snot means an ugly person or someone that's not attractive. Anyway, it's a stupid saying."

Her sudden change in topic momentarily yanked Clay out of his depressed state and made him chuckle. "Okay, that's funny. I do have to say, you Irish have a colorful way of speaking. He said something else, some long word, or rambled a chain of words together that I couldn't understand. He spoke them so fast, that I don't even know how to repeat it back to you."

"Most likely a filler, like the words *ya know* or *the likes*. Most of the young Dubliners use them out of habit. I find their use of them annoying."

"That doesn't surprise me." Clay walked back inside the workshop and took a seat on a step that led up to the loft. He took a minute to get situated before he mentioned, "I wish I had remembered my Bible."

"Your Bible? Why?"

Clay found that amusing and answered, "For the obvious reasons—it calms me when I read it."

"Calms you? It's full of rules that are impossible to follow. How can you find comfort in something that always points out your faults? I should think it would only make you more miserable."

"Ah, spoken like a true skeptic."

"Sorry, Catholic school was brutal. I was always in trouble. Never could stay within the parameters of the school's rules."

"Who would have thought Emer O'Farrell was a troublemaker?"

"Not a troublemaker, just not a rule follower."

"There's a difference between the two? What was it? Sneaking boys in after hours?"

"Typical. Go straight for the naughty stuff."

Clay laughed and was feeling more at ease with the doctor. He enjoyed listening to her share a few tales of mischief that she had gotten into at boarding school. Clay slid around on the step he sat on and leaned back against the banister as she spoke. Every now and then, he would interrupt and have her translate a word she had used that he didn't understand. Before he knew it, he found himself enjoying their conversation, and the guilt that he had felt earlier from not being allowed to go with Billy and the others had faded.

CHAPTER 4

The Emerald Island Nightclub always had huge crowds on the weekend. The line outside proved it to be so tonight. It surprised Eddie to see the large number of people stretched from its door to the street corner. Derrick strolled right to the front of the line and greeted the bouncer with a fist bump. The large man stepped aside and let him in without question. Eddie followed in behind him.

Inside, the dance floor was full of young men and women moving to the music. Following Derrick through the sea of human bodies dancing was easy enough. However, his getting through the second round of bouncers wasn't. Derrick's appearance parted the human barricade the security guards were providing and let him go up the stairs. Eddie, a few steps behind him, got stopped. He tried to explain that he and Derrick were together, but the two men didn't budge. Frustrated and on the verge of hitting one of them, a whistle from above caught one bouncer's attention. Derrick leaned over the banister and yelled, "He's wit me! Let 'im up. Come on, Eddie, stop faffin' 'bout!"

The two men stepped aside and let him pass.

The upper level was for private parties, and tonight, Ronan Gallagher had reserved the entire floor for his friends. When Eddie reached the top step, Derrick seemed pumped up and eager to have some fun. He slapped Eddie hard on the shoulder and ushered him over to Ronan, as if they were old buddies. Before Derrick could introduce Eddie, Ronan caught sight of them and yelled, "Howya, Deek! Who's the ol' bag o' wind with ya?"

"Oi, Ronan, lay off! This is Eddie, my mate. He's in town for a few nights. I thought I'd show 'im a good time and get 'im fluthered."

"Great! Oi, Brenda, fetch a couple pints of the black stuff for my friends and shots o' whisky, would ya?"

Eddie sat down next to Derrick, looking around as if he was in awe of his surroundings; all the while his body moved to the rhythm of the music. Brenda returned with the drinks and Eddie nodded his head in thanks. Her appreciation for his manners didn't go unnoticed. Ronan leaned forward and said, "She's a nice ride, but ya can do better. I promise, the night's young." Then, eyeing Derrick, he said, "After yer drink, go down and find us a few pretty girls. I'm in the mood for some fun!"

Ronan dropped a shot of whiskey, glass and all, into his pint of beer, causing it to overflow onto the table. He didn't seem to care; he just picked up the glass, put it to his lips, and chugged the beer and whiskey mix until both glasses were empty. He yelled something incoherent while shaking his head. Derrick laughed and did the same with his beer and whiskey. He even gave the same response afterward. When it was Eddie's turn, he slung his head back, but before he could get the drink down, he choked and spewed the contents from his mouth, dumping the rest all over the floor. A roar of laughter rang out from everyone that saw what happened.

Eddie stood up laughing while brushing off his shirt and pants. "I'm off to the jacks, be back in a jiff!"

Stepping around the table, Eddie headed for the stairs and made his way toward the men's restroom. Once away from prying eyes, he took his phone out and made a quick call. It was short and to the point. He said, "I'm in!" then took a quick glance at his screen and announced, "I got it," before he disconnected and put the phone back in his pocket.

In the men's restroom, Eddie took his time cleaning up. He hoped Derrick and Ronan were well on their way to getting drunk. Once they were, it would be easy for him to look intoxicated right along with them. Though Eddie enjoyed an occasional pint, he wasn't a big drinker and if given a choice, he would never choose dark beer. He had never acquired a taste for liquor, largely because it smelled awful, so he hadn't had to fake the gag reflex earlier. He was lucky he hadn't puked.

He tossed the paper towel in the trash and was reaching for the door when it flew open. A young man ran in, barely making it to a urinal before he spewed all over it and the floor. Those closest to him hurled swear words at him, and one guy even pushed his face down in the urinal, full of vomit, for getting his shoes dirty.

Eddie left the restroom without giving the drunk a second thought. As far as he was concerned, the guy got what he deserved. *No one should ever go out and get that plastered.*

Not wanting to leave Derrick alone for too long, Eddie pushed his way through the crowd and was about to take the stairs when he collided into a pretty redhead. The drink she carried got knocked out of her hand and spilled all over the bouncer blocking passage to the second floor. Eddie jumped between the young woman and the furious security guard. "Sorry, buddy. My fault. I didn't see her. Look, I'm sure Ronan will pay for your cleanin'."

The man glared at the woman and pointed toward the entrance. "Out with ya! Go on, out with ya!"

"Actually, she's with me, do ya mind? Ronan's lookin' to have a wee bit of fun. You'll not stand in the man's way, will ya?"

The big guy didn't like it, but he stepped aside and let them through. Eddie offered the young woman the stairs first and then followed. Seeing a pretty redhead with Eddie surprised Ronan and Derrick.

Ronan could barely contain himself and yelled, "Oi, Eddie, where d'ya find the beautiful coppertop?"

"Downstairs. She doused the security with her drink. I thought it best to save her. Sorry, lass, what's your name?"

"Claire. And thanks, this is my first time in the club. Getting tossed tonight would've been a bust."

"No bother. This is Ronan and Derrick. Would ya like to stay for a drink?"

"Yeah. That'd be grand. Thanks."

"Claire, come and sit with me. No need ta hang with the ol' bag o' wind. Come on." Ronan patted the seat next to him and then shouted over at the waitress with his finger moving in a circular motion, "Brenda, drinks all around!"

*   *   *   *   *

At one thirty the next morning, Derrick and Eddie dragged Ronan out of the Emerald Island Nightclub. Claire had her arm draped around Ronan's waist, trying to steer him to the car. The two sang "The Gypsy Maiden" an old Irish folk song, and every now and then, Ronan would swing his arm out, emphasizing a long note, which inevitably caused them to stumble.

Derrick made it to Ronan's black Mercedes first, held out his hand to his friend, and said, "Keys."

"No way! My car. I drive!" Ronan insisted.

"Right and miss the long ride home with the ginger? Sit in the back with 'er and enjoy 'er. Eddie and I won't be a bother ta either of ya. Right, Eddie?"

"Nope, enjoy. The girl looks like she wants to play."

This perked Ronan up. He looked at Claire with salivating lust. "Oh, aye, I think I will. Thanks, lads!" Ronan tossed the keys to Derrick, who unlocked the car. He even opened the back door for his friend. Claire insisted Ronan get in first, but just as he did, she slammed his head into the roof of the car, knocking him out cold. Grabbing a fistful of his hair and belt, she hurled him into the back seat.

"Hey! Whaddaya do that for?" Derrick shouted.

"And you didn't think I could pass. Now get in and drive! This took far too long. Now get moving!"

Eddie lips twisted up on one side, displaying his cheerfulness when Derrick looked his way. "Ya knew and said nothin'?"

"Yeah, well, she's magic, isn't she? Ya did tell her boss none of her agents would pass because they'd be too old and ugly."

Derrick growled at them and got in. He started the car and threw the lever in reverse. Then, draping his arm over the front passenger's seat, he looked over his shoulder and backed out of the parking space. "You're gonna have a hard time explainin' the knot on 'is head."

"Just drive, you idiot!" Claire shouted. "He's drunk and fell into the car. It's not that hard."

Eddie made a quick phone call, stating, "We're on our way," and then hung up. Those were the last words spoken until they made it to Brian Gallagher's property.

*   *   *   *   *

If evil had a face, it would be in Brian Gallagher's likeness. Despite his unpleasant disposition with his business dealings, he was a staunch believer when it came to family. In all his twenty-nine years of marriage, he had never cheated on his wife. He had even killed a few women who tried to seduce him. What good he had in his life came from his wife, Angela, and he loved her dearly. She was everything he wasn't: sweet, kind, caring, and very loving toward him and their children. They had three boys; Ronan was the youngest and the most trouble, but Brian loved him.

What disappointed him most about his son was that he couldn't hold his liquor. It angered him to see his boy passed out on the couch, but knowing Derrick was with Ronan gave him some peace of mind. His son's friend always brought him home in one piece, and he was very grateful for that. Of course, Brian made it very clear to Derrick that if anything ever happened to his son, he would kill him. He made sure the young man never forgot it.

Tonight, however, Derrick not only bought his son home, but also strangers. Brian was very suspicious of those he didn't know. But this morning, one of the new faces just happened to be a young lady—a beautiful redhead. All Brian could ever see when he saw a pretty face was money. And this face was gorgeous.

Derrick had finished with his apologies for Ronan's state and went into the introductions. "Mr. Gallagher, this is my mate, Eddie, from Cork. He's a Yank, but he's been livin' in Ireland for the past fifteen years. He's been a help in findin' some o' the girls I bring ya.

And this here's Claire, she's Ronan's date. Eddie found 'er at the club. He's a good eye."

Brian studied Eddie for a moment and then the young woman. When he held out his hand, Eddie shook it and said, "You've a fine home, Mr. Gallagher. Thank you for welcomin' me here."

"Fifteen years of Ireland has you nearly sounding like us. Still a bit of Yank in you, though."

"My Chicago accent is still fightin' to be heard, sir."

"Allister, pour the man and this pretty lady a drink. Eddie and Claire, please have a seat."

"Thank ya kindly, Mr. Gallagher, but I canna drink another drop, unless of course it's coffee bein' offered."

Brian frowned but nodded to Allister to get the coffee. "And you?"

Claire seemed drunk but managed, "Yeah, coffee would be grand, thanks."

Derrick quickly added, "Thank ya kindly, but no coffee for me."

"That's good, because I'm not offering anything to you. Get Ronan up to his room! Put him to bed and pray he doesn't die in his own vomit. Or it will be your last night alive."

If Derrick was frightened of Brian Gallagher's threat, he didn't show it. He pulled Ronan to his feet, put his arm around his friend's waist, and then draped Ronan's arm over his shoulder. Once he was sure they wouldn't fall over, the two staggered out of the room, leaving Eddie and Claire alone with Brian.

Allister brought in the coffee and set the tray down on the table in front of the couch. Brian took a seat in the chair across from them and crossed one leg over the other while resting his chin on one hand, as though he was in deep thought.

"Le Penseur, the Thinker," Claire said.

Brian's eyes bore deep into Claire's soul.

Unnerved by his stare, she said, "I'm sorry. The way you're sitting reminds me of the famous bronze sculpture by Auguste Rodin. It's one of my favorite pieces of art." She glanced around the room and smiled. "I can't help but admire all your artwork. Originals, all of them. Francisco de Goya, Picasso…and a fabulous landscape by Rembrandt. You have a keen eye, Mr. Gallagher."

Claire's comment brought Brian out of his private thoughts and back to his guests. "My wife, Angela, is the collector. You've an eye yourself."

"My studies at the university were in art. When my mother and father were alive, they'd take me and my sisters to the museum every weekend. We'd spend hours trying to replicate our favorite portraits with colored pencils or chalk," she said with a slight laugh. "We were never any good at it, but my dad always took our drawings with him to work and decorated his office with them."

"Sorry to hear about your parents. Where are your sisters?" Brian was curious.

"One lives in London and the other in Boston with her American husband. I don't get to see either of them much anymore. I swear, I could fall off the planet and neither would ask about me for years." The cheerfulness in Claire's eyes faded.

"Well, we'd miss you. Wouldn't we, Eddie? A pretty lass like you."

"Oh, aye, I would. You've no aunts or uncles, or the likes livin' near ya?"

"No. It's just me, which I'm okay with. I'm happy. I've applied to a few galleries around Dublin for a job. I haven't heard back from any yet, but I'm hoping I'll hear something soon."

Gallagher's eyes gave away his delight. Claire had done her job convincing him that she would make him a lot of money, and he grinned when he said, "Derrick's right, Eddie, you can pick them."

The gratification that came from knowing he had power over people's lives never ceased to amaze Brian. It gave him a great deal of satisfaction to watch Claire's body language go from calm to fear. It was a moment he quiet enjoyed and pleasure that never grew old.

At first, Eddie avoided eye contact with Claire. Then, shrugging his shoulders, his mouth twisted upward and he asked, "Oi, lass, you enjoy a good ride, don't ya?"

"What?"

"Come on, hitchin' up with me and the boys tonight, ya had to know it wouldn't be free. You'd have to give a little."

Claire bolted up, but Allister blocked the only exit to the room. Eddie rose to his feet and said, "Mr. Gallagher, sir, I didn't know what a catch we had, but we've a keeper. I think ya could get a cool fifty thousand for her easy, if not more. We don't find a lot of gingers, well, not as pretty as you, darlin'."

Allister pulled his gun from its holster while Eddie grabbed Claire's arm. She tried to jerk free, but he had a firm grip on her. With her free hand, she swung at him and missed. Then a rash decision to sink her teeth into his arm put an end to her fight. Eddie's fist collided with her face, causing her body to go limp, and fall into his arms. He threw her over his shoulder and followed Allister out of the house to a new black Toyota Hilux pickup.

With a great deal of care, Eddie placed her in the back of the truck and climbed in next to her. He leaned back and placed Claire's head on his lap. Gazing down at her, he pushed a strand of hair from her face and stared at her for the longest time. When the truck lurched forward, Eddie placed his arm over her shoulder to keep her from rolling around.

As he watched Gallagher's house disappear, he balled-up his fist and hit the side of the truck. "Sweet, Jaysus, please, we're needin' some help here!"

*   *   *   *   *

Once Derrick was sure Ronan wouldn't die in his sleep, he went downstairs and found Eddie and Claire gone. Their whereabouts confused him. The mugs were full of hot coffee and Gallagher sat in his chair smoking a cigarette. Derrick watched as he blew the smoke from his lungs. His boss pointed to the couch, indicating he wanted him to sit down. Derrick wiped the palms of his hands on his trousers before taking a seat.

"You've gone and made a mess of things. A mess I have to clean up." Gallagher took another drag from his cigarette as he eyed the young man. He flicked the ashes into a small ceramic bowl and blew the smoke toward Derrick before he continued. "A mess I don't want to clean up, but if I don't, my organization is at risk."

"Um, I'm sorry, Mr. Gallagher, I've no idea what yer speakin' 'bout. I've done as you've asked. I'd never do anything ta lose yer trust. Not ever!"

"Oh, but you have, boy, you have. You've brought strangers to my home. Into my house, where my wife's sleeping. You've no business doing so, and you know the rules."

"Seriously, Mr. Gallagher, Eddie's my mate. He helps me find girls in Cork and other places around the country so not ta be pickin' from the same spot." Derrick's eyes moistened while he tried to persuade Brian to believe him.

"I've no doubt the man's who you say he is, but you shouldn't have brought him here, lad."

"But the lass…she's perfect for ya! I'm tellin' ya the truth, he's the one that found 'er for ya. I'm sorry, really I am, but no harm will come to ya because of 'im. I promise!"

"Oh, I'm absolutely sure he won't be a problem."

Derrick's eyes widened. He knew Eddie would be dead soon, if not already. He actually liked the guy. But sitting across from his boss, he feared more for his life than Eddie's. He slid back onto the couch when Gallagher stood up.

"Come on, boy, all's well. Just remember to never bring strangers to my home again. I'll walk you out."

Getting up slowly from the couch, Derrick nodded his thanks for giving him a second chance. He led the way outside with Gallagher following. He turned to his boss when he remembered he had arrived in Ronan's car.

"I'm sorry, sir, I've no means ta get back ta Dublin."

Just then, a truck pulled in and parked. Allister got out and said, "It's done."

Gallagher reached out his hand and snapped his fingers at Allister several times, who in turn handed him his gun. Derrick couldn't run fast enough. Gallagher shot him in the back of the head before he got five feet away.

Handing the gun back to Allister, Brian ordered, "Have someone clean up this mess!"

"Right away."

Gallagher walked back inside the house and found his wife, Angela, at the foot of the stairs. "What is it, Brian? Who's shooting?"

"I'm very sorry to wake you, dear. Just a rat. The lads got carried away and shot it. Go back to bed."

CHAPTER 5

The first group to make it back to Patrick's workshop was the team sent to stakeout Gallagher's place. They arrived at six thirty in the morning. Clay flew down the stairs and bombarded them with questions. From the looks on their faces, he could tell something was wrong and that the mission must have gone awry.

Connor, the team leader, said, "You'll get filled in when Patrick returns. He'll be here shortly."

Clay stormed outside, slammed the door behind him, and yelled, "Augh!"

He balled his fingers into fists and desperately wanted to hit something. Instead, both fists went to his face, and he collapsed on his knees. Pain shot through him like a bolt of lightning when he did. The hard ground jarred his ribs, reminding him they hadn't healed. He stayed in an upright position, sucking in air through clenched teeth. It took a few seconds for the pain to subside.

A black Land Rover pulled up at the same time Clay collapsed. Billy jumped out of the vehicle and ran over to him. "Hey, man, what's going on? You okay?"

"Something happened at Gallagher's place and no one will tell me what it was."

"Get up. Let's go for a walk."

Clay stood, held his side, and took in a deep breath before he followed Billy down the road that led to the stream. Clay didn't speak—he waited for Billy to say what was on his mind.

"Derrick's dead, and they lost Eddie."

Shocked, Clay stopped and stared at him. "How did they...?" Clay clasped his hands on top of his head. "Ah geez, and what about the shipment—you missed it too, didn't you?"

The expression on Billy's face answered the question before he uttered one word. "We're not sure what happened to the shipment. Kate thinks someone got word to Gallagher. She stayed behind to find out who. Brian Gallagher keeps a tight ship and has people everywhere. Kate has known for quite some time that she has a mole in her office but isn't sure who it is. They must've given Gallagher a heads-up, and he had the shipment redirected. All we found were empty containers."

Every emotion that Clay felt rushing through his body blew up inside him, leaving him mentally and physically drained. Staying focused on their conversation was difficult. He paced from one side of the road to the other, making sharp turns with each direction change, an action he hoped would calm him.

"So Kate doesn't know who it is that tipped off Gallagher?"

"She's had her eye on an agent and now she's sure it's him. The man's in custody and Kate's questioning him as we speak."

"Do you think he'll talk?"

"Maybe." Billy ran his hand over the top of his head. "Listen, I'm sorry this didn't go down the way we had all hoped it would. Gallagher has survived a long time because he hasn't made any mistakes—well, until now."

"What do you mean until now?"

"The agent Kate sent is with Eddie. She has a tracking device on her and it's still giving out a strong signal. We know where she is. Kate wants to hang back, so they not only get the girls but also the other shipment. Patrick, his team, and I are leaving here at noon to meet up with the director."

"But my sister could be with the agent. What happens if something else goes wrong and you miss Kayla again?"

"I know this is hard for you, but you need to understand, there are other girls involved. I'm not here just for Kayla. Remember, I came to Ireland because of another girl. I'm helping with your sister's case because I think there's a good chance they're together. It isn't just Kayla anymore. We want them all, and I promise we're going to get them all."

Having been reminded that Billy's wasn't there just for his sister, was disappointing. He had forgotten about the other girl Billy was searching for. He hated that Kayla wasn't his only motivation. Clay knew he was being selfish, wanting everyone to concentrate on finding his sister. Now he understood that wasn't the team's objective. He wasn't even convinced that Billy could keep his promise to him or the girls, but he needed to let it go. No amount of arguing would save Kayla. He grudgingly said, "Yeah, okay. Whatever."

Being upset at him wouldn't help his sister's plight either. Truth be told, he was grateful that Billy was honest and didn't spare his feeling. With that realization, the tension he was feeling gave way. He could sense Billy's stare and knew he had more to say. He nodded to his friend that he was ready to listen.

"Okay, so something positive came out of last night. Patrick's team has video footage of Brian Gallagher killing Derrick with his righthand man, Allister, handing him the gun. He's going to jail one way or another, but getting the girls back will shut him down completely and will be a tremendous victory for us."

Clay tried to understand why they just didn't arrest him now. He figured it was because Gallagher had a huge operation; taking him down wasn't enough. He was positive Kate wanted everything. Gallagher was only a tiny piece of a rather large puzzle that he couldn't see. His only concern was finding Kayla and no one else.

"What am I supposed to do while you're gone?"

"You should go home."

"I'm not going home!" Clay snapped. "Besides, I don't have a passport. Derrick and his thugs took it, remember?"

"I suggest you go to the American embassy and tell them you got robbed and need a new passport. Then go home. I won't lie to you—this could be over with tomorrow, or in a month, or possibly longer. Go home, Clay."

"I'm not leaving without my sister!" Clay jabbed his finger in the air only inches from Billy's chest and yelled, "And I expect daily updates!"

The outburst startled Billy, but he didn't move; he just stared at Clay.

His eruption surprised even himself. Clay knew he was being unreasonable, but he didn't care. What did matter, was that Billy was tiring of him fast and he needed to find a way to fix that.

"Listen, man—"

"How much of a donation will it take?" Clay asked, cutting Billy off. "A hundred thousand dollars? Two hundred? Give me the name of the organization, and I'll have the money wired to them. I'm not leaving! And just so you know, I was going to donate anyway, but now you get to set the price. One that will allow me to stay and get daily updates."

The frustrated look on Billy's face was enough to let Clay know that his outburst had pushed Billy right to the edge, and it was going to cost him. "Fine! HMSC, Harper's Ministries, Save a Child. The organization is out of California. It's run by the Harper family. Their daughter, Linda, went missing in 1997 and was found in 2000. She's now the charity's CEO."

"So is it safe to say I'm going with you?"

"Yeah, you bought yourself a ticket to go as far as Killybegs. But that ticket only gives you access to information and nothing more."

"What's Killybegs?"

"It's not a what, it's a where, and it's northwest of here. The operations might not be in Killybegs per se, but it will be the closest place to civilization you'll get, and that's where you'll be."

"Where will the operations take place?"

"In the ocean. The Atlantic Ocean, to be more precise."

A puzzled expression shot across Clay's face. He was sure he had his geography right and that the Irish Sea was to the east of Ireland and the Atlantic to the west. "Okay, wait. I'm confused. Aren't we near the Irish Sea?"

"Yeah, we are, but they aren't. I'm not sure how Gallagher's people moved them so fast, but Kate does, and at the moment, the agent's beacon shows she's out in the Atlantic Ocean somewhere."

"Ah, geez."

*   *   *   *   *

The ocean was violent. Eddie had never felt this dizzy in his life. His world was rolling in every direction with each wave that hit the fishing vessel. It was all he could do not to vomit. He and Claire had been tossed into a storage room at the bottom of a large trawler with seven other young women. For whatever reason, Gallagher hadn't had either of them killed, which Eddie credited to divine intervention by his Savior, Jesus Christ. God wasn't done with him yet, and he was grateful for it.

Another thing Eddie couldn't comprehend was why he was there. The women he understood, but a grown man that had no value in the market of human trafficking, he didn't get. Allister had pushed him onto the fishing boat and ordered him to stay with Claire. He did as he was told because there was no way he would ever leave Claire alone.

The moment he realized they were in trouble, Eddie had actually contemplated climbing out the back of the truck and running to safety. Allister would have been none the wiser, but that would have meant leaving Claire.

For the first leg of their voyage, he moved around freely. It wasn't until they boarded a trawler that his situation changed, and he became a prisoner. When he carried Claire's drugged body into the storeroom, someone from behind clobbered him in the back of the head. Eddie lifted his hand to the spot and felt a knot.

He heard a moan and turned his head toward the sound. It was Claire. "Good, she's wakin' up."

Eddie slid over to get closer to her. He hadn't meant to hit her as hard as he did, but he had knocked her out cold. He felt terrible for hitting her at all but thought it was the only way to protect her. Had he known Allister was going to drug her, he wouldn't have hit her at all. Then he remembered his arm and the teeth mark Claire left after she bit him. His hitting her had been a knee jerk reaction to her teeth sinking deep into his flesh.

He leaned in close and whispered, "Oi, you okay?"

Placing a hand on her face, she answered, "Ah, criminy, my head is killing me."

"Sorry about that. I meant only to slap ya open-handed, not a full-on fist to your face. But I had nothing to do with druggin' ya."

"You hit me with your fist. What an idiot! Ah, geez, I'm gonna be sick." Claire leaned over and Eddie barely got the bucket under her before she spewed. She lifted her head after she spit the rest of the nasty taste out of her mouth. Looking in Eddie's direction, she asked, "Where are we?"

"On a trawler in the Atlantic Ocean somewhere."

"What? How'd we get to the Atlantic?"

"Boat, car, another boat, and now we're on a trawler."

Claire panicked for a moment and felt around for something on her person. There was a sigh of relief when she found what she was searching for. Eddie informed her, "They took our phones if that's what you're lookin' for?"

"No. I don't need the phone. I've a tracker in my dress. Thank goodness, it's still there."

Hearing that Claire had a tracker on her released some of the anxiety he was feeling. Hopefully, it was doing its job and Billy and Patrick knew where they were. However, with all the rocking and rolling the trawler was doing, he didn't think it mattered. The merciless sea would swallow the ship long before anyone found them.

He gave pause to his fears and thought of the scriptures where Jesus and his disciples were on a boat during a violent storm. It terrified the disciples and Jesus said to them, "Why are you afraid, you of little faith?"[2] Eddie swallowed back the bile coming up his throat and said out loud, "Apologies, Jaysus, for doubtin' ya."

Claire slugged him hard in the chest. He curled into a ball in case another fist was on its way. "You're not blaming God for this one, Eddie! This is all on you!"

"Ouch! No blamin' here, just a word of gratitude from one of His humble servants."

"Gratitude for what? We're out in the middle of the ocean in a storm, no less! Not much to be thankful for now, is there?"

"We're alive, are we not, lass?"

---

[2] Matthew 8:26 (CSB).

Claire let out a frustrated groan. "Ugh! You're right. I'm just scared and feeling a little helpless at the moment."

"I as well."

"Have you found any of the girls?" Claire's body shuddered from the cold.

"Oh aye, we've several bodies lying about. I tried to wake them, but they're all doped up. A few have their eyes opened, but they're not speakin'."

"Brilliant! So you've no clue if Kayla's on board with us?"

"You've plenty of time to ask them yourself. Don't think we're goin' anywhere—not anytime soon."

"Then give me a hand."

The trawler rocked up, down, and sideways, making it hard for Claire to stay upright. Eddie wasn't doing much better, but between the two they managed to stand and stepped over a few stored items that had fallen to the floor. Once on his own two feet, Eddie stated the obvious, "It's a wee bit chilly in here."

"You think?" Claire replied snidely. "If the temperature drops any more, I may as well be wearing nothing. My jacket and dress aren't meant for winter." Someone moaned. Claire stopped talking for a second, and then ordered, "Hand me the bucket."

"Aye." When Eddie reached for one of the five-gallon containers rolling around, the trawler hit an enormous wave and sent him flying into Claire, knocking her to the floor.

"Get off, Eddie! I'm on top of someone."

The girl groaned and said something in a language similar to Italian or Spanish. Claire rolled over, doing her best to get off the poor woman. She, along with Eddie's help, pulled her to an upright position so they wouldn't step on her head should another wave knocked them to the ground. They moved around the storage area, doing their best to sit the girls up as they did. Claire felt around and found another young woman crushing a smaller girl.

"Help me!"

Eddie lifted the larger woman for her so she could pull the smaller body from underneath. They were too late.

"This one's dead," Claire announced. "She either died from the drugs or from suffocating."

"Ah, geez. Can ya tell who she is?"

"She's just a child. Nine or ten at the most. Poor thing." Claire felt around some more and hit bare flesh. "There's one more in the corner. Give me a hand."

"Right." Eddie braced himself on the hull with one hand and with the other he reached for the girl's head. He felt moisture and advised, "Easy with this one. She's a gash on her forehead, but she's breathin'."

The woman mumbled something when they repositioned her. Neither could understand what she said. Claire leaned in closer so she could hear better and asked, "Come again?"

"Help…Clay."

"Kayla! Is your name Kayla Warner?"

"Kayla?" The young woman's brain struggled to process the words. Finally comprehending the question, she whispered, "Um, yeah."

"Right then," Eddie said as he situated himself next to her. "Aye, your brother's been looking for ya, girl. He'll be glad to know you're alive."

Lifting her hand to the cut on her head, Kayla murmured, "He'll be…so mad. Don't tell—"

"No, he's not mad, Kayla, just concerned," Claire informed her. Then she asked, "Are you okay? Do you know what they gave you?"

Kayla's fingers crawled over the cut on her forehead. "Ouch." Her hand, too heavy to hold up anymore, dropped to her lap.

"You've a wee cut. Best to leave it. The blood has dried, and it's not bleedin' at the moment."

"Did you hear anything, Kayla? Do you know where they're taking us?" Claire asked. Kayla didn't answer. She had passed out again. "It doesn't matter anyway, we've no way to get word to anyone."

A weak voice behind them said, "*Na Cealla Beaga.*"

"Where?"

"*Na Cealla Beaga.*"

"The shipping port in Killybegs?"

"No, near Killybegs," the woman corrected. "I'm cold."

"Aye, lass, we're all freezin'. Hang on just a bit longer. We've been at it for near an hour," Eddie said in a consoling tone. Then he asked, "How ya doin', I mean, other than bein' cold?"

"Okay, just a little groggy."

"What's your name, lass?" Eddie asked.

"June."

"How long ya been with them?"

"I'm not sure. Only a few days, I think."

"Today's the twenty-eighth of May," Claire advised.

"Eh, yeah, I dunno. Maybe five or six days."

Eddie continued with his questions. "Where'd they take you from?"

"My fella, he's a bit of a chancer," June answered. Then, focusing more on Eddie, she managed, "He likes to gamble, and he got in over 'is head. He couldn't pay the money back and some blokes broke 'is legs and took me for payment."

"Well, he got what he deserves then, but not you, lass. Be careful with your next choice of men. No need to get mixed up with an eejit who takes risks."

"Not sure I'll have a choice. I overheard the guards say they were shipping us off to North Africa."

"Aye, lass, we plan on messin' that up for them just a wee bit."

Claire got up and felt her way over to the door. Eddie followed her. What light they had was a single bulb over the hatch that kept flickering on and off. Eddie reached for it and twisted the bulb in tight. Once he released it, he saw Claire at the door pushing and pulling on the lever. It didn't budge.

Eddie tried it but gave up when the lever wouldn't move. "It's no use. It's locked and there's nothin' either of us can do to change that."

"Then look for something that we can use as a weapon."

Together, they searched the storeroom. The only things found were buckets, slickers, and towels, along with other odds and ends, but nothing they could use as a weapon.

June extended her hand to no one in particular and said, "Here."

Eddie glanced in her direction and saw she was holding up a small pocketknife.

"Eh, not sure what it'll do, but I'll not turn a nose up to it. It's better than nothin'. Thanks, lass."

No sooner than Eddie had the knife in his hand, the boat hit another wave that sent his body flying. His back slammed into the door, and he landed with a thud. The wind knocked out of him, and he gasped for air. When his lungs filled with oxygen once more, the hatch behind him opened, scaring him half to death. He flung his body around to see who was there. A young man's face peered through, and then a glaring light shone on Eddie, causing him to shield his eyes with his arm.

The flashlight's bright beam moved from him to Claire and then around the small storage compartment. As soon as the light shone on one of the drugged girls, there was a gasp and then the words "Holy Mary, mother o' God! Da! Da! They're people in here. Da, what have ya done?" the young man yelled behind him.

"Never you mind, boy. Get on with ya!"

"What do ya want me ta do, Da? I came home ta help ya fish, not ta haul doped girls around in the bottom of the boat."

"Then outta my way, boy!" the older man yelled as he pushed past his son, grabbing the flashlight from his hand as he did. He aimed the light at Eddie and asked, "All's well, mister?"

Eddie covered his face again from the glaring light while trying to calm his nerves. He took two deep breaths and yelled, "No!"

Claire took over and explained, "One girl is dead. She's been dead for some time."

"Chris, go get 'er!" the older man ordered.

"I'll not do your dirty work for ya. I'll not be a part of it!" Chris's voice was just as firm.

"You there," the older man kicked Eddie's foot and ordered, "Go get 'er and bring 'er up. She needs ta go over. Bad luck ta carry the dead on board a ship."

"It's no bad luck, Da! Put 'er in the cooler."

"I'll not put her with the fish!"

"What fish? We've none on board! Apparently, ya don't fish any-more. You've gone and got sucked in with Gallagher and 'is band of eejits! Da, I—"

Eddie got up slowly and held onto the hull of the trawler as it continued to rock in every direction. Carefully, he moved over to the dead body, trying his best not to step on the other girls, or worse yet, fall on them. Swaying over the dead child gave him pause, and he said a quick prayer. "Please, sweet Jaysus, forgive me for what I'm about to do."

He lifted her up and over his shoulder with ease. With the added weight and the trawler rocking in every direction, he had a hard time staying upright. The short trek across the storeroom to the hatch was a near impossible feat. Before he stepped through the opening, he said, "I'll do it for ya, but the ginger and I get a few minutes of your time after I'm done."

"Ya canna make demands, mister. I'm the captain of this vessel and you'll do as I say!"

Eddie rolled the girl off his shoulders into the arms of the cap-tain and offered, "Then my luck has run out, and I don't care what-cha do to me. But I'll not do your dirty work for ya, if you've not the mind to give me and Claire a moment of your time."

The captain growled at Eddie and pushed the girl back into his arms. Glaring at Claire, he ordered, "Get up, woman! Ya heard the man. You're in need of some fresh air and a swim."

Eddie's anger boiled over, and he yelled, "You, eejit! She's with the garda. She's one of the honest ones and has a tracker on her. Ya also should know, the ARW is involved. Ya need to speak with us, not toss us overboard. We can help."

"Ah, geez, Da! The ARW? Da, they're not the garda. Gallagher has no hold over 'em. Ya've got ta listen ta the man."

"Not sure you should've told them who I am," Claire said. "But I'm definitely in no need of fresh air tonight, nor a swim. So I'll be happy to join you in that conversation, especially if Gallagher's the main topic. I'm sure he has a man on board with you. You can tell him nothing about us."

"Oh, aye, we do, but he'll be no harm to ya. He's too busy flushing 'is guts out," the captain explained. "But a deal's a deal. The dead girl goes and you, fella, are tossin' 'er over."

Eddie glanced down at the lifeless body in his arms and went pale. He hoped he could forgive himself for what he was about to do. He looked back at the captain and nodded his head in agreement. Claire was about to protest when the captain stepped in front of her, saying, "You'll be next, girl, if ya say another word."

She clamped her mouth shut and took a step back. The sea was fierce, and she knew there would be no surviving a night like this in the water. When the captain followed Eddie out, Claire moved toward the exit. Chris waited for her to go through before he stepped out and locked the hatch behind him.

"I'm sorry 'bout this, miss. I didn't know 'bout any of it. My ma said my da's been strugglin' with his debt, but I didn't know it was this bad," Chris whispered as he followed behind Claire.

She glanced back at him and offered, "It'll only get worse for him if he doesn't assist us. And throwing the girl overboard won't help."

"My da's a suspicious man and has no belief in God. I'm convinced it's only mine and my ma's prayers that have been keeping 'im afloat all these years. He'll not budge on the girl, nor you, if you try ta interfere."

Claire got the message loud and clear. Eddie would do it to keep her alive, and for that, she was grateful. She watched the captain follow Eddie up the companionway. The hatch at the top of the stairs opened up to the savage storm that was raging outside. A wave crashed into the trawler, knocking everyone off balance and scaring Eddie enough to make him step back.

The captain stepped around him to open the hatch. Before he did, he eyed Eddie with a warning, "Wasting time will only get ya killed. Toss 'er in when a wave's leavin' or you'll fall over yerself. I'll open the hatch after the next wave hits, then yer on yer own."

Eddie didn't even have time to argue because when the next wave hit, the hatch flew open and with the firm hand of the captain on his back; he pushed Eddie outside. The force of the Atlantic

Ocean was far beyond anything Eddie had felt before. Being out in it, with its violent winds and monstrous waves, was the scariest thing he had ever experienced in his life.

He had no control over his legs and when the next wave hit; it slammed him against the trawler with his feet flying up in the air. He fell hard on his tailbone and slid several yards across the deck before the trawler hit another wave that propelled him back onto his feet. The next wave shot over the trawler and latched on to Eddie. With a violent jerk, the dead girl flew from his arms and crushed him against the side railing. Then a huge depression between the waves dropped the trawler into a deep dive. Suddenly, Eddie was floating in midair. When he came back down, his body missed the vessel and went into the raging waters.

Terror consumed Eddie as the water suck him under, but before he had time to give in to death, he slammed into the side of the trawler. Frantically, he reached out for something to hold on to, and felt two hands latch onto his arm. The next wave lifted him and sent his body flying over Chris's head. The two men landed on top of one another in a heap. Chris didn't falter. With incredible strength, he lifted Eddie and hauled him back inside.

Eddie collapsed, coughing up salt water. After several heaves, he fell back against the bulkhead to catch his breath. He looked up at Chris in total amazement. The young man's strength and courage astounded him. Chris had to have nerves of steel to go outside in the storm like he did to save him.

Fear had paralyzed Claire when she saw Eddie's drenched body collapse against the wall, shivering. He had escaped death only by inches. Once Chris pulled him to his feet, Claire couldn't help herself and lunged at him, crushing him with a bear hug.

"I thought you died!" she cried out.

He hugged her back. "Oh, aye. It's good to be alive, but I lost the girl. I've no idea if she went over."

She released Eddie's neck and grabbed his wet face, pulling it close to hers. "The sea has her now. Nothing else can be done for her. Let's see if we can get the captain's help. I want off this boat!"

"Aye, lass," he agreed and slipped his hands from Claire's shoulders to her arms. "I'm with ya there." Then, taking in a deep breath, he released her and turned to Chris. "I've no words to tell ya how grateful I am that ya came for me. Thank you isn't enough."

"Oh, aye, it is. God must not be done with ya yet, or He wouldn't have spit ya outta the water the way He did. One minute I see ya goin' over, then…well…it was like a cannon shot ya right outta the water at me! It's a miracle given straight from heaven. I've seen nothin' like it before."

He would have to agree, but nonetheless, Eddie was grateful for the young man's heroism, and said, "Aye, it is, but just the same, you've some courage goin' out there after me and that's somethin', so thanks."

The captain's huff made Eddie and the others look at him. Now that Eddie had his senses back, he said, "We need to have a word with ya, and a satellite phone or radio, if ya have one."

"Aye, we do," the captain said. "Come on then. We'll have a drink of somethin' hot, and ya can explain how yer gonna help me out o' this mess with Gallagher."

*   *   *   *   *

The gale force winds, along with the downpour of rain, had been raging for hours outside. Clay had experienced nothing like it before. Fresno had its usual dust storms and even a few rain showers, but this was scary. The owner of the inn had told him storms like this were commonplace for this part of Ireland. Because of it, Clay was happy to be indoors, sitting by the fire in a comfy chair.

Finished with his last call of the evening to his secretary, Clay leaned back and stared out the window. Marsha would wire the money in the morning to Harper's Ministries. With the donation taken care of, Clay chuckled to himself at the hefty price tag Billy put on his being there. He didn't care—it was for a good cause, and he would be happy to donate to Harper's Ministries on a monthly basis after this.

Spinning the cell phone between his finger and thumb, he thought of Emer. With another spin, he caught it as if it were about to fall from his grip. He leaned forward with his elbows on his knees and tried to talk himself out of calling her. His phone showed 1:30 a.m. *Probably not a good time to call.* He really didn't need to tell her anything because there hadn't been any new developments. Just as that thought passed through Clay's mind, Billy rushed into the lounge where he was sitting.

"We just got word, buddy! They're alive!"

Clay nearly dropped his phone and had to grab it in midair. "What? Who's alive? Did they find Kayla?"

With a huge grin, Billy answered, "Yeah, buddy, she's on the trawler with Eddie and Claire."

The phone Clay held slipped from his fingers and dropped to the floor. His hands went to his face and slid over the top of his head. His sister was alive and with Eddie. This was beyond great news!

"Wait! Who's Claire? And you said trawler? In this weather? Are they insane?"

"Claire's the agent that Derrick drove out to Brian Gallagher's place," Kate answered as she came in behind Billy. "We have Brian and Ronan Gallagher in custody. We lost Allister and his goon, Craig. But we'll find them, I promise."

"Wow! When did you get here, Kate?" Clay asked. "I figured you'd be in Dublin working on this. Wait, if you're here, then you must be bringing in the trawler."

Having the director of the AHTU in Killybegs had to mean something. What brought her this far from Dublin only left Clay with more questions, but before he could ask any of them, Kate informed him, "We're not bringing the ship into port."

"Wait! What?" Clay yelled, dumbfounded. "What do you mean? My sister's out there, and I want her brought to shore...like, right now!"

Kate gave Clay a sympathetic look. "Your narrow-minded thinking is making you blind to a much larger picture that I'm focused on. It involves a lot more people than you and Kayla. Clay, there's—"

"Please," he begged.

"Clay, I don't just want the trawler, I want the South American ship, the *Crystalline*, and its cargo. I can't have it if I bring the trawler to shore. The *Crystalline* hasn't arrived yet. Once it does, I'll have them both brought in."

"I don't understand. Can't you find the cargo ship some other way?"

"I can't get another ship out there right now. The storm is causing havoc for us, and the trawler is already waiting at the rendezvous point. This weather is going to hold for another hour at least. Once it passes, then we'll move in as fast as we can. Until then, the trawler waits for the *Crystalline*. Claire will go as one of the girls and her tracker is giving us a bright path straight to her and your sister."

Clay twisted around and collapsed in the chair behind him. His faith was dwindling again. He knew he was hanging on to the human aspect of all that could be physically done. He wished he could focus on the spiritual part of what God was capable of doing, but he couldn't. All he could think about was getting his sister back.

"I don't believe this. This doesn't seem right. Something's going to go wrong, I just know it! Can't you get Gallagher to tell you where the *Crystalline* is heading? Wouldn't that be much easier?"

"Even though we have a video of Gallagher killing a man, he's not speaking. He wants a deal, and the deal he wants, I'm not willing to give him. My goal is to bury him, right along with his organization. His being out of the picture is an enormous victory for Ireland in the fight against human trafficking. You have no idea just how big a win it is for us. Half, if not more, of all human trafficking in Ireland will stop. Not to mention the drugs and other things that Gallagher has his greedy hands in."

"Sorry, buddy." For the first time since Kate had entered the room, Billy spoke. Clay had almost forgotten he was there. His friend's words lacked any sympathy when he explained, "It's going to take longer than we'd hoped. Had it been sunny outside and a calm ocean, Kayla would be on her way home to you. I get that it's frustrating, believe me. That's why it would have been better for you to go home. These setbacks come with the job. We get so close only to have something happen that's out of our control. Like tonight's storm. No one wants to risk more lives when we know where the trawler is. So we sit and wait."

Patrick came into the room and asked, "Kate, you ready to go? I'm set if you are."

"Where are you going?" Clay inquired as he got up from the chair.

"Over to the captain's house, to have a word with the man's wife," Patrick answered.

"The captain?"

"Yeah, the captain of the trawler. The wife's awake and waiting for us to come by. We'll not be gone long, but you need to stay here. This is the AHTTF business. Try to get some sleep. Nothing can be done about your sister 'til the storm dies down."

"I can't sleep," Clay said as he sat back down. "I'll be sitting here when you return."

When the last member of Patrick's team left with Kate and Billy, the only sound Clay heard was the pulsating throb that pounded against his skull. It caused his mind to scatter in every direction. Then out of nowhere, he heard the soft, reassuring voice of his mother breaking through all the noise in his head. Hunched over, with his elbows on his knees, Clay rubbed his temples. He did his best to listen to his mother's words and closed his eyes to concentrate.

"Ask, and it will be given to you. Seek, and you will find. Knock and the door will be opened to you," he heard his mother's sweet voice say. Matthew 7:7 was a favorite verse from the Bible that his mother used to quote when he was a boy. The memory brought a smile to his lips. He used to think if he asked for something in Jesus's name, he would get it because the Bible clearly stated that he would. His mother would laugh and was happy to inform him that that wasn't what it meant. The older he got, the more he understood it was about trust—trusting in God to take care of the things that were out of his control. The mess Kayla had gotten herself into, he knew he should turn over to God, but Clay was having a hard time doing that.

Remembering the morning his parents died, Clay's mother had said something odd to him, or at least he thought it was strange at the time. Now he wasn't so sure. They were his mother's last words of wisdom before she died. She had quoted another scripture she loved as she walked out the door for the last time. "Trust in the Lord with all your heart, and do not rely on your own understanding; in all your ways know Him, and He will make your path straight."[3]

Those two Bible verses made more sense to him now than they ever had before. Clay fell to his knees and prayed.

*   *   *   *   *

Clay gave up waiting for Kate and the others to return and went to his room. Taking a hot shower helped somewhat with the jitters; however, he knew he wouldn't be able to sleep. He lay in his bed trying not to think about his sister, but his mind always drifted in that direction. So he decided to make a phone call to take his mind off everything.

He heard two rings before a groggy voice said, "'ello?"

Happy to hear the doctor's voice, he teased, "You dropped your 'h' again."

"It's three thirty-six in the morning, I'll drop the 'o' in a minute." Emer's voice was waking up.

"No need to be mean. I called with news. Some good and some not so good."

"Oh, aye? Start with the not so good bit."

The wind outside his window had calmed, and the howling that had come with it was down to a whimper. Clay, stretched out on his bed, found it odd that the first person he always thought to call was Emer. Now, having her on the other end of the phone, he felt more at ease. He didn't understand the calming effect she had over him, but he recognized that she did, and with all that was going on, he was glad for it.

"Derrick, the young man that took my sister...well, he's dead."

"G'wan, yer coddin' me?" Emer seemed more awake now.

Clay's lips parted into a slight grin. "If I knew what that meant, I could answer you."

"Oh, Clay, I'm so sorry to hear that. He was your only lead. So what happens now?"

---

3   Proverbs 3:5–6 (CSB).

"Codding?"

"What?"

"Codding. What does it mean?"

"You're kidding, or pulling my leg," she answered. "You don't seem to upset about Derrick's death."

Clay thought about how he felt and offered, "I am sorry for the guy, but he chose his life. Because of that choice, he's dead. I can't help but wonder how many girls he persuaded to trust him or outright abducted that are dead, or worse, living out the rest of their lives in slavery—all because of him."

"I get it, I do. But murder, whoever the recipient is, is wrong."

"You're right." There was a tinge of guilt in his voice. "I know I sound heartless, but just knowing what the guy did for a living makes it hard to feel sorry for him. Don't get me wrong—when I heard he was dead, I was devastated. But my reason for feeling that was mostly because of Eddie and my sister. He was our only link to them."

"I understand. We have a saying in Ireland, 'If you lie down with dogs, you'll rise with fleas.' It means, if you choose to be in the company of bad people, you're going to pick up bad habits yourself. Being around the likes of the Gallaghers, I'm not surprised by Derrick's lifestyle."

"No, me either. I just can't help but think, now that he's gone, someone's daughter will come home safely tonight because he won't be around to take her from them."

"True," Emer agreed. "It's scary knowing the world has people in it that will take whatever they want with no consideration for those around them. So what are you going to do now?"

"Well, the good news is, Kayla's alive, or at least she was a little over an hour ago. The AHTTF got an agent on board a trawler, the same trawler my sister's on."

"Oh, Clay, that's wonderful news. Wait. You said trawler. Where are you?"

"In a town called Killybegs, up north somewhere. I'm still kind of lost around here."

"It has a huge fishing port, I think. I've never been, but I read about the place in my economics studies while at the university."

Clay put one arm behind his head as he lay stretched out on his bed. "I'm beginning to think I've seen more of Ireland than most Irish people. But as far as Killybegs goes, I haven't seen much of the place. There was a terrible storm tonight that I thought would blow the inn over. I've been inside a car most of the day and sitting by the fire most of the night. I feel completely useless, though I paid to come. I was hoping for updates, but now it looks like I'll be at the port to welcome my sister home."

"Hold on. I thought you said they found your sister. Why isn't she with you? And what do you mean you paid so you could be there to get updates?"

"Okay, maybe I should explain a few things." Clay sat up to adjust the pillows behind his back and got comfortable. "Because of the storm, they couldn't get anyone out to rescue Kayla and the other girls. The trawler was supposed to meet up with another ship from South America, called the *Crystalline*. The AHTTF wants that ship and its cargo. Because the agent has a tracker on her, they know where she and the trawler are. Claire, the agent with the task force, convinced the captain to help them if she'd help him out of all this Gallagher mess. At the moment, Kayla, Eddie, and Claire are still somewhere out at sea, waiting to meet up with the other ship. That's all I know."

"And the money?"

"Oh, that." Clay chuckled. "I more or less paid a huge chunk of change to Harper's Ministries. Billy works for the organization. They find trafficked girls and boys and bring them home or find them someplace safe to live. My donation bought me a ride up here and the promise of getting updates."

"Really?"

"Yeah. I would sell my business back home if it helped get my sister back. There's eight years between us. My mother had several miscarriages before Kayla was born. She's a miracle child. My mom spent a month in the hospital with complications during her pregnancy with Kayla. My sister is all I have left."

"I understand. I don't get along with my family much, but if something ever happened to any of my siblings, I would be up in arms about it too."

"I'm sure you would."

Changing the subject, Emer said, "I finally got a lock on my office door."

"Really? Lily didn't shanghai the locksmith this time?"

"I outwitted her. I'm rather pleased with myself."

Clay laughed. "Careful, she might have done something you're not aware of yet."

"Not possible. Anyway, I have an early start in the morning. I best be off. Good night, Clay. Best o' luck to ya and yer sister. Give me a ring when ya have 'er. Sometime well after three o'clock in the mornin' would be best."

There was laughter in Emer's voice, and Clay knew she was teasing him and wasn't mad that he had called, but he understood the polite warning. "Thanks for talking to me."

"Don't think I had much say in the matter. Talk to you soon."

Emer hung up, leaving Clay to his own thoughts again. He set the phone down on the table next to his bed and slid back under the covers. He had to readjust his pillows a few times before he got comfortable. He was beyond exhausted and ready for sleep, but it didn't come. His mind and body had drained completely from agonizing over Kayla. At times, he was so angry at her for leaving her friends and going with Derrick and then guilt washed over him, and he felt terrible for even being the slightest bit upset at her. The tug of war between the anger and guilt was tearing him to pieces.

Maybe I should go home.

Rolling over onto his side, Clay lay staring at the digital clock that read three fifty-nine. The team hadn't returned from their meeting with the captain's wife. Was that another thing for him to worry about? What did the captain's wife have to say that would take this long to explain? The numbers changed to four o'clock. "Ugh!" Clay growled. He rolled over and stared at the black sky through his window. Flustered, he gave up and pulled the covers over his head to block everything out of his mind. He didn't move from that position and lay in silence, waiting for Billy and the others to return.

CHAPTER 6

Stretched underneath the covers, Clay woke with headache from the constant pounding he endured throughout the night. He untangled himself from the sheets and blanket, swung his long legs over the side of the bed, and sat for a second to get his bearings. It took him a moment before he remembered where he was and about Kayla. He shot a quick glance over at the clock next to his bed. The digital display showed eight thirty.

An urgency rushed through him that launched him toward the door. Without thinking, he opened it and ran down the hall to Billy's room. He knocked several times, but there was no answer. His knocking quickly changed to pounding, but Billy still didn't come.

"Oh my!" a woman's voice gasped.

Clay turned to see an older woman with a surprised expression on her face, staring at him. Confused, he looked down at himself and was shocked to find he only had his boxers on and nothing more. "Eh, good morning. Um, sorry...I'll...if you'll excuse me, I should probably get dressed."

"Oh, yer no bother at all! I quite like the view. Not seen one like this in, well...ever!"

Embarrassed, Clay tried to step around her. However, the woman wouldn't budge and stood in the middle of the hallway, forcing him to press up against the wall to squeeze pass her. She lifted her fingers just enough to let them slide across the ripples of his stomach muscles when he did.

He heard her say, "Oh my. Very nice indeed."

Clay couldn't get in his room fast enough. He threw on his clothes, grabbed his toothbrush, and ran down the hall to the bathroom. After making himself more presentable, he ran back to his room, threw everything on his bed, and slammed the door behind him. He ran down the stairs, taking two at a time. The woman he had met upstairs now blocked him from exiting the inn.

"I'm sorry, excuse me please. I'm in a hurry."

"Oh, aye! You and the rest of the town. Shame though, I liked ya better in yer kex."

"What do you mean?"

"Yer underpants."

"No, I mean, the part about the town being in a hurry?"

"Oh, aye. A trawler arrived this mornin' and you'd think the town's folks had never seen one before today."

This time, Clay forgot his manners and pushed past the woman and sprinted toward the port. The police had the area blocked off, and onlookers crowded in tight to get a better view. Patrick and his men mingled in with the authorities, combing the trawler for evidence. Clay had to fight his way through the crowd and once he made it to the caution tape, he ducked to go under it. A big, burly Irishman, the same height as Clay, grabbed him by the collar of his jacket, and said, "Not so fast! You're not allowed ta pass the line. Now back with ya!"

"You don't understand, I'm with them." Clay pointed at Kate and Patrick and then yelled, "Patrick!"

Patrick lifted his head in Clay's direction and waved him through. The police officer let him go and Clay ran over to where they stood. When he got closer, he could tell something was wrong.

"What is it? What's going on?"

Patrick's facial expression was grim. Terror froze Clay in place while he waited for him to explain what had happened.

"Everyone on board is dead. The entire crew. Captain and all."

The breath Clay had been holding in blew from his lungs. The worst day of his life was the day the police came by his office and told him that both his parents were dead. Or so he thought. That moment couldn't compare to how he felt now. He thought his heart was going to explode and everything around him suddenly went black.

A firm hand grabbed his arm and then his waist. Patrick caught Clay and lowered him to the ground. Then something under his nose blasted him out of his spiral, and he jerked his head back.

Through fits of coughing, Clay asked, "Oh, man, what is that stuff?"

Patrick dropped the vial on the ground next to him and helped Clay back to his feet. "Ammonia carbonate. It works every time."

"I think it shattered a few brain cells."

"Can't have you going over in a heap." Patrick didn't let go of Clay until he was steady. "Kayla wasn't on board. Neither was Eddie or Claire."

"What?" Clay asked, trying to regain some of his composure.

Kate joined in the conversation by saying, "The *Crystalline* must have made it to the rendezvous point, taken the cargo and sailed off."

"I really wish you would quit using the word *cargo*. My sister and the others taken are hostages or victims or something else other than cargo!"

"Right, Clay, I'm sorry." Kate regretted her choice of words. "Claire said there were seven girls on board, including your sister. One, they found dead, the other six were alive but heavily drugged. Allister, Gallagher's righthand man, must have contacted the ship somehow and told the captain we were on to him."

"Okay, what about the tracker? Is it still sending a signal?"

Neither Kate nor Patrick answered, but their body language let him know they lost it too. He couldn't believe it and shook his head in disbelief. Then, taking a step back, he walked in a circle, lost in thought, until Billy's sudden appearance made him stop.

"The captain's youngest boy isn't on the trawler, but they found a dead girl tangled up in the fishing net."

"Come again?" Kate asked.

"Remember the Captain's wife, Mrs. Dunne, told us that her youngest boy came home to help his dad and brothers. He had been on a mission trip with World Charities for two months before he came back home."

"That's right. I've forgotten his name. Do either of you remember it?" Patrick asked.

"Yeah, it's Chris. It's short for Christian. His mother went home to get a picture of him for us. She said he's twenty-two, and that he's a big kid."

"Okay, I'll have my people do their best to find out who the dead girl is," Kate said, lacking her normal confidence. "You said Chris has been working for World Charities? I've heard about them. They pretty much have free access into any port worldwide."

Not sure where any of this was going, Clay offered, "I know Roman. We met a few years ago at a fundraiser that a friend of mine in Fresno organized for him. Not that it's important, but his mother, Madison Richards, was there too. Since then, I've had lunch with Roman a few times. He's a great guy."

"The actress?" Kate asked. "Isn't she married to the musician, Jason Walker?"

"Yes. She and Jason started the two charities, Roman just runs them. We're not best buds, but my company donates to both World Charities and Charities USA. Roman always returns my calls, but I'm not sure what he or either charity can do for us."

"World Charities has, what…five ships now? More importantly, it has connections. Could you give me Roman's direct line?" Kate asked.

"Sure. Um, they have six ships. Australia just gutted an old navy sealift vessel and donated it to World Charities. I received a letter about it last month. They need donations to help get it stocked up with medical supplies and equipment, so it would be a fully functioning ship in its fleet. And yes, you're correct, Roman has contacts all over the world and never has to ask twice for anything. Give me a minute, and I'll get his numbers for you."

Clay had his phone out when he walked away to call his secretary. There was an eight-hour difference, and he knew Marsha would be home. He did the calculations in his head. It would be late, but she was the only one that could help.

Marsha was twenty-four and smart. She liked to hang out with friends, but during the work week, she never went out much, except to church or church events. She should be home, he just hoped she would be awake. He would find out soon enough. He punched in her phone number from memory.

She answered on the third ring. "Hello?"

"Hey, Marsha, sorry to be calling so late."

"You didn't wake me. I'm up binge-watching a TV show. I could use the break. Any news?"

"Yeah, they lost her," Clay whispered.

"They what? Oh my word, I'm so sorry. Is there anything I can do to help?"

"Yeah, there is actually. Can you text me all of Roman Jones's numbers please? I need them quick."

"Oh sure, let me get my laptop." Clay heard Marsha rustling around for something and then typing. A few seconds later, her voice announced, "Done. I sent you all three numbers. I also sent you his brother Monte Jones's number. He lives in Texas."

"Thanks, Marsha. I'll call you later. Sorry again for calling so late."

"Any time. Oh, before you go, the pastor asked me to pass on to you that the church is praying for Kayla."

Just knowing there was an army of salvation warriors out there praying for his sister, gave Clay comfort. "Would you tell him thank you for me? You have no idea how much I appreciate hearing that. Thanks again."

He disconnected without saying goodbye and made his way over to Kate. He handed her his phone with the numbers she needed on the screen. He watched as she entered them into her phone. When she finished, she made her first call. "Hello. Is this Roman Jones?" There was silence for a brief moment. "Mr. Jones, I'm Director Kate Walsh, with the AHTU, in Ireland." She walked away to have a private word with him.

A tall, slender woman, in her mid- to late fifties, interrupted the three men as they watched Kate pace back and forth as she spoke to Roman. "Excuse me, but I've the picture of my boy." Mrs. Dunne's eyes were moist and red from crying. She handed the picture to Billy, and he thanked her.

"Um, ma'am, I'm Clay. I'm sorry for your loss." He angled his head just enough to make eye contact with her. "My sister, Kayla, was one of the young women on board your husband's trawler."

The woman, who was on the brink of collapse, burst into tears, and barely got out, "Oh, aye, I'm verra sorry for all the trouble this mess has caused ya. I told my husband not to do it. He was thick headed, but he didn't deserve this. Neither did my boys. That man, Allister, put a gun to 'is head and threw a bucket o' money at 'im. I know my Cappy's burnin' in hell for what he's done."

Clay took Mrs. Dunne in his arms and held her tight. As stupid as her husband had been, she hadn't been part of it and had become another one of Brian Gallagher's victims. The thought of her losing her entire family and family's reputation, all in one day, was enough to break his heart.

She cried in his arms for a few minutes before she stepped out of his embrace. Her grief had drained her physically. Because of it, she could only manage a weak nod of thanks for his kindness before she turned and walked away. Clay felt helpless. He wanted to do something for her, but he didn't know what. It wasn't until Mrs. Dunne had some distance between herself and Clay that she turned to face him. "My boy, Christian, he's a good lad. He's a boy after Jaysus's heart. If he's alive, he'll be doing the Lord's work, I can promise ya that."

Another woman came alongside Mrs. Dunne to console her. She put her arm around her friend and guided her back toward the crowd of onlookers. Clay watched as the burly Irish officer lifted the tape so they could pass, and then they disappeared. He continued to stare at the cluster of spectators for a few seconds after he lost sight of Mrs. Dunne and her friend. Someone in the group caught his attention.

A suspicious-looking man in the crowd watched as the police worked. If he was trying to blend in with the people around him, he did a poor job. He had a gray hoodie pulled over his head, doing his best not to be noticed. Clay caught a glimpse of his face and recognized him right away. He was one of the men that had beaten him up and dumped him on the side of the road.

Grabbing Billy by the jacket, Clay dragged him a few feet toward the man while shouting, "The guy in the hoodie!"

Billy caught sight of him and yelled, "Go right, go right!"

Clay did as ordered. Patrick noticed his friends chasing someone and shouted at Kate before he ran after them. She looked up from the phone and saw the three men in pursuit of a young man in a black coat and gray hoodie. She shouted, "Thank you!" into the phone and took off running.

Billy bulldozed into the crowd, knocking someone to the ground. He didn't stop to see if the guy was okay; he kept his eyes locked on the young man in front of him. When the suspect saw Clay and Patrick on his right, he jumped up and slid over the top of a parked car, changing his direction, and ran up another street.

The woman Clay had met earlier that morning was bent over fixing the lace on her shoe. When she stood up, her umbrella slipped, and the young man's feet got tangled up in it. His body flew a few feet before his face smashed into a red mailbox. The sudden collision made Clay stop and cringe.

"Ouch! Now that's gotta hurt." Clay chuckled.

Billy yanked the kid up by his collar and flung him around to face Clay, as if he was showing his friend his catch. "I take it you know him?"

Blood gushed from the man's nose.

"Oh, yeah. Paybacks are fun to watch. He's the one that kicked in my ribs."

Kate slowed when she was close enough to see his face. "Craig!" Then looking around, she asked, "I wonder if Allister's here?"

"Unfortunately, this kid is in no condition to talk right now." Billy held the dazed young man up by his collar and arm.

Kate glanced past Billy at the woman holding her broken umbrella. "Sorry, ma'am. Are you all right?"

"Oh, aye, I am dear. Though my parasol's been in better condition."

The sound of Kate's voice was a mixture of concern and compassion. "I'll be happy to buy you another one. You're staying at the same inn we are, yes?"

"I am. But I'd much rather another gander at the young man here in 'is kex. Oh, what a holy sight he was! He made this ol' girl's heart flutter," the woman said, smiling up at Clay.

All eyes fell on the rather tall, handsome American, waiting for some kind of explanation. Clay's cheeks flushed beet red, and he stuttered at first, saying, "I…I may have…left my room without getting dressed this morning when I went looking for Billy."

"Good thing I wasn't in my room or I would've punched your lights out."

"Oh, no, ya wouldn't. He's a glorious body. Rock hard to the touch, with tiny ripples."

Kate's giggles turned into full-blown laughter. At one point, Clay honestly thought she was going to fall over. Billy and Patrick too. The older woman seemed unfazed by the reaction she got from his friends when she shared her earlier encounter with him. She locked eyes with Clay and said, "Oh, aye, glorious indeed."

With a delightful sigh, the woman took her broken umbrella and walked away, leaving them to their fits of laughter. Clay could only grin. He couldn't be upset at her even though she had taken advantage of him while he stood half naked in the hallway. He was becoming very fond of Irish women.

Patrick, who was still grinning, said, "Right, come on, Billy, let's get this idiot over to medical so they can have a look at him. What a fool! Staying to watch the aftermath of his handiwork."

"You're being too nice, Patrick," Billy said as they hauled the young man back to the dock.

*   *   *   *   *

"Right, genius, we've got you on murder. If you want to go down for all the murders, then so be it. But I should think you a wiser man than that. Where's Allister? Give him to me and a deal can be made." Kate sat across the table from Craig in the interrogation room, waiting for his answer.

"I dunno where he is! He gave me orders to sit tight, so I did. When you hauled the trawler in, I knew somethin' wasn't right. Honest, I dunno where he is."

"You understand, you're going to jail for murder? You, being a young man, will never see the light of day if you don't give me something."

"I didna kill anyone! Not ever! I'll tell you whatever you're needin'. I'm always lookin' for someone to hop on, and Allister knows it. I only like fightin'. Allister ordered me to batter the yank up a bit, and nothin' more. That's all I done."

Clay watched through the two-way mirror as Kate interviewed Craig. His ribs were sore from all the running he had done, trying to catch the young man. He glanced over at Billy, who was watching the interrogation with him and Patrick, and said, "He's not lying about being the one who beat me up. Allister, Derrick, and another guy held me down while Craig beat the tar out of me."

"What do you think, Patrick? Is he telling the truth?"

Patrick eyed Billy and then glanced over at Clay before he answered, "Aye, he is. I'm sure he knows nothing more."

The three men went back to watching Kate's interview with the young Dubliner. Fifteen minutes of questioning had passed before Craig said something that caught the attention of both Kate and Patrick. Clay saw Patrick tense up with the word *Liffey*. He recalled Eddie had mentioned something about the River Liffey, but he couldn't remember what he said. Whatever it was, the mention of the river triggered a reaction from Kate and Patrick. Clay decided not to ask him about it and went back to listening to the interrogation.

"Then you've heard of the *Crystalline*?" Kate asked.

"Oh, aye. Been on it too. It's a River Liffey cruise tour boat. Gallagher owns the company, not with 'is name on the papers, but an ol' school mate runs it. It's a legit business, one of many that Brian Gallagher owns."

"If that's true, then it wasn't the *Crystalline* that went to meet the trawler?"

Craig looked at Kate as if she was crazy. "Of course not! That weather would've destroyed the *Crystalline*. No, it were another fishin' boat, not as big as the one you brought in. This one can go down the Liffey a bit. The *Crystalline* meets the fishin' boats in the bay and will take the girls from 'em and take 'em into Dublin."

"The bay?"

"Oh, aye. Dublin Bay, at one of its many fishin' ports."

Kate wrote down a few notes before she asked, "Why did Brian Gallagher have the girls shipped over here, when he was only going to send them back to Dublin?"

"Dunno. Just the way he does things. He likes ta keep 'em movin'."

"And I thought you said you knew nothing?" Kate scoffed while tapping her fingers on the table. "What's the tour company's name?"

"Alison's River Liffey Boat Tours."

"Alison's?"

"Oh, aye, she's a mate of Brian's wife, Angela. The boat company belonged to Alison's da. The business was runnin' aground, and Gallagher gave 'er the money to keep it afloat."

"So Alison's in cahoots with Gallagher?"

"Yer as daft as they come, woman. No, it's 'er brother that captains the boats."

The director jotted down a few more things and even cracked a smile when he called her daft. Looking up from her pad, she eyed Craig, asking, "And?"

"Oh, ya needin' a name, are ya? It's Anthony McCormick. He's not the pleasant sort neither. If he knows yer comin', he'll get rid of everything. If ya get my meanin'?"

Kate tensed up. It was obvious she didn't like hearing Craig say out loud what Clay assumed she already knew. His sister and the other young women were in danger. Allister was tying up loose ends, but Clay, like the others, hoped they would get to the girls before Allister did.

"Do you know Thomas O'Leary? Or his girlfriend, June Donnelly?"

"No, I can't say that I do. Why?"

"June was one of the women on the trawler. I'm told her boyfriend had both legs broken. I thought you might have been the one to work him over."

"No. Honest. Ask 'im yerself. He'll tell ya it weren't me."

"I will as soon as I find him."

"I thought ya said the man's legs were broken? He canna have gotten far now, can he?" Craig smirked.

Ignoring his snide remark, Kate rose from her chair. "Okay. Thank you very much for all your help."

Craig stood up too. "Right, I'm off then."

Laughing, Kate said, "Now who's daft? You're under arrest, Craig, for the murder of all those on board the trawler. For kidnapping, extortion, assault, and anything else I can find to throw at you. I'm going to see to it that you die in prison. Which might be sooner, rather than later, especially once Gallagher finds out you've talked."

Craig's face paled as he collapsed on the chair. The three men watched the young man flounder in mental agony.

"I almost feel sorry for the dumb kid," Billy said.

"I'll not shed a tear for him. He knew what he was getting into, especially hooking up with the likes of Allister," Patrick argued.

"I said almost." Billy chuckled.

The door opened, and Kate's head popped in. "Come on. We've a drive ahead of us."

"What about Craig? Are you going to leave him here?" Billy asked.

"Yes. He'll be safer here. If I move him to Dublin, Gallagher will have him killed, and I still need him alive. I have to make a quick call to the commissioner and take care of Craig's arrangements. I'll meet you back at the inn"—Kate looked at her watch—"in say, twenty minutes?"

"Yeah, sure," Clay answered as if Kate was directing her comments to him.

Patrick ran his fingers through his hair while eyeing Clay and asked, "And what about this one?"

Stunned by Patrick's question, Clay didn't know what to say. Billy jumped in and answered, "He's with me."

"Okay then. I'll see you all in twenty minutes." That was it; Kate disappeared when the door to the observation room closed, leaving the three men to their own thoughts.

Patrick was the first to break the silence when he opened the door. "Okay, gents, let's be off. You heard the lady, we've a bit of road ahead of us."

The men had to hike back to the inn. It was cold, even with the sun out, but the wind had died down considerably. The storm from the night before was nothing but a distant memory. Clay walked behind Patrick and Billy, listening as they discussed the recent developments in the case. He wasn't sure what any of it meant, but he didn't want to ask too many questions out of fear his companions would grow tired of him and send him back home. Kate could force him onto a plane heading back to California, and he didn't want that. Besides, he had helped in the case by giving them Craig.

If the kid hadn't decided to watch the police pull in the trawler, Kate would have never known Craig was there. Nor would she have gotten the information that she now had. Clay's reasoning was useless unless he verbally defended his being there with the director and Patrick. He decided against it and let it go.

Going over everything that Craig had told Kate made Clay smile. He wanted to chalk it up to good ol' Irish luck, but he knew better. Divine Providence was at the helm of this; he was sure of it. All those prayers back home had to be helping direct this good fortune. For a man who said he knew nothing, Craig had been a fountain of information.

Craig thought it had been just a casual exchange of words with Kate and, that when it ended, he could leave. Clay shook his head at the stupidity of the young man. The dumb kid didn't have a clue. He got sucked into Gallagher's world, and he didn't even understand the trouble he had gotten himself into, nor the high price he would soon pay because of it.

Once word got out Craig had been captured and given Kate the information she needed on Gallagher's method of transporting girls around Dublin, Brian Gallagher would surely have him killed. *Poor kid.* Without realizing it, Clay's thoughts had taken him all the way back to the inn. He heard giggling and then Billy say, "You've got a fan club, Clay."

The woman that had seen him in the hallway in his underwear, stood outside the inn with a friend, gossiping. She stared at Clay, nodding at him while she explained the huge role he had played in her morning.

He didn't mind being the topic of conversation, but when he got close enough, he stopped, leaned toward them, and said, "You can't be that bored that I'm all you're talking about this morning. Besides, it's not polite to spread rumors."

"Oh, rubbish! It's nae gossip if it's true and one look at ya, she'll know that truth be told!"

The woman had a sweet disposition and good humor. Clay couldn't help himself; he liked her. He offered his hand to the first woman and said, "I'm Clay Warner."

Shaking it ever so lightly, she said, "This here's my sister, Louise, and I'm Catherine. It's a pleasure ta meet ya, Clay—all of ya." Catherine grinned with the last of her words.

Wagging his finger at her, he joked, "You're a very naughty woman, Catherine."

Both women laughed. Louise was happy to inform him, "I've told her that her whole life."

"Well, it was a pleasure to meet you both. Have a wonderful day."

Billy and Patrick were already inside the inn and halfway up the stairs when Clay left the women. He took two steps at a time and went straight to his room. It didn't take him long to gather his stuff. Grabbing the backpack Patrick had given him, he tossed what few belongings he had into the bag.

On the way up to Killybegs, Patrick had stopped for gas and Clay was able to buy an extra T-shirt. He bought underwear and socks when Ian had taken him to town to buy his phone. With the clothes he had purchased and those he currently wore, he didn't have much. He didn't mind traveling light, but he would have to wash his clothes often, which took time.

A book came to mind that he once read where the main character owned nothing at all. He would buy pants and shirts at the Salvation Army and gave them his dirty clothes or threw them away.

It wasn't a bad idea, but he didn't think he even had time for that. Everything that was happening now was happening fast. Every night he had spent in Ireland since his arrival had been at a different location. None of the places he ended up were of his choosing, but like now, he would go wherever the lead to Kayla took him.

Making sure he had everything, he glanced around the room one last time. As he did, a final thought slipped from his lips, "Hang on, Kayla. God's got an army of soldiers coming for you. Just hang on, sis."

When he stepped out of the room and closed the door behind him, he found Billy waiting for him. Grateful to see his friend, he said, "I'm—"

Billy handed him something. "This is from the captain's wife, Mrs. Dunne. Last night, she asked if I would mind giving this to you. How your faith came up, I don't remember, but she gave me this Bible to give to you."

Clay smiled out of bewilderment at the book he had longed to have in his possession. Now, holding it in his hand, an unexpected sense of relief washed over him. He didn't understand the strange feeling. Staring down at the Bible, he said, "I don't know what to say. I didn't think to pack mine. I wanted to travel light and didn't bring it. Thanks for this."

"You're welcome. But like I said, Mrs. Dunne gave it to me to pass on to you."

"That's weird. I mean, I only met her today. I feel bad for her. I wish there was something I could do for her."

"You can. Pray for her. Pray we find her other son alive, right along with Kayla. That's the best gift you can give her."

As Clay unzipped his backpack and slipped the Bible in, he promised, "I will. I definitely will."

CHAPTER 7

Each time the fishing boat hit a wave, it reminded Eddie they were still in the ocean, somewhere off the coast of Ireland. With no window for him to look out, he didn't know what part of the Irish coast they sailed. That information would come soon enough, for now he was grateful for a somewhat calmer sea.

Chris, along with the rest of Eddie's traveling companions, was unconscious. The attack on the trawler had happened so fast that no one on board knew what was going on at first. Thinking back on it, Eddie couldn't believe how brazen their new captain had been when he lined his vessel up with the trawler and his men boarded, taking it over during the storm. If it hadn't been so terrifying, he would have thought it a swashbuckling pirate movie. Instead of swords, high-powered guns were used. How he and Chris hadn't been shot by the rapid gunfire, he couldn't explain.

During the takeover, the men boarding the trawler murdered the captain, his two older sons, two of Gallagher's men, and three crew members. Eddie remembered Chris diving at him, taking him to the floor when the shooting started. When all the smoke cleared, they were the only two men spared. Their attackers had taken them hostage along with the young women.

Somehow their new captors knew about Claire's tracker. One man ripped all her clothes off. She fought and screamed the entire time, fearful he wanted more than just her clothes. Chris had tried to stop him but got hit in the back of his head with the butt of a gun, rendering him unconscious.

Drugging the woman guaranteed there wouldn't be any flailing when the men transported them from the trawler to the fishing boat. The only reason Eddie could think of for his being alive was they needed him to help transfer the girls and Chris from the trawler to the other vessel.

Seeing Claire lay on the floor with nothing on angered Eddie. He set the girl in his arms down in the corner of the small compartment, and glared at the guard. "The lass is worth nothin' if ya let her freeze to death!"

"Why don't ya lie with 'er, ya ol' coot, and have a wee bit o' fun wit 'er—that'll keep 'er warm."

"Are ya sick in the head, man! Gallagher's not payin' ya to manhandle his product now, is he? Get her some clothes and keep your head attached to your body. She's cash money to be made, and Gallagher will be none too pleased if she dies."

"Why d'ya care? The boss is selling ya wit the girls anyway, yer nothing to 'im."

"Maybe so. But unless ya have some kind of death wish, I suggest ya find somethin' to cover her with. Go on, get the girl some clothes, will ya?"

"Ah, she's a looker that one is," the guard said. "Maybe I'll lay wit 'er myself and keep 'er warm."

The way he looked at Claire made Eddie sick, and he wanted to punch the guy in the face. Instead, he yelled, "Seriously! Come on."

"Oh, aye, I'll get the lass some clothes." Then he stepped out of the small room and locked the door behind him.

Eddie did his best not to look at Claire. He checked on Chris and felt around on the back of his head. He found a knot the size of a golf ball, but there was no blood. Setting Chris upright was a challenge because the young fisherman was twice his size and solid muscle, but he managed to get the lad situated before he helped the women.

Next, he moved over to Kayla and checked the gash on her head. No fresh blood. He worried that transporting her from the trawler to the boat had reopened the wound. With the storm rocking both vessels, he had lost his footing and landed hard on the deck with her in his arms. At the time, he didn't know if her head had hit something on his way down. He was grateful it hadn't. "Aye, lass, you'll be fine. Here ya go." He heaved her next to Chris, using him as a cushion. He hoped that if the boat bounced around too much, Chris would protect Kayla's head.

The door unlocked and a guard stepped in, tossing clothes at Eddie. Before he got "Thank you" out, the door closed. "Well, ya've no manners, but I thank ya kindly just the same."

He scooted over to Claire and with his eyes diverted, he felt for her head. He did his best to get the shirt over it, but instead, got it tangled up in the sleeve. Frustrated, he yelled, "Come on, eejit! Suck it up. Help the lass out and get her dressed. It's not like ya did this to her."

It didn't matter. Eddie felt like a creep taking advantage of Claire and didn't like it. He moved fast, only taking a peek to get the right body parts in the correct hole. Once he had the shirt on properly, he slipped on the sweatpants. The clothes were far too big for her, and he had to pull the string around her waist tight, leaving its excess hanging down to her knees.

"Right. Here ya go, lass." Eddie picked Claire up under her arms and moved her next to Kayla. "Sit right here. Aye, that'll do."

Pleased with himself, Eddie found a spot on the floor and sat down. With his knees pulled up to his chest and his elbows resting on top of them, he bowed his head and exhaled. For the first time since this ordeal had begun, he felt like he could take a minute to breathe.

An hour had passed when he heard a groggy voice whisper, "What happened?"

Eddie looked up and saw Kayla staring at him. "Hey," he said as he moved closer to her. "You okay?"

"Yeah, I think so. My head hurts." She lifted her hand and felt the wound at her hairline.

"Easy, girl. You've a gash there. The bleeding has stopped but ya need to leave it be."

"What happened? Where are we?"

"Still at sea. I'm thinkin' we're headin' south. As to what happened, ya went to a party instead of goin' back to the hotel with your friends. Do ya remember that bit?"

"Yes." Her grogginess couldn't hide her flushed cheeks. "How do you know my brother?"

Understanding her need to move on, he answered, "He asked for my help in findin' ya, and I agreed to do so. Not that it's doin' either of ya any good now."

"Your accent, are you—"

"Born in Chicago, but I've been livin' in Ireland for the last fifteen years. I'm soundin' more Irish these days."

"Oh...I think I'm going to be sick."

"Sorry, lass, there's no bucket. Try to breathe and think of somethin' else."

Kayla took small breaths and swallowed. She looked over at the young man passed out next to her. "Who's he?"

"Chris. He's the young man that helped us while we were on the trawler. His da was the captain."

"My brain's a little foggy, but if you're here to help me and he helped us, then why are we crammed in this tiny room on another boat?"

Eddie's lips formed a lopsided grin. "As best laid plans go, ours went awry. We're alive and that's the best we can ask for. The bonus is, there's no storm."

"Hmm, uh." Claire was coming around.

"Hey," Eddie said. "Ya okay, lass?"

Hearing Eddie's voice, Claire roused. Her body jerked awake, and she grabbed fistfuls of her clothes. She looked down and cried out, "My dress!"

"Aye, lass, they took it."

She pulled out the collar of her shirt, glanced down, and then leaned her head back and closed her eyes. "Augh!" Claire took several deep breaths before she opened them again and looked straight at Eddie. "Thank you."

"I'm sorry for what happened to ya."

"They didn't...they didn't do," Claire's body shuddered, "do anything, did they?"

"No lass. They were goin' for the tracker is all."

Claire's shoulders slumped, and her eyes blinked a few times before keeping them open. Then she pushed herself up to a better sitting position. "I'm sorry. I'm Claire. I'm with AHTTF."

"AHT—what?"

"Yeah, it's the Anti-Human Trafficking Task Force."

"What?" Kayla asked, stunned. "How long have I been out? And what... I mean, I don't know what I thought...but human trafficking? That didn't even cross my mind. What an idiot! You must think me stupid...which I am. Oh, geez, what have I done?"

"No need to be hard on yourself," Eddie said. "You're an innocent that walked into the lion's den, is all. We've the best of the best looking for us. They'll find us, lass. I've no doubt about it."

A noise came from the other side of the door. When it flew open, two armed men stepped in and grabbed Eddie. Kayla screamed and Claire got a foot to her shoulder when she tried to get up to help. "Watch yourself, woman, or you'll be next, and ya don't want that. The boys haven't been to shore in weeks. A pretty thing like you would go a long way on morale with the lads."

Eddie added, "It's okay."

Claire held her breath and froze in place, exhaling when the door closed. She looked at Kayla who had tears streaming down her face. Frustrated, she slammed her fist on the wall and screamed.

*   *   *   *   *

The guards dumped Eddie onto a bench seat at the table. Seeing the man that had driven him and Claire from Brian Gallagher's place surprised him. He took a quick glance over at the guards and then back at Allister. Grateful that his host wanted to chat, Eddie relaxed and sat upright.

Allister took up the whole bench across from him. He leaned against the wall with one leg propped up on the seat. While he scrutinized Eddie, he tapped his fingers on the table as if he was deciding on something. Eddie waited patiently for the man to share his thoughts. It wasn't until Allister slid his leg under the table and clasped his hands in front of him, that he spoke.

"I'm at a loss as ta who ya are." The expression on Allister's face made it very clear that he was enjoying himself. "The girl, well, I'm sure she's with the Garda Síochána, but my guess is you're not."

Eddie just stared at Allister.

"Ah, well, I'm sure ya don't care what becomes of you, but if I choose ta give the lads a girl for a wee bit of fun that would open that mouth of yours, would it not?" Allister had Eddie's attention now, and he knew it.

"I'm lookin' for a friend's sister, is all. It's the American ya have stashed with the others."

"Ya think me an eejit?" Allister slammed his fist on the table. "Are ya workin' with the Garda Síochána? I aim ta know who it is you're workin' for!"

If anything happened to him, Eddie could handle it, but if something happened to the girls because of him, he would be devastated. In order to protect the women, he was going to have to answer Allister honestly. That meant giving him all the information, holding nothing back. He held Allister's gaze and said, "I work with a group of retired gentlemen from the ARW."

Allister's brow lifted. The guard sucked in air and blew it out with a whistle, before he said, "The lads and I didn't sign on ta fight the ARW, retired or otherwise. The garda's different, they take the cash."

"Shut up, John!"

Eddie let John squirm for a few seconds before he continued. "Oh, aye, the lads hate traffickers and there's no amount of money to sway their thinkin'. And just so ya know, the director of the AHTU is leadin' the charge. You've her agent and she'll want her back, alive and unscathed."

Allister tapped his fingers on the table again, lost in thought. Then he ordered John, "Tell Duff ta set course for the island we spoke of, and not ta forget ta radio ahead ta bring in the other cruisers. We'll wait it out a few days, then split up and meet as planned. I've some unfinished business that needs tendin' to before I can leave."

*   *   *   *   *

Though Eddie knew Ireland well, he didn't know its coast-line. So catching a glimpse of it didn't help. He had no clue where they were, nor where they were heading. Locked back in the small room with the others, Eddie stewed over the lack of information he had. The fishing boat changed course a few times, and though he tried, he couldn't get his bearings. When the boat slowed down and the engine's hum altered, he knew they had arrived at their final destination.

All the ladies were awake, very alert, and terrified. Eddie was at a loss about how to console them. He was sure that once they were all off the boat, he'd be dead. Allister had no need for him. The man had to know that no matter who he sold Eddie to, he would fight to be free and wouldn't stop until he was. The only option was to kill him. Eddie couldn't understand why he hadn't done so already.

"You said Allister mentioned an island. Did he say which one?" Claire asked.

"Aye, he did but didn't give a name. If I had to guess I would choose Dingle Bay, possibly Tralee Bay. There's only a few islands there, so it must be somewhere near or past Dingle Bay."

"One of the old military outposts."

"My thoughts too, lass. Listen, ya have to take care of Kayla and these others. My thinkin' is, Allister has no use for me and once on land, I'm as good as dead."

"What? Please, we have to do something!" Kayla burst into tears right along with the other five girls.

"Not to worry, lass. I've played around in this dark world far too long. It was bound to catch up with me. All ya lasses listen to Claire and you'll be okay."

He was lying. Claire fully understood what would become of them if he died. While the women were sleeping, Eddie had explained to Claire his thoughts on what would happen. He was sure they would split girls up and would rendezvous later. He hoped that Kate would find them before then.

The door unlocked and opened with armed men stepping through. They grabbed the girls and pulled them to their feet. Eddie put his hand on Chris to keep him from doing anything stupid that would get him knocked out again, or worse, killed.

"Up with ya!" a man yelled.

Eddie and Chris got up, and the guard shoved them both in the back, pushing them toward the door. Once outside, the light from the morning sun was blinding. Eddie tripped over a rope and Chris grabbed him so he wouldn't fall. When Chris pulled him back, he whispered, "South of Dingle Bay."

Now knowing their location, Eddie hadn't a clue what good it would do them. Chris was a fisherman and knew the coastline of Ireland like the back of his hand. Maybe, between the two of them, they could figure out how to get off the island and back to the mainland.

The guards led the group to an old bunker and forced them to sit in the corner of the underground room. The metal door looked new and slammed shut with a loud echo. The only light that came in was from two small slits in the cement wall at the ceiling's edge. They were only large enough to allow light and fresh air in, and nothing more.

Standing, Eddie asked Chris, "Ya sure we're near Dingle Bay?"

"Oh, aye, I am. My da fishes all around Ireland in the Atlantic. I know my coastline."

"I figured ya did." Eddie scratched his head. "Any thoughts on how we get outta here?"

"None. You?"

"Nope. Claire?"

"No. We're outnumbered, and we don't have any weapons. I need you both alive, so no stupid moves from either of you. Got it? Kate and the others will come. They have to have found the trawler by now."

"There are no clues left behind on it, and with the tracker gone, they've no place to look. We've been switched between two boats since the trawler. Though we've a bit of time. Allister said he had a few things to take care of."

"Tying up loose ends, no doubt," Claire concluded. "I need a phone, or a radio, to get word to Kate."

"Aye, lass, but you'll not get one. We'll have to pray."

"Pray? You're giving up, Eddie."

"No, lass, not givin' up. Just askin' for a wee bit of help is all."

Chris got to his feet. "I'm of the same mind-set. Prayin' is all we can do for now. Any of ya lasses care ta join us?"

All the girls got up and formed a circle. Kayla only hesitated for a moment, saying, "I walked away from God awhile back. I'm not sure He'll want to hear from me."

Chris took her hand and assured her, "He's a lovin' father, and yer his daughter that's come home. The angels are singin' a glorious song in yer honor because of yer returnin'. Never forget that, Kayla."

She gave him a weak smile and squeezed his hand as a thank-you gesture for his kind words and then bowed her head. Right when Eddie began to pray, the door swung open, and a guard pushed Eddie to the floor and aimed his gun at Chris. Claire grabbed Chris by the arm and held him back.

John walked in and latched on to Kayla's hair, rolling it up tight in his fingers so she couldn't get away. She screamed.

"Come, darlin', the boss is bored and wants to have a wee bit o' fun with ya."

Claire yelled, "No!" A gun's barrel pressed up against her forehead.

John pointed to June and ordered, "Up with ya, girl!"

The other women huddled in the corner, crying. June wouldn't move. The guard aimed his gun at one of the openings at the ceiling and shot off a round and then aimed it back at Claire. "Up with ya now, woman, or I'll just kill 'er."

John dragged Kayla out by her hair and June followed. The door slammed shut and locked. Chris ran to the door and beat his fist against it several times, begging Allister's men to bring the women back.

"So much for praying!" Claire said bitterly.

"It's all about trustin', lass. Allister won't kill them. They're cash money and if he's on the run, he'll need all the money he can get."

"Well, what Allister's about to do to Kayla and June, they'll wish he'd kill them."

"There's no arguin' against that. I would imagine it's gonna get worse before it gets better. Chris, you still up for praying, lad?"

"Oh, aye, I am."

They formed a circle once more, and this time, even Claire felt compelled to join in. They all bowed their heads and Eddie prayed.

CHAPTER 8

The long ride back to Dublin from Killybegs lacked the usual, mundane boredom that normally came with long drives. With Kate in the front seat and Patrick driving, a lot of brainstorming took place. Each idea they explored; Kate delegated that job to someone. When she finished her calls, she glanced over at Patrick and studied him for a few seconds.

"I hate this," she said.

Patrick never took his eyes off the road when he asked, "Hate what?"

"All of this!" she snapped. "I'm sorry. I'm just frustrated. I know we can't save everyone, but I need these girls back. Every last one of them. Including the South American shipment."

"Kate, we're working on it. We've got a lead and location. We'll find them."

"We have the name of a boat," Kate grunted. For her, it wasn't enough. "When I first wrote that report for the Blue Blindfold Campaign back in 2016, I had only skimmed the surface of human trafficking in Ireland? Now, getting a firsthand glimpse into Brian Gallagher's world, I never knew how imbedded it was in our country."

The seriousness of the conversation between Patrick and Kate made Clay a little uneasy, and he asked, "What's the Blue Blindfold Campaign?"

Kate turned slightly in her seat to get a better look at Clay. "Blue is the color used for human trafficking awareness, like pink is for breast cancer. Blue Blindfold is annual report on human trafficking in Ireland. I wrote an extensive account on the commercial sex trade, forced labor, and the fishing industry a few years ago. Unfortunately, at the time, I didn't have a full understanding of just how bad it was here."

"Just how bad is it?"

This time Billy answered. "You have to understand, the number I'm about to give you is just an estimate, but there are close to, if not more than, thirty million people worldwide held in bondage."

"Ah, geez," Clay said, shocked.

"Yeah, it's pretty grim. What people don't realize is that not all trafficking has to do with sex. Victims of modern-day slavery include forced labor, organ removal, marriages, and of course, prostitution. The brunt of them are young women and children in the commercial sex trade."

"I had no idea."

"Though most victims are from poverty-stricken countries, color and status have no bearing on whether a person becomes a trafficker's next target," Kate added. "If someone is in the right place at the wrong time, he or she will become a victim, like Kayla did. Most cases go unnoticed because the victims are in plain sight. Escort services are one example. Even though the ladies working through these types of agencies do so openly, they have pimps controlling them. The trafficker's methods of coercion may vary, but almost every victim I've interviewed has said the same thing; horrific physical or sexual violence is involved. Then in other cases, where abductions occur, the captors are so brazen, they walk their abductee right out in the open. The coercion used in these cases don't differ from the escort services.

"A great example of that was the young woman in Berkley, California, they found after eighteen years of captivity," Billy offered. "Her captor walked her and her daughters onto the University of California campus in Berkley, and it took the event manager at the university to see that the young girl's behavior was off. Think about how many people they walked past before they came face-to-face with the one woman that noticed something was wrong."

Patrick nodded and asked, "Yeah, and wasn't there a lass in Utah that was seen in public after nine months of being abducted?"

"Yes," Clay answered, remembering both stories.

"Asia, being the worst," Billy said, "has boys and girls as young as nine years old hustling men on the street for sex, right out in the open, and no one, not even the government, does anything about it."

"A nine-year-old? Seriously? Who would—?"

"Very sick individuals," Patrick answered before Clay could finish. "Men that have children…have daughters at home that are none the wiser that their loving father's a pervert."

"The sad fact of the matter is," Kate continued, "there are only thirty-two countries out of one hundred ninety-five that are in full compliance with the Trafficking Victims Protection Act. The TVPA is the standards outline for every country to follow."

Disgusted mostly with himself for not being more aware, Clay said, "I didn't know about any of this. Why isn't it talked about more? I mean, I've seen movies on the subject, but they didn't open my eyes to the problem."

"People are so wrapped up in their own lives, or they simply don't care because it's not happening to them," Kate explained. "I have to say though, there are more campaigns exposing it and more activists fighting against slavery now than ever before. People are noticing the severity of trafficking humans now, which is a good thing."

A phone rang. It was Kate's, and the conversation ended. Clay thought about what he had learned as he watched Kate write the information given to her in a small notebook. He wished he had been more knowledgeable about this before now, but it wouldn't have helped Kayla. She would have done what she did out of spite.

Clay and his companions sat quietly while Kate spoke on the phone. He had a lot more questions but would do the research online when he had more time. He made a promise to himself that he would get to know Harper's Ministries on a personal level. Billy and the others had opened his eyes, and he would never allow them to be closed again on the subject of human trafficking.

*   *   *   *   *

By the time they made it to Dublin, it was late evening. Kate announced, "Okay, gentlemen, that's it. I have everything set. Alison O'Kelly's family and her brother, Anthony McCormick, have been under surveillance since we left Killybegs. If either sneeze, I'll know about it the second it happens."

"I take it they haven't sneezed yet?" Clay asked seriously.

"No. I've not heard a thing which seems a bit odd."

"Do you think someone warned them to stay home?" Patrick inquired.

"Maybe," Kate said, hopeful. "How much farther?"

"Almost there," Patrick answered.

"Where are we going?" Clay asked.

"You're going on a boat ride down the Liffey."

That surprised Clay, and he eyed Billy who explained, "They're looking for a boat that transports girls around Dublin."

Clay nodded that he understood. He wasn't sure he could handle another setback. With his eyes closed, he did the only thing he could do and said a silent prayer.

$$* \quad * \quad * \quad * \quad *$$

A massive manhunt for the *Crystalline* on the River Liffey had been underway long before the team arrived at the dock. Having read a little about the river before he had arrived in Ireland, Clay knew it was a major artery for Dublin and cut through the city center, separating the north from the south. Referred to as simply the Liffey, was the primary source for drinking water and generating electricity for Dubliners, a major tourist attraction, and a popular place for recreation. Though the River Liffey didn't offer many places to hide, it had several smaller tributaries and canals that would make the search for the boat long and tedious.

When Clay got out of the car, the dock was crawling with people. Agents were everywhere, gearing up for the hunt. He overheard Patrick telling Billy that this was the largest campaign the AHTTF had ever done. Patrick and Kate worried that, because of the size of this operation, leaks were inevitable. Hearing that caused a sick feeling in Clay's gut.

Before anyone in the director's group got on board one of the police boats, a man in his thirties, well groomed, jogged toward Kate, calling out to her. He was an inspector in the Dublin police force and someone she recognized right away.

"Killian, what do you have for me?"

Slightly out of breath, the inspector answered, "Eh, Director, we've word on the suspect you asked us to find. Thomas O'Leary—he's the boyfriend of one of the girls from the trawler." He looked at his notes to make sure he got the woman's name right. "A June Donnelly. They found him dead in his flat."

"Criminy! Allister is cutting off all ties. Do we have a location on him yet?"

"No, sorry, I've no news about him."

"How did O'Leary die?" Patrick asked.

"He hanged himself."

Kate looked at him incredulously and asked, "How did a man with two broken legs hang himself?"

"With a little help, I'm sure. Grossman's on it and will let me know his findings as soon as he's done with the autopsy."

"Thanks, Killian." Kate paused for a moment and then in an authoritative tone she ordered, "I want Allister found, and I want him found now!"

"On it!" Instead of walking back to his car, Killian ran.

Kate didn't linger and ordered everyone on board. Each boat pulled away from the dock, one after another. Clay was happy to be on the move again. Instead of being forced to wait at the hotel, Patrick spoke to Kate earlier on his behalf, and she allowed him to be a part of the team patrolling the River Liffey. However, Kate gave him a strong warning before their departure: if he so much as caused an ounce of a problem, she would have him handcuffed, dragged to the airport, and put on a plane heading back to California.

He took her warning seriously and stayed out of everyone's way. He even refrained from asking questions, though there were a few times he had to stifle the urge to do so internally. Instead, he sat back and listened.

The radio chatter was confusing, and the language being spoken around Clay didn't help either. He desperately wanted to know what was going on and that frustrated him. Billy seemed to understand the terminology and language and fed him tidbits of information, but that only added more questions to the cluster he already had floating around in his head.

Billy must have sensed Clay's need to know more and explained, "We're looking for a cruise boat called the *Tourmaline*."

"Wait—I thought we were looking for the *Crystalline*?"

"The police found it drydocked, waiting for repairs. The *Crystalline* is one of five tour boats owned by Alison O'Kelly and her brother. Word must have gotten out that the police were looking for it, and Anthony McCormick sent it in for repairs."

"When did the name *Tourmaline* pop up?" Clay ignored the little voice in his head advising him not to ask too many questions, but Billy didn't seem to mind.

"Kate's agents found the *Crystalline* a few hours ago, and there was no evidence that indicated Kayla or the other girls had ever been on board. With the *Crystalline* out of commission, the task force had four other tour boats to concentrate on."

The *Tourmaline* dominated the radio chatter from the moment Clay boarded the police patrol boat and was now the entire task force's primary focus. He couldn't help but wonder why the police were now concentrating on this one boat and asked, "So why the *Tourmaline*?"

Billy simply answered, "It's missing."

Where the *Crystalline* was an ivory color cruiser, the *Tourmaline* was blood red. Each tour boat was a different color, but they were all the same make and model. It was a common River Liffey faring craft used for day trips only. Few tour companies offered nighttime dining excursions that slowly navigated the river while enjoying a quiet evening with family and friends. Alison, on rare occasions and for the right price, would rent boats out for nighttime parties. The scheduling records showed that the *Tourmaline* was on a private party cruise.

Excitement erupted on the boat when word came that a search party had spotted the *Tourmaline*. The River Liffey cruiser was halfway to Athy on the Barrow. Patrick glanced over his shoulder at Billy and Clay and said, "Right, gents, we're only a few minutes from the location. Fingers crossed."

The boat traveled along the Grand Canal just east of the River Barrow. Though the Grand Canal went all the way to the River Shannon, the largest river in Ireland, it had limited access because of low-lying bridges and dams. The River Barrow, simply referred to as the Barrow, was 120 miles of open river that a boat like the *Tourmaline* could easily navigate all the way to the Celtic Sea. It was the second largest river in Ireland and was one of three rivers known as the Three Sisters. The rivers Suir and Nore were her siblings.

The helmsman, Mark, a retired Irish Navy man, navigated the Barrow as fast as he could. Clay's jitters had taken over. He bit the inside of his mouth in an effort not to yell at Mark to go faster.

Once at the location, bright lights shone on the red tour boat. There was no movement on board that Clay could see as the boat pulled up to the forty-eight-passenger cruiser. At Patrick's request, no one was to board her until he got there.

The *Tourmaline's* rear hatch was open, but the window screens were pulled down and no one from the other boats could see inside. An eeriness swept over the men and dampened the mood of everyone on board.

Patrick's eyes narrowed. "This doesn't look good. Take us in slow and steady, Mark."

"Oh, aye," he replied.

"Right, gents, this is it—stay alert." Then Patrick pointed at Clay and ordered, "You stay put!"

Mark lined the police patrol boat up to the rear of the *Tourmaline* with ease. Patrick jumped on to its back platform with no effort at all. Billy hopped on after Patrick did but didn't follow him inside.

With his flashlight on and weapon drawn, Patrick stepped down into the *Tourmaline*. "Ah, geez, it's rancid!"

The stench was overpowering. Patrick gagged and put the back of his hand to his nose, hoping to block the odor. He shined his light all around the inside until the beam illuminated the carnage that caused the horrific smell. Two lifeless bodies, an adult male and female, were on opposite sides of the boat. Blood was everywhere.

Patrick whispered, "Whoever did this had vengeance on their mind."

The woman's mutilated body was unrecognizable. However, Patrick recognized the man shot in the chest right away from a photo he had seen earlier.

"Kate won't be happy about this," he said over his shoulder.

Billy gagged and backed away to get some fresh air. "Who are they?"

"If I had to guess, I would say it's Alison O'Kelly and her husband. I recognize him from a photo Kate showed me."

Crouching down on the back platform again, Billy looked in and asked, "I thought she had them under surveillance? I'm just guessing, but this happened a while ago and not tonight. If I'm right, then who have the police been watching all this time?"

Patrick shook his head at his friend while saying, "I've no idea. I'll radio this in to Kate. What a mess."

Both men had seen a lot while in the military, but the brutality of these murders shook them up. Patrick took the steps up and stood next to Billy. "This was our only lead. Kate was right, we've nothing."

Billy released a frustrated sigh. He was about to step back onto the police patrol boat when he turned and faced Patrick. "Why do you think they butchered her the way they did?"

Patrick eyed his friend for a moment and then glanced back inside the *Tourmaline* before he answered. "Maybe a warning to Anthony not to screw things up."

"Or maybe he already screwed things up, and this is what happened because of it," Billy surmised.

"There's no telling. We've got to find Anthony...hopefully alive."

"Didn't Kate say Alison had three kids?"

"Yeah, she did. Two girls and a boy." Patrick's face paled. Taking in a deep breath, he went back down inside the cruiser. With his flashlight on, he searched between each row of seats for the children.

A sigh of relief blew from Patrick when he found no sign of them. "I'll check the helm!" he yelled back at Billy.

With the helm's door closed, the only course for Patrick to take was to walk through the muck of blood that covered the floor. "Criminy, this is disgusting!"

"You all right in there?" Billy asked.

"Oh, aye. This is just nasty business," he answered. "Almost there."

Patrick grabbed the handle to the helm's door with his flashlight hand, while he kept his gun aimed at it. "Oi, anyone in there?" With no answer, Patrick pulled the door open and shone his light all around the empty cabin. Tension expelled from his entire body. "They're not here!"

"Am I allowed to say thank goodness?"

"Yeah, you are. My hope is, they weren't here to see this done to their parents."

"You and me both," Billy agreed. "You know I've dealt with the Ukrainian mob before, and I thought they were butchers, but I have to admit, they were mere kittens compared to Gallagher's henchmen."

Patrick sat down on the bench closest to the exit and unlaced his boots. He took them off and set them on the bottom step. Forensics would need them once they came and did a thorough inspection of the *Tourmaline*. Once done, he stood and took the steps up to the platform. "I think I would have to agree with you. This is beyond inhumane." In two long strides, Patrick was back on the police patrol boat and asked, "Can you hand me the radio, Mark?"

"Aye."

One look at Patrick, Clay knew that whatever had happened on the tour cruiser wasn't good. Even Billy looked awful. Scared of hearing the details, he ran his fingers through his hair and then locked them behind his head. He took slow, methodical breaths, hoping to calm his nerves. When he made eye contact with Billy, his friend whispered, "It's not her."

Clay unlocked his hands, leaned forward, placing both of them on his knees and blew the air from lungs with the words, "Ah, sweet Jesus, thank you," coming with it.

Patrick held the radio mic so tight that his knuckles were white. He put the mic close to his lips and took in a small breath before he called out, "Kate, come in, over."

"Here, Patrick. We'll be at your location in five, over."

"No need. The girls were never here. Alison O'Kelly and her husband are dead. No sign of their kids or Anthony." Patrick paused for a moment and then advised, "Kate, it's brutal, over."

Silence filled the air.

Thanking God for it not being his sister might have been insensitive. Two people were dead. From what Craig had told Kate during the interview, Alison had known nothing about the human trafficking side of the business that her brother had gotten involved in with Brian Gallagher. After seeing the expression on the faces of both Patrick and Billy, he knew the word *brutal* wasn't even close to describing what they had seen. Clay suddenly felt sick to his stomach.

"Right, the garda can haul the *Tourmaline* in after forensics go over it. I want you to meet me back at the dock. This is sloppy, and I need to clean up a few things before we regroup. Over." Kate sounded frustrated.

"Aye. On our way. Over."

*　　*　　*　　*　　*

Kate had invited Clay, Billy, and Patrick's team over to her house for a late dinner. Her husband was an excellent cook and had prepared a feast for them. After the meal, he offered everyone coffee and then took the kids upstairs to bed, leaving Kate and her guests to discuss the case. Clay, for the first time since all of this started, didn't want to be a part of the conversation. He had heard enough of the gory details from Billy, so he excused himself and went outside.

Bundled in a thick coat, Clay sat on Kate's patio trying to make some sense of the day's events. Of course, he couldn't. This dark and very dangerous world he was getting glimpses of, scared him. Knowing Kate's responsibilities required her to work cases like this every day, and that she enjoyed doing them, surprised him. Her marriage and children added to his wonder as to why she would take on such a job.

The glass door to Clay's left slid open. Once the door closed, Kate took a seat in the chair next to him. She pulled her coat tight around her and propped one foot up on the table. "You okay? You haven't said much since we got here. I'm a little concerned."

Leaning forward and placing his elbows on his knees, Clay answered, "Yeah. I just don't know how you do it. Seeing the expressions on Billy's and Patrick's faces when they came off the *Tourmaline* was enough for me."

"To be honest with you, I more than likely would have puked had I seen the carnage. Killian brought the pictures over from the crime scene, and they're gruesome. My job isn't like this most days. However, Gallagher is in a class of his own and hires nothing but the most deranged individuals he can find. The more unhinged they are, the more likely he can keep his people in line. Allister is the worst of them. I believe Brian's wife is the only sane person in his circle."

"His wife?"

"Yes, He's been married to the same woman for the last twenty-nine years. I have her under house arrest and she's been very cooperative. She knew her husband's dealings weren't all on the up-and-up, but the human trafficking part—well, she didn't have a clue. Giving Alison the money for the River Liffey cruise tour company was her idea and Brian gladly did that for her. Had she known he was going to use the cruise line for human trafficking, she would have found another way to help her friend. It devastated her when Killian told her about Alison and blames herself for her friend's death."

Clay nodded that he understood. Leaning back in his chair, he eyed Kate. "Can I ask you something?"

"I'm an open book. Ask away."

"On our drive from Killybegs, Billy said something that caught my attention. It kind of freaked me out a little. I mean, this is all horrible business, but he said that some traffickers use their victims for organ harvesting. I don't get it. I thought there were rules and guidelines that doctors and hospitals had to follow...like ethics.

Don't they use only organs from known healthy donors who have recently passed away?"

Kate didn't have to think too hard on how to answer that question. "A few years ago, a concerned Indian official invited me to New Delhi, India, for a conference on how best to stop organ removal from their citizens. He invited me because someone gave him a copy of the Blue Blindfold report that I wrote. I explained organ harvesting wasn't an area I knew much about, but the man was in dire straits. Because I didn't know much about the topic, I called a friend, Dr. Williams, and asked him to join me. What Dr. Williams shared at that conference scared even me."

"How? What scared you?"

"Dr. Williams lectured on cultures that offered their citizens cash for their organs. India is one of the worst. Iran even has a legal market for organ harvesting. China used to. The Chinese government allowed doctors to take the organs out of executed convicts. However, they finally put an end to that practice, but that was only as recently as 2015."

"Wow."

"Wow, is right. Each country is gauged by the TVPA standards, and they're divided into tiers—tier 1 being in complete compliance with the standards and tier 3 being in the 'I don't care' category. Iran has been at a 'I don't care, tier 3' since they started gauging countries, and China, even after changing their ways, has fallen back into a tier 3."

Clay didn't understand and asked, "You mentioned TVPA before. What does it stand for?"

"It's the Trafficking Victims Protection Act. It's more or less a way to gauge whether world governments are in compliance. Many countries just don't care, especially when harvesting brings in millions of dollars."

"Oh…okay, so if Iran, China and I'm guessing India still practice organ removal, how do they go about taking the organs out of someone who's alive?"

"You'd think that would be the tricky part, but it's not. There are several ways actually. One way is by abductions. The reapers, who are black market doctors, just cut out what they need and release the person. Or they find a poor family, which is extremely easy to do in countries like India and China, and pay them for their parts. Another way is that the harvesters pay a family member for a relative and that person is killed outright for all their organs."

"Ah, geez!"

"Clay, you need to understand, there are so many facets to human trafficking—all money oriented and all terrible for the victims. Seventy-one percent of all those trafficked are women. That part alone is a ninety-nine-billion-dollar global business. Brian Gallagher isn't a millionaire, he's a billionaire."

Fear for Kayla, Claire, and the girls on the South American ship washed over Clay, paralyzing him for a moment. There weren't enough people like Kate to stop the buying and selling of humans, especially with that much money being made. Clay hadn't thought it was possible for him to admire Kate any more than he already did, but knowing she was fighting against human trafficking daily, his admiration for her grew.

Since he had arrived at Kate's house, Clay had done a lot of thinking about his being there. He was torn between staying in Ireland and going home. The daily updates and the emotional rollercoaster he found himself on were killing him. He wasn't like Kate and the others, and it was becoming too much for him to handle, especially knowing Kayla was caught up in the horrifying world of trafficking.

He looked at Kate and said, "I think I'm going to go back to Ian's house. That's if you don't mind me staying in Ireland while you track down my sister."

"Ian?"

"Yeah, he and his wife, Mary, are the couple that helped me. Ian found me when Allister and Craig dumped me on the side of the road. They put me up for a night. They live just outside a small town, near someplace called Cork." Clay chuckled. "I have no clue how to get back there, but I called Ian, and he invited me to stay for as long as I like."

Checking her watch, she said, "Criminy, it's almost two. Yeah, listen, get in touch with your embassy today before you go. I'll send you with some paperwork that will allow you to stay for a few months if need be."

Her comment surprised him. "A few months? Do you think it will take that long?"

"Clay, I've no idea where Kayla and the others are. With Allister loose and on a massive killing spree, I've no idea how long it will take to find the girls or him. But," she said, leaning forward, "I think it's a good idea for you to go stay with your friends and let us deal with this."

"Thanks, Kate, for everything."

The glass door slid open and police inspector Killian's head popped through. "We have 'im!"

Kate jumped out of her chair and asked, "Who?"

"Anthony McCormick. And he's scared out of his wits."

Clay followed Kate back inside the house and closed the door behind him. Patrick and his team were gearing up to leave when Kate asked, "Where's he being taken?"

"The local garda station."

"I want him redirected. Have them—"

Patrick cut in, "Kate, we'll take him to my place. Find out where they are, and we'll escort Anthony ourselves!"

"Do it, Killian!"

"Kate, do you mind if I tag along for this? I promise to stay out of your way. I'll leave for Ian's afterward."

"Yeah," Patrick answered for her. "I'll see to him once we've had a chat with Anthony."

Clay was grateful. "Thanks."

*   *   *   *   *

It was 3:00 a.m. when Patrick pulled onto his property with Anthony in tow. The man looked like he had been in a fight and lost but was able to stand on his own. Kate offered Anthony the chair opposite her. Patrick took the only empty chair at the table, whipped it around and rested his arms on its back when he sat down. The rest of the group stood around the table and listened.

Kate had the folder that Killian had given her with the gruesome pictures of Alison and her husband. She opened it and laid one picture down at a time on the table in front of Anthony. He couldn't look at them and turned his head away.

Agitated, Kate tapped her finger on a picture of Alison's mutilated body and said, "Look at what your dealings with Brian Gallagher have done. Look!"

Anthony's entire body shook as he cried out, "Ah, sweet Jaysus, what have I done? Please, forgive me!" His head dropped, and he wailed in agony over the savage murder of his sister. Anthony placed his balled-up fists over his eyes and yelled, "He's crazy! She'd nothin' ta do with the business. The eejit didn't need ta kill 'er!"

"Why did Gallagher have Alison killed, Anthony? And why so barbarous?"

"I dunno! Honest! She'd nothin' ta do with the business." Anthony wiped his eyes as he gasped for air. He couldn't stop crying and had a hard time speaking.

Kate gathered up the pictures from the table, put them back in the folder and handed it to Killian. "I'm sorry, Anthony, but you've had a hand in the destruction of so many families, I'm finding it hard to have any sympathy for you. I'm looking for the last group of girls taken from the trawler. Do you know where they are?"

Anthony trembled. His facial muscles tightened, clamping his mouth shut. He quickly wiped his eyes while his head bobbed up and down, lost in thought. When he finally made eye contact with Kate, the frail, despondent man that once sat across from her, was gone. Anthony's vitality had returned. "Oh, aye, I do!"

Everyone in the workshop tensed up. Patrick stood, flipped his chair around the right way, and then sat down again. He scooted closer to the table, asking, "Where are they, Anthony? Be a good lad and tell us where they are."

"I'll give ya everything ya ask for, but you've got ta give me protection, or I'll not tell ya a thing."

Before Kate could argue with him, Clay had positioned himself at one end of the table, gripping its sides. He leaned in low, only inches from Anthony's face, making him push back in his chair, but it didn't move. Once Clay was confident that he had the man's attention, he spoke with an almost eerie calm.

"Every time you transported someone's loved one down the river to the next boat, I'm sure you thought it was just business, nothing personal, right? How does it feel now, Anthony? Is Alison's death just business as usual? Or has it gotten personal enough for you? My sister, Kayla, was on that trawler. You need to understand—it's extremely personal for me, and I want her back! My sister, like yours, didn't deserve this. Now, you can do one of two things. Either help us and save my sister and the girls with her, or you can have more deaths piled onto your ever-growing list of crimes. No deals! Got it? You'll tell Kate everything she wants to know, and you'll do it now!"

With Clay's last words, he slammed his fist down hard on the table, causing both Anthony and Kate to jump. Anthony's face paled, and he swallowed hard. His eyes went from Clay to Kate and back again. He knew his life was finished, no matter what he did. He took one last look at Clay before he turned to Kate saying, "Dingle Bay."

"What?"

"They shipped them to one of the islands around Dingle Bay."

"How long will they keep them there?" Patrick asked.

"As long as they need to. The islanders are no match for Gallagher's muscle—Allister and his men—so they say nothin' and mind their own business."

"Patrick, I don't want to include any other agencies in this. I don't know who I can trust right now, except those in this room. I need you to deal with this as quietly and as quickly as you can."

"Understood."

"Billy, are you okay to go with them?"

"Yeah, I most definitely am."

"Clay, I'm fully aware that without your help, we wouldn't have found Craig. Not to mention getting Anthony here to talk; however, I need you to go to Ian's house as planned and wait this out. Will you do that for me?"

Clay was angry at Anthony, but when Kate spoke to him, some of that rage dissipated, and he answered, "Yes, I can. I mean, I will, as long as you keep me informed about what's going on."

Kate had the sweetest smile, and it softened Clay's anger even more. "I'll personally call you with every detail, no matter how small."

The promise of getting updates from Kate was enough for Clay. All the tension drained from his body and there was a spark of amusement in his voice when he stated, "Um, you'll have to point me in the right direction because I don't know how to get there. Oh, and maybe a ride to a bus or train station."

"It's on the way to Dingle Bay. You'll ride with us," Patrick offered.

"Gentlemen, I can't stress enough how important it is that you speak to no one. I'll go back to Dublin and get some house cleaning done. Someone will pay for screwing up the surveillance I had on Alison and Anthony." Then she asked Anthony, "Do you know where your nieces and nephew are?"

"Ah geez, I dunno. Please, ya have ta find 'em!" Anthony choked back his grief and offered, "I'll tell ya anything…everything ya need ta know. Just find 'em!"

"Our list of victims has just increased by three, gentlemen." Kate's mind was working fast. She faced Killian and ordered, "I need you to go pick up Craig in Killybegs, but only you. Transport him back here. Because of the leaks at my office, Patrick, I hope you don't mind me using your place as my temporary headquarters?"

"No, not at all. I sent the girls away for a while. I'll call the wife and tell her to extend her visit with her sister."

"Great, thanks. I have two close friends in the Garda Síochána that I trust with my life. I'll have them transferred to me. It shouldn't take long. They can stand guard over Anthony and Craig when he arrives. I'll stay here until they get here. The rest of you, get going. I want this finished by tonight, if at all possible."

Killian took a package out of his bag and handed it to Kate while Patrick and his men grabbed their gear. He spoke in a low voice so Clay couldn't hear. She opened it and eyed its contents. She and Killian looked over at Clay, grinning, before she closed the envelope.

Kate nodded her thanks to the inspector and without a word to anyone, he hurried out the door and headed for his car.

Clay heard the car's engine start and the sound of its tires as it left the premises. He knew Killian had a long drive to Killybegs to pick up Craig and didn't blame him for his sudden departure. Kate stared quizzically at him, which made him feel as if he had done something wrong. She glanced down at the large envelope, gave an exasperated sigh and walked over to him.

"This is for you. But you might want to wait and open it later, when you're alone." Then with an odd expression, she added, "I thought Patrick said you were a Christian."

Confused by her comment, Clay glanced down at the package. The label was addressed to him in care of Kate Walsh at the Anti-Human Trafficking Unit in Dublin and had been opened. It was from Emer. He couldn't imagine what it was she had sent him, but he would have to wait to find out its contents later. Patrick's voice pulled him away from his thoughts, and he thanked her. He opened his backpack, slipped the package in, and forgot about it.

Patrick and his men grabbed the last of the gear needed. They carried out wetsuits and diving tanks and loaded them into the two Land Rovers. Kate had fallen into the same rhythm as Patrick and was on her cell phone spouting out more orders. This left Clay alone with Anthony—they were the only two that weren't in motion.

As Clay glanced down at the man, he couldn't believe that he actually felt bad for the guy. Giving in to some unknown force, he found himself crouched down next to him. He took one of Anthony's hands in his and studied him for a moment. Anthony lifted his eyes just enough to see Clay staring at him.

Not giving him time to react one way or another, Clay offered, "If there was ever a time in a man's life to come to God, it's now. With every fiber of my being I hate you and all that you represent. But there is a small part of me that understands that you weren't just lashing out at me and my sister, but you were, and most likely still are, fighting against God. Because of that, I know, at some point, I'm going to have to find a way to forgive you for your part in all of this and trust God's justice will prevail. Just having you sitting in front of me shows me that God is winning."

Clay took a moment to shake off his sudden need to cry. He didn't understand what it was he was doing, but something inside compelled him to speak to Anthony. For the first time in Clay's life, his faith came first, and the need for him to share it was extremely powerful.

Locking eyes with him once more, he said, "Matthew 6:15 says, 'But if you do not forgive men their trespasses, neither will your Father forgive your trespasses.' So I want you to know that I need to forgive you. That I have to forgive you. But I also want you to understand that God can and will forgive you, even without my forgiveness. You'll have to pay for what you've done according to Ireland's laws, but your spirit will be God's, and no one can take that from you."

Clay released Anthony's hand and opened his backpack. He pulled out a small book and handed it to him. With a slight chuckle, he said, "I can't believe I'm doing this because a dear woman just gave this to me, but I want you to have it. It's a Bible. The entire book is important but start with Ephesians chapter 1. Wherever you read the word *us*, replace it with the word *me*. 'Jesus Christ, who has blessed *me* in the heavenly realms,' 'For he chose *me*,' 'In love he predestined *me* for adoption,' and so on. Pray for His forgiveness. Each time, before you open the Bible to read, pray and ask God to give you understanding. Let God into your heart, Anthony. When you do, all the fear and hate bottled up inside you will no longer be your companion, but God will. Let Him in and He'll show you what genuine love and peace feels like. I promise."

A tear dropped on the cover of the Bible and Anthony wiped it off. As he sucked in air, he brushed his hand across his face several times to wipe the moisture away. Then, peering up at Clay, who was now standing next to him, he said, "I'll not make it ta heaven. I don't deserve ta go!"

"If it was based on whether we deserve to go to heaven, none of us would make it. It's a gift. Not from me, but from God. He gives it freely. You just have to reach out and take it. I promise you won't regret it."

Anthony looked down at the Bible in his hands and laughed with tears streaming down his cheeks. "I've never held a Bible in my hands before, not once." Then, nodding his head, he held it up with one hand and announced, "I'll do it! Thank ya for yer kindness. And for what it's worth, I'm truly sorry 'bout yer sister and, more importantly, for my part in all this."

"I appreciate that. I'm sorry about Alison. She didn't deserve to die the way she did. No one does."

Anguish contorted every muscle in Anthony's face, and he sobbed uncontrollably. He drew the Bible close to his chest and held it tight while his body shook. Clay honestly felt bad for him. He had done all that he could and would let him deal with his grief alone. He picked up his backpack, slung it over his shoulder and did an about-face. When he did, he noticed Patrick and Kate, along with the others in the room, staring at him in complete astonishment. He shrugged their curiosity off and made his way outside without saying a word.

"Okay, now I'm totally confused," Kate confessed.

"About what?" Patrick asked.

"The package he received." Kate didn't wait for Patrick to ask what she meant; she rushed to catch up to Clay.

Once outside, Clay stopped. He didn't know where he was going, but he needed air. He decided to go for a short walk and made it a few yards from Patrick's workshop when he heard his name being called. He turned around and saw Kate jogging toward him. She slowed to a walk as soon as she caught up to him but didn't stop. Clay guessed he was going to have company.

The two ambled in silence down the road that led to the stream. Clay could only guess what was going through Kate's mind. She probably thought he was some crazy religious zealot. The thought made him chuckle. "You think I'm nuts, don't you?"

Kate never looked at him; she stayed focused on the path in front of her. "No. Not even close. I've met a few American missionaries before and I'm sure they think all Irishmen and women are going to hell in a handbasket of some kind." She glanced over at him and finished with, "You're different somehow."

"Me, a missionary?" Clay scoffed. "You're crazy! I'm no missionary. Not even close. Although I do donate to World Charities and Charities USA, but I'm sure that doesn't count for anything."

Kate smiled at him and then faced forward again. "What you did back there was nice. I have nothing but disdain for the man myself, then you go off and practically forgive him."

"I didn't forgive him. I said I needed to, and that I wanted to, but I never forgave him. I have too much anger and hate imbedded in me right now to forgive anyone. I'm hoping, when I'm away from all of this, that I can get my head on straight."

"When I was a small girl, my uncle was a devout Christian. He read the Bible daily and prayed earnestly for his family. His love for God was as real as they come, and my dad hated his brother because of it. Of course, my dad was like a lot of folks—payday came, and he was off to the pub to drink it all away. My uncle, on the other hand, secretly gave large portions of his earnings to my mother, to stash away someplace safe so my father would never find it. My uncle was a good man and didn't have a family of his own. Because of that, he felt it was his job to help my family financially. You remind me a lot of him."

Clay grinned at Kate and explained, "The sad fact of the matter is, your uncle was a better man than me. When my folks died, I just went through the motions. I went to church every Sunday morning and Wednesday night, wrote out my tithe check each month, supported whatever cause the church asked me to support, but it was all done with little or no feeling at all. It took Kayla to go missing for me to realize that."

"I'm sorry about your parents, Clay. Is Kayla your only sibling or do you have others?"

"No, she's it."

"I know you're not married, but do you have a girlfriend back home, waiting for you?"

"No, not back home."

"You've had time to meet someone here?" That surprised Kate. "Dr. Emer O'Farrell is a woman? The one that sent the package?"

Clay laughed. "Yeah, she's a woman. But no, she's not really. I mean, she's the doctor that took care of me after my run-in with Allister and Craig. She has a fiery temper, but I think she's kind of cute. She thinks I'm an idiot for trusting in God the way that I do."

"A temper, huh? And she caught your eye? And to top it off, she's not a Christian. Well, that explains a lot." Kate found that somewhat amusing but let it go. With a more sober expression, she explained, "I need you to prepare for the worst, Clay. Kayla may already be dead."

Those words stopped Clay from taking another step.

She faced him and continued, "Allister's severing all his connections that link him to Brian Gallagher. The video of him handing the gun over to his boss doesn't mean a thing. He'll claim he didn't know Gallagher's mind at the time and didn't know he was going to kill Derrick. Craig and Anthony are the two that will put Allister in prison for a long time. I have to keep them safe. The problem is, I have no idea how involved Allister was in your sister's abduction. She may be dead if she saw too much. I know this is hard for you to hear, but I don't want you to have false hope."

Clay's eyes watered, and he quickly wiped them. He knew what she meant and had fought hard not to think about that. Now, with Kate telling him to prepare for the worst, he couldn't help but think she was already dead.

"Hang on to your faith because you're going to need it more than ever now." Kate gently held Clay's arms. Her touch made him expel the breath he had unknowingly been holding. "Good or bad, I'll keep you informed, I promise."

"Yeah, thanks. Um, thanks, Kate, for everything. For putting up with me. I know I haven't made it easy for you and the others."

"I meant what I said back there. If you hadn't recognized Craig in the crowd at Killybegs, I would have been none the wiser. You've helped. What's the doctor's name again?"

"The doctor?" Her question confused him at first. "Oh, Emer O'Farrell."

"Go get to know the doctor a bit more. She obviously has a sick sense of humor." There was a slight chuckle in Kate's voice when she spoke. "And don't worry about the embassy. I know where you'll be, and I have some pull in the justice department. You can stay until we find Kayla, or until you're ready to go home. All right?"

"I'd forgotten about my passport." Clay let out a sigh of gratitude. "Yeah, thanks. You have my phone number, correct?"

"Yeah, I sneaked it off your phone when you gave it to me with Roman Jones's numbers."

"Oi! We're off then. You coming, Clay?"

With his name being called, Clay turned around and saw Patrick at the top of the road. "I guess this is it. I'll wait for your call, but please don't leave me hanging. I know I've said this a dozen times already, but thank you for everything you've done."

Instead of a handshake, he gave her a hug. She hugged him back, saying, "You're welcome. We'll speak soon, I promise."

* * * * *

By the time they neared the village close to Ian's farm, it was early morning. Connor drove while Patrick rode in the front passenger seat with Billy and Clay in the back. The rest of the team rode in the other Land Rover, following them. Clay was thankful to be traveling with Patrick and Connor because he got to eavesdrop while they hashed out their plan.

What they decided on would be intense and involve a lot of swimming in the frigid ocean. The team would have to go unnoticed as they sneaked onto each island. Grateful he sat this one out, Clay said a silent prayer of gratitude for these fearless men. Whatever the outcome of his sister, it had been an honor for him to have met them.

With everyone sure of what they were going to do, the discussion drifted to a lighter topic. Clay's mind wandered off the conversation and onto the package that Emer had sent him. Curiosity got the best of him, and he reached for his backpack and pulled out the large envelope. When he opened it and slid out the contents, his eyes widened.

"Whoa!" Disbelief shot across Clay's face when he saw the two thick magazines he held in his hands.

Billy saw his expression and glanced down at them. He was just as surprised as Clay was. The only difference—Billy laughed. "Seriously, Clay! Who knew?" Hearing Billy's outburst, Patrick shifted around in his seat to see what was so funny.

The look on Clay's face was priceless. Patrick glanced down at the magazines and said, "That explains Kate's confusion." He reached back and took one to show Connor.

Embarrassment didn't even come close to explain how Clay felt.

Billy guffawed, "Who'd send you dirty magazines? And send them through Kate's office?"

"Poor Kate—she hands you these and then watches you give your Bible to Anthony," Patrick added. "She was struck dumb, and no wonder!"

Mortified, Clay couldn't fathom why Emer would send him magazines with naked women in them, fully knowing that all he wanted was a Bible. "I...I don't get it," he said, perplexed. "Why would she send these to me?"

"They weren't just sent to you. They were expressed to you! Not just to you, but to the AHTU, no less! Ah, this is brilliant!" Patrick howled. "All packages have to be opened by someone before they go to Kate! Especially if they aren't marked confidential. The entire department is aware of your package by now!"

The roar of laughter was deafening as Clay sat in shock, staring at the magazine. Then the muscles in his face lifted on one side of his mouth. "Lily!" He shook his head and barked, "I'm gonna kill her!"

"Ah, no, killing, along with those dirty books you're holding, goes against every fiber of your faith." Clay could see Connor grinning through the rearview mirror. "Who's the lass that sent them to ya?"

He couldn't help but find it humorous, but the embarrassment he felt kept him from laughing. "She's a young woman who likes to prank her boss."

Connor laughed hard, and like the others, he was having a hard time holding it together. "Well, she's pranked the entire task force and Kate right along with ya! They'll be razzin' Kate for harboring a man that's in ta lookin' at dirty pictures of ladies while she's fightin' so hard against such atrocities. The irony is brilliant! I'd love to meet the lass that has a mind as gifted as hers."

Humiliated once again, Clay pulled out his phone to call Kate but then thought better of it. He would explain it to her later. Instead, he found Emer's contact number and pushed the phone icon. It rang twice before he heard Emer say, "Hello, Clay. How are you?"

Clay's companions stopped laughing so they could eavesdrop on his conversation. He realized it but didn't care. "It's good to know you've been practicing your pronunciation of 'hello.'"

"Oh, I have. Do you like it?"

Clay grinned and said, "Actually, I liked it better when you dropped your letters. It's more you."

"Well, you have the proper side of me when I'm awake and have had a cup of coffee."

Remembering that his buddies were eavesdropping, he said, "Hey, just so you know, I have an audience listening on my end."

"Really, and what would they find so interesting about a chat you're having with me?"

"Ah, well, that's the funny part." The snickering was back, but the men kept their laughter to a hushed murmur. "The package you sent to me, in the care of Kate Walsh, at the Anti-Human Trafficking Unit, in Dublin—"

"Great! I'm glad you got it. Wasn't sure where you were staying, so I sent it to her. I hope that's okay?"

Ignoring his friends heckling, Clay forged ahead. "Yeah, no, Kate was cool about it...somewhat confused by it, but she didn't mind."

"What do you mean somewhat confused by it?"

"So apparently, when a package arrives at the AHTU in Dublin, someone in the mailroom has to open it first, you know, to make sure there's nothing in it that would harm anyone."

"Yeah, so? It was only a Bible. No harm to anyone unless they read it," Emer said, playfully.

"Um, I didn't get a Bible from you. Instead, I received two very colorful…yet very disturbing magazines with naked women in them. Okay, well, I never actually opened them, but I'm sure they're filled with pictures of nude women."

Billy and Patrick couldn't contain their laughter anymore. Connor tried his best not to laugh. Instead, he snorted, which caused him to fall in with the others, making the noise level in the vehicle increase. On the other end of the phone, there was nothing but dead silence. Clay swore he heard Emer growl just before she yelled, "That idiot! I give her a simple task to do, and she still manages to mess it up! I'll fire her!"

Clay joined in with his friends and laughed. "You can't fire her."

"Stop laughing—it's not funny! Oh, I'm…Oh my…wait. That means Kate saw them too!"

"I'm sorry to say she did. She was a tad confused by them. Especially knowing me and my faith. She did ask me a lot of questions about you though."

Emer was fuming, and Clay could hear her temper flare without hearing her words. "She must think me a fool!"

"I told her you thought I was an idiot for putting my faith in God and the Bible. So I'm guessing she thinks either I'm a liar and a pervert, or you're testing me."

"I may not have the same beliefs you have in God, but I would never test you. I've no doubt that holy fire would come down on top of me if I did."

Clay laughed. "Well, Lily doesn't seem to have the same fears."

"She'll be fearing me this morning when I get to the clinic. I canna believe she'd be such a stook! And before you ask, it's an idiot or fool and she's both today!"

"There you are!" Clay teased. "That didn't take long for you to release that old neighborhood dialect of yours—with coffee and all."

"This isn't funny. Kate must think me a buffoon!"

Still laughing, he promised, "I'll call her later to explain it wasn't you, but that Lily sent them. Your reputation won't be tarnished for too long." Clay now knew why Lily liked to mess with Emer so much. It brought her down to earth and made her human. "Do me a favor, hold your wrath, at least for another hour or so, would you?"

"Why?"

"I'll be there in about an hour. I'd like to be the one to talk to her and return the magazines."

"You're coming here? Why?"

"There's nothing I can do right now. Kate's going to let me stay in Ireland for as long as it takes. It's been a hit and miss so far. I just need to stay in one spot while they look for Kayla. Hopefully, I'll get some work done while I wait."

He could tell Emer had softened to the idea of not saying anything to Lily. "I'll be here when you arrive."

"Thanks, Emer. I'll see you soon."

When Clay put the phone back in his pocket, Patrick handed him the other magazine and offered, "So your character hasn't been corrupted after all. Kate will be glad to know that. What you did for Anthony was nothing short of amazing. You're a good man."

Slipping both magazines back into their envelope, Clay glanced up at Patrick. "I didn't do what I should've done, which was to forgive the man for his part in all of this. I'm still angry. I'm even mad at my sister, and I hate myself for feeling that way about her. She didn't deserve this, but then again, she's the one that went with Derrick. There's always a source, you know, a starting point to every problem. If my sister had just gone back to the hotel with her friends, if Derrick hadn't been a jerk and invited her to the party, if she hadn't been so trusting…and the list goes on. Then there's a part of me that can't help but think she's the reason that Gallagher's organization is crumbling. That, because of her, human trafficking will end in Ireland, at least for a while. I'm sure some other idiot will resurrect it, but because of Kayla, Gallagher's done."

"Someone may try, but with Kate leading the fight against them, they'll fail." Patrick's words were absolute, and Clay didn't doubt them for a minute. Patrick respected Kate, and it was clear he did every time he mentioned her by name.

"Kate…she's pretty amazing, isn't she?"

"Aye, she is. And she'll not let up 'til she ends human trafficking completely in Ireland. But you're correct. Because of your sister, we've brought down a powerful man and his organization. We have so much information on Gallagher's business, that there'll be no place for him to hide the girls."

Clay took some comfort in knowing that. Then, remembering the envelope, he put it in his backpack and tossed the bag in the rear cargo compartment. He leaned back in his seat and smiled when he thought about Lily. "When this is all over, Connor, and you get a break, I know a pretty young lady that you should meet."

"Oh, aye?"

"Yeah, she has a great sense of humor. You're just her type."

Connor positioned himself so he could see Clay better in the rearview mirror and smiled. "The lass that sent you the dirty books? She did get ya ta squirmin'."

"Yeah, she did. I would love to see how well you fare after spending some time with her."

That brought back the laughter. The rest of the ride consisted of bragging rights to successful pranks that each man had pulled off during his youth. Clay was no match for them and was glad he'd met them as fully matured men. He was a wimp, even next to Lily, but he loved her sense of humor and didn't mind being pranked by her. He wished he was as quick-witted and could prank her back but then thought better of it. She got him good, and he couldn't help but smile.

CHAPTER 9

Connor exited Motorway 8 and headed in the direction of the farm. When he got close to the small village near Ian's, Clay tapped him on the shoulder. Without looking back, he asked, "Yeah?"

"Hey, do you mind pulling over here? I'd like to stop by the clinic first. I'll find a ride to Ian's later." Clay reached over the back seat and grabbed his backpack.

"Aye. Best o' luck ta ya."

"Thanks, Connor." Then, turning to Billy, Clay added, "Don't forget your promise—dead or alive, I want to know."

Billy nodded. "I promise."

Before Clay got out, he said to Patrick, "Thanks again for everything you've done for me and my sister. I want you to know I'll be praying for all of you—for Eddie and Claire too. May Jesus guide and protect you."

Once out of the car, Clay shut the door and waved before he headed for town. Patrick watched him for a few seconds and then said, "Let's go get the man's sister, gents!" He did a drum roll on the dash of the vehicle before he sat back in his seat.

Clay glanced over his shoulder as the two vehicles did a U-turn. He had mixed emotions about not going. Part of him wanted to go with them, but the other part was more logical and knew he would only get in their way. The emotional rollercoaster ride he had been on was killing him. The fact that he'd been able to keep all the pain he felt bottled up inside, surprised him.

Morning temperatures in Ireland never seemed to change. Fiercely cold with a hint of moisture hanging in the air. This morning, Clay had dressed warm enough and kept the chill at bay. As he walked toward Emer's office, he tried not to think about his useless-ness. Readjusting his backpack on his shoulder, he mused, "I may not be able to help physically, but I can pray. I guess there's no better time to do that than now."

His prayer, at first, bounced all over the place, from one person to another. He'd remember an incident that directed his petition for God's blessings on that person, and then something else would pop in his head about someone else. Because of the random directions his prayer went, he decided to focus on his sister and those looking for her. Finally, with his mind cleared and with purpose, he poured all his efforts on Eddie, Kayla, and Claire.

When Kayla disappeared, it upset Clay that he lacked the skills needed to find her. However, God had placed the right people in his life, and inadvertently in Kayla's, with the necessary skills to get the job done. It didn't matter if he was useful or not. God was in control, and even if he got a call with bad news, Gallagher was finished. Kayla had done that, along with Eddie and his amazing friends.

Determined to stay focused on what God had already done and not on what he couldn't do, Clay pushed the pity party he had been hosting out of his thoughts. Without realizing it, chastising himself and praying for his sister and friends had taken him to the outskirts of town and to the street that led to Emer's office.

He could see the clinic at the end of the road, which naturally made him think of the beautiful doctor. His exhaustion and useless-ness melted away, and his spirit brightened at the thought of her. His lumbering stride picked up with eagerness and purpose until a car pulled alongside him and made him stop. He bent down to see who it was, but he didn't recognize the man.

"Oi, Clay! It's good ta see ya."

"Hey, how are you?"

"Grand. Just grand. Sorry ta hear about yer sister. Any news yet?"

It never ceased to amaze Clay that everyone in town knew who he was and why he was in Ireland. He found it both funny and creepy. This morning he leaned on the humorous side of it all and took no offense to the man's question. "No, not yet."

"Sorry ta hear it. That's rotten, that is. Me and the missus are keepin' her in our prayers. Keep yer chin up, boy. She'll be home before ya know it."

"Thanks. I hope you're right."

"Are ya off ta see Emer?"

Clay put his head down, grinning. He knew he must be stirring up the gossip pot pretty good around town and found the man's probing funny. "Ah, yeah, as a matter of fact, I am."

"Not sure she's a full shillin', but if that's what ya like, she's perfect for ya. Have a nice day. I'll tell Ian and Mary I've seen ya."

Trying not to laugh, Clay bit the inside of his mouth and thanked him. Back in motion, he jogged the rest of the way to the clinic. Not slowing when he got to the door, he used his shoulder to open it, unintentionally barreling into the office.

A young mother with a small boy glanced up and politely smiled at him. Her son coughed, and she lost all interest in Clay and tended her child.

Realizing his blunder, he mumbled, "Sorry."

Lily's eyes lit up when she saw him and bellowed, "Oi, Clay! It's good ta see ya! Emer's with a patient and has another in front of ya. Take a seat and I'll let her know yer here."

"Hey, Lily. It's good to see you too." Not missing a beat, he slipped the backpack off his shoulder, set it on her desk and smiled down at her. "Actually, I need to speak with you."

"Oh, I like where this is goin'. Whaddaya need?"

"You know, I met this guy while I was in Dublin, and he really wants to meet you. He loves your wicked sense of humor."

Lily's cheery demeanor never changed when she asked, "Really? How does he know that I'm wildly spirited? You talkin' about me ta strange men?"

"Oh, no, I didn't have to." Clay pulled out a large yellow envelope and tossed it on the desk in front of her. "He got to see it first-hand. Come to think of it, so did the director of the Anti-Human Trafficking Unit. Kate, the director, had them hand delivered to her after someone in the mailroom opened it. You know, to make sure it didn't have explosives in it."

She picked up the envelope and pulled out the magazines. The puzzled expression on her face only lasted a few seconds. An outburst of giggles replaced it. "Oh my, I bet you went scarlet red!" Then the muscles on her face gave away her concerns. "Oh, my brother will be flippin' mad! They're 'is! I must've gotten the labels wrong. Oh, Clay, this time it was an honest mistake. I wasn't trying ta mess with ya."

"I was speechless when I pulled them out. I couldn't understand why Emer would send them to me," Clay said in a lighthearted voice.

"Oh, no, she sent ya a Bible," Lily replied in a matter-of-fact tone. Then, as if zapped by a lightning bolt, she shot straight up and out of her chair with her hand over her mouth. "Criminy! Oh, my brother's gonna be heated." She guffawed at the irony of her mistakes. "He's no need for God in 'is life, none at all. Ah, well, it serves 'im right, doesn't it? I hate those filthy magazines showin' up at my house anyway."

"Why does he have them mailed to you?"

"He's a wife, and she doesn't like them either. He pays me to send 'em to 'im in an envelope so she's none the wiser. She's not stupid—she knows! He's a slacker. The Bible will do 'im some good. Give 'em here. I'll have a nice fire with 'em tonight."

"Sure." Clay picked up the package and handed it to her.

Lily glanced down at the label and laughed. "Oh, this couldn't get any better now, could it?"

Clay wasn't sure what she meant and asked, "Why?"

"It's got Emer's name all over it, doesn't it?" She laughed. "Pranked her and didn't even know I did. It's brilliant!"

"Along with me and the director of the AHTU." Clay wasn't angry; he was just pointing out that the joke went further than Emer.

"Aye, it did. Truly sorry about that. No harm done…right?"

One brow lifted when Clay's mouth curled up on one side. "Yeah, no harm done. But I wasn't kidding about Connor. You'd like him."

"Are you trying to get outta yer date with me?" she teased. "No matter, I know you've eyes for our lass in there. Not ta worry, you're off the hook."

Clay's face turned bright red. "Look, I barely know her. So you and the rest of the town need to slow it down just a little."

The door to the examining room opened, and a man walked out with Emer following. The gentleman didn't slow down; he continued toward the door with only a nod to Lily and a "Howya" to Clay.

Making eye contact with the stranger, Clay said, "Hi," and waved as the man left the clinic.

Emer's face lit up when she saw Clay. "You made it!"

Facing her, he answered, "Yeah, just having a word with Lily about our package mishap. It was a simple mistake. No need to fire her."

"What?" Lily yelled. "Come on, Emer, ya have ta see how ridiculously funny it is?"

"Mrs. Kennedy, why don't you take Thomas in. I'll be just a minute." Emer gave the impression everything was business as usual.

The mother and son got up and went into the examining room with the door closing behind them. Emer glared at Lily. This was the conversation Clay had hoped to avoid. He stepped in front of the doctor, placed both hands on her shoulders, and tried to neutralize the situation before it got out of hand.

"Emer, I'll call Kate right now and let her know it was Lily, and that the two packages got switched. She'll laugh about it. Now, Thomas seemed really sick and could use your magnificent healing touch. Go on. Everything will be okay."

Her anger defused, and she agreed, "Yeah, okay."

"Great, um, can you meet me at Sean's for lunch?"

"At the pub?" Emer asked, slightly confused. "I thought you didn't like going into pubs?"

"Sean has the best fish and chips in town, and I need to eat. Besides, his place doesn't stink of beer."

"Yeah, okay." Then, peeking around Clay, she added, "And Lily, consider yourself lucky that he's a good sport about the mix-up."

"Thanks, Clay," Lily chimed in. Then to Emer, she assured, "I'll get Mr. O'Brien's prescription over to Dean right away."

"Great. See you ladies later. I have a few calls to make." Clay grabbed his backpack and left. He took out his phone and called Kate. He hoped she would find the mix up funny, and more importantly, that she wasn't getting razzed by her subordinates. He smiled when she answered on the second ring.

*   *   *   *   *

The usual lunchtime crowd packed into Sean's pub. Clay had been there for an hour. Once customers started pouring in, he was never alone. Strangers came over to talk to him, mostly about his sister. However, a few were compelled to involve themselves in the imaginary love affair between him and their local doctor. It was an intrusion he couldn't stop, no matter how hard he tried. Instead, he gave a cordial nod, thanking them for their concern.

When Emer arrived, it was as if she had the power to part water, and those still lingering close to him stepped aside and went on with their business as if neither of them existed. Clay couldn't help it and smiled when he stood to greet her.

"What's so funny?"

Clay leaned toward her and whispered, "This town is what."

She knew what he meant and added, "I'll never get used to them knowing all my business."

"Apparently, what they don't know, they make up. If they aren't telling me about my sister—like I'm not caught up on her news already—they're filling me in on our relationship."

"Our relationship? You and me?" His last comment mystified her.

"Oh, you haven't heard? They all think I could do much better than you," he said, grinning.

Emer's temper radiated from her eyes. They darted from one table to another, and Clay could see she didn't like anyone speculating about them. Then she launched out of her chair, saying, "Why, I—"

Clay reached over the small table and placed his hand on her forearm. "It's not worth it. They'll still talk, and really, I'm not worried about it. You shouldn't be either."

"I'm the town's only doctor. It's my reputation." She hesitated for a moment and then sat back down. Emer eyed Clay for a second and concluded, "You're enjoying this way too much."

Clay couldn't help it and laughed. "Just a little."

Sean set down two plates of food. They both looked up at the same time and said, "Thank you."

"Not a problem. I'll have yer drink right out to ya, Emer. Give me a sec."

Emer and Clay sat in silence until Sean returned with her drink. "Thanks."

Once Sean left, Clay asked, "What does it mean that you're not a full shillin'?"

She looked up from her food and glared at him.

He put both hands up, saying, "Hey, I was told that—I didn't say it."

"I hate this town!" she said in a huff.

"I'm still waiting."

She crossed her arms and stared at him for a few seconds. Right before she answered, one side of her mouth curled, giving a lopsided grin. "Something like, half crazy."

"Huh, only half?"

Emer picked up a french fry and threw it at him, hitting him on the nose.

"Half crazy and juvenile. Nice!" He bent over and picked up the french fry from the floor. When he sat upright, Emer had crammed three fries in her mouth while grinning at him. Clay enjoyed seeing the doctor's silly side, though it surprised him.

"Well, let them talk," she said once she swallowed her food.

"Thanks for buying a Bible for me. That was nice of you."

"You seemed sad, so I thought it would help. A lot of good it did you."

"It's the thought that counts. I'm heading over to the church after lunch to have a talk with the priest."

"What? You're going to talk to the vicar? Aren't you a Baptist?"

"Well, yeah, but at this point, I'll go into any church to pray. And besides, what's wrong with the vicar?"

"As you Americans like to say, he has one too many screws loose."

"Is this the Catholic schoolgirl coming out of you, or genuine concern for my faith?"

"Neither. I just wanted you to know he's not your usual man of God." Then very casually, she said, "Look, I'm off this weekend. We'll go to Cork and get a room. There's a missionary there that you should meet."

A woman at the table next to them leaned over to her friend and whispered something, causing them both to smile at Clay. He in turn couldn't help but poke fun at Emer for adding more fuel to the town's gossip and said, "Get a room? Together? I'm not that easy." The two women giggled and Emer's cheeks flushed beet red.

Embarrassed, Emer leaned in closer to Clay, making sure he would be the only one to hear her. "Criminy! I meant we could stay one night together in Cork..."

Clay laughed outright at her blunder. "Seriously, what's with you and your wanting to sleep with me?"

This time, several tables around them erupted in laughter. Emer shot up from her chair, mortified, and ran outside. Clay had to move fast to catch up to her. Once he did, he grabbed her by the arm and pulled her around to face him. "I'm sorry! Really, I am." He chuckled. "I'm just having some fun at your expense. I'll stop. I promise."

She glared at him for a few seconds before she spoke. "Clay, they already think I'm a fool!"

"No, they don't. Well, not all of them anyway." He playfully nudged her with his shoulder.

His boyish charm always seemed to soften her spirit, and staying angry at him was impossible. "Ugh! I just couldn't seem to get my foot out of my mouth, could I?"

Clay grinned. Then he slipped his hand into hers and continued to hold it while they walked.

"You do understand," Emer continued, "you're only adding to the gossip more by holding my hand?"

"Well, if we're going to get a room together this weekend, don't you think we should at least hold hands first?" Emer pivoted on one foot and slugged him hard in his shoulder with her free hand. "Ouch!

Okay, okay, enough! So tell me about this missionary. How is it you know about an American missionary living in Cork?"

Now fully enjoying herself, she answered, "I found out about him when I bought the Bible for you. Bethany told me about him. She owns the bookstore here in town. She met him two weeks ago and said he seemed like a real man of God. Her words, not mine."

"Do you think she'll give me his name and number?"

"No—I have it already. I called him and told him about you and your sister." Clay stopped and pulled Emer around so she was facing him. Surprised by his sudden reaction, she said, "I'm sorry! I hope that was okay? He offered to pray for you and Kayla. I didn't think it would be a problem."

"No…it's okay. It's just one of the nicest things you could have done for me, but I'm a little confused. You don't believe in God, yet you're catering to my faith. I was sure you thought I was an idiot for believing."

"Clay, I've never met anyone like you before. If there are Irish Christians, which I'm sure there are, I've not met them, not a true Bible-reading one anyway. Don't get me wrong, I'm sure there are quite a few God-fearing Christians in Ireland. I just don't have any within my circle of friends."

"You have a circle of friends? That could be scary."

"Ha-ha. Okay, so I haven't met anyone like you. I don't know what it is—maybe it's that you're living your faith and not telling everyone about it. You're not condescending or preachy. It's just who you are. Because of that, it's easy for me to want to help you."

Still holding Emer's hand, Clay had them walking again. "Thanks. Even for the Bible I didn't get. I can't believe you took the time to go buy one for me. Mrs. Dunne—she's the wife to the captain that owned the trawler—gave me a Bible while I was in Killybegs. Why, I don't know. I hadn't even met her at the time. She gave a Bible to Billy to pass on to me."

"She did? Well, my efforts were for naught."

Clay slipped his free hand into his jeans' pocket and chuckled. "Actually, I gave it to this guy, Anthony. He's a human trafficker. I thought he needed it more than I did."

His comment left Emer dumbfounded, and Clay knew it. Knowing her personality, he could only imagine the intellectual tongue lashing she would have given the man, or anyone who made a living selling humans. Her giving Anthony a Bible wouldn't have been an option.

Her voice was soft when she said, "I'm sorry, Clay, that must have been hard."

"What? Giving him a Bible?" He chuckled. "That was the easy part. Forgiving him is a whole different story."

Emer scowled and faced him. "You didn't...did you? How could you forgive such a vile piece of rubbish?"

"I couldn't, but...I know you're the last person who wants to hear a quote from the Bible, but if you'll indulge me just this once. In Colossians 3:13, it says, 'Bear with each other and forgive one another if any of you has a grievance against someone. Forgive as the Lord forgave you.' I'm not perfect by any means, and at the moment, I have enough rage pinned up inside me to last several lifetimes."

Another thought came to mind and he started walking again, heading toward the clinic. "It's weird—it's like the Holy Spirit keeps nudging me to utter those three simple words, 'I forgive you,' but I can't. I mean, I couldn't. I just gave him the Bible and told him a good place to start reading and walked away. Anthony was crying because his nieces and nephew are missing, and Allister had his sister and brother-in-law brutally murdered. Kate thinks Allister has the kids, hoping to keep Anthony quiet."

Emer said nothing. Her eyes watered, and she quickly wiped them. She stared at the road for a few seconds before she looked at Clay. Then she volunteered, "I'll close the clinic for the day. I don't want to leave you alone. You shouldn't be alone. I'll tell Lily to—"

"Listen, Emer," Clay interrupted, facing her. "I would love to go to Cork with you this weekend, but you should know, Patrick and his team are going to an island Anthony told them about. He said that's where Allister might be, and hopefully, my sister and the other girls are there too."

"On an island? Where?"

"Um, he said, Dingle Bay, I think."

"The military used the islands during the war as lookout posts. Some of them have occupants, and others don't. Quite a few islands have well-fortified forts or bunkers that are of no use to anyone. Not even for tourism. I suppose they would be a perfect place to hide people or drugs."

Having made it to the clinic, Clay gave Emer's hand a slight squeeze and said, "That's what Patrick and Kate told me. Hopefully, this will all be over with tonight."

Emer placed one hand in the middle of his chest, leaned in and kissed his cheek. Without a word, she stepped inside the office and was greeted, not only by Lily, but by a man she didn't know. Clay accidentally bumped into Emer, unaware she had stopped. He grabbed her around the waist so not to topple her over.

"Howya, Clay and Emer. This is Noah Smith. He said you called 'im, and he had ta come."

The man held out his hand to Emer first then to Clay. "Sorry for coming unannounced, but after our conversation, Doctor, I felt I needed to be here. Clay, I'm very sorry to hear about your sister. I hope you don't mind my coming?"

Clay let go of his hand and freed him from his worry. "Uh, it's a free country, or so I'm told."

"He's the missionary I told you about."

"Oh, wow! You just saved us a trip. We were planning to head down to Cork this weekend to find you."

There were four patients in the waiting room. Clay knew Emer needed to get back to work, but before she did, he asked, "Maybe you can come by Ian's and Mary's tonight after work?"

"Yeah, sure. Mr. Smith, it was nice to meet you."

Noah nodded at the doctor, picked up his bag, and followed Clay outside. Before Clay had time to close the door, he heard Emer directing one of her patients into the examining room. Her shift from consoling him to performing her job amused him and made him smile.

"Listen, I have to stop by the pub and pay a bill. Emer stormed out of the place so fast we didn't have time to eat or pay the check."

"If you don't mind, I would love to grab a bite to eat myself."

"Glad you said that because I'm hungry, and Sean's pub has the best fish and chips in town."

$$* \quad * \quad * \quad * \quad *$$

Seeing Clay again thrilled Ian and Mary, and both were happy to meet Noah. Mary caught the men up on all the scandals going on around town, even the one about Emer and Clay going to Cork for a romantic weekend getaway. Noah laughed at Clay when he tried to correct her. She carried on talking as if she hadn't heard a word he said. He let it go and verbally stated to Noah, "I'm glad Emer isn't here to listen to all the sordid details of our nonexistent love affair."

There were a few chores around the farm that Noah and Clay volunteered to help Ian with before they called it a day. Once they finished, the men went inside to clean up for dinner. It was well past six when Emer arrived.

Mary poked at her husband as if to prove that the rumors about Emer and Clay were true. Ian whispered to her, "Auch, no, Mary, leave 'em be," then he followed her into the kitchen to help with dinner.

Oddly enough, Emer felt comfortable around Mary and Ian. She was able to relax and didn't feel like she was under a microscope, being judged the way she was by so many people in town. She appreciated the kindness the couple always showed her.

All three guests insisted on cleaning up after the meal. Mary fought against it but, in the end, lost the battle. Emer enjoyed the time she spent cleaning the kitchen. She mostly listened as the men and Mary discussed various topics while they did the dishes.

Once everything had been washed and put away, Clay and Noah went to find Ian, leaving the two women alone. Emer stood in the middle of the kitchen, looked around, and announced, "Well, that's it. Looks like we got it all."

"Oh, aye, ya did," Mary agreed while putting a bowl away.

"It was very nice of you to invite me to dinner. Thank you. The food was marvelous."

"Ah, it's kind of ya ta say. I love ta cook and haven't cooked like this in a long while. It's mostly me and Ian now that our boys are grown."

Emer had forgotten that Ian and Mary had two grown sons. She saw the joy that Clay ignited in the couple because of his being there. Both sons lived in Dublin with their families and neither came home to visit their parents much anymore. Mary had told her once that her boys were happy in the city and had no plans of moving back to the country. Speaking about them saddened her. Now, having the opportunity to see Mary interact with Clay, Emer could tell how much she missed her sons. Clay had filled a void in Mary's life, much like he had done in hers.

She shook the thought of Clay from her head, folded a towel and lay it on the counter. "How are your boys? Have you heard from them?"

Mary's voice lost its cheerfulness when she answered, "Ah, no, lass. Ian called them the other day, but they must have been out."

"I'm sorry to hear that. Well, at least you have Ian. It's just me at home."

"I would think Clay would keep ya company a wee bit."

The doctor's eyes widened, and she said what she had wanted to say at the pub. "I'm sorry, but Clay and I are just friends. The rumors that are going around town are just that, rumors. Clay has his mind on his sister, not romance. You understand that, don't you?"

"Auch, aye, I know it's not true. Just havin' a wee bit o' fun with the two o' ya. But if ya gave it much thought, you'd know yer a perfect match for one another."

Emer smiled at her sweetly and left it at that. She heard a cell phone ring and then Clay's voice. She and Mary hurried to the sitting room to see if the call was news about Kayla. When they appeared, Noah motioned for them to come in. Both women quietly found a seat and sat down.

"Billy? Is everything okay? I didn't think—"

Clay had been pacing when he caught sight of Emer. Her presence had a calming effect over him, and he felt less agitated. The pacing stopped, and he stood straight. His voice was strong and clear when he said, "Okay, thanks. I'll be up, no matter the hour, so please call me."

He briefly covered his mouth with his hand before he spoke. "That was Billy. They're about to check out another island, and I shouldn't expect a call until later tonight, possibly early morning. There are two more islands to investigate. But getting to them is going to take some time. That is, unless they get lucky and find the girls on the next one."

Noah stood up and announced, "This would be a good time to pray. Ian...Mary, do you mind?"

"Not at all. Please, go ahead."

As weird as it was for Clay to see Emer join the circle, it was weirder for her to be a part of it. Holding hands with Clay and Mary, she bowed her head when Clay did. He gave her hand a light squeeze, but then, as if he knew she might bolt and run, he kept a firm grip on it. Noah started the prayer, with Clay finishing it.

When the prayer ended, Mary gave Clay a hug and left the room crying. Ian followed to comfort her. Noah shook Clay's free hand and said, "It's hard to imagine, especially in a situation like this one, that anything good is going to come out of it. We need to remember that the Bible says, 'And we know that in all things God works for the good of those who love him, who have been called according to his purpose.'[4] If everything you told me is true, then I can't help but think God wanted this very wicked organization to come down and he's using your sister's abduction to do it."

This surprised Emer. "Why would God do such a horrible thing to Kayla...to any of those girls?"

Clay motioned for her to take a seat on the sofa, and he sat next to her.

Noah sat down across from them and explained, "The hardest part for all of us to accept is that we are part of God's plan, He isn't a part of ours. Isaiah 53:4–5 says, 'Surely he took up our pain and bore our suffering, yet we considered him punished by God, stricken by him and afflicted. But he was pierced for our transgressions, he

---

[4] Romans 8:28 (NIV).

was crushed for our iniquities; the punishment that brought us peace was on him and by his wounds we are healed.' The prophet Isaiah foretold this hundreds of years prior to Christ's crucifixion. God had preordained Christ's suffering. What we thought was evil transgressions against God, turned out to be God's mercy and grace given to the world through his son, Jesus Christ."

Noah gave Emer a few seconds to think about what he said before adding, "We all need to remember, it's during our time of weakness that teaches us to depend on God. Paul even explains it in 2 Corinthians 12, where he reveals he 'was given a thorn in my flesh' and said, 'Three times I pleaded with the Lord to take it away from me.' But instead of taking it away, God told him, "My grace is sufficient for you, for my power is made perfect in weakness." There are several passages in the Bible that urge us to continue to ask God for help, but we are never to expect God to answer our requests the way we think He should."

"So why pray if all He's going to do is punish us by not answering our prayers?" Emer asked.

"That's a reasonable question. What we see as a punishment, God uses for His glory," Noah explained. "God didn't do this to Kayla. Terrible men did. Just as in Jesus's crucifixion, evil men nailed him to the cross, not God. Is Kayla, like Jesus's crucifixion, part of God's plan? I believe the answer is yes. God is sovereign, no matter the outcome. If God predetermined Jesus's crucifixion, then it's safe to say that God has had an ultimate plan, one He set in stone from the very beginning of time."

Clay nodded in agreement. "Emer, do you remember the story of Joseph? His brothers sold him into slavery because their father favored him over them."

"Yes, I do."

"Okay, so in Genesis 50:20, Joseph tells his brothers, 'You intended to harm me, but God intended it for good to accomplish what is now being done, the saving of many lives.' The harm Brian Gallagher intended for Kayla is now being used for good and will save a lot of lives. In Ephesians 1:11 it says, 'In him we were also chosen, having been predestined according *to the plan* of him who works out everything in conformity with the purpose of his will.' All that means is, God has a plan we aren't aware of and it's going to play out according to His will and not ours. Because of God's sovereignty, it isn't how great our faith is, but how great God is despite our lack of faith. He's in control all the time."

"The hardest part for us as Christians is giving up control," Noah added. "We get angry when things don't go the way *we* want. If you think of Job and the extraordinary suffering he experienced, he still fell to the ground and worshiped God, saying, 'Naked I came from my mother's womb and naked I will leave this life. The LORD gives and the LORD takes away. Blessed be the name of the LORD.'"[5]

"Look, I don't want you to think I'm special or that even Kayla is, but Brian Gallagher has been doing this a very long time. I just can't help but think my coming here, looking for my sister kick started his destruction. I didn't tell you this, but there was a young girl found dead on the trawler."

"What?"

"Yeah, they found her body tangled up in the fishing net. Somewhere, someone's missing her. They may or may not be looking for her. It's the same for the other girls: no one came for them, not because they didn't want to, but maybe they didn't have the means to or even knew where to start. I missed Kayla, and I had the means to look for her. I'm beginning to believe what Noah said is true. My sister is the means that God is using to destroy Gallagher and his organization."

The turmoil flaring inside Emer over what they said turned her insides out. Some of what Clay and Noah said made sense, but if God was all knowing and all powerful, why would He use girls to fight His battles?

She glanced up with moistened eyes and saw Clay staring at her. Wiping them, she said, "With all of my intellect, I never could understand that part about God. It's what put a wall between us."

Clay wrapped his arm around her while offering, "I understand. It's our human nature, with its free will, poor choices, and the battle between right and wrong that constantly tugs at us from within."

---

5   Job 1:21 (CSB).

Noah agreed, "God gave us the right to choose and because of our human nature, we choose poorly sometimes. He's having to clean up our messes, and unfortunately, we have to help Him do it."

"I know I don't need to state the obvious, but we…meaning all people, die every day. We get sick, we hurt. We even have a lot of moments when we're happy, but as Christians, we always have the comfort of knowing Christ is with us, carrying us sometimes, but always loving us," Clay added. "It wasn't until I came to Ireland, looking for Kayla, that I was reminded of that."

"That's why I came here after you called, Emer," Noah explained. "I couldn't imagine going through something this traumatic and not having Jesus in my life. God needed me to be here with Clay and you during this time."

Emer lifted her head from Clay's shoulder and stared at Noah. Clay slipped his arm from around her and took her hand in his. "If it's understanding you want, then it's understanding you'll get. You just have to let Christ in. I thought I needed the Bible, but I've always had God's words with me, I just wasn't listening."

"The Bible you gave away to the human trafficker?"

"Yeah. When I gave Anthony the Bible, I realized then that I didn't need it. Don't get me wrong, I need the Bible for my own personal time with God, but His words are imbedded right here." Clay pointed at his chest. "I know God's in control and I'm going to let Him keep control. If anything happens to Kayla, I'll be crushed, but I know I'll be okay because of my Lord and Savior. He's given me a lot of wonderful people to help me get through this. You being one of them."

Emer offered a weak smiled. She could feel herself being drawn to something or someone more powerful than her own understanding. It scared her, and she stood up abruptly and wiped her eyes. She reached out her hand to Noah, saying, "Thank you for coming. I need to go home. I had a day full of patients today and I'm exhausted." Then, facing Clay, she offered, "I'll have my phone by my bed. Please call me the minute you get word."

"I'll take you," Clay offered. "You shouldn't be driving home like this."

She gave Clay a hug and held on to him longer than she intended. "I'll be fine. It's not far, and I could use the time to think."

"I'll walk you out."

She placed her hand in the middle of Clay's chest and said, "No. I'll manage. I'll talk to you soon."

Ian and Mary came downstairs as Emer opened the front door. Looking up at them, she said, "Thank you for the wonderful dinner." Before either could say a word, Emer went outside and closed the door.

Clay watched as Noah ran back into the small sitting room to get something, and then just as fast saw him run out the front door. This left Clay to explain to his hosts, "She said she's exhausted and wanted to go home."

"Oh, aye," Ian agreed.

"She'd tears in her eyes. She's broke up with all this dreadful mess."

Realizing Mary was correct, he reached for the door when it suddenly opened. Noah stepped back inside, saying, "I almost forgot to give Emer the Bible I brought for her. I have two more if anyone needs one."

"We've one upstairs that I'll go fetch," Ian said. "Go on Mary, get off yer feet for a bit."

She did as her husband suggested. The two young men followed her into the sitting room where Noah grabbed his bag and took out two Bibles.

"Here, this is for you."

"Thanks, Noah, for thinking to bring them," Clay said.

"It's what I do." He chuckled.

Ian was back with his Bible in hand and took the empty seat next to his wife. Clay got comfortable in his chair and opened his. Noah said, "If you'll turn to 2 Corinthians chapter 1, verses 3 and 4, I'll begin, 'Praise be to the God and Father of our Lord Jesus Christ…'"

CHAPTER 10

The phone call came in at three fifty-six the next morning. Only Clay and Noah were up. The noise from the phone broke the long silence that had been looming over the two men for almost an hour. Clay's hand shook when he pulled the phone from his pocket. He put the speaker on so Noah could listen. It was Kate.

"Clay, I'm sorry it's taken so long for me to call."

"It's okay, you're busy. Did Patrick find them?"

Kate's silence was enough to let Clay know something was wrong. When she answered, he could hear the sorrow in her voice. "Yes and no. I've some bad news: Eddie's dead."

Clay's muscles slacked and the weight of his body sent him crashing to the floor. Noah grabbed him by the arm to steady him. Then kneeling next to him, he made sure Clay stayed in an upright position.

In a rushed voice, Kate added, "They didn't find Kayla. She's still missing, so are Claire and two other girls."

Hunched over, Clay didn't move. He considered Eddie a good friend and couldn't believe he was dead. He tried to focus on Kate's last words, but with the lack of sleep and hearing the news about Eddie, it took him a few seconds to grasp.

What Kate said about his sister and the other women wasn't good news. However, there was room for hope. When he sucked in a deep breath, his back straightened. He held it in for a few seconds before he let it go and repeated the intake of air until the light-headedness subsided. He placed his hand over Noah's and whispered, "Thanks."

Noah eyed Clay for a moment before he released his arm and stood.

Clay was afraid to ask Kate his next question but forged ahead and did so. "What happened to the other girls?"

"Patrick found their bodies next to Eddie's."

"Ah, geez! How did they die, Kate?"

Her hesitation to answer right away spoke volumes. Any kind of death involving human trafficking would be ugly, Clay got that, but he wanted to know.

"A gunshot to the head. I'm sorry I don't have better news for you. Patrick and his team captured two of Allister's men, and they're talking. The team is heading to the next location they think Allister is hiding. I'm flying there now. In another hour or so we should have more news. Sit tight—there's still hope."

Kate didn't give Clay time to ask any more questions. She ended the call with, "I'll talk to you soon," and disconnected before he could respond. Tossing his phone near the fireplace, he sat down on the floor with his knees pulled up to his chest and covered his face with both hands. He sat in that position for quite some time.

Noah picked up the phone and put it on the table before taking a seat in the chair closest to the fire. He said nothing, giving Clay time to comprehend the news he had just received. When Clay finally dropped his hands from his face, he whispered, "This can't be happening. I can't believe he's dead. Ah, geez!" Clay pushed himself up from the floor and paced the small room for a few seconds before adding, "I'm not sure you're aware of this, but Eddie had been looking for his sister for the last fifteen years."

"No...I didn't know that."

"Well, he had. Eddie spent the last fifteen years helping other families find their missing loved ones, always hoping he would find his sister too. Instead, he dies helping me find mine. I don't understand how he could do it, knowing what the cost could be for him."

Noah got up and stood next to Clay, stopping only inches from him. "Don't go there. He was doing what he needed to do. Eddie knew the risks that were involved and more importantly, he understood the pain you were going through. He couldn't save his sister, but he must have felt he could save yours. In some strange way, maybe his death will help them find Kayla."

A mixture of intense anger and grief overcame Clay. "How? How could his dying help save my sister?"

Clay covered his mouth and went quiet as if thinking how best to answer his own question. Then, running his fingers through his hair, he thought about the last time he saw his friend and the conversation they'd had. He admired Eddie and the passion he had for finding abducted girls, who'd unwillingly got sucked into the terrifying world of human trafficking.

He understood he could never save his own sister, but there was nothing to stop Eddie from finding others that needed saving. Clay recalled what Eddie told him about his job—that it was his wife, and the young women he brought home to their families were his children. His only purpose in life was to fight against human trafficking, a fight that ultimately took his life. Clay hoped more than anything that Patrick and Billy would find his sister and the other women alive, so Eddie's death wouldn't be in vain.

Noah stared at Clay for a second before he answered his question. It was obvious that Eddie's death had been a huge blow. Noah spoke with compassion when he quoted John 15:12–13, "'Greater love has no one than this, to lay down one's life for one's friend.' Eddie was a warrior and for the last fifteen years he's been fighting in an endless war. I think he knew that. I'm sure Patrick and the rest of the team understand that too. Satan is winning a lot of the battles; Eddie's death is proof of that. It's something I'm sure all the warriors fighting in the same battle are fully aware of. They also know that God will ultimately win the war, and that's why they stay to fight… even to their deaths."

"If I hadn't called him…he would still be alive."

Placing his hand on Clay's shoulder, Noah shook his head. "That's not true. God knew the time, the place, and the circumstances concerning Eddie's life and his death. It's 'God's will be done,' not 'our will.' We both may think it's not fair, but as men of faith, we have to trust Him in all things. We don't get to pick and choose."

Noah was right, but the hurt and guilt Clay felt because of Eddie's death was very real to him. "I need to clear my head. I'll be back shortly. Why don't you try to get some sleep?"

"Do you want company?"

"No. I need to be alone, but I'm glad you're here," Clay said, sincerely.

*   *   *   *   *

It was cold when Clay stepped outside, but he didn't notice. The full moon above filled the night sky with it's an illuminating light and the ground with its moving shadows. He stumbled a few times as he headed up Ian's dirt driveway. When he reached the main road, he kept walking toward town.

From the moment Clay had met Eddie, he had considered him a friend, even though he didn't know him well. The memory of Eddie's accent—a mixture of both Irish and American, made him smile. Ireland had done her part in transforming him into one of her own.

Any hopes of finding Eddie's sister had vanished because no one would be looking for her anymore. The police had given up a long time ago. Clay would make it his mission never to let Eddie's or his sister's memory die. He wasn't sure how he was going to do that, but he would find a way.

Now, more than anything, he wanted to help men like Eddie fight against human trafficking. He didn't have the skills or even the know-how to help find girls, but he could financially back those that did. He could even drum up donations for the cause.

Not sure how to organize fundraisers, he would have to hire someone who knew the ins and outs of running a charity. Roman Jones's family had built World Charities and Charities USA from the ground up. Once Clay explained all that he had witnessed these men and women doing, he knew Roman would help.

Before Clay knew it, he found himself standing in front of the clinic's steps. He thought it odd that he always seemed to find his way to Emer. For the first time, he admitted to himself that he enjoyed her company and liked thinking about her.

The sound of his phone ringing snapped him out of his thoughts. He took the phone from his pocket and answered, "Hey, Emer."

"Is everything okay? Noah gave me a ring and said that Kate called you…with bad news. He asked me to call. What happened?"

Clay expelled his breath and sat down on the steps before he answered. "They didn't find Kayla. She wasn't where they'd hoped to find her. They have one more place to look."

"Oh, I'm so sorry."

"Yeah, me too." Clay choked up and had to take a second before he continued. "Yeah, sorry—it's a lot to take in right now."

"Where are you?"

"Funny thing about that, my paths lately always seem to lead me to you, either with a phone call or in person."

"Clay, where are you?"

"Sitting on the steps of the clinic."

"Come around to the back of the building and take the stairs up to the flat. I'll have a cup of coffee waiting for you. I'll even make you breakfast. Wait! You drink coffee, don't you?"

Clay stood and walked toward the back of the building. "Yeah, I do. As long as you have cream and sugar."

"That's the only way I drink it. The door's unlocked."

*   *   *   *   *

Angry over the loss of his friend, Billy's determination to find Kayla and Claire was far greater than it had been. He hoped that if he and the rest of the team found the women, they would find Allister. Pledging an oath to himself, he would never allow Allister a day of rest. Billy promised he would hunt the man down until his last breath. He hoped Patrick and the others were of the same mind.

Every muscle in Billy's body ached, and he was beyond exhausted. If it wasn't for the adrenaline kicking in, he would be flat on his face. Sleep would come, but not until he had Allister in his clutches. With the new lead, he prayed for that to happen sooner rather than later.

When the small plane landed, Billy watched Kate push passed the attendant who barely had time to get the door opened and the stairs down before she got off. She ran over to where he and Patrick were waiting and, without stopping, jumped into the lead vehicle. Patrick looked at him and shrugged and did the same. No orders were necessary, Connor sped off in the direction he knew he needed to go with Niall, Harry, and Gerard following his lead in the car behind them.

"Okay, we've a positive ID on one woman, June Donnelly, twenty-one years old, from Dublin. She's the one Claire told us about when she called from the trawler. Thomas O'Leary was her boyfriend, and he owed money to Gallagher. He's the one Killian found hanged with two broken legs. I have someone notifying her family as we speak. We're still working on the other girls. We don't know if their Irish, but their pictures are being sent out all over Ireland. Killian will let me know the minute he hears something. He said he's also combing through the list of runaways and that Interpol is doing its part."

"Good. But just so we're clear, Allister is ours, Kate. Anyone else we find you can have, but he's ours." Patrick's voice didn't allow any discussion in the matter. She didn't argue with him. Her only concern now was to find Kayla and Claire. Anything else would have to wait.

"I have a friend at the local garda in Kinsale. She's not positive, but she thinks Allister is tucked away on a boat at the harbor. She's working on which one, but she really doesn't have much to go on. Did Allister's men say anything? A name of a boat? Or an exact place?"

"Only that he was hold up at the Kinsale Yacht Club, at the marina."

Kate got on the phone and passed on the information to someone on the other end. There was a brief silence before Kate said, "Okay, we'll be there in a few minutes."

She dropped her phone in her coat pocket and sat back in her seat. Patrick looked over his shoulder at Kate and asked, "Are you in charge or do we have to go through someone else?"

"The commissioner has given me full authority. As soon as we have Allister in our sights, I'll give him a call. There won't be time for anyone to tip Allister or his men off that we're coming."

Clearly pleased with the answer, Patrick faced forward as Connor sped toward Kinsale. The roads were wet from rain, and narrow at times, but it didn't slow Connor down. He raced through the downtown area, only slowing for intersections and sharp corners. Because of the hour, traffic was light. Connor pulled the Land Rover into a parking space near the marina. When the team exited the vehicles, a woman in her mid- to late forties was waiting for them.

Ellen Boyle was the lead inspector for Kinsale's police and a close friend of Kate's. She welcomed each team member with a handshake and a warm smile. "Right, we've narrowed it down to twelve possibilities, but knowing Gallagher and his lifestyle, Allister is probably on Brian Gallagher's rather large yacht."

Surprised by that, Kate asked, "Gallagher has a yacht here?"

"Yeah, he does. It arrived three days ago. I'm guessing he planned to use it to transport the girls out."

"Actually, that's what Allister is hoping we'll think," Billy chimed in. "My thought is something a lot less noticeable and not as obvious."

"Billy has a point," Kate agreed. "Possibly something close to it, not as fancy, but powerful and in a place that will give him full view of the yacht just in case we raid it."

"Well, that leaves us with four boats, still in the yacht classification, and they're definitely large enough to house him, the women, and a few of his men." Ellen lay the map on the hood of her car and pointed. "There are two cruisers docked at the end of the marina that would give Allister an unobstructed view of Gallagher's yacht, and also easy access to the harbor and out to sea. I suggest we hit all four boats and Gallagher's yacht at the same time."

"We don't have enough people to do that," Kate said, pointing out the obvious.

"I've got that covered. There's equipment in our van that will block all cell phone signals. Here, take these." Ellen handed radios to everyone and then explained, "I'll call my team that's on standby. None of them know who it is we're tracking. They'll get that information when they arrive. No one will have time to let Allister know we're coming."

"Okay, gents, let's gear up!" Patrick ordered. He and his men grabbed their vests and weapons out of the back of the vehicles, and without a word, they headed toward the marina.

Kinsale was an enchanting town nestled into its harbor's hillside. As picturesque as the harbor itself was, its genuine beauty lay within the town. The colorful buildings only enhanced its unique character as did the cobblestones roads, laid hundreds of years before.

Pubs, taverns, and restaurants lined the streets and served some of the best food Ireland had to offer. People from all over the country traveled here, mainly by boat, to enjoy its southern coast and food. But now, even with all its splendor, it would come under attack for unknowingly harboring human traffickers.

The yacht club had one entrance to the boats through a locked gate. Ellen had already gotten the electronic key from the club's manager. He was none the wiser as to why the police needed it. He did his best to stay out of the authorities' business when they checked boats that came into the harbor. Whenever the police showed up, it normally meant a routine custom's check.

Before Ellen opened the gate, she advised Kate, "If you're going for the two at the end, my team and I will take the other three. They've just arrived. Remember, there are civilians living on these boats. Please don't accidentally kill someone. That's a mess neither of us want to deal with."

"Right, gentlemen, you heard the inspector. Keep the gunfire to a minimum."

Ellen pushed open the gate and held it for everyone to go through. Her team didn't slow down and followed her in. Ellen spouted out orders to the new arrivals with a quick explanation of who it was they were going after and the boats they would search.

Kate, along with Patrick and the rest of his team, sneaked down to the last dock. The two cruisers they would board were on opposite sides from one another. Billy, Patrick, Connor, and Kate took the large craft on the right while the other three, Niall, Harry, and Gerard, took the boat on the left.

Billy crept onto the boat first, when gunfire rang out on the other side of the marina. Kate waved her arms frantically for the men to continue with their search of the two boats.

With more urgency now, Billy and Patrick moved fast, cutting through the cockpit and entering the upper salon. The stairs that led to the lower staterooms were behind the helm. Billy gave Patrick the lead and followed him down. They were narrow, which made it hard to get more than one man down at a time.

The first door Patrick opened was a bathroom. The second door he tried was locked. He pointed at the third door and Billy nodded that he was ready. Patrick leaned on the wall behind him and with everything he had kicked the door open, shattering the trim.

With perfect timing Billy went for the other stateroom door and threw his body into it, not checking if it was locked. Billy found himself face-to-face with Allister. Gunfire came from the room next door, followed by screaming. The sudden intrusion startled Allister, but it didn't slow him down. He jumped out of bed and reached for his gun. Billy opened fire on him before he had a firm grip on his weapon. Allister's shoulder exploded, and he fell back onto the bed. Kate grabbed Billy's arm to stop him from firing another shot.

"You got him! Don't kill him." Kate slid past Billy and picked up Allister's gun. She moved with haste to the other side of the bed and knelt down next to a young woman on the floor, crying.

"Shh. It's okay. You're safe now." Kate gently pushed a strand of hair from the teenager's beaten face and pulled the sheet off the bed. "It's okay—it's over. Here, wrap this around you. What's your name?"

"Sophie Cleary," she cried, covering herself.

In a soft reassuring voice, she said, "Sophie, I'm Kate. I'm the director of the AHTU in Dublin. I want you to go upstairs to the upper salon and have a seat. I'll have medical come in and check on you, and then you and I will have a little chat, okay?"

Sophie's crying made it hard for her to speak, so instead, she nodded. Kate helped her to her feet. When Sophie saw Allister on the bed glaring at her, she cried more.

Slugging Allister hard in the face gave Billy a great deal of pleasure, but having his hand around the man's neck, squeezing the life out of him was almost intoxicating.

Allister struggled against the death grip that had him pinned down. He grabbed Billy by the wrist with his good hand and tried to free himself. This only added more pressure to his throat.

"Keep it up, you piece of garbage, and I'll break your neck!" Billy growled.

"We still need him," Kate said.

Allister laughed while holding onto Billy's wrist. "You've got nothing on me. The girl will never talk!"

Kate held Allister's gaze and grinned. "You're an idiot. You're not playing with the local garda—I have Craig and Anthony. You shouldn't have killed Anthony's family, and Craig…well, he's just plain stupid and gave you up without a care in the world. Can you feel the task force's chokehold on you?"

Billy squeezed Allister's neck a little harder, emphasizing her words. Doing so made it more difficult for him to breathe, but that didn't stop his anger from boiling over. He tried to lunge forward, but Billy leaned into him, and with his free hand, punched him hard in the face. Allister fell back onto the bed, unconscious. The sound of Patrick's voice broke through Billy's rage, and he turned to face his friend.

"Claire and Kayla aren't here. Ellen radioed and said they found one young woman half dead. An overly combative officer killed two men on Gallagher's yacht."

"I want that officer in custody. I want to make sure he's not helping Allister clean up his mess," Kate ordered.

"Got it. Connor took the other two blokes upstairs."

"Great. I'll let Ellen comb through the evidence here. I want to know where Claire and Kayla are. Keep all of Allister's men separated. I don't want them to have a chance to talk to one another."

With Kate's last orders, Patrick ran up the stairs. Billy grabbed Allister by the hair and pulled him up to a sitting position. Then, crouching down just enough, he threw Allister over his shoulder, announcing, "I'll be happy to take this trash out for you."

Kate stepped aside to let him pass. Billy took a step and then stopped when a thought came to him. He turned around a little too fast, smashing Allister's head into the door when he did.

"I can't stress it enough; we need him alive."

Grinning, Billy said, "A little headache never killed anyone. Ladies first."

Kate laughed. "I'm not joking. I need him coherent when I talk to him."

She climbed the stairs ahead of Billy and heard a thud and then a thump, with Billy saying, "Oops, sorry about that, buddy," and then there was another bump.

"And without causing him any brain damage," she begged.

Billy only grinned.

Medical arrived and had given Sophie a warmer blanket. "We need to take her to the hospital," a medic announced.

"Connor, go with the girls. Take Niall, Harry, and Gerard with you. Your eyes are never to lose sight of either of these women. I don't care what the doctors say. Do you understand?"

"Yeah, don't worry. They'll never leave my sight."

"Connor, talk to them. I want to know where Claire and Kayla are. I won't be far behind you. If they know something, call me right away." Then, remembering something else, she asked, "Connor, would you take Allister to the car? If Billy takes him, there might not be much left of the man."

A goofy grin replaced Connor's serious demeanor when he replied, "Sure." He took Allister from Billy and swung him over his shoulder, but before he stepped out onto the deck, he turned, causing Allister's head to hit the glass when he did. "Thanks for sharin', Billy."

"Enjoy. There's a few light posts along the way."

"Oh, criminy. Get him to the car minus the brain damage!" Only partially upset, Kate said under her breath, "I wouldn't mind having a go at him myself."

*   *   *   *   *

Between Ellen and Kate, the mess at the marina had wrapped up quickly. Ellen gave Kate the run of the police station, primarily the interrogation room. She sat across from Yegor, a man she had no knowledge of prior to now. Ellen combed through his background, looking for anything that would give Kate leverage. Once she had enough information, she opened the door and handed her a folder. While Kate scanned over the file, Ellen asked, "You're not from around here, are you, Yegor?"

The man didn't flinch. Kate looked up and said, "Ukrainian mob. My, you've been a busy boy, haven't you? What brought you to Ireland?"

When Yegor's lips parted to form his best smile, his teeth were yellow from years of smoking. "I come for sightseeing. I love Irish people. Very friendly."

"We are friendly. However, we're not very agreeable to those who kidnap our young girls," Ellen offered.

"No kidnapping. They come to me freely. I can't help if I'm a charming guy and women love me."

Kate's expression didn't change. "I'm going to keep it very simple, and you need to be very honest with me. Can you do that for me, Yegor?" She didn't wait for him to answer. "Here's some information about me I feel you should know. I really hate human traffickers. I'm the director of the Anti-Human Trafficking Unit and am overseeing the Anti-Human Trafficking Task Force operations right now. Unfortunately for you, that makes you my prime target. I will bury you right along with Allister and neither of you will ever walk this planet a free man again. For now, your ties to the Ukrainian mob don't interest me. I'm only interested in two women that have gone missing. I want to know where they are. Give me that, and maybe we can work out a deal for you."

This made Yegor readjust his slouching position and sit upright. "You give me a deal just for the girls? What girls? I know nothing about any girls."

"Then our conversation is over. Ellen, charge Yegor with murder, kidnapping, rape, weapons violations, human trafficking; and I'm sure you can add drug charges to his list of crimes."

Yegor leaned forward, placing his elbows on the table and waved his hands while saying, "Girls? I know nothing about any girls. But Allister tell me interesting story that I share with you."

"I'm listening."

As if waving off the situation he found himself in, he nonchalantly offered, "I do nothing with them, but Allister tell me he dumped two women overboard."

Kate tried to hide the fear and anger that bolted through her and asked, "Where?"

He shrugged his shoulders. "I tell you, I know nothing. Ask someone else. I am here visiting a friend is all. Nothing more."

"Just visiting a friend, huh? Well, you're going to prison for a long time just for being on the boat with Allister."

"You ask, and I give you answer!" Yegor drilled his finger into the table. Neither Kate nor Ellen seemed concerned about his outburst. In a much calmer voice, he said, "I know nothing more. So you give me deal, yes? I walk. I never touch the girl. You ask her."

"I said I would give you a deal if you told me where the girls are. Since you don't know anything, I have nothing to offer you, except a lifetime in prison. And then, of course, there's Interpol that will want a piece of you."

Ellen joined in by explaining, "Apparently, you and your boss, Olsen Popova, like to sell girls all over the world. When I ran your prints, it flagged Interpol, and they're on their way. Too bad—Irish prisons are pure luxury compared to those in Turkey, and for whatever reason, the Turkish government wants you."

The combative belligerence that shot across Yegor's face let both women know Ellen had scared him. "I tell you all I know! Allister tell me, he get rid of two, maybe four girls. He had two with him and the other brought here from London. I know nothing more...!" His sudden pause made Kate and Ellen glance at one another. He was holding something back and both women could see he was giving it some thought as to whether he wanted to share it with them. "I give you vessel with South American girls, only if you make me deal!"

"You have my attention. Give me the name and where it's heading. If the authorities get to it and find the cargo, we'll discuss a deal."

Kate wrote down the information Yegor had on the cargo ship transporting the girls from South America. This was the ship they had lost during the storm and the one she thought had rendezvoused with the trawler.

Billy's connections back home had been correct. What she got wrong was the name of the boat believed to have met the trawler. The web of lies surrounding Brian Gallagher's organization was unraveling. Kate now understood just how big his business really was, especially now that she had one of his associates from the Ukrainian mob sitting across the table from her.

"I need to call the commissioner. Keep at it, would you, Ellen?"

"Sure."

*　　*　　*　　*　　*

Clay sat at a small table in Emer's kitchen. He was on his second cup of coffee, watching her cook scrambled eggs. Once cooked, she split them up onto two small plates, added the buttered toast next to the eggs, and handed him a plate.

"Juice? I have orange or cranberry apple, if you would prefer?"

"Thanks. The coffee's fine."

Emer set her plate and coffee down across from Clay and took a seat. "Eat up before it gets cold."

"Thanks, Emer. You didn't have to do this, but I really appreciate it."

Using her fork and toast to scoop up her eggs, she said, "You're welcome."

Clay took a bite of eggs and nearly choked on an eggshell. Before he could tease Emer about it, his phone rang. In his rush to answer it, he dropped his fork and watched it bounce toward the floor. In an ill-contrived attempt to catch the fork, his phone nearly went into his eggs. Emer latched onto his hand, stopping the collision. Her touch calmed his jitters somewhat, and he nodded his thanks.

"The fork will survive. Answer the phone," she said tenderly.

He read the name on the screen. "It's Billy."

"It could be good news."

Still slightly hesitant, Clay answered the phone. "Hey, Billy."

"Clay, Kate asked me to call and give you an update. We have Allister. I wanted to kill him, but he's alive."

With both elbows on either side of his plate, he covered his face for a second. Then he stood and walked around in the small kitchen. "Kayla wasn't there, was she?"

"I'm sorry." Clay heard the sadness in Billy's voice. "From this point on it will be a recovery. Allister threw Claire and your sister overboard—"

Clay's knees buckled, and he dropped to the floor, crying out, "No!"

Emer jumped out of her seat and knelt down next to him, wrapping her arms around him. She held him tight while he cried. Taking the phone from Clay, she said softly, "Billy, this is Emer."

"Hey, I'm sorry to give him the news over the phone. His sister's dead, along with the agent that was with her. Just let him know that Kate won't quit until she's found their bodies. She has every seaworthy vessel out searching for them as well as every village along the coastline. Because this is such a huge case, the commissioner is giving Kate everything she needs. Let Clay know I'll call as soon as they've found Kayla."

Billy hung up without a goodbye and Emer dropped the phone on the floor next to her. She put both arms around Clay and hugged him. "I'm so sorry."

Clay's body shuddered as he cried.

Devastated for him, Emer tried to console him. In doing so, she blurted out, "I had a guinea pig once. I know that's weird coming from me, owning a flea-infested rodent, but anyway, it died. It was the first surgery I ever did. It was stiff as a board by the time I found it. The only thought that came to mind was to cut it open, which I did. It was my first official surgery. I said that already, didn't I? Oh, well, I was only eight at the time. I took one of my mother's cooking knives, and cut it open—"

The expression on Clay's face was one of pure confusion. He wiped his eyes and stared at her. She let go of him, but didn't move away. "Yeah, I know not the smartest thing to do to my pet, but my curiosity got the better of me. I opened up my guinea and found his heart, his lungs, his liver...everything, really. When I was done, I put all his tiny parts back inside and stitched the little guy up with a needle and thread. I put him in a box, took him out to the garden where I dug a deep hole, and buried him."

Emer's cheeks glistened from the tears she could no longer hold back. She tried to smile but, instead, wiped her eyes and nose with her sleeve before continuing. "My mother was so sweet, she went to the store and bought me another one. It was a beautiful white one; anyway, it died very quickly, and it devasted my mother see me heartbroken again. However, in my eight-year-old analytical mind, I understood the wooden cage carried whatever disease the first guinea had and would kill any animal I put in it."

Completely dumbfounded, Clay couldn't help but ask, "What did you do with the wooden cage?"

Emer's lips curled up when she answered, "I burned it. What my mother thought was heartache over the loss of another stupid guinea pig, was actually my frustration that I couldn't use the crate anymore. I asked for a metal one because I could clean it with a powerful disinfectant. My mother said she couldn't bear to see me in such pain again and refused to buy me another cage."

Clay's eyes reflected a glow of appreciation for her mother. "She was trying to protect you from another heartache."

"Yes. When I think of death, I don't know why I always think of that silly story." She chuckled and sniffled at the same time. "I don't know what she would have thought had she walked in on me dissecting the first guinea."

Clay smiled. "She probably would have thought you were insane."

Emer leaned against the kitchen cabinet. Clay scooted back and did the same. Once situated, with his long legs stretched out, he said, "Life just keeps moving, even when we're gone. It did when my folks died, and it will with Kayla too. Thanks, Emer, for being here with me. I know we can't replace people the way your mom tried to do with the guinea pig, but for whatever reason, it's important to me that you were here when Billy called."

Emer chuckled through her sniffles. "I live here, you buffoon!"

"You do, don't you?" Clay gave a slight laugh. "Huh. Well, I'm glad I walked here. By the way, that was a really stupid story to use to console me."

"I know it was." Emer laughed. "I just didn't know what to say, and I couldn't stand seeing you cry."

This time, Clay draped his arm over Emer's shoulder, squeezed her tight, and held her for a few seconds. He kissed the top of her head before he removed his arm. "Thanks." Then Clay let out a very agitated, "Ugh!" while he shook his head. "Enough! Um, listen, I'm not really hungry, but I could use some air. Will you walk back to Ian's house with me?"

"That has to be ten kilometers, if not more!"

"Ten kilometers sounds far, and since I don't understand kilometers, I'm guessing it's about six miles. Since I walk less than a fifteen-minute mile, I'm sure it's close to that. Come on, it'll be good for you…and me. It's your day off and Mary's a superb cook."

Emer looked at him with a calculated stare and asked, "And what's wrong with the breakfast I cooked you?"

Clay remembered the phone call, and for a moment, there was a lapse in his cheerfulness. He swallowed back the knot forming in his throat. Emer took his hand and was about to say something when he answered, "I don't know how to tell you this, but there were eggshells in mine. Not only are you not very good at consoling people, but you can't cook."

She balled up her fist and hit him square in the chest, laughing. "Let me grab my jacket." She got up from the floor, ran to her bedroom, and came out, slipping it on.

Once on his feet, Clay went outside and took the stairs down. She locked the door and trailed behind him. The morning was chilly with dark gray clouds giving the impression it was going to rain. Clay wished he had put on a sweater under his light jacket. He walked as if on a mission, and Emer struggled to keep up with his long strides.

"If you don't slow down, you'll be walking alone!"

Clay took Emer's hand and laced his fingers through hers as they walked, causing her to glance over at him. Clay had a very natural way with people. No one had ever been comfortable around the young doctor, not even Emer's parents. Her personality was such that it always put a large barrier between her and others. But from day one, he had managed to maneuver around her temper and sarcasm without a scrape.

"Sorry, I'm cold."

"You're in Ireland. It's always cold."

With a slight squeeze to her hand, he said, "It's cold but breathtaking. I think I get why Eddie stayed."

Sorrow washed over Clay at the mention of his friend.

"Eddie's the man that you met at Sean's pub, right?" Emer asked. "He sounds like a unique individual. I can't wait to meet him."

Clay shuffled to a stop in front of her. He hesitated for a moment and then said, "Yeah, he was. Um…he's dead. I'm sorry, I should have told you earlier."

Emer placed both hands on his face. "I'm so sorry." Then she slid her arms around his neck and hugged him, causing a natural reflex of his arms going around her waist, and he held her tight. Tears welled up in both their eyes as they stood motionless.

Finally, Clay drew back and turned around purposefully. He had them in motion again, heading toward Ian's farm. "Come on—if we keep this up, we'll never get there."

Emer only nodded in agreement. This time she took Clay's hand as they walked. The exercise was therapeutic for them. Clay told her about the first day he met Eddie, and learned about his sister, who had been missing for the last fifteen years. From there, he moved on to Kayla. Emer laughed at the stories he shared about his sister. If either were feeling the chilly air, neither showed it. Before they knew it, their conversation had taken them all the way to Ian's farm.

Mary went into overdrive when she saw them. "Yer chilled ta the bone! Ian, tend ta the fire, will ya? I'll see ta the coffee and tea."

Clay reached for Mary, saying, "Slow down. Let me give you a hand."

"Auch, no! Sit by the fire and warm yerself."

"Clay, I got this." Noah's tone didn't allow room for argument. "Do as Mary said, and I'll give her a hand."

It only took Mary and Noah a few minutes to get everything ready. Clay sat on the floor near the fire and leaned against the sofa where Emer sat, with her leg resting against his shoulder. Mary patted Emer's other leg when she sat next to her and offered, "Here, lass, drink up, it will warm ya."

"Thank you."

"Have you heard anything?" Noah asked.

"Yeah, I have," Clay answered in a sober voice. "It's a recovery now, not a rescue."

The words took a minute to register with everyone in the room. Mary's hands went to her face, and she whispered, "Oh, no. I'm so sorry for ya, Clay." Emer held Mary close as tears trickled down the older woman's face.

"Aye, laddie, terribly sorry for ya. Ya've a home here as long as you need."

"Thanks, Ian. You and Mary have been amazing, and I appreciate everything you've done for me."

"What happens now?" Noah asked.

"I don't know. I dropped the phone when Billy said it was a recovery." Clay looked up at Emer for an explanation.

Her fingers touched the back of Clay's head, and she smiled tenderly at him before she answered, "He said Kate wouldn't stop until she's found both women. Claire, one of Kate's agents, was with Kayla. Allister threw them both overboard."

Mary couldn't help herself and wept even more. Her entire body shook and Emer tightened her hold on her. Ian wiped his eyes and stared at the fire. "I canna believe Ireland, with all her beauty, has such a dark side to 'er."

"We're all given a choice and unfortunately, not everyone chooses wisely," Noah stated.

"Come on, Mary, let's make ourselves busy and see to breakfast." Emer stood up and offered her hand to the older woman. "It'll help clear our minds."

She got up willingly, taking the doctor's hand, and the two went to the kitchen. Clay jokingly yelled out, "Don't let Emer anywhere around the eggs!"

"Shut up, Clay!" Emer countered.

* * * * *

Patrick put the headphones on and spoke into the mic. "Let's go!"

The helicopter lifted off the ground and ascended over Kinsale. Those in Dingle Bay had already been in the air for twenty minutes, along with ten others stretched out from Kenmare to Rosscarbery Bay. Because Patrick had insisted on being part of the air search, the chopper leaving Kinsale waited for him and was the last one in the air.

Anxiety had Patrick's blood pumping through his veins at a higher rate than normal. He could feel his heartbeat and tried to slow it down by controlling his breathing. He hated that this had turned into a recovery instead of a rescue.

In the short time he had known Clay, Patrick had come to like him. Not finding his sister alive was hard to accept. His team had been relentless in tracking down Allister, who always seemed to be one step-ahead of them. That infuriated Patrick even more.

His hope was that Kate would find all the people that Gallagher had on his payroll within Ireland's government. Brian Gallagher had finagled his way into the pockets of officials a long time ago and now had spies imbedded deep in every facet of the government. Flushing them out would take time. He was confident Kate would do it, even if it took her years to do so.

"Right, lads, keep an eye out for anything," the pilot ordered over the headsets. "Even if you're not sure, tell me and we'll make a quick flyby. Better to be sure than not."

The mid-morning sun shimmered over the water, causing shadows. The pilot crisscrossed the ocean and coastline, hoping to find the women. Patrick held his binoculars to his eyes and focused on moving his head in an orderly fashion, up and down the coast, so he wouldn't miss anything.

Kate had also ordered seacrafts of every kind out to search for Kayla and Claire. Fishermen, private yachts, and sailboats were all part of the massive hunt. Patrick saw them below, making sweeps closer to the shore. Just seeing them gave him the reassurance he needed that everything was being done to find the two women. The boats, Patrick knew, had been searching for hours, long before the helicopters had.

The call came in at six o'clock that evening that a search party on foot had found the bodies of two women at Courtmacsherry Bay. A search party found them washed ashore and had called the local police. Patrick was heartbroken but relieved. They could keep Billy's promise to Clay; dead or alive, his sister would be returned to him.

Kate waited for Patrick when he got off the helicopter. He jogged over to her, but instead of trying to speak over the noise, she waited until they were in the Land Rover. Billy and Connor were already inside.

"It's them, Patrick. I've called Clay, and he's on his way here."

"You're having the bodies brought here? Why?"

"The commissioner ordered Grossman here."

"Why is Dublin's chief coroner coming to Kinsale?"

"We have a mess and Ellen's requested the extra help. The commissioner wants answers now, not tomorrow."

Patrick ran his hand over the top of his head and asked, "How long before the bodies arrive?"

"Maybe fifteen to twenty minutes. Honestly, I don't know, I'm only guessing."

"How long before Clay arrives?"

Kate sighed. "Again, I have no idea, but if I had to guess, I'd say in thirty to forty-five minutes."

Patrick looked at Billy and said, "Okay, you and I will wait for Clay to get here."

"Absolutely," Billy answered.

"Kate, where did you tell him to go?" Patrick asked.

"I told him to head straight to the morgue at Kinsale Medical, on New Road. Listen, I have to meet with Ellen. We have the cargo ship from South America to tend to. After I take care of some other business, I'll be heading back to Dublin."

"Do you need Connor?" Patrick asked.

"No. I want you both with Clay when he IDs his sister. Just get me over to Ellen. She won't mind shuttling me around until I leave."

Patrick leaned back and slapped his hand on the back of Connor's seat. "Let's go find Ellen." Then, glancing over at Kate, he added, "You finally got Brian Gallagher and Allister, didn't you? It must feel good?"

Shifting around in her seat, she eyed Patrick and corrected him by saying, "*We* caught them. I couldn't have done it without you." Then in a more subdued voice, she added, "We lost a lot of good people in the process, but they didn't die in vain. So yeah, it feels good, but the hurt that comes with it weighs heavy on my mind. When you stopped by my office and told me about Brian Gallagher's involvement in Kayla's abduction, I thought it would lead to another dead end. But this...this I wasn't expecting. Five years the AHTU has been after Gallagher—five years! Now, all because of a pretty California girl and her brother, we have him and his entire organization by the throat."

Patrick nodded. "You're right, of course, what an utter waste of live."

No one in the Land Rover added anything more. Yes, it was a monumental victory for Ireland, but it wasn't without deep battle wounds. The cost had been high for everyone. With the loss of Eddie and Derrick, the trawler's crew, Alison O'Kelly and her family, and a ship full of innocent girls, plus what Kayla and Claire had gone through, it would be hard to rejoice in their victory.

They all knew the body count would continue to rise the more the authorities dug into Brian Gallagher's network; more families destroyed because of his twisted world, and there was no celebrating that. The mess left behind in Gallagher's wake would take years to clean up. Those in high places would run for cover, doing their best to hide any tracks that led from Gallagher to them. No agency would be without a scarring, starting with the police. Judges and politicians were knee deep in the muck of Gallagher's organization. Anyone involved in this case knew that, and because of it, it dampened any mood for celebration.

"One day," Kate said. "One day I'll celebrate—maybe I'll add in something big, like my retirement. However, that day will have to wait. There's too much to do before I can close this case."

Patrick looked at her, saying, "You retire? Never. You're to entrenched in your job just like I am. No one will ever be able to fill your shoes."

"Yes, well, my shoes right now are hurting my feet and I'm in need of a new pair. After I close this case, I'm switching to a more comfortable shoe."

CHAPTER 11

Patrick and Billy wanted to be at the hospital when Clay got there. As it was, they wouldn't make it there before he did. Clay had called and said he and Emer, along with a friend, Noah, had just arrived.

Neither had paid attention to the time. Kate asked if they would help tie up a few loose ends, which they had been happy to do. However, the task took longer than intended and was the reason for their delay.

Checking his watch for the third time, Patrick sat impatiently in the front passenger seat while Connor sped through the streets of Kinsale. Turning onto New Road, Connor said, "The bodies must have just arrived."

The announcement snapped Patrick from his thoughts. He looked up and saw the ambulances. He slapped his hand hard on the dash and ordered, "Forget the parking lot—pull in behind them!"

Three bright yellow and green emergency response vehicles were parked in front of the medical center. Connor slammed on the brakes and parked behind one of the ambulances. Patrick and Billy couldn't get out of the car fast enough and had their doors opened before Connor came to a complete stop. The three men ran behind the last gurney being wheeled in. Patrick saw Clay and rushed over to him.

"Sorry. I wanted to be here when you arrived."

Clay wasn't paying attention to him. He watched as EMTs wheeled the bodies in, one at a time. He had a puzzled expression on his face and asked, "Emer, why would they have oxygen masks on dead bodies?" Hearing Clay's comment, Patrick slowed and watched the ambulance personnel move quickly toward the elevators.

"They wouldn't," she replied. "Hang on!"

Emer ran alongside one gurney and disappeared into the elevator with it. Patrick took his phone out and called Kate. The second he heard her voice, Patrick demanded, "Get down here now!"

Disoriented, Clay hadn't moved. Seeing his friend's state, Patrick grabbed him by the shoulder and hauled him onto the other elevator. Billy and Connor fell in behind them with Noah squeezing in last. Pushing the second-floor button several times in the hopes it would help the elevator move faster, Patrick repeated, "Come on, come on!"

"I don't get it, they're dead, right?" Clay asked no one in particular.

"There were three bodies, not two," Connor added. "Who was the third?"

No one answered either question. As soon as the doors opened on the second floor, Patrick moved with determination, dragging Clay out of the elevator with him.

Unlike the first floor, people were moving in every direction. Patrick grabbed a male nurse with his free hand and asked, "What's going on?"

Before he could answer, a voice from behind said, "I was told I had autopsies to do on two young women, but apparently, they're alive."

Patrick let go of the nurse, turned around and found the coroner, Dr. Grossman, standing behind him. "Wait, what are you saying? Kayla and Claire are alive?"

"Barely, but yes. Along with a big lad. They're near frozen to death, but they're very much alive."

The news surprised everyone. However, the information sent Clay in a spiral, causing his body to slack and his knees buckle. Patrick still had him by the collar and when he felt his weight, he latched on to Clay's arm before he collapsed. Noah caught him from behind and kept him from falling to the floor. Connor grabbed a chair, and the three men eased him down on it.

Billy placed his hand on Clay's shoulder and offered, "Hang tight, buddy. I'll find out what's going on."

The elevator doors opened, and Kate and Ellen stepped out. Before Kate could ask what happened, Patrick said excitedly, "They're all alive!"

"What?"

"Yeah, Dr. Grossman said there was a big lad with them. I'm guessing of course, but I think the young man might be the captain's missing son, Chris."

Kate turned to Dr. Grossman with her hand held out. "Norman, thank you for coming."

"Yes, but now I'm not sure I'm needed."

"You're needed. We have five bodies that just arrived downstairs. Ellen will take you to them. I want to know about the dead girls and only one male right now. The garda shot and killed the other two men. You can examine them last."

"Right—I'll let you know my findings as soon as I'm done."

"Thank you."

The coroner followed Ellen to the elevator. Kate watched as the door closed behind them before asking, "So no one has said anything?"

"No," Patrick answered. "Everyone's been moving so fast. I haven't been able to ask anyone what's going on."

Kate looked down at Clay before she positioned herself in front of him and knelt down. "Your sister has a fighting chance now. Don't give up."

Eddie's death had acutely affected Clay, but being told Kayla's rescue had become a recovery had crushed his soul. The lack of sleep only added to his disposition. He rubbed his inflamed eyes and whispered, "I had come to terms with the fact that she was dead. If she dies now, I'm not sure I'll be able to handle it."

"I don't know how it happened, but she's alive and I, for one, am going to hang on to the hope that she'll survive. The entire hospital's personnel are on this."

Tears trickled down Clay's face. Kate leaned in and wrapped her arms around him. When she released him, she placed one hand on his cheek. "You should know that I sincerely care about you, and because of it, I have stepped over that imaginary line that no one in my position should ever cross. This case has become personal for me." Letting her hand drop, she stood up, announcing, "I'm going to see what's going on. Stay put."

Before she could, Emer appeared. Seeing the director, she said, "You must be Kate. I'm Emer."

Kate's facial features expressed one of those "Aha, it's you!" looks, while saying, "It's nice to have a face to go with the name."

The doctor immediately flushed red but forged ahead with the information she had. "They have a brilliant medical team here, so all three are in excellent hands. Kayla, Claire, and the young man are being treated for severe hypothermia. Whoever found them was smart enough to know that hypothermia can cause a person to seem dead when they aren't. Their rescuers did all the right things until the emergency personnel could get to them. I informed the doctors of the possibility of drugs in the women's systems. They're doing a complete exam on them now." Emer knelt down in front of Clay, took his hand in hers, and said with sincerity, "Kayla's going to be fine."

Clay blew out his breath. Emer placed both hands on his face, kissed his forehead, and forced him to make eye contact with her. He relaxed and whispered, "Thank you."

Emer stood but didn't step away from him. He clasped his hands around the inside of her knee and rested his head against her hip while she combed her fingers through his hair. "Would someone mind getting Clay some coffee?" she asked.

"Yeah, sure—I think I could use some too," Billy answered. "Does anyone else want coffee?"

"Yes, most definitely! I'll give you a hand," Noah offered.

Connor came back with a few extra chairs. Everyone thanked him and arranged them in a row against the wall. Before they got situated, a nurse came through the double doors and called out, "Dr. O'Farrell?"

"Yes."

"Would you come with me? Dr. Lowell has requested that you join him."

"Yes, give me a moment please." Emer cupped Clay's face in her hands and whispered, "Do what you do best—and pray." She bent down and kissed his forehead once more before she followed the nurse down the hall and through the doors.

Kate, having watched the tender moment between the two, said, "She's gorgeous, Clay. I understand the attraction."

He crossed his arms at his chest and stretched out his legs, trying to get comfortable. With a slight lift to one side of his mouth, he offered, "She's mad because everyone thinks there's something going on between us."

That made Kate, Patrick, and Connor laugh. "Well, it's no wonder, the way the two of you interact with one another," Kate said, pointing out the obvious. "You and Emer are the only ones oblivious to it."

Clay's smirk turned into a full-blown grin. Then, resting his head against the wall, he changed the subject. "I'm surprised that Chris was found with my sister and Claire. Don't get me wrong, I'm very grateful he was, but I can't imagine what Allister's reasoning was for keeping him alive. Do you think someone should call his mother?"

"No," Kate said, shaking her head. "Not until I'm sure it's him and the doctors tell me he'll be okay. I feel it would be best for his mother if she didn't know until we had news that was based on facts and not on assumptions."

Clay sat up from his slouching position, placed his elbows on his knees, and looked past Patrick at Kate. "I would want to know you found him, no matter what state he's in."

"He's right, Kate," Patrick agreed. "Mrs. Dunne has lost everyone. Emer said they'd be okay. You should call her."

Outnumbered, Kate exhaled, stood from her chair, and took her phone from her pocket. Before she made the call, she said, smiling, "You're impossible, Clay. As I said earlier, you made me step over a line that I'd sworn I would never do with my job, and that's allow myself to become personally involved with a case. It's no wonder Emer's in love with you."

Taken aback, Clay didn't know how to refute her comment. It didn't matter anyway because Kate had disappeared down the hall to phone Mrs. Dunne. Patrick and Connor could only laugh at him.

Billy and Noah came back with the coffee and handed them each a cup, with Billy asking, "What's so funny and who's Kate talking to?"

Connor, still grinning, took the cup being offered him and said, "Thanks. She just enlightened Clay on a few things concernin' Emer and is now callin' Chris's ma."

"Ah. Where's Emer anyway?"

"A doctor asked her to join him," Patrick explained.

"Is that a good thing?" Billy asked curiously, still holding two cups of coffee.

"Let's hope so," Patrick answered. "She'll let us know if anything changes."

Clay took a sip of coffee and pulled out his phone. "Thanks for the cup of Joe. I need to call Ian and Mary. I know they're worried sick about me. Besides, I have some good news to share with them." He got up from his chair and walked to the other end of the hall.

Seeing Clay smile for the first time in weeks, filled Patrick with unsurmountable joy. He was happy for him. Now that he could take a breather himself, Patrick allowed his mind to take him through the chain of events that had led him and his friends to this very moment. It was nothing shy of a miracle. He lifted his eyes and his coffee cup upward and said, "Cheers and thank you, sweet Jesus."

Patrick's companions did the same, each echoing, "Amen."

*   *   *   *   *

The monitor beeped softly while Clay slept in the chair, with his upper body resting on Kayla's hospital bed. He had been by her side for the last three days. During that time, he hadn't let go of her hand except for the times he had to eat or go to the bathroom.

Not wanting to wake him, Emer moved quietly to the other side of the bed. Pleased with Kayla's vitals, she took her other hand and could feel its warmth. This roused Kayla from her sleep, and she blinked up at the doctor. Her cracked lips and dry throat didn't allow her to speak.

Emer had never been one to become overly excited about anything, but seeing Kayla's eyes open sent a jolt through her body. She reached over and shook Clay from his sleep. "She's awake!" He shot out of his chair. With his mind blurred, his eyes darted in every direction until he heard Emer's voice again. "Kayla's awake."

Slightly disoriented, he leaned in closer to his sister, repeating Emer's words, "She's awake." Kayla's hazel eyes transfixed on to his. He took a strand of her hair and tucked it behind her ear. "Hey, you. Welcome back."

The wet towel Emer placed on Kayla's lips seemed to please the young woman. The moisture from it trickled into her mouth. When her lips finally parted, she whispered, "I'm sorry."

"There's nothing to be sorry about. I'm just glad you're alive."

A tear fell from the side of Kayla's right eye as she blinked. She tried to lick her lips, but her mouth was still too dry. Emer applied Chapstick to them and put the moist towel in Kayla's hand. "You've been heavily medicated and can't have water right now except through this wet towel," Emer explained. "Just suck on it. Sorry, you'll have a full glass of water when the doctor says it's okay."

Nodding that she understood, Kayla's eyes fluttered and then closed.

Concerned, Clay yelled, "Kayla?"

"She'll drift in and out of consciousness for the rest of the day, which is normal."

He glanced over at Emer and then back down at his sister. "She's going to be okay, isn't she?"

"Yes, she is."

There was a light knock on the door before Kate and Billy entered the room. Clay let go of his sister's hand and said, "Hey."

"How is she? Any change?" Billy asked.

"Um, yeah." Clay wiped his hand across his mouth and added, "She just woke up. Well, for a second anyway."

Emer moved next to Clay, placed her hand on his arm and said, "I need to let the doctor know. I'll be back in a few minutes."

"Yeah, sure, and thank you."

Billy stepped aside to let her pass. "Just curious, she wouldn't have any available sisters, would she?"

"Men!" Kate said, glaring at him in a joking manner. "Claire woke up an hour ago, but Chris is still out. His mother has arrived and is with him now."

Clay glanced back at his sister. She was still asleep. "Eh, listen, I would like to talk to Mrs. Dunne if you don't mind?"

"Feel free to do so." In a more serious tone, Kate said, "Claire told me that if it hadn't been for Chris, she and Kayla would be dead. Allister ordered their execution and that's when Chris broke free and tackled the girls, taking the three of them over the side of the boat. Allister's men shot at them, but thankfully missed. Chris swam both girls to shore. How he managed it, I don't know."

"Geez. That kid's amazing." Clay dragged his fingers through his hair and took another look at Kayla. "I know she knows about some of those that died. But I think it will break her heart when she finds out just how many died trying to save her."

"You should be the one to tell her," Billy advised. "The media hasn't let up. This is the biggest news story in Ireland and it's going global. She'll hear about it one way or another—either from you or them."

"You're right. I should tell her sooner rather than later, but for now, I'll keep the TV off. When I'm sure she can handle it, I'll fill her in on everything. She needs to rest. However, I'd like to talk to Chris's mother right now if you wouldn't mind staying with Kayla while I'm gone? I'll just be a few minutes"

"You remember what room Chris is in, don't you?" Kate asked.

"Yeah, I do."

"I'll stay here with your sister while you're gone. I'll send for you if she wakes up."

"Thanks, Kate."

*   *   *   *   *

Clay found Mrs. Dunne in Chris's room, slumped in a chair next to his bed. If she heard the door open, she gave no sign that she had. She never took her eyes off her son. Clay understood. He cleared his throat before he asked, "Mrs. Dunne, um, I'm sorry to bother you, but I was wondering if I could have a word with you?"

Not looking in his direction, she answered, "Hum?"

He stepped around in front of her. "Mrs. Dunne, do you remember me?"

Seeing Clay brought her out of her trance and when she stood, she fell into his arms. Clay held her while she wept.

With the rest of her family murdered, Chris was all she had. Clay empathized with her. However, he had had time to heal from his parents' deaths. Mrs. Dunne was still grieving the loss of her husband and two older boys.

After a few minutes, Clay released her, lifted her chin with the tips of his fingers and forced her to look at him. "I lost my parents a few years ago. Kayla is all I have left, so I want you to know I understand the pain you're feeling. I know your faith lies with God, but grief has a way of pulling you in directions that you don't want to go. Even in your darkest hour, trust in Him and healing will come. It'll take time, but I promise you there is healing. Just don't make the mistake I did and walk away from God."

"I canna. He's the only one to have held me together all these years. I knew nothing good would come outta Cappy workin' with the likes of Brian Gallagher. But he would nae listen—the ol' coot!"

"I'm not willing to lay all the blame on your husband. Gallagher had his ways of forcing people to do what he wanted. He had another fisherman's boat torched because the man refused to work for him. One thing I've learned from all of this is forgiveness goes a long way. You're going to have to find a way to forgive your husband. Once you do, you and Chris can move on."

She nodded in agreement. Then looking over at her son, she explained, "My husband said Chris was weak. My baby would nae cuss or drink. Nor was he foosterin' with the floozies. He were nothin' like 'is older brothers. They were like their da, always gettin' in trouble for somethin'."

There was a light rumble of laughter coming from Clay. "I'm sorry my Irish isn't that good, 'Fostering with the floozies'?"

That made Mrs. Dunne smile. She wiped her eyes and corrected Clay by saying, "Foosterin', meanin', messin' and floozies, meanin' ladies lackin' in the morals. Don't get me wrong, he liked the women, he just wasn't ready for one. Workin' for World Charities was a dream of 'is. When he got the job, 'is da was angry, but I told my boy ta go and not ta worry about 'is da. I did nae want Chris involved in this mess with Gallagher. A lotta good it done me."

"I'm grateful he was there for my sister and Claire. He saved their lives."

"He did? How d'ya know?"

"Claire's awake. Kate spoke with her, and she said that if he hadn't been there, she and Kayla would be dead."

"It does nae surprise me. He was nae weak like 'is da thought. Just look at 'im, you can see he's strong as an ox, and he loves the Lord. He's a good lad."

Clay couldn't agree more. "Um, listen. I don't want you to think I'm assuming anything here, but I want to give you something, and I hope I'm not out of line doing so."

Confused at first by what he meant, she unfolded the paper he gave her and saw it was a check. Then, shaking her head, she said, "No. I canna take the money. No, no. Here. I canna take it." She pressed the paper into Clay's chest and let it go.

Not prepared for her to release it, Clay watched the check float toward the floor. He quickly reached for it and caught it in midair. "I'm sorry. I hope I didn't offend you by giving this to you? It's just with…Well—"

"Yer a good man. I canna take it. Yer sister nearly lost her life because of my Cappy. I canna take your money. Thank ya, but no."

"Kayla will have to take responsibility for her part in all of this. Your husband didn't make her leave her friends." Clay didn't want to play the blame game. What happened, happened. There was no way to change any of it now. "If you or Chris ever need anything, just call. I'll leave you my number. Please call me anytime, day or night. Mrs. Dunne, this isn't your fault and people can be harsh. This," Clay held up the check, "was only to help you get a fresh start. That's all."

"Thank ya kindly, but Chris and I will manage."

Clay wished she would take it but understood. He put the check back in his pocket and took his business card out and handed it to her. She hesitated for a moment before taking it. "Day or night, it doesn't matter, just call me if you or Chris are ever in need of anything."

"Aye, I will." She looked up at him and said, "However long the day, the evenin' will come."

"I'm sorry?"

"It's an Irish saying, 'The bad stuff doesn't last forever.' Me and my boy will be fine. The Lord will see to it."

"Take care, Mrs. Dunne."

He headed down the hall, back to Kayla's room, when his phone rang. Taking it out of his pocket, he looked at it and saw it was Roman Jones. He stopped to answer it. "Hey, Roman, thank you for returning my call…"

*   *   *   *   *

Three more days had come and gone, and Kayla grew stronger. Hearing the doctor say she could go home overjoyed Clay. He took a seat in the chair next to Kayla's bed and held her hand. She playfully begged him, "Please, Clay, enough with all this mushy brother stuff."

Grinning, he said, "I can't help it, I thought I lost you. Do you know how scary that was for me?"

In a more subdued tone, she said, "I know. I'm so sorry."

"No more apologies. Although we need to have a serious talk."

The underlining tone of stress in Clay's voice gave Kayla chills. She shrugged them off by saying, "Don't worry, my partying days are over. Noah has been wonderful. When you went to shower and get a bite to eat, he was kind enough to read the Bible to me. I've been such an idiot. I'm so grateful God didn't give up on me."

"Noah's become a good friend. I'm glad he could do for you what I couldn't."

Kayla swallowed. "I know you said no more apologies, but I'm going to have an apology tour coming up soon, as well as a thank you one."

Clay rubbed the back of his neck as if choosing his next words carefully. Kayla realized that whatever her brother needed to talk to her about was slightly more serious than her begging forgiveness from everyone. She said nothing more and waited for him to tell her what she needed to know.

"I'm not sure how much you remember, but once we walk out these doors, you're going to hear about it. I need to explain everything that took place on my end... I mean, I know you're not telling me everything that happened to you, and that's okay, but there are few things you're not aware of that you need to know."

"I gathered from some of Kate's questions earlier that there were a lot of bad things that happened."

"Yes...more than a lot." Clay brought Kayla's hand to his lips and kissed it. Then letting it go, he stood up and paced in front of her bed. "I called this guy, Eddie. He was amazing. I know you would have liked him right away. But anyway, I called him to see if he could help me find you." Clay combed his fingers through his hair as he thought about his friend. "Um, someone abducted his sister fifteen years ago. Like you, it happened while vacationing here in Ireland. Ever since her disappearance, all he's done is search for abducted girls and brought them home."

"Yes, I knew him." Kayla was near tears thinking about Eddie and barely got out, "You're right, I did like him."

"I figured you would." Clay avoided making eye contact with her. She could tell he was struggling with his own emotions. When he finally looked at her, he said, "I don't know if you saw him die or if you even knew he died, but Allister killed him. Well, we think he did. He hasn't been talking much. Also, the young man that invited you to the party, Derrick—he's dead."

"I remember Eddie," she whispered. "He kept reassuring me that everything would be okay. Allister...I...I watched him—" Overcome with grief, Kayla placed both hands over her face and wailed, "I'm so sorry!"

Clay rushed over and sat on the bed next to her. "Hey, hey. I didn't mean to upset you, but you're going to find out from the media, if not from me. Listen, Kayla, it's not your fault. Allister did this, not you."

"It is because of me! If I hadn't left my friends… The memory of it is so vivid! Chris tried to block my view, but…" She shivered as she stared into Clay's eyes. "Claire screamed at Allister when she saw Eddie's body. Allister just laughed and dragged her over to him. I was so scared, I thought he was going to kill her too."

Clay took her hands in his. "I can't stress enough that none of this is your fault. Noah reminded me that God knows the when, the where, and all the circumstances of our life and death. Eddie's job always seemed to lead him down into a cesspool of degenerates, but he did it to bring girls and boys home to their families. He never took the glory, and he never gave up hope in finding his own sister. You need to understand—he chose that life."

"Chris said they murdered his dad and brothers."

"Again, Sis, not your fault. The captain chose to work for Gallagher—something was bound to go wrong." Clay settled in closer to her. "People died because Derrick took you, not because of you. Kate said for the first time in her five-year endeavors to bring Gallagher down, it took a girl from California to mess things up for him. Brian Gallagher's world fell apart, piece by piece, and as hard as he tried, he couldn't stop it from unraveling. He thought killing people would fix his problem. The only thing is, his network was so vast that he could never kill everyone."

Kayla whispered, "Who else died?"

"Look, I know you'll hear about it from the news or some reporter, and because I don't want you to get blindsided, I'll tell you. Allister had a woman, Alison O'Kelly, and her husband killed. They were innocent in all of this—it was her brother that worked for Gallagher—they just got caught up in all this mess like you did. Their children are still missing."

Overcome with grief, Kayla's hands went to her face, and she cried. Then she grabbed the box of tissues and took one out to wipe her eyes and blew her nose. "I'm sorry, I just don't want to hear any more. It's too much."

"I get it. Living it every day and seeing the faces of Patrick and his men when they found the aftermath was enough for me. How these guys do it every day, I don't know." Clay stood and walked to the foot of the bed. "When we leave here, we'll stay with some friends of mine at their farm. Unfortunately, we can't go home until Kate says we can. You'll have to sit down with one of her officers and answer their questions. I'm guessing we can go home in a couple of weeks."

"Won't I have to stay for the trial?"

"You may have to come back for it, but it won't be for some time. I think the court system here is slower than back home."

"Will you come back with me?"

That made Clay smile. "Yes, of course."

A nurse walked in and handed Clay a plastic hospital bag with Kayla's belongings. "The doctor has cleared your sister. She can go home, if you'll sign the release forms."

"Yeah, okay." Clay handed Kayla the plastic bag and followed the nurse out.

Kayla slid out of bed, opened the bag given to her, and pulled out the dress she had been wearing the night she made the worst decision of her life. She threw it across the room at the same time Emer walked in. Surprised by her sudden appearance, Kayla ran over to pick up the dress and crammed it back inside the bag. She stared at Emer as if she had been guilty of more than just throwing her dress across the room.

The compassion in Emer's eyes when she smiled put Kayla's spirit at ease. She placed a small suitcase on the bed and unzipped it. "I have some clothes for you. I didn't think you would want to wear what you had on when they found you. And as sweet as your brother is, I know he wouldn't think of purchasing anything for you. I hope I got the right size." Emer shook out a green sweater, held it up, and asked, "Is this okay?"

"Oh, Emer, thank you so much!" Kayla rushed toward her, took the sweater, and gave her a quick hug. "You're the sweetest ever. I love it!"

"Thank goodness," Emer said relieved. "So you like the color and style?"

"Are you kidding, it's beautiful." Kayla dug through the rest of the clothes in the suitcase, and her face lit up. Without warning, she did an about-face and gave Emer another hug. "These are perfect. Thank you so much."

Emer instinctively wrapped her arms around Kayla's waist, and they held each other for quite some time.

"What's this then?" Emer asked. "They're just clothes and I'm happy you like them, but really, there's no reason to cry."

Letting go, Kayla took a step back and wiped her eyes. "I know. I can't help it. Thank you so much."

"Get dressed. There's a very handsome young Irishman in the hallway that would like to have a word with you."

"Chris?" Kayla's spirits brightened.

"Yeah. Go on, I'll let him know you'll be out in a minute."

Kayla went into the bathroom to wash her face and comb her hair. She got dressed and put her socks and shoes on. Satisfied with her new look, she walked out of her room feeling like a human again. She found Emer in the hall talking to Chris while her brother leaned against the wall, scrolling through messages on his phone. Clay stood upright when he saw her.

"Hey! Look at you. Where did you get the clothes?"

"From Emer," his sister answered. Then, facing Chris, she said, "Hi. Are you going home today?"

"Aye, I am. You all right then?"

"I am." Kayla's eyes watered. "Um, thank you for saving my life. Claire's too. I don't even want to think about what would have happened to us if you hadn't been there." Kayla walked up to Chris and put her arms around him. He returned the hug.

"I just listened ta the voice in my head, tellin' me ta jump. Your gratitude will have ta go ta God, not ta me."

"Believe me, I haven't stopped thanking Him. But you listened to Him. So thank you."

Clay held out a piece of paper to Chris. Seeing it, Chris released Kayla and took it from him. His eyes grew in size when he realized what it was. "I'm sorry, what's this for?"

"A check. Your mother wouldn't take it, but I need you to. I don't know how the people in Killybegs are going to treat her, or you, when you go home. With your dad and brothers gone, she may not want to stay there. This should help with whatever decision she makes. I also called the bank that held the loan on your dad's trawler. I asked them if they wanted a trawler or the cash. Of course, they want the cash, so as soon as the AHTU or the AHTTF releases it, there's a buyer for it in Greece. You can thank your boss for that one."

"My boss? Roman Jones?"

"Yeah. He and I discussed the trawler, and he wanted to help. Because of his connections, he found someone to buy it. Roman also wanted you to know there's a job waiting for you at World Charities whenever you're ready. A fulltime paying job. That's if you want it?"

"Oh, aye, that's grand news!"

"Anyway, your mom won't get much for the trawler, mainly because your dad owed too much money on it. But she'll get a small amount back. With this check and what she'll get from the trawler, she'll be okay."

"Aye, she will. I canna think what ta say," Chris said, amazed. "Thankin' ya seems too small a word for all ya've done for me and my ma. But it's all I have ta offer. So thank ya kindly for this."

Clay held out his hand to Chris. "There are no words to express how grateful I am that you were there for my sister. If you ever make it to California, look us up. Oh, and I gave your mother my business card. Don't hesitate to use it if either of you need anything."

"Thank ya, I will. I have ta go—my ma's waitin'. Take care of yerself, Kayla, and you too, Clay."

Backing up, Chris nodded his head in appreciation to Clay and Kayla before he turned and jogged toward the elevator. He and his mother waved at them as the doors closed. Clay picked up Kayla's suitcase, took his sister's hand, and headed for the elevator. Emer walked beside them and glanced up at Clay.

"What is it, Emer? I can tell you want to ask me something."

"Not ask. Tell you something."

"Which is?"

"You're very kind."

Kayla looked at her brother with admiration and agreed, "He has his moments. How much money did you give him?"

"Not much."

"Your brother donated a large sum to a charity that finds missing children."

That information stopped Kayla dead in her tracks. She looked worried and asked, "Because of me?"

"Listen, it's only money. I can go home and make the money back in…well, never mind. Just know I'm not broke, and I would have sold my business if it would have brought you home."

Kayla threw her arms around his waist and squeezed him tight. Clay dropped the suitcase and wrapped both arms around her and kissed the top of her head. "I'm so sorry for all the heartache I've caused you. Thank you for coming to find me." She lifted her head and looked up at him with tears streaming down her face. "I love you."

Clay drew her closer to him. "Sis, you're all I have left. I had to come. I love you too. Now come on; if we keep this up, we'll never get outta here and Emer needs to get back to work."

Noah was waiting for them downstairs. As they approached, he reached for the suitcase. "Here, let me take that. The car's just outside. I called Ian, and he said their house is ready for all of us. I told them I could get a hotel, but he wouldn't hear of it. Are you okay with me staying another day?"

Holding both Kayla's and Emer's hands, Clay grinned at his friend and announced, "If you can get us through that mob outside, then you can move in with me permanently!"

Noah laughed. "Then you better follow me. The car's out back. The media is as thick as locusts out front."

Clay did an about-face with the women in tow and followed Noah down the hall and through the back of the hospital. When they stepped outside, the cool air hit them, but it didn't slow them down. Clay opened the car door for his sister and Emer and shut it once they were in.

Looking over the top of the car at Noah, Clay offered, "I know a lot of terrible things have happened, but having my sister back is a miracle. Part of me feels guilty for being so happy and the other doesn't. Is that wrong?"

Noah gave an understanding nod. "Don't feel guilty for having your sister back. Miracles are a beautiful thing to see, and it's okay to be happy to have Kayla back. As it for Mrs. Dunne and Claire's family. Remember, a lot of good came out of this horrible mess."

"You're right." Clay did a light drumroll on the top of the car and added, "Let's go and get these ladies home."

CHAPTER 12

It had rained most of the day, which only added to the prison's eeriness. Once he was inside, Clay didn't think it was too bad. Not until the prison guard led him through a series of mechanical doors and barred gates that slid opened each time a loud buzzer went off. Once through a barrier, a door or gate would close with a loud clanging noise before the next one would open.

Clay knew he could never survive in prison and was glad he had chosen the life that he had. Being a criminal and living in the shadows was no way to live, especially knowing there were places like this, waiting to house those who got caught. No, he liked his boring life and couldn't wait to get back home to it.

The last barred gate he went through opened to a hall with several iron doors, each with a small window. The guard took Clay to the last door at the end of the hall, waited for the electronic lock to be released, and then opened it for him. When he walked into the room, he saw Anthony in handcuffs, sitting at a small table. The Irishman had to lift both hands to wave at him.

"Howya, Clay! It's good o' ya ta come."

"Yeah, well, you'll have to thank Kate for that. She's the one that pulled all the strings to get me in to see you." Clay took the only other chair at the table and sat down.

"Aye, I'll tell her. She's comin' in later today ta see me. I wanted ta tell ya that I know what I done was wrong and I'm willin' ta pay for my crimes. And thank ya for givin' me yer Bible. It was the best gift ever given ta me."

Relaxing a little, Clay said, "Listen, I told you that God would forgive you, even if I didn't." He paused for a moment and then offered, "Kayla and I had a long talk about you when Kate told me you wanted to see me. I want you to know we both forgive you for any part you had in Kayla's abduction. It's hard to imagine that either of us can forgive anyone who sold girls for a living, but there you have it. We forgive you."

Anthony put his head down and wiped his eyes. "I thank ya, Clay. Tell yer sister I send my thanks, would ya? And I want ya both ta know I'm givin' Kate everything she asks for, and more. I have names, places, countries, and I even know where most of the money is. I kept a ledger of it all. I'm not askin' for a deal either, I want ya ta know—I'm givin' it freely to the authorities."

"You know Gallagher will have you killed," Clay said, with a quizzical look.

"Oh, aye, I do. He's the devil if there ever was one. He'll die for his crimes too. I'll see to it." Then with a slight laugh, he added, "Auch, no, who am I kiddin'. God will see to it that the man gets his due justice. I'll just be the tool used ta see that it happens. Givin' my life ta Christ was a grand gift ya gave me. I'll never forget ya because of it."

"It's a gift from God, not me, but you're welcome."

"Aye, it's true, but just the same, thanks." Anthony took a moment and then asked, "I've a favor ta ask ya, Clay, knowin' ya owe me nothin'."

"Sure, what is it?"

"The director of the, eh…" Anthony stopped. "I canna remember the letters of the task force."

"AHTU? Kate?"

"Yeah, that's it. The director told me you're startin' a charity, one that will link ta other charities ta fight against human traffickin'. Would ya mind much ta add Alison's name to it? Ya know, in honor of her. So her kids will know their ma was a kind woman?"

Clay smiled and offered, "I was going to name it after my friend, Eddie. He died helping my sister, but I know he wouldn't like me drawing attention to his name. So yeah, I'll call it the Alison O'Kelly Foundation Against Human Trafficking."

Anthony's body shook as he wept. Clay's heart went out to him. His sister was dead because he worked with Brian Gallagher.

Thankfully, his nieces and nephew had been found at a neighbor's house. Alison's quick thinking saved her children when the home invasion happened, and they were able to run to safety. However, now they were without a mother and father because of the choices Anthony had made. He would have to live with that for the rest of his life.

Clay reached over the table and took Anthony's hands. The guard moved toward him, but he quickly explained, "I'm only going to hold his hands so we can pray."

The guard stepped back and watched as the two men bowed their heads. Anthony never let up on the tears while Clay prayed over him and his family. When he stood to leave, Anthony looked up at him, mouthing, "Thank you."

Smiling at the Irishman, he offered a parting quote from the Bible: "Forgive, and you will be forgiven."[6]

With those last words, Clay headed for the door. It unlocked, and the guard held it open for him as he walked out. Down the long hallway, toward the first round of barred gates, Clay took one last look over his shoulder. The gate slid open, and he stepped through. The sound of it sliding shut behind him sent a chill down his spine. He was never so happy to leave a place in his life as he was then.

Connor had been waiting for him in the parking lot when he came out of the building. "Not a pleasant place ta be, is it?"

"No, it's not."

They opened their doors at the same time and got in. Connor started the car and pulled out of the parking lot as Clay glanced at the side mirror. The tension in his body disappeared as he watched the prison get smaller. "Thanks for being my chauffeur today. Driving through Dublin would have been a nightmare for me."

"Glad ta do it. The next bit won't easy but should be quick."

Clay only nodded that he understood.

Their next stop was Eddie's apartment. Billy had asked Clay if he would mind giving him a hand with Eddie's things. Since he had to be in Dublin to meet with Anthony, he agreed to help. He and

---

[6]   Luke 6:37 (NIV).

Kayla wouldn't be heading home until after Eddie's funeral, and he wanted to help in any capacity he could. He hoped this job would be easier than the visit he had just had with Anthony.

Even though Eddie had made his home on the west side of the city, Clay remembered how much he had loved the Irish countryside. Not knowing if Eddie had family back home in Chicago, he offered to pay the funeral expenses.

Ian and Mary wanted to help, so Clay let them pick the perfect place to bury his friend. The couple told him about a cemetery near them that was in the plush hills of Ireland's countryside, and Mary promised she would tend to all the details. Clay was grateful for her and Ian's help. With all the funeral arrangements taken care of, the only thing left to do for Eddie was to box up all his stuff.

*   *   *   *   *

It took Connor thirty minutes to drive to Eddie's apartment from the prison. He pulled into a parking space and both men got out. Connor pointed to the building in front of them. "Eddie's flat is just up the stairs. Billy's already there."

"Great."

Clay followed Connor upstairs, taking two steps at a time. At the top of the landing there was a single apartment door. It had been left open and the men went in without knocking. Neither were prepared for what they saw. A surprised whistle came from Clay as he entered the small apartment. Whatever he had been thinking he would find; this wasn't even close to it.

Maps and pictures covered one entire wall. Each picture, mostly of men, had a piece of paper attached to it, full of information about that person. Included were photos of various properties and buildings with arrows made with a marker going from each picture to a place on the map. There were images of fishing vessels and even a photograph of Alison O'Kelly's River Liffey Boat Cruises tacked to the wall.

The kitchen table had open files scattered across the top of it, along with pads of paper with Eddie's thoughts written on them.

Each file had detailed information dedicated to one person. At the end of the table, neatly stacked files had the word *home* written across the front of them in big bold letters. Clay picked up two pictures he found lying on top of the messy table. The two eight-by-ten photos were of Brian Gallagher and Allister.

"I know. I was just as surprised as you look."

Clay glanced over at Billy and then back at the pictures. "What is this?"

"I don't know. But I called Kate because Eddie has a lot of leads here. I mean, he has stuff on people I've never even heard of. I figured Kate has the manpower to go through all these files. I counted twenty-seven boxes, all filled with folders just like these. There's one box filled with intel on a Saudi family, Ali and Omari something. I've forgotten their last name. And of course, there are several boxes full of intel on the Gallagher family. Eddie never said a word to me about any of this, and he and I were good friends."

Connor took a quick peek inside the bedroom before he went in. Glancing around the room, he found more maps and photographs of men tacked to the wall. One picture, in particular, caught his attention. He pulled it from the wall and pointed at it, hitting the photo several times as he did. "I know this face! It's Oslo or Olsen or something like that."

"Olsen Popova." Billy came in and took the picture from Connor. "He's one slippery dude. He's part of the Ukrainian mob."

While studying the bedroom wall, Clay remembered something. "Didn't Kate say she had a Ukrainian in custody?"

Both Billy and Connor looked at Clay and answered, "Yeah."

Billy pulled out his phone, as did Connor. The men went in opposite directions so they wouldn't talk over one another. Clay didn't want to eavesdrop on either conversation, so instead, he browsed through all the news clippings he found tacked up on another wall. Scanning them, he realized the articles were about missing girls. Some clippings were ten years old, if not older.

He took down the one in the center of all the other news clippings and read it. It was an article from a local Irish newspaper. The story was similar to Kayla's, down to the young woman's brother coming to Ireland looking for her. Her name was Tina, seventeen years old, from Chicago. She was Eddie's sister. Surprised by his find, Clay did the numbers in his head; she would be thirty-two now. When Billy came back into the room, Clay said, "This is Eddie's sister, Tina."

Billy took the clipping and looked at it. "Yeah, she was his life's work. She's the reason he worked so hard to find other girls. I'm only guessing, but I think in his hunt for her, he stumbled onto all this. Some of these girls we worked on together. Some we found, others we didn't. But it looks like he never gave up on any of them."

Clay heard him but was focusing on the article about Tina. "Billy, I don't want her forgotten. You need to find her."

"Whoa there, buddy! Don't you think we've tried?"

"Yeah, listen, I'm sorry. I know you both did. However, that was before you had Gallagher. Anthony told me today that he has a ledger with all the details of where Gallagher has his money, where he sent the girls, and all the people involved in Gallagher's organization. That, with all of this, should help you find her."

Billy took in a deep breath and sighed. "I don't know. There are so many fresh leads of other girls to follow, this would only take away from finding them."

"I understand you still have to look for the young woman that brought you here to Ireland, and I'm sorry she wasn't among those already found. But who knows, something here might lead Kate to her, leaving you free to focus on Tina."

"Man, I don't know. That's a leap—"

"Well, Patrick and the lads are on their way ta help," Connor chimed in. "It's the least we can do for the man after he gave his life for the cause."

"Okay. Kate said not to touch anything. She's on her way. When I mentioned Olsen Popova, she went nuts. She's gathering a team and will be here within the hour."

*   *   *   *   *

Kate and her agents arrived thirty-five minutes later. Having Yegor, one of Olsen Popova's men, in custody was huge for Kate, and she couldn't believe her luck. She was coming around to Clay's belief that it was Divine Providence—God's intervention—that was clearing the path for her and her agents. Everything seemed to just fall into her lap.

"I can't believe this," she said. "You never knew he had all these files?"

Billy glanced around the room one more time before he answered, "No, I didn't have a clue. Do you think any of this is useful?"

"Are you kidding! His file on Olsen Popova is thicker than mine, and I thought mine was thorough. Interpol barely has a file on him."

"How did Eddie live?"

Confused by Clay's question, Billy asked, "What?"

"I mean, how did Eddie make a living while he lived here?"

"He worked with me finding girls, and I split the reward money with him if there was any, or he got paid by the charity. But as you can see for yourself, he lived a frugal life. There's nothing expensive in this place."

Clay agreed. There was nothing personal in the apartment either. Everything he was looking at in the room was there for one reason only—to find abducted girls. "Weird. Eddie and my story are almost identical." Then facing Kate, he said, "Listen, something doesn't feel right. Allister shot Eddie—Kayla and Claire said he did. My sister told me that Allister killed him only after he said something to Eddie. What was it that Allister said to him? I mean, he didn't kill Chris. Was he planning to sell him? If Allister could have sold Chris, he could have sold Eddie too. You even said traffickers will sell men, just not as often. I mean, he could've sold them for their organs if nothing else, right?"

"Yes, that's true. What are you getting at?"

"Do you think Allister knew who Eddie was all along and just played dumb when he showed up at Brian Gallagher's house? I remembered something that Allister said to his men when they dumped me on the side of the road. He told Craig and the other guy not to mention my being here to Gallagher. Why? Why didn't he just kill me instead of beating me up?"

Kate looked at him quizzically. "You think, in Allister's sick mind, he wanted to keep you alive to torment you over your sister's abduction? You think he was doing that to Eddie?"

"A few years ago, a California couple got attacked in Paris, and the men that assaulted them took their two young girls. Does anyone here remember that story?"

Connor snapped his fingers several times while saying, "Yeah, yeah, yeah! It was that Popova guy! He supposedly snatched the Americans comin' out of a restaurant. Even told the da, 'I want you ta live the rest of your life knowin' what's gonna happen ta your girls.' His men proceeded ta rape the wife, right in front of him and their daughters. This Popova guy is one depraved individual."

"That's the family! Listen, Allister could have done the same. I mean, apparently, there's some connection between him and this Popova guy. Allister left Eddie and me alive because he knew we would never give up looking for our sisters. Eddie's and my stories are identical, right down to my coming to Ireland to look for Kayla. Eddie even told me he had gotten beat up for his efforts just like I did."

"Right, I get that, but why do it if you know you're going to sell the girls anyway? There's no reason to make Eddie suffer unless Allister had his sister close." Kate stared at Clay as if he had the answer to her question written across his forehead.

"My point exactly!"

"So you think Allister has had her all this time, and he knew that Eddie never left Ireland?"

"My guess is, Allister knew where Eddie lived. That way he could make calls or send pictures to him every now and then, just so he could keep twisting the knife already left in Eddie's back."

"This is still all speculative."

"Okay, so just hear me out for a minute. I come to Ireland and in less than five days my search leads me right to Allister. I come along and Eddie drops everything to help me find Kayla. I mean, look at this place, Kate." Clay pointed to a picture of the Alison's River

Liffey Tour Company. "Eddie knew about Anthony McCormick's connection to Gallagher. I mean, I hate to state the obvious, but you didn't even know about his sister's tour boats involvement. Eddie was getting close."

Nodding her head, Kate said, "True. Go on, I'm listening."

"I think he finally figured out that his sister never left Ireland. With all the dead end leads he followed, he must have realized someone was pulling his strings to keep him going in circles. I think Allister kept Tina close so he could taunt Eddie. Not killing me was Allister's greatest mistake. Kayla was a fresh lead that led straight to Tina. I don't think Eddie or Allister understood just how close Eddie was until they were standing face-to-face in Brian Gallagher's living room."

"You think Allister recognized Eddie?"

"I think they knew who the other was, maybe not personally, but Allister and Eddie most definitely recognized each other. Look at all the boxes around here that have Brian Gallagher's name on them." Clay picked up Allister's eight-by-ten glossy and held it up to Kate. "How could they not be aware of who each other was?"

"Kate, you've got to get inside Allister's head somehow," Billy begged. "The psycho must've gotten a lot of satisfaction from knowing Eddie was still in Ireland looking for his sister. The guy is certifiable! He more than likely had tabs on him, you know, so the nutcase could keep twisting the knife in Eddie's back. Then, in walks Clay, another American, looking for his sister. Allister probably thought he could toy with him the same way he did with Eddie. The only difference this time was that Derrick, the idiot that he was, hand delivers Eddie to Allister at Brian Gallagher's house."

"Also," Clay interjected. "Derrick took Kayla to Brian Gallagher, and then I came looking for her. Everyone at the bar said they saw Kayla with Derrick and that she left with him. When I arrived, the police had told me that my sister more than likely wasn't in Ireland anymore, and rightly so. It took me four days to get to Dublin. That was more than enough time to get her out of the country. But that didn't stop me, I still went around asking about Kayla. Which begs the question, why was my sister still in Ireland? Did Allister like the idea of playing cat and mouse with me too? When I got close, Allister ordered Derrick, Craig and this other guy to beat the ever-living daylights out of me and dumped me on the side of the road."

"Aye, it's all a game to Allister," Patrick added. "I'm seeing a sparkle of light here Kate. Maybe when Allister saw Eddie standing in Brian Gallagher's house, he knew his theatrics had caught up to him. He had to get rid of Eddie. My bet is, he didn't do it without saying something to him about Tina first. I'd bet my life on it—Allister knows where Tina has been this whole time."

Kate gave some consideration to what the men said. Then, looking at Billy, she explained, "He's not talking. He wants a deal and I'm not willing to give him one."

"Can ya give the man a bread crumb?" Connor asked. "Have him give ya somethin' ta prove he's an honest bloke. Ask him about Tina's whereabouts and if she's where he says she is, give the man a crumb and nothin' more."

Kate folded her arms and regarded Connor. Then, glancing at Billy and Clay, she said, "Yeah, maybe I can. But just so you know, the man's not much into chitchatting. I'm not sure how to get him to open up."

"Then let me talk to him," Clay offered.

"That's out of the question!"

"Why? He didn't kill me, and in his sick, depraved mind, he wanted me to suffer the same way he made Eddie."

"Absolutely not! However, I know the perfect person to have speak to him. She'll surely have his knickers in a bind." All three men looked puzzled. Kate, please with her choice, announced, "Claire. He thinks she's dead. I haven't had time to enlighten him about her and Kayla's survival.

CHAPTER 13

It was midafternoon when Claire arrived at Allister's holding cell. She had done several interrogations with harden criminals before, but today would be her hardest. When Kate had asked if she would do it, every fiber of her being screamed "No!" but she loved her job, and she wanted to get back to work. Doing this for Kate would not only prove to her boss she was ready, but also to herself.

As she walked through the prison, the memory of Allister's foul breath and coarse hands touching her bare skin filled her mind. She bit her bottom lip hard in an effort to push the repulsive memory away. Each step taken, had to be forced, but she never faltered as she fought to control her emotions.

The only audible sound heard were heels clicking down the hall with intent. Hearing he had a visitor, Allister sat up from his cot and waited for the person to come into view. If Claire's sudden resurrection surprised Allister, he didn't show it.

However, any anxiety she had prior to coming face-to-face with the man who'd raped her had been replaced with fierce arousal from the inner most depths of her soul and with it, a strong, unwavering force. There was contempt in her voice when she said, "Hello, Allister. I bet I'm the last person you expected to see again."

"Alive but not without damage." She heard the spiteful snickering in his voice, which made the hair on her neck stand on end. "Ya remember the small party we had, don't ya, lass? I quite enjoyed it."

"You mean the part where you raped me? Oh, yeah, I remember it very well. So do Kayla and Chris." Allister flinched when she mentioned their names. "From the look on your face, you hadn't heard they survived too? Chris is a powerful swimmer and swam his heart out, getting Kayla and me to shore. Kate had everyone searching for us and thankfully, someone found us pretty quick—fast enough that I still have all my fingers and toes." She held up her hands and wiggled her fingers for him to see.

A guard placed a chair next to Claire and stepped away. She thanked him and sat down. Allister's lips curled into a taunting grin as he stood and leaned into the bars with his arms draped through them. "Ya miss me, do ya, lass? Want ta reminisce about our night together? Oh, aye, you're quite the beauty. I'll enjoy havin' your company for a wee bit. It gets a bit lonely down here."

"You know, I was worried about that. I think the general population will be good for you, especially when Gallagher finds out what you did."

With a sinister grin, Allister said, "All I've ever done is protect the man. I have nothin' ta fear from him."

"Huh. Eddie was a huge mistake, wasn't he?" Claire leaned forward with her elbows on her knees in complete control. "And Clay too. You should've killed them both, but you didn't. Why was that? Do you have a rare sickness when it comes to Yanks? Or are you just sadistic? You made Eddie suffer fifteen years over the loss of his sister, Tina. Were you hoping to do the same to Clay?"

Allister's expression went from surprise to anger very quickly, and he slapped both hands hard on the cell bars before taking a step back. Claire had him and didn't stop. "That's right, Allister, you keep that mouth of yours closed tight. Gallagher will cut your tongue out himself and cram it down your throat for toying with both men. That game you played with Eddie and Clay ended up taking down Brian Gallagher's entire empire. Maybe you need to be reminded that we have Anthony, and because of him, we now have Brian's money—all of it! From every country he had it stashed in, the AHTTF now has it all. They had it wired back to Ireland, you see." Claire leaned back in her seat and added, "Kate plans on using it to fight against human trafficking. She has it because of your sick mind and the need to play games with the Americans."

"You're bluffing!"

"Am I?" Any mistrust Claire had in her ability to confront Allister was long gone. It was as if she had an imaginary noose around his neck, and she was controlling his air flow. The power she felt over him was exhilarating and her next words she hoped would be a powerful blow to his psyche. "Kate's doing the paperwork as we speak. You'll be in the same cell block with Brian Gallagher by nightfall. Let me enlighten just a wee bit. When I'm done here, I'm off to see the man and get him up to date on your idiotic plan. I'm sure he'll find it all very interesting. How does it feel? I'm only offering you what you offered me. Only, I think Gallagher will succeed at killing you."

"Make a deal with me! I'll give ya more than Anthony can."

"Give me Tina."

Allister looked troubled by her request and shook his head.

"Give me Eddie's sister, Tina! I know you know where she is."

He shook his head again and, this time, yelled, "No!"

"You know where she is. You wanted Eddie to suffer, and you couldn't do that if you sold her to the highest bidder. She was a real treasure of pain that you could inflict on Eddie whenever you wanted. When you whispered in Eddie's ear right before you shot him, you told him, didn't you? You told him about Tina. I saw the look on his face right before you shot him. Where's Tina, Allister?"

"Aye, I do, but ya canna have 'er." His voice was an odd mixture of anger and sadness.

Claire eyed him for a moment and then asked, "Why not? She's still alive. I know she is. Wait. You've gone and fallen in love with her, haven't you?" Claire shot out of her chair in complete defiance and took a step toward his cell. "Oh, my word! You've a warped and depraved mind. What was it you told Eddie just before you killed him?"

Allister's eyes bore into Claire with such hatred, that she had to fight the urge to step back. Then, without warning, he yelled. "Yes, she's alive!"

A rush of adrenaline shot through her body and it was all she could do to keep both feet on the ground. With renewed confidence, she repeated her question, "Where is she?"

His lips twisted and curled into a devilish grin. "You want ta know what I told 'im?" He leaned into the bars so Claire could see him better, and without so much as a flinch, he said, "I told 'im his sister was the mother of my children."

Totally taken by surprise, Claire yelled, "She's what?"

The howl of laughter he bellowed reverberated through the hall. Claire's chest tightened and her body flushed with heat. Allister had opened the gates of hell and this time she couldn't control her emotions, which only added to his enjoyment. When he finally quit laughing, he added, "She's the mother of my children, lass! For fifteen years I've bedded her. She stays with me because of 'em. We've five wee ones. If she ever left me, she knew I'd kill 'em, and her too."

Horrified, Claire stuttered, "You've…you've had her here…in Dublin…this entire time? What a sick twisted pervert!"

Allister was enjoying himself. "Oh, aye, lass. Call me what ya like, but she's been my pleasure for quite some time. Kayla was my next conquest, until that eejit, Derrick, brought you and Eddie ta Gallagher's place!"

A sour taste filled Claire's mouth as her face paled. Allister had gotten inside her head, and he knew it. She didn't care and screamed at him, "Where is she, Allister?"

"I'll not say without a deal." An eerie calm washed over him, causing her nerves to unsettle again and made her take a step back from his cell. Allister leaned into the bars again and calmly repeated, "I'll not say without a deal."

Furious now for letting him get to her, she bellowed, "The only deal you'll get is the one that has you in general population where Gallagher can reach you if you don't tell me where you have her!"

Allister's face went near purple this time and spittle spewed from his mouth when he yelled back, "I'll nae tell ya, if ya threaten me with that again! Now make me a deal!"

Taking him by complete surprise, Kate casually stepped out of the shadows and greeted Allister with an authoritative poise. She touched Claire on the shoulder when she did and said, "I'll take it from here. Thank you." Then, eyeing Allister she offered, "This is what I'm willing to offer you. Until your trial, you'll stay in isolation, I'll give you two hours of park time, alone, every day—one in the morning and then again in the late afternoon. I will allow you access to reading material, nothing violent or sexual of course, and movies with a G rating, and on Sunday, I'll allow you to choose your evening meal. That's it."

"You call that a deal? I want visits, and I want my choice of prison."

"No visits. Besides, you don't have any friends."

"I've a boy, fourteen. I want ta see 'im."

"No! Absolutely not."

"A visit with the boy, or no deal."

Kate glared at him for a moment and then said, "Okay, but only if he wants to see you. And it's a one-time visit, and that's it!"

Agreeing to the terms, he reluctantly gave Kate the address. The second she was out of Allister's earshot, Kate was on the phone to Patrick. Once outside, both women ran to the car and got in. The director gave the driver the address and then was on her phone again, barking out more orders. When she ended the last call, she put the phone in her pocket and faced Claire. "You were brilliant in there. Thank you."

Placing her hand over her stomach, Claire said, "Thanks for letting me do it. But I um…I allowed him to get inside my head. I'm sorry about that."

"Interrogations are hard when you have a personal connection to the person you're interrogating." Kate's expression softened, and she gave Claire a reassuring smile. "I shouldn't have let you go in, but I knew once Allister saw you, he would open up. It had to be either you or Clay, and I would never allow Clay anywhere near him. With that said, had I known everything, Claire, I wouldn't have let you in to see him either. Why did you leave the part about your being raped out of your report?"

"I didn't leave it out, I just didn't point it out," she answered, shifting in her seat and looking out her window.

Upset by her casualness, Kate said, "Does your therapist know?"

"You mean the shrink? Yes, she does." Claire's posture straightened while making eye contact with her boss. "I'm doing everything that's required of me to get back to work. I can't cry anymore over what Allister did to me. Yes, that disgusting pig raped me and I'm working through that…" A chill swept through Claire's body, causing her goose bumps. She rubbed her arm in an effort to get rid of them. With a frustrated sigh, she said, "Believe me when I say the horror I felt when Chris knocked Kayla and me overboard left me with night terrors of drowning. I don't even like swimming in pools!"

Taken aback, Kate stared at her. Claire was sure her boss didn't know if she should laugh or cry. Being raped, as horrible as it was, wasn't the only thing she had to deal with. Her thoughts not only tormented her with the rape, but also with Eddie's death and her near-drowning experience. She was grateful Kate said nothing more about it. Instead, her boss shared, "Patrick and his team will meet us at the address Allister gave us."

Happy the focus was no longer on her, she said, "The address… I recognized it. It was one that Eddie had marked in the file he had on Allister. I saw it when I helped go through the folders at the office."

"Yes, it is. Eddie was so close—just inches away from finding Tina. It's very sad, really."

"It is," Claire agreed. "If he had come to us with all his findings, I can't help but think Gallagher and Allister would have been in prison a long time ago."

"True, but he was a meticulous man, and though he had a lot of information, he couldn't tie the pieces together. If he didn't tell Billy about what he had, he must not have felt he had enough evidence."

"That, or maybe he was afraid Billy would think he was crazy." Claire let out a heavy sigh and then looked at Kate. "Is Clay going to meet us at Allister's place?"

"Yes, he is. I asked Patrick to bring him. That boy has a head for law enforcement, I'll give him that."

"Kayla said he works with computers, or some kind of computer imaging for hospital equipment. He's rich."

"Yeah, I know. I did a background check on him. You wouldn't know that he's wealthy, not the way he acts around people or cares for them. I like—"

"We have company, Director!" the driver said nervously as he looked at the rearview mirror.

Two black Land Rovers pulled up fast alongside the car. It frightened both Kate and Claire until they saw Connor grinning and waving at them. Then, just as fast, he and the other vehicle slowed down and fell in behind them.

"Connor! Criminy, he scared me. Remind me to yell at him later," Kate said, placing her hand over her heart. Claire just laughed, even though it had frightened her too.

"Who's in the other car?" Claire asked.

"Gerard was in the passenger seat, so my guest is the rest of Patrick's team."

Nothing more was said, and Kate's driver drove as fast as he could through Dublin's city streets. It wasn't until he had the car on the motorway that he was able to pick up speed. The two Land Rovers kept a tight tail behind him, mimicking his every move.

*   *   *   *   *

Allister's property was twenty minutes southwest of Dublin. When they arrived, the gate was wide open. Because of it, the driver maneuvered the car onto the estate with a great deal of caution. He followed the road that led to an old-fashioned cottage.

"I can't believe this is it," Kate said, surprised. "Knowing Allister's demented mind, I would have never thought him capable of owning such a place. I was leaning more toward some dark creepy hole in the wall, but this…it's too beautiful and inviting to be his."

"My thoughts too," Claire said in complete astonishment.

Three barking dogs ran up to the vehicles, doing their jobs announcing their arrival. A young teenager ran out of the house, calling the dogs back. When he saw the strange men with the guns, he ran back inside. A few seconds later an attractive young woman, in her early thirties, came out, holding a toddler. She handed the child to her son and ushered him back inside. There was a brief argument, and then the young teen did as he was told.

Billy, Clay, and Kate walked toward the woman together. Clay held out his hand and introduced himself, then Kate and Billy.

"Are you Tina?" he asked.

"Yes."

"Do you have a brother named Eddie?"

Both hands went up to her face, covering her mouth. Tears welled up in her eyes. With a shaky, muffled voice, she cried out, "Yes! Please, no! Please, don't tell me Allister finally did it? He killed him, didn't he?"

"I'm sorry, Tina," Clay answered.

Tina grabbed a fist full of Clay's dress shirt and jacket and cried. He held her and could almost feel her pain as she trembled in his arms. She stayed pressed against him for a few minutes. Kate and Billy let her have the time she needed to come to terms with the news that her brother was dead. When she finally let go, she asked, "How did he die?"

"He died saving my sister."

Confused by his answer, she asked, "Saving your sister? From Allister?"

"Yes, from him and his boss, Brian Gallagher," Kate replied.

Tina had a hard time breathing. She walked over to a bench facing the garden and sat down. Clay followed and sat beside her. Patrick and Billy fell in behind Kate and stood quietly while they listened.

"Eddie never gave up looking for you. You were his life's mission, and while searching for you, he helped countless other young women find their way home. My sister being one of the them." Clay's voice was compassionate, but when he reached out to her, she pulled away. Realizing his mistake, he dropped his hand and offered, "Sorry. You have nothing to fear from us, and I'm sorry we're having to tell you about your brother. Allister must have recognized him right away. I think your brother knew that his coming face-to-face with Allister put him on borrowed time."

Tina cried. This time her body shook so hard that Clay was sure she would rattle him right off the bench. When he put his arm around her this time she didn't flinch and let him.

Through bouts of tears, Tina asked, "Where's Allister?"

Billy knelt down in front of her and answered, "In jail, waiting for trial." With moisture filling his eyes, he paused momentarily and took in a deep breath. Then he added, "Your brother and I were good friends. He and I worked on a lot of cases together. Eddie had a huge role in taking down Brian Gallagher and Allister. Both men will rot in prison for their crimes. Kate, here, will see to it."

Genuinely grateful to hear that, she wiped her eyes and said, "Thank you."

"When was the last time you saw Allister?" Patrick asked.

"Um, he hasn't been here in weeks. He has this place wired with cameras and sensors, so he knows my every move. Two weeks ago, all of his security left without a word. They just disappeared. I knew Allister was still watching us though because he called to remind me that he was."

"I spotted a few cameras when we drove up," Patrick offered.

"Well, he's not watching now," Kate stated. "Most of Gallagher's men have been caught, and those that haven't are on the run."

"You need to understand, Gallagher's men are not Allister's men. He had his own little realm, or kingdom if you like, that Gallagher knew nothing about."

This surprised everyone. "Gallagher didn't know about you?" Kate asked.

"Oh, no! Gallagher was all about his business and family. His men were loyal to him, and he only allowed them whores, nothing permanent like a family. He had a woman killed because one of his top men fell in love with her and talked about getting married."

"That shouldn't surprise me, but it does," Kate stated. "How did you find out?"

Tina eyed Kate. "Allister happily shared it with me, even bragged about being the one to have killed her. It was his way of reminding me what he could do to me. So you have to believe me when I say the children and I were his best kept secret, along with this place. The men he hired to watch over us, he paid—not Gallagher. And they were all very loyal to him."

Clay got up from the bench and walked around for a few seconds before he stopped next to Kate. "Two weeks ago? Didn't you arrest Gallagher then?"

"Yes, I did."

"Wasn't that also around the same time Allister started his rampage and began killing everyone, trying to tie up loose ends?"

"Yes, it was." Kate was listening but still not following Clay's thoughts.

"If he had killed Anthony and Craig, there wouldn't have been anyone to point the finger at him. Allister was set to take over Gallagher's organization, I'll bet you anything. He almost succeeded."

Glancing down at Tina, Clay realized her mind was someplace else. Then, in a near whisper, he heard her say, "I saw Eddie once."

Stunned, Clay didn't know what to say and just stared at her. It was Kate that asked, "Come again?"

Tina wiped her eyes. "Yeah. It was about a year ago. Allister told me he was living here in Ireland." She sat up straight, sniffling back her tears. "I guess I should explain. One day, my oldest child, Sam, started asking questions as to why I couldn't go out. That's when I told him the truth about his dad. Sam's a good boy and loves me very much. When Sam confronted his father about it, Allister decided it was time for Sam to learn the family business. He thought he could turn Sam into the monster that he was."

Tina took a moment to catch her breath. She glanced up at the three men and then at Kate. It was clear the young woman's nerves were unraveling. No one attempted to console her this time, instead they gave her the few seconds she needed to calm down.

"My boy," she continued while rubbing her hands together, "came home crying after his first night out with his father. Allister beat me severely that night because of it. I thought I was going to die. After that, Sam never cried again and with every outing, he hated his father even more. After I healed, Allister took me somewhere in Dublin, and we sat in the car for hours. That's when I saw Eddie. He was walking down the street, smiling, like he didn't have a care in the world. Allister told me he would kill my brother if I ever left him or said another word to the children about him. That day I swore an oath to myself that I would protect my brother, and I never spoke to the children about their father again."

A commotion coming from the house made everyone turn to see what was happening. Connor came around the corner, dragging

Sam with him. Tina shot up from the bench and begged, "Please, he's no harm to anyone!"

"Claire's inside tending to the other children. This one had a gun. We thought he might shoot us, but it's not loaded."

"Sam, honey, they're here to help," his mother cried while reaching for him.

"Da will see them!" The teenager ashen face trembled with fear and anger as he yelled. "He'll kill you because they're here. I won't let him hurt you. Not ever!"

"Your father's in prison, and he'll never hurt anyone again," Kate assured him.

Connor freed the teenager, and he ran to his mother. She wrapped her arms around him. "It'll be okay, son, I promise. That evil monster will never drag you out on another job, or hurt me, ever again." Tina glanced over at Kate and asked, "Do you mind if we go inside? I'll make some tea and coffee, if anyone cares for some?"

"That would be lovely, but before we go in, do you know if your husband—"

Tina froze in place while facing Kate. Her jaw tightened and eyes narrowed as they locked on to the director's. "Let me be very clear. Allister was not my husband! He raped, drugged, and beat me every day during that first year. And believe me when I say I fought hard against him. Once I found out I was pregnant with Sam, I stopped fighting and let him have his way with me. After Sam was born, I fought him again, but instead of lashing out at me, he went after my son. So whatever ill, misconceived notion you have of my life here, please understand, there may not be any bars keeping me in, but make no mistake, I am a prisoner here."

Kate touched Tina's shoulder and offered, "Please forgive me, I'm sorry for my poor choice of words, but can you tell me if you're aware of a workshop or someplace on the property where Allister went, but he never allowed you to go?"

Tina pointed when she spoke. "Do you see those walls that line the fields? Allister never allowed me to go past them, not ever. Whatever lies beyond them, I don't know."

"I do!" Sam shouted when he stepped away from his mother. "Da took me there a bunch of times. He buried a body in one of the fields. I'll show you where."

Not surprised that Allister hid his crimes on his property, Kate asked, "Would you mind showing Patrick and Connor?"

Shrugging his shoulders, the teen answered, "Don't care who I show."

"Harry. Niall. You lads stay vigilant. Gerard you'll come with us," Patrick ordered.

Harry nodded. "Yeah sure, boss, no problem."

Not bothering to tell them to follow—Sam ran toward the back gate. Patrick, Connor, and Gerard had to run to catch up to the young man. Kate watched the men for a few seconds before she continued toward the house.

Billy hollered, "Patrick hold up, I'm coming with you."

Kate waved him on while she followed Clay and Tina inside the house. To all their surprise, the interior was just as welcoming as the exterior. The place was immaculate and charming, almost picturesque. There were no walls separating the kitchen from the dining and living room, making it one large open area. Natural light filtered in through the windows, creating a warm atmosphere. The sweet aroma of something baking only added to its ambiance.

"Wow," Clay said.

Kate added, "Knowing Allister, I can honestly say I'm stunned that he lived here. I wouldn't have thought he had any taste at all. Obviously, Tina, you had a great deal of influence with the decorations."

"He bought this place fourteen years ago, but the renovations took six months to complete. When he moved me here, I had nothing but a mattress. The fact that Allister allowed me any comforts at all surprised even me," Tina explained. "Since I couldn't go furniture shopping, he gave me magazines and catalogs to choose from."

"Well, the place is cozy. I half expected you to be living in some dark, dreary place," Kate added.

"That dark, dreary place…well, it existed every time Allister came home."

Tina's last statement put a halt on the conversation, but not with what Tina was doing. She filled a kettle with water and placed it on the stove. After she turned on the coffeemaker, she took the cups out of the cabinet and set them next to the cream and sugar on the kitchen island.

If Clay had to guess, this was Tina's first time to have guests in her home. Allister probably didn't allow anyone from his world to come here. The house was his very own private fantasy world that he created with her and their children.

Clay watched Tina with curiosity as she worked. She was trying hard not to cry. Not sure what he should do, he asked, "Can I help?"

"Thank you, but no, it's all done. Who would like coffee?"

"I would, thanks," Kate answered.

Clay followed with, "Yeah, that'd be great."

Claire stood up from the couch and said, "I'll have tea, thank you."

Tina pointed to the tea bags that she had set next to the cream and sugar. When the kettle whistled, she offered, "Please, help yourselves."

The atmosphere in the room wasn't jubilant, but everyone's earlier anxieties had evaporated. Clay noticed it. He watched the women make their drinks. Each seemed to be unfazed by the fact they were standing in the same room with a woman that had been missing for fifteen years. It was as if this was just another normal day, hanging out with an old friend. Clay shook his head in awe of them.

"Are you going to stare at us, Clay, or join us?" Kate asked.

"I'm sorry, this seems all so natural to you. I mean, this is Tina!" he said with both hands pointing at her. "Eddie spent the last fifteen years of his life looking for her, and she's been here this entire time."

Kate took a deep satisfying breath and offered, "I know, it doesn't make any sense, does it? These kinds of moments, for me anyway, are very rare. I thought a cup of coffee would help us all ease into it."

Tina bowed her head for a second. When she raised it, tears seeped from her eyes.

"Oh, man, I'm sorry, I didn't mean to make you cry." Forgetting about the coffee and her previous reaction to his touch, Clay took her in his arms in two quick strides. When he was sure she was okay, he took her hands in his and said, "I'm sorry, I'm just having a hard time getting my head around all of this."

"It's okay, believe me, I get it," Tina whispered.

"You understand you're not a prisoner in this house anymore. You and your children are free to come and go as you please."

Slipping her hands from Clay's, she took a step back, wiped her eyes, and tucked a strand of hair behind her ear. "I don't want to doubt you, but I'm too scared to leave, even knowing Allister's not coming back."

"You don't need to worry about anything. I know I'm not your brother, and I would never try to replace him, but you and the kids will be okay. Kate will see to everything here, and where she can't help you, I will. It's the least I can do for Eddie. He was an amazing guy, and if it wasn't for him, I wouldn't have my sister back." Then nodding at Claire, he added, "She's alive because of him, and we can't forget, he led us to you."

Tina covered her face with her hands and wept. This time Kate took her by the shoulders and guided her over to the dining table. Clay pulled out a chair and Tina sat down. Claire set a cup of tea in front of her while Kate took a seat next to her.

"It'll be okay. Clay's right, though. We're here to help. Do you have family back home in America? Anyone that we can call?"

"Yes…I think I still do. My mom and dad, an aunt and cousins." Tina settled down as she thought about her family. Her once vacant eyes now had a glimmer of hope. "I have a cousin, Donna. She and I were like sisters growing up."

"I'll ask Billy if he has any phone numbers," Clay offered. "We were going to bury your brother here in Ireland, but if you think your family would rather have him home, I'll take care of all the arrangements."

"I don't know," she said, honestly.

"No need to worry about that now. We've plenty of time. However, if you think you're up to the task, I need ask you a few questions?"

A toddler came up to her mother with her arms held high. Tina scooped the child into her arms and cuddled her. "Yes, you can ask me anything. I'm just not sure I'll have all the answers."

CHAPTER 14

Tina had a hard time believing she could leave the property where she had been a prisoner for the last fourteen years. It frightened her knowing what Allister would do to her, or the children, if he ever found out they'd left. The only time he allowed her to leave the premises was the day he had taken her to see her brother. That had been over a year ago.

The land and the house that sat in the middle of it had been her sanctuary. As beautiful as both were, they held too many horrible memories—ones she desperately wanted to forget. However, when Allister wasn't home, which was most of the time, she had felt safe there. Driving away, leaving all she knew behind, was terrifying.

When Tina learned her mother and father still lived in the same house in Chicago and even had the same phone number, it surprised her. They were on their way to Ireland to pick her and the kids up and take them back to the United States. She hoped seeing her parents would help make the transition easier for her and the children.

Kate had talked her into leaving Allister's property, accompanied by Clay and Billy. The cottage and the land were now under the AHTTF's control. An extensive search of both would take her agents months to do, rather than weeks.

Clay and Billy had been kind enough to take her and the children to a friend's farm in southern Ireland. Ian and Mary were happy to have them in their home and even fell into the doting grandparent's role with the kids. However, none of it seemed to matter; she couldn't quite shake the fear that Allister had instilled in her. In the back of her mind, she worried he would find her. There was some comfort knowing Clay and Billy were always close by.

Today, that fear was alive and well. Tina was having a hard time relaxing. She sat on a small sofa next to Kayla, in Dr. O'Farrell's apartment, worrying about everything. She glanced over at Kayla, who smiled back at her. That small gesture seemed to melt away some of the tension she was feeling.

She didn't understand her connection to Kayla, but she was sure it had something to do with Allister. The two got along very well, like a sisterly bond or such. Whatever the case, Tina enjoyed being around Kayla, as did all her children.

Their conversations over the last several days had been unrelated to either of their dealings with Allister. But today, Kayla wanted a private word with her, and Emer had offered her apartment, so they could talk without interruption. It was a conversation Tina had been dreading, but she understood the need for it.

"Are you sure your brother can handle all the children?"

"You're kidding, right? He loves kids and will have them spoiled by the end of the day."

With complete admiration, Tina said, "He and Billy have been so kind to me. They've been very protective of my family."

"I hope that doesn't bother you. Clay's been that way ever since my parents died. I'm afraid I've broken his heart more than once in the last few years."

"Is one of those moments when you came here, to Ireland?"

"No. My trip was a gift from my parents. It's just how I acted when I got here."

"Oh."

The words that followed, lacked Kayla's usual eagerness to share what was on her mind. Her movements seemed slow as if she was sinking into herself and away from the rest of the world. When she finally spoke her voice was low, almost inaudible. "I know Clay doesn't blame me for what happened, but he should."

On the verge of crying, Kayla reached for her glass of water, took a sip, and set it back on the table. With nothing more to say, she leaned back on the sofa lost in thought.

"Are you okay?" Tina asked.

"Yeah, I was just thinking, if I hadn't been such a jerk to my friends and gone with Derrick, none of this would've happened."

Tina understood. "Me too. Like you, I went to a pub with school friends. I was the youngest in my group, but they don't card you here, so I didn't have a problem getting in. That's when I met Allister. He took a liking to me right away and kept flirting with me, even after I asked him to leave me alone. Some of my classmates told him to bug off too. A lot of good it did me. He slipped something in my soft drink and somehow separated me from my friends. I don't think they even noticed I was missing. Allister made me pay every day for making a fool of him that night."

Kayla reached over and took Tina's hand while inhaling a deep breath. She let it out slowly before she said, "Um, my brother doesn't know what I'm about to tell you, or at least I don't think he does. I asked the doctors not to say anything to him, but whether they did… well, I was unconscious for a few days while in the hospital, so I just don't know. I'm rambling. Sorry."

Kayla stopped talking and closed her eyes for a moment. Tina understood whatever her friend wanted to share with her, still had to be very raw. When Kayla's eyes opened, they were wet and red. She wiped her face with both hands and barely got out, "I'm sure Emer knows, being a doctor and all, but she hasn't asked me anything about it. So…anyway…anyway, Allister…well, he…he raped me. He slapped me so hard across my face—numerous times. At one point he choked me, and I honestly thought he was going to kill me. Then he…"

"I know." Tina reached for Kayla's hand and said, "He was an evil man. But he can't harm either of us, ever again."

"It's just…" Kayla said as she swallowed. "He told me, when he was lying next to me, that I was soft like his girl, Tina. I thought what a sick pervert, to rape me and then tell me he enjoyed me as much as he did his girlfriend. I felt sorry for her, knowing she was giving herself freely to him, and she knew nothing about him being a rapist."

Tina shook her head in disbelief, but when she spoke, she held her chin up. "Allister has always taken what he wanted. I don't think there's a woman on this planet that has ever given herself freely to him."

"I realize that now, but at the time, I didn't know."

Allister was a disgusting pig, and knowing he had used her name while in bed with another woman made Tina sick to her stomach. The thought of him mentioning her at all was disturbing. She didn't think it was possible to hate him any more than she already did. The sick fantasy he created in his mind about their life together, made her skin crawl.

Before she could say anything, Tina had to swallow back the bile that was making its way up her throat. Once she was sure she wasn't going to be sick, she said, "He told me once that he loved me. He had just…well, he had just finished having sex with me, and I guess he thought there was a tender moment between us, and he said, 'I love you.' I was so scared that he expected me to say it back. When I didn't, I thought for sure he'd hit me. The days following his confession, I noticed the beatings were less frequent, and he was gentler with me. When I didn't reciprocate his feelings, oddly enough he wasn't angry, but he came home a lot less. A month would pass and I never saw him. Then a year ago he started coming home more frequently. That was around the same time he began taking Sam out with him over the weekends and wouldn't bring him home for days. He knew it drove me crazy."

"I'm so sorry. Sam is such a sweet young man. If he's scarred from his dad, you wouldn't know it."

"I know, he hides it well. My biggest fear is that he'll turn out like his father, especially knowing the things Allister exposed him to."

"I understand. Whatever Allister subjected Sam to must have been horrible, and he most likely did it, hoping to…" Suddenly, Kayla's eyes widened, and she blurted out, "Oh, my gosh, I told your brother!"

Confused by her comment, Tina asked, "You told Eddie what?"

Kayla's eyes filled with tears. "I told him what Allister said about his girlfriend, Tina. Eddie completely freaked out! At first, I thought it was because Allister had raped me, but then I realized it was because of something else. Eddie kept repeating your name. Allister had baited me. He had to know I would tell Eddie what he said. When Allister came back in the room with Claire, Eddie jumped up and attacked him. That's when Allister pulled his gun and said he was an idiot to think he didn't recognize him. Now I remember what it was Allister said to your brother. It was 'Tina's the mother of my children,' and that when Eddie went ballistic. If Allister hadn't killed Eddie, your brother would have ripped him to pieces."

Aware of how cruel Allister could be, Tina knew he had enjoyed telling her brother he had fathered her children. That information alone would have sent Eddie over the deep end, which it had clearly done. Allister would have never let Eddie see her again. He would have killed her if he hadn't killed Eddie.

She got up from the sofa and wandered into the kitchen. "Can we go for a walk? I'm suffocating in here."

"Yeah, sure." Kayla got up and grabbed her sweater and handed Tina her jean jacket.

After locking the door behind her, Kayla followed Tina downstairs. Neither were familiar enough with the town to know where they wanted to go, so they just walked. "It's nice to go wherever I want," Tina said once Kayla was beside her. "I keep thinking Allister is stalking me, though. It's a feeling I can't seem to shake. It's something I'll have to work on, I guess, if I'm going to have any chance of a normal life."

Kayla cracked a weak smile. "I was dumped in the bottom of a ship during a terrible storm. I'm kind of grateful they drugged me, so I missed most of it, but when I came around, I thought I was going to die. Saying I was frightened out of my mind hardly describes how scared I was. All I wanted to do was go home and sleep in my own bed and never leave it again. I saw things that I can't get out of my head. Horrible things I've only seen in movies. Seeing them with my own eyes…well, let's just say, staying in bed with the covers pulled over my head seems like the only logical thing for me to do. Especially now that I'm afraid of my own shadow."

"Even with your brother around?"

"Yeah…no, I feel safe around him. But I want to go home and sleep in my bed. I question every measly sound I hear at night while everyone else is asleep. Don't get me wrong, Emer's a great room-mate, but she couldn't stop me from getting scared last night. Every sound I heard creeped me out. I slept on the floor, next to the couch where Clay was sleeping."

"I woke up this morning with Billy asleep in a chair outside my bedroom." Tina smiled when she recalled finding him slouched over in the most uncomfortable position. "I'm not used to this kind of protection, where the one guarding me is there to keep people away from me and not to keep me locked up."

A woman's scream frightened them, causing both to jump and spin around at the same time. Tina and Kayla saw an older woman fighting with her bicycle while yelling obscenities at the clinic. Lily stood at the door begging, "Come on, Mrs. Murphy, I canna sched-ule an appointment without ya! Blimey! You crazy ol' bat!"

Smiling, Kayla took Tina by the arm and led her to the clinic. "Lily!"

"Oh, howya, Kayla."

"My brother said you and Emer had some colorful tactics when dealing with your patients. Now I understand why."

"Ah, never mind about the ol' coot. She's too old ta listen any-way. Come in. Ol' lady Murphy was the last patient today."

"Thanks," Kayla said as she stepped inside.

"Lily, make the appointment for Mrs. Murphy next week and call her with the day and time that she should be at the hospital. The stupid woman won't listen to reason when it comes to her health." Giggling caused Emer to turn around. When she saw Kayla and Tina, she offered, "Sorry, I didn't see you there."

"Geez, Emer. Clay said you had a one-of-a-kind bedside man-ner," Kayla teased.

"Oh, aye, the doc's a class act," the receptionist added.

"Shut up, Lily!" Emer snapped, while smiling. "That woman will forever be a pain in my neck."

Kayla and Tina laughed. Clay had warned them about Emer and her temper, but seeing it firsthand was funny and just the dis-traction they both needed.

"I'm meeting Clay and the kids," Emer continued. "Are you done with your talk?"

"Actually, we were heading into town ourselves. Would you like to walk with us?"

"Yeah, that would be grand. Let me grab my keys and sweater and I'll be ready to go." Then, turning to Lily, she asked, "Lock up, will you?"

*   *   *   *   *

Kate knocked on the door several times before Clay opened it. He stepped aside to let her in. "Hey, how was the drive? Oh, let me take that for you." He took her coat, hung it on the rack by the door.

"I flew in to Cork and took a rental. Cut my time in half."

"Nice. Thanks for coming here to meet with Tina. She and Billy are waiting for you down the hall. Can I get you some coffee?"

"No, thanks. I'm wired up enough."

Clay nodded and led her to the sitting room. He excused himself, allowing her some privacy while she talked to Tina and Billy. Kate had called the meeting, but instead of making Tina come to her office in Dublin, she decided to make the trip out to the farm to speak with her.

What Kate was about to ask, she knew would upset Tina, but there was no way to sugarcoat the question. However, sitting in front of her, Kate struggled to get the words out.

Fidgeting wasn't normal for the director. This case had become personal, something she should have never allowed to happen. She couldn't do anything about it now and needed to get this meeting started. "I have to ask you something, primarily because I made a deal with Allister so he would tell us where you were. Anyway, if he gave up your address, I would…well, he wants a visit with your son, Sam. It will be—"

"No!" The question horrified Tina. She stood up abruptly and paced the small room. As she moved around the tiny space, she rolled her hands over one another. Then she suddenly stopped and faced Kate. "I don't want him to!" she yelled. "Sam can be hotheaded sometimes, and I know he'll want to go just to shout at Allister. I don't want you to ask him." Then she begged, "Please, don't ask him."

"It's one visit and only if Sam agrees. I need to ask you, do you think Sam wants to see his father? Sam's still a minor. The problem is, his father still has some rights where it concerns his children. His solicitor is pushing for the visit."

Agitated by the request, Billy snapped, "This can't be happening. Look, Tina's parents are here and after the memorial, they're all planning to fly back to the States. Allister can't interfere with their leaving, can he?"

"Honestly, I don't know. I don't know if Allister will let it go after he sees his son. But now with his solicitor involved, you might not get to leave as planned."

Despair and fear washed over Tina as she sat down and wept. Neither Kate nor Billy knew what to do. Billy got up and said, "Hold on." He went to the door, opened it, and yelled, "Clay!"

"Yeah! Coming. What is it? What happened?" Clay ran out of the kitchen and stopped in front of Billy with his eyes darting from him to Tina. Seeing her cry put Clay in panic mode. "What's going on?"

"Do you know anyone at the American embassy?"

The question confused him. "I'm sorry, I don't. Why?"

Kate got up and asked, "What are you thinking, Billy?"

"I'm thinking after the memorial, we take Tina and the kids to the American embassy in Dublin and get them protection. Allister can't touch them there."

"Well, that's all good and well, but they can't stay there forever," Kate reasoned.

Billy snapped his fingers, trying to recall something, "What's his name? Your friend, Roman something or other?"

"Roman Jones?" Baffled by all the questions, Clay said, "Okay, Billy, you need to back up a bit and fill us in on what's going through that head of yours. You're only feeding us broken thoughts."

Tina stood next to Billy. He glanced over at her and exhaled. "Okay, if the court is even entertaining the idea, as sick as it is, that Sam has to see his father, we need a way out for Tina and her family.

I did this once before when I found a girl in Istanbul. The authorities wouldn't let me take her home because the family that owned her had issues with her leaving. They had convinced the courts that the girl's family owed them a great deal of money because they had paid for her, fed her, given her shelter, and so forth. I sneaked her into the American embassy and put her under diplomatic protection. The ambassador got her out of the country and her family didn't have to pay a dime."

"You've got to be kidding!" Clay said.

"No, I'm not."

"Okay, wait a minute. We do things slightly different in Ireland than they do in Turkey. I have more faith in our courts than that," Kate assured him. "However, if it looks like the court is going to be in favor of Allister, then we have a backup plan. I'll personally drive them to the embassy. But we give the system a chance first."

Billy seemed to be in another world.

"I think Billy's lack of sleep is finally catching up to him. Hey, Billy? Snap out of it. We won't let anything happen to Tina or the kids. Allister can only have a mental hold on us and nothing more. Don't let him get inside your head."

The blank stare lasted only a second, and Billy shook his head, saying, "Yeah, you're right. I just..." Billy took a deep breath and glanced over at Tina. "Sam's not going to see Allister, I promise."

Tina wiped the moisture from her face with her hand and whispered, "Thank you."

"Okay, now that's settled, I have a few other things to work out with you," Kate calmly stated. "If you would have a seat, we'll get through them and my job for today will be done."

"Yeah, sure," Tina agreed.

CHAPTER 15

E ven though Eddie's body was being sent back to Chicago, a memorial service was held for him at the old church Mary had suggested. Behind the church was a timeworn cemetery that recorded the long lineage of many local families as far back as the 1400s. The church's history was such that it had survived quite a few uprisings and battles. It was one of Ireland's finest historical landmarks and a place fitting to hold Eddie's service, especially knowing how much he had loved Ireland.

Clay stood at the pulpit. The church was at full capacity; friends and strangers alike had come to show their respect. Eddie's story was headline news across the globe, and the media had swarmed in on the small church. However, inside the sanctuary, the attendees were spared all the cameras and chaos that came with the media frenzy.

Keeping his eyes locked on Tina and her family, Clay pushed the pandemonium going on outside the church out of his mind and began the service. "We've come to say goodbye to a son, a brother, an uncle and a dear friend. Eulogies are meant to be a time of remembrance, to celebrate the life of our loved ones who have left us. I hope those speaking today can put Eddie's memory in some kind of perspective for Tina and the rest of her family—and help them understand what kind of man he was. When I met Eddie..." Clay paused, thinking back to their first encounter with one another. "Wow, I'm sorry. My life since I arrived in Ireland has been one big blur. I think it was a little over a month ago when we first met. I needed help to find my sister and with one phone call, Eddie strolled into my life. Though I didn't know him well, I considered him a friend."

After Clay looked over his notes, he folded them and slipped them into a Bible. Then, stepping out from behind the podium, he looked out at the audience. "Eddie loved Ireland and spoke about her history as if he was a native. Even knowing she had a dark side to her, he still loved her. His destiny started here and sadly ended here. While he searched for his sister, he was instrumental in bringing home over thirty girls—all strangers, all in need of saving. In the end, his job ultimately took his life but not his legacy."

Then taking a moment, Clay closed his eyes to focus on his next words. Once he was sure of what he wanted to say, he made eye contact with Eddie's sister and offered in a tender voice, "Tina, he loved you so much and never stopped looking for you. It was because of that love; my sister is with us and countless other girls are sitting safely at home today. Eddie was a man of integrity. He was honorable and selfless. He was a man who loved, with every fiber of his being. And the best part about him—he's my brother in Christ, and I will have the honor of meeting him again one day."

Moving back behind the lectern, Clay picked up the Bible, took out several small pieces of paper, and opened it to the scripture that he wanted. His eyes skimmed over the verses before he spoke them from memory. "'Brothers and sisters, we do not want you to be uninformed about those who sleep in death, so that you do not grieve like the rest of mankind, who have no hope. For we believe that Jesus died and rose again, and so we believe that God will bring with Jesus those who have fallen asleep in him.'[7] This, ladies and gentlemen, gives me a great deal of comfort. There is hope through Christ, and because of Him, there's no need to feel sad for Eddie. He's with his Savior."

Then, holding up handwritten sticky notes. Clay said, "I found these tacked to the wall in Eddie's apartment." He glanced at the director of the AHTU. "Sorry, Kate, I probably should have told you I took them, but they're only scriptures, nothing more."

Kate mouthed, "It's okay."

He nodded his thanks and continued. "This one is from 2 Corinthians. 'He comforts us in our affliction, so that we may be able to comfort those who are in any kind of affliction, through the

---

[7] 1 Thessalonians 4:13–14 (NIV).

comfort we ourselves receive from God.' This was Eddie. He turned a horrible situation in his life into something good by helping others, like me, who were experiencing the same thing. I'm a beneficiary of his afflictions."

Moisture filled Clay's eyes, and he quickly wiped them. "Eddie was hurting, but it didn't stop him from helping others. Um…these other notes kind of confused me at first when I found them. I mean, knowing what the wall in his apartment meant to him. The first one is Jeremiah 29:11, which says, '"For I know the plans I have for you"—this is the LORD's declaration—"plans for your well-being, not for disaster, to give you a future and a hope.' And then again in John 16:33: 'I have told you these things so that in me you may have peace. You will have suffering in this world. Be courageous! I have conquered the world.'" I think Eddie knew that if he couldn't change his suffering, he would find a way to prosper from it."

Looking at Kayla, Clay explained, "Eddie told me, 'With a wee bit of luck and a whole lot of grace from the good Lord above, we'll find your sister.' I remember being surprised when he said that. I thought he was just pacifying me because of my faith." He smiled at his sister and then set his gaze on Tina. "But instead, these scriptures solidify his devotion to God and wiped out any doubts I had about Eddie's sincerity. I remember his most profound words. 'I've faith that God will one day bring my sister home, yet I believe it won't be me that does it.'"

Holding up the Bible in his hand, Clay excitedly said, "This is Eddie's Bible, and I stayed up all night reading the notes he'd written. He'd made the scriptures personal to him. Listen to this," he quickly flipped through the Holy Scriptures, found the page he wanted and read from its margin, "'I consider my suffering in this present time won't compare with the glory that God will reveal to me because everything works together for good of those that love Him and serve Him.' He personalized Roman 8:18 and 28 to fit his life. I mean the man's faith astounds me. If I only had an ounce of it…"

When he spoke his next words, it was with less animation. "Eddie knew God would bring you home, Tina. Why did he believe so profoundly that you would be found? Simply put, it's because of

God's promise. Eddie wrote that promise down in his own words next to Deuteronomy 31:8. 'The LORD himself goes before Tina; he will never leave her nor forsake her. Do not be afraid Tina or discouraged.'" Then, turning to another scripture, Clay read, "Though Tina walks through the valley of the shadows of death, please don't let her fear the evil that surrounds her, let Tina know You are with her, Jesus. Eddie believed God had placed a shield of protection around you. He knew Christ would protect you when he was gone, no matter where you were."

Clay's eyes glistened while offering his final thoughts. "Eddie doesn't want us to weep for him, no more than he wants us to praise him for the work he did. His search may have started with Tina, but in the end, it helped him to be the servant God had intended him to be. He's safe now, in his Savior's arms. I won't weep for him because that's not what Eddie would want. I will rejoice because of him and am so grateful to have had the honor of knowing him."

Tina dabbed her eyes with a tissue as Clay took the steps down from the pulpit and walked up to her. He gave her a hug and kissed the top of her head. Then turning his attention to Sam, he swallowed the teen with his embrace, nearly crushing the young man. When he let go, he took Sam's face in both hands and said, "Sam, your uncle has given you a gift, a powerful example to follow. You treasure it and hang on to it! It will help you when you hit that fork in the road. You can either be your uncle's nephew or your father's son. That path between right and wrong, good and evil, will always be in front of you. Choose wisely and always remember what your uncle did *for* you, not what your father did *to* you." Clay handed the young man the Bible he had used during the eulogy. "This was Eddie's. You'll find all his notes and thoughts in its margins. I know he would want you to have it."

Through tears, Sam said, "Thank you. I promise to read all of it."

Happy to hear that, Clay shook the young man's hand and then glanced over at his mother. "These are for you, Tina. They're the scriptures that Eddie handwrote and had tacked all over his walls in his apartment."

"Thank you, Clay. Thank you for everything you've done for us," she said, weeping.

"You need to understand, I didn't do anything. It was God and all the people he brought together: your brother, Kate, Billy, Patrick, and his team. They're the ones you should thank. I got to sit back and watch a real honest-to-goodness miracle unfold. I'm glad you're safe and going home. That's all Eddie ever wanted for you."

She hugged Clay and repeated her thanks. He gave her a reassuring smile before he took the empty spot next to his sister, wrapping his arms around her. For the first time in weeks, he felt free from all the bottled-up anxiety he had carried with him. He had his sister back and that was a glorious feeling. But even better than that, he had his faith back, and that was a feeling of insurmountable joy.

Claire stood at the lectern and cleared her throat. The mic carried her voice. "Sorry." Clay looked at her and grinned. Comforted by that simple action, she said, "I'm Claire and though I don't have scriptures to offer, I do have a story to share with you about Eddie. Even though I have no doubt he was a gentleman, he punched me in the face so hard it knocked me out."

The sanctuary fell silent and Claire's face turned red. "Eh, I probably shouldn't have started with that, but it was a punch that ultimately saved my life. It stopped the men from doing anything to me. You see, Eddie knew if I was awake, the men would have... well, let's just say he saved me from anyone having their way with me. When we were on the trawler, I remember him saying, 'Apologies, Jesus, for doubting you.' and I slugged him so hard for trying to blame God for the predicament we were in." Her eyes glistened as she recalled the bittersweet moment. "Then he said he wasn't blaming Him. They were just words of gratitude from a humble servant. I'm not a religious person so it confused me as to why we should be grateful, and Eddie simply said, 'We're alive, aren't we?' At the time I was so angry at him, but I knew he was right."

Taking a tissue from a box on the stand next to her, Claire dabbed her eyes and glanced over at Tina. "He saved my life several times during the short period we were together, and he always shrugged it off by saying, 'No thanks to me, just to God.' Honestly, who saves someone and then gives credit to some imaginary being?" Claire choked and wiped her eyes again. "Your brother, Tina, taught me more about God's mercy than a lifetime of church and gave his life without a second thought. If I only had an ounce of his bravery, kindness, selflessness, and passion, I would be a better person. There will never be a day that goes by, that I won't think about him. I just…I just wanted you to know."

Claire stepped down from the stage and gave Tina a hug before she went back to her seat. Billy was the last one to speak about Eddie. He filled in the last fifteen years of his friend's life for his family as best he could. It was a tribute to a man who had dedicated his life to find his sister, and because of that commitment, his sister was finally going home.

Noah, who had returned from Cork to help with the service, made an announcement at Kate's request. "Because the media has planted themselves everywhere around the church, Kate has asked that you allow the family to leave the sanctuary first please. Now if you'll all bow your heads, I'll pray."

*   *   *   *   *

The chaos outside the church made it difficult for the police to push back the crowd. Once Tina and her family were in their cars, the drivers moved away from the church and headed to Ian's.

At the farm, Ian and Mary welcomed everyone. The house was full with Eddie's mom and dad, his aunt and cousin, and a few women he had helped over the years, and Patrick and his team. Emer and Lily were invited, along with a few locals that had offered Clay support when he needed it the most. Because of the large crowd, Tina was somewhat overwhelmed and sneaked off to find a quiet place outside.

Emer found her lost in thought, near the gate to the cow pasture. "Hey, you okay?"

Startled, she whipped around, placed her hand over her chest, and exhaled slowly. "Wow, yeah, I didn't hear you come."

"Sorry. I didn't mean to spook you."

"That you can't apologize for. I'm naturally a nervous person, thanks to Allister."

"Yes, I should have remembered and called out to you, sorry," Emer offered. "You're not used to this many people being around you either, are you?"

"No. Seeing my parents has been the best thing ever, but their doting over me is making everything close in around me. I just needed to escape for a few minutes. Is that a terrible thing to say?"

Emer leaned against the small wall that went around the field behind her and folded her arms. She glanced at the house before she answered, "No, it's not. You were a prisoner for fifteen years and only had your children and...well...anyway, not a lot of people in your life during that time, and now you'll never be alone. That's a huge adjustment—something your family will have to understand. Your children don't seem to mind though. They're playing with the other kids, enjoying themselves."

Tina smiled in the direction of the house. "That's a blessing, isn't it? It'll be easier if I'm the only one needing space. My parents have been great with the kids, and the children love having grandparents. It'll all work itself out, I'm sure."

"This may be a stupid question, but Allister...did he have a family outside of you and the children?"

Never having thought about it, Tina answered, "Honestly, I don't know."

Emer gave her an understanding nod.

"I mean, I don't want to seem heartless, but I don't care if he does. When I leave Ireland, I want to leave everything about him here. I hope there will come a day when I won't think of him or ever have to utter his name again."

Pushing herself away from the wall, Emer stood in front of Tina and said in a more serious tone, "I hope I'm not stepping over some imaginary boundary, but I want you to understand, this will be a huge adjustment for you and your children. I see what Kayla's going through, and she only had to deal with that monster for a short time. Don't expect to get over this just because you're free and out of Ireland. Allister had a mental hold over you that would crush anyone's spirit. When you go home, find someone to talk to. A professional or a good friend. You may be free physically, but not mentally, and that will take time."

"Thanks. I know you're right, but it's hard for me to talk about this. Clay and Billy are the only ones I feel safe around and when I say something, it's like they know immediately what I'm talking about. Trying to do that with my family or even my cousin, Donna… well, it's going to be hard. All I see in their eyes is sympathy and not understanding."

"It'll take time. I don't know Billy well, but Clay…well, it doesn't surprise me you trust him. He has that effect on everyone he meets. You needn't worry too much. Your family will help you get into a daily routine. You'll get busy with your children's school and all the things you did before with your kids. Find a therapist, a good one you feel comfortable with. The first one you go to might not work out for you, but you need to keep looking until you find someone, and when you do, stick with him or her. You need to tend to both your physical and mental health for the sake of your family. Your children need you to be strong for them."

Tina wiped a single tear from her cheek and promised, "I will. Thanks, Emer, for everything. Clay talked a lot about you on our drive from Dublin to here. You're everything he said you'd be."

Emer laughed out loud. "I'll kill him!"

"Now, there's the woman he spoke so much about," Tina said, laughing with her. "I knew you couldn't hold in that feisty personality of yours for too long."

"Exactly how did Clay describe me?"

Tina stepped away from the wall and draped her arm through Emer's. "Seriously! I saw ol' lady Murphy wagging her fist in the air at you when she left your office the other day. Clay was dead on."

Emer jokingly growled. "Ugh! I hate this town."

Both women laughed and headed for the house. Before Emer opened the door, Tina said, "Thanks again for everything. One thing you should know that Clay said about you, something Mrs. Murphy obviously doesn't see, is you're the prettiest and smartest woman he had ever met. And he said that while surrounded by women. Believe me when I say he took the onslaught of heckling that followed like a real trooper, but he never recanted what he said."

That made Emer blush. She opened the kitchen door, offering Tina to go in first. The aroma of something sweet hit them the moment they entered. Mary and Kayla stood by the stove, delighted their brownies had cooked to perfection. Clay was looking for something when Emer saw him and froze with a surprised expression. The awkwardness was obviously mutual when Clay caught sight of her. He stopped what he was doing and stared back. Tina saw their reactions and grinned. Then, turning to Mary, she asked, "Is there anything I can do to help?"

"Oh no, child, everything's taken care of. Ya need only tend ta yer family." Then, grabbing a tray full of rolls, she faced Emer and asked, "Here, lass, would ya take these and put them in the bun holder?"

Pulled from her stupor, Emer answered, "Yeah, sure."

Kayla set the pan of freshly baked brownies on the table. "Clay, hand me the knife, would you?"

Still staring at Emer, he mumbled, "Huh?"

Kayla looked at her brother and then at Emer and chuckled. "The knife please?"

Snapping out of his gawking, he searched the counter for the knife. Emer had it in her hand and handed it to Kayla. Mary didn't miss the exchange either and commented to no one in particular, "Oh my, ya canna blame the boy! She's a beauty ta look at. What will he do when he's gone?"

"Long-distance relationships are hard, but doable," Kayla said, smiling.

Embarrassed by the comments made by Mary and Kayla, Clay bent down and opened the bottom cabinet looking for another serving dish for Mary. He quickly glanced up at Emer and was surprised she wasn't getting upset with them for talking about their nonexistent relationship. Instead, he found her grinning at him.

"Maybe we should just get it over with and have a baby," Emer stated nonchalantly.

Clay pulled out what he was looking for and then stood up too fast, hitting the open cabinet door above him. He grabbed the top of his head and eyed Emer. "Wait! What?"

"Oh, aye, you would make grand babies," Mary said cheerfully.

Kayla giggled while she cut the brownies into small squares. Emer didn't miss a beat and answered him, "Let's have a baby—you know, start a family—together. Besides, the town has us practically married anyway."

Clay couldn't believe his ears. "The problem is, we're *not* married."

Mary took a pan to the sink and said, "Did ya not spend the weekend together?"

"Did we? Is that what the town's saying? Then it must be true."

Emer's comment left Clay speechless. He couldn't believe she was riding the rumor train and seemed to be enjoying it.

"Oh, aye, lass, it is!" Mary turned on the water and washed the dish as if this was a normal everyday discussion.

"There you have it! Now you have to make an honest woman of me. I'll be shamed with the entire village knowing what we've done."

Clay stared at her. Emer didn't normally joke around like this. "Okay, wait a minute." Clay waved his hands in front of him. "We haven't even gone on a date yet."

"Really? I count two. And all those late-night phone calls have to count for something. Not to mention, I've seen you in your kex."

"Kex? What are kex?" Kayla asked.

"My underwear!" Clay answered, never taking his eyes off Emer. "You stormed out of the only meal that would constitute as a date because of the town's gossip about this nonexistent relationship of ours," he reminded her.

"She's seen you in your underwear and you called her in the middle of the night? I've never seen you in your boxers, and I'm your sister!" Kayla stared at her brother, grinning. "Clay, you never call anyone at night, not ever. High school was the last time you ever called a girl just to chit-chat."

Clay looked at his sister and was about to say something, but Emer beat him to it. "Oh, yes, I have, and he did."

"Oh my, I've some words ta tell the ladies in the mornin'," Mary chimed in.

Clay glanced over at Mary and could see she was enjoying herself at his expense. "Okay, I get it. You three ladies are toying with me, but that's okay, I'm an easy target."

"So you're saying you don't want children with me?"

Clay turned red. "Well, I didn't—"

Kayla raised her hand. "Yes please! I would love to be an aunt."

"You don't have a vote," Clay informed his sister.

"You do put a lot of stipulations on our having children. Going on dates and so forth. And to think, all I thought we had to do was have sex."

Mary laughed outright, as did Kayla.

"So that's it!" Clay snapped jokingly. "You think I'm easy and I'll sleep with you because you're drop dead gorgeous and you suggested it?"

"No. Apparently, we have to go on a few dates first." Then Emer looked at Clay shyly and asked, "You think I'm drop dead gorgeous?"

Flustered, Clay answered her question with one of his own. "Do all Irish women drive men crazy or is it just you?"

"Are you calling me a floozie?"

"Ha!" Clay pointed his finger at her. "Finally, a word I don't need translated." Taking a step forward, Clay placed both hands on Emer's shoulders and asked, "Would you like to have dinner with me?"

"Slow it is then," Emer sighed. "Yes, I would love to have dinner with you."

Clay slipped his arms around her and held her. "And yeah, I think you're beautiful."

When he pulled away, he lifted her chin and kissed her on the lips. Mary sniffled and Kayla draped her arm around her. Emer laughed and slugged Clay in the middle of his chest while saying, "I never kiss on the first date, so now you'll have to wait until the third, possibly the fourth date, before you get another one."

"You'll make babies with me, but you won't kiss me?"

"A ring, pal," Emer said, pointing to her wedding finger. Then with an arched eyebrow, she added, "Besides, I'm sure Jesus would take offense to you taking advantage of a new believer."

Her last statement left Clay stunned. Fully aware of the impact it had on him, Emer picked up a tray full of food and took it into the dining room, very pleased with herself.

Kayla laughed and said, "Oh, boy, are you in trouble! Mom and dad would have loved her though. You know that, right?"

Clay grinned and said with little thought, "Yeah, I do. Here, let me take that for you."

CHAPTER 16

The sound of feet echoing in the hall didn't sound like his son's. Allister pressed his face against the metal bars so he could see who was coming. The guard only said he had a visitor and nothing more. A second set of footsteps made Allister smile. "Ah, yes, Sammy, my boy." He took his chair, placed it in front of the bar door, and then sat down and waited.

The steps slowed and a woman's voice said, "It's okay, he can't hurt you."

Feet shuffled and Allister grinned. "Ah, come ta me, my boy. Come ta Da."

His euphoria faded when a woman came into view. Baffled for a moment as to why he was seeing Tina and not his son, Allister anger heightened. His eyes bore into her as if trying to penetrate her soul. It was the same cold, hateful look she had seen each time he'd beat her.

"Hello, Allister." She took a deep breath and shuddered. Tina had rehearsed what she wanted to say to him several times before she came. She had even practiced in front of Billy, Sam, and Kayla a few times. Now standing opposite of Allister, the confidence she had walking into the prison was gone.

"Ya seem frightened, darlin'."

Tina pushed her shoulders back, exhibiting her self-assurance. "Seeing you behind bars, I must say, is almost satisfying. But what will be more satisfying is seeing your reaction when I share some news with you."

"I'm sure I can request conjugal visits. You would like that, wouldn't ya, Tina? Feelin' my body up against—"

"Sorry, Allister, this time I don't have to listen to you. However, you need to pay attention and listen carefully to what I have to say.

The court ruled against Sam coming to see you—*ever*. See, I went before the judge yesterday morning because he wanted to hear what I had to say. When I was done, the judge looked at your solicitor and asked if you were ready to confess to multiple counts of rape, abduction, kidnapping, and physical abuse for the last fifteen years— charges, that would sentence you to a lifetime of prison. When your solicitor said he would have to confer with you, the judge announced that while he did that, he should let you know there would be no visits with any children."

Allister yelled, "*Augh*! You stupid woman! I'll have Sammy. He's mine!"

"Actually, I haven't even told you the best part yet. It gets better. Because there are no birth records, the judge was kind enough to exopodite my request for them. And guess what? Your name isn't on any of the documents."

Allister lunged at her through the bars. "I'll kill ya! Sammy's mine. Ya've no idea the things he's seen or done for me, ya dense woman!" Then seeing the defiance in Tina's eyes, he added, "Are ya challengin' me, darlin'? If ya are, then ya need to know, Sammy boy—"

Her voice was bold and showed no sign of fear when she answered, "Oh, I'm fully aware of what you did to *my* son. But Clay told him something at my brother's funeral—he told him, he could either be his father's son, or his uncle's nephew. Sam chose Eddie's memory over yours! He's talking to the police and showing them where you hid all the bodies that you were stupid enough to bury on the back side of your property. Did you think he did all of those terrible things out of some sick love he had for you? You're dumber than I thought. He did them to keep me safe." She took another bold step closer, just inches from his grasp. "And he kept me safe, didn't he?"

Obscenities gushed from Allister's mouth, while he swung his hand out trying to grab her. The air swirl in front of her face, but she didn't flinch. Her lips curled on one side as she stood her ground. She taunted him, and he hated it. This was the first time since her abduction, he had no control over her. Allister's face darkened as he screamed at her. Spittle spewed from his mouth, spraying everywhere. "I'll kill Sammy and all those brats o' yers! I'll slit their throats while ya watch, just like I did yer eejit brother! Oh, aye, lass, I killed him and it was a sweet pleasure ta do so."

The knife she had expected to be thrust into her heart hit its mark. Knowing it would come didn't make it hurt any less, but she wouldn't let Allister see her pain. "I'm fully aware of what you did. Yes, you hurt me. But I'll not shed one tear for you. When you die no one will care, not me nor my children. There's no one in this world that loves you. However, I loved my brother, and I will carry his memory with me forever. When I walk out of this disgusting place, I'll never think of you again."

"Ah, sweet lass, every time ya look at our wee ones, you'll see me. There's no escapin' it!"

"Actually," her temper quieted, "I'll look at them as the gift they are—from a gracious and loving God. They're what He used to keep me sane over the years. I've thanked Him for the last fourteen years for those children, starting with the day Sam was born. See, I never thought of them as being yours to begin with. And now I have the documents to prove it. Goodbye, Allister."

Tina walked away and didn't look back. Allister shouted every profanity he could think of, but instead of making her shudder, her confidence grew.

Kate kept pace with her stride and said, "You did great. One more stop. Are you ready for this?"

"Yes, I am. I'm very ready."

*   *   *   *   *

The women walked through a string of corridors with mechanical doors. Each time they waited for the sound of the buzzer and then the heavy door would slide open. Tina's nerves rattled the moment one closed behind her. What courage she had left was in threads by the time she and Kate passed through the first wing of the prison.

Patrick and Connor met them on the second floor, where three different prison guards escorted them to another isolation wing. Instead of cell bars, this wing had iron mechanical doors, each with a small window. There was another loud buzzing sound and a lock being released before the guard pushed the door open and stepped into an interview room. Patrick and Connor trailed in behind him. Neither Kate nor Tina entered the room until Patrick gave his nod of approval.

A foul musty odor hit Tina and Kate at the same time, making their noses crinkle. The dull gray walls and no windows enhanced the already gloomy atmosphere of the prison. The only items in the room were three chairs and a table placed in its center. Brian Gallagher occupied one chair with his hands and feet chained, and two large guards standing behind him. Connor pulled out a chair for Tina while Patrick did the same for Kate.

Gallagher, not knowing the reason for the impromptu visit by the director of the AHTU and a woman he had never seen before, said, "I'm not talking to you without my solicitor, so you're wasting my time."

"Your time? That's rich coming from you. I should think you would like some adult conversation."

"Your kind of conversation I don't need. I've done nothing wrong! I'll be out before you know it."

Unfazed by his outburst, Kate stared at him. "You needn't talk, you just need to listen. This woman has something to share with you."

Gallagher glared at Tina, making her shudder. "I've no memory of her. Anything she has to say about me will be lies."

Tina took a quick glance at Kate, who patted her arm and said, "What she has to say, you're going to want to hear." Then, nodding at Tina, she added, "Go on. It's okay."

"Um, well, I have no desire to be here any longer than I need to, so I'll just say it. I'm the reason for the collapse of your organization."

Gallagher's facial expression changed, letting both women know they had his attention.

Tina continued, "I might have been the reason, but I'm not the cause. I'm Allister's dirty little secret that he kept from you for the last fifteen years."

Now very interested in what she had to say, Gallagher pulled his chair closer to the table and with his fingers laced together, he placed his hands in front of him. "I'm listening, girl."

"He abducted me fifteen years ago and kept me on property he bought a year later. He had his own fully functioning organization, with his own men. My brother came to Ireland looking for me. I was told you met Eddie the night you killed a young man. See, when you took the other American girl, Kayla, her brother also came here looking for her. He found Allister within a few days of his arrival, but Allister didn't kill Clay, just like he didn't kill my brother. Instead, he enjoyed tormenting them."

Gallagher's jawline worked back and forth as his anger rose.

"Allister knew where Eddie lived. It was easier to taunt him that way. I'm sure he thought it was funny, controlling my brother's emotions the way that he did. Actually, he did it to both of us. He laughed at me every time he said anything about my brother."

It was difficult for Tina to continue, and she stared down at her hands trying to gain control over the raw emotions she was feeling. Before one tear fell, she wiped her eyes, took a deep breath, and slowly exhaled. Then, glancing at Kate, she said, "Sorry, I thought this would be easier."

"You're doing fine. Go on."

Lifting her chin, she made eye contact with Brian once again and said, "But God had other plans and brought Eddie and Clay together. I don't know all the details, but I was told your son, Ronan, liked my brother and invited him to your home. Allister must have recognized Eddie right away, and I'm only guessing, but I'm sure Allister freaked when he saw him. You were never to know about me or the other world he created that didn't include you. That's how he kept me under control, you see. He threatened to kill my brother and my children if I ever tried to leave him."

"You gave him children?" Gallagher asked in disgust.

"Not by choice." Tina's voice was weak, and she fought not to cry.

Kate reached over and placed her hand on Tina's arm. "It's okay, just continue. We have plenty of time. Gallagher doesn't have any place he needs to be."

Gallagher's eyes were intense as he stared at her and agreed, "No, I don't."

Tina swallowed hard and blurted out, "Allister told me once that he would take your place one day soon. That the Ukrainians you worked with preferred to do business with him. He bragged about the millions he was making behind your back. How he was cutting into your business and profits, and you were none the wiser. He was very proud of that fact."

"Why are you telling me this? What is it you hope to gain?"

Sitting up straight, she looked him square in the eyes and explained, "I'm leaving Ireland and have been told I won't have to return. The AHTTF has more than enough to keep Allister in prison for several lifetimes. His men scattered when the authorities arrested him, leaving no one to do his bidding. You, however, have a long reach, even from prison. I know Allister will lie to you, and I wanted you to know the truth. I also want to make sure my family is free from all of this. You can make that happen."

"Aye, but you've told me all I need to know, lass. Why should I care what happens to you or your brats?"

Tina bit her lower lip, cleared her throat, and then said, "Allister told me once that you valued family. I understand it's mostly yours that you appreciate, but I'm begging you to let mine go. We're no threat to you."

"You're going to find out anyway," Kate interjected. "Allister went on a killing spree, not to help you, but to help himself. He was ready to take over your organization. With you in prison, who would run your business for you?"

Gallagher didn't answer, he just glared at the director as she continued with her narrative.

"If you won't say it, I will," Kate offered. "Allister, of course, and that would place him right where he wanted to be. He had been building his own empire, just waiting for the right moment to squeeze you out of yours. Eddie's sudden appearance must have propelled it forward a bit early, is my guess."

Kate struck a nerve. Gallagher ground his teeth back and forth, mulling over the information the women had given him. He was not a man who did favors for anyone. But he hated disloyalty even more. The one man he had trusted with his life and the life of his entire family had deceived him.

His lips curled, showing his yellow teeth and with it a deep guttural noise escaped just before he said, "Oh, aye, lass, you're free to live your life as you please and where you please. There'll be no harm to come to you or your young ones, from me or Allister. I'll see to it."

Anticipating to plead her case more, Tina released the breath she had been holding and said, "Thank you."

"Great!" Kate slapped her hand on the table, jarring both Gallagher and Tina. "We're done here."

Before Tina and Kate got up to leave, Gallagher said, "One last thing, Director. This favor I'm doing for the girl, now you do for my wife. Leave her be. She has no knowledge of my dealings. As Allister did for the lass here, I did for my wife. I love Angela, and I want her to be free from you and all this. Make it happen, and I'll keep my promise to the lass."

"You haven't heard then?"

"Heard what?"

"Angela's no longer under house arrest. We released her last week. We've allowed her to keep a few paintings from your home, which I'm told are quite valuable. She's gone, Brian. She packed up her art and moved."

Gallagher simply nodded that he understood. Standing, Kate placed a hand in the middle of Tina's back and guided her toward the door. Once they stepped out of the room and the door closed behind them, Tina collapsed in Patrick's arms. He held her as her body trembled.

"It's okay. It's over now," Kate said in a reassuring voice. "There's nothing to hold you back. You're free to go. He'll keep Allister in check, I'm sure of it. Gallagher doesn't know everything the AHTTF has on him yet, and once Allister finds out I've had a chat with his boss, he'll tell me everything I need to know about the organization. I now have them working against one another."

Tina stepped out of Patrick's embrace and wiped her eyes. "Thank you. That had to be one of the hardest things I've ever done. But I would do it again if it meant keeping my children safe."

"They're safe," Kate said, looking at her watch. "We need to get you to the airport. Your flight leaves in a few hours, and I need to get you through airport security."

"Then we best get going, ladies," Patrick said, nodding in agreement.

"Thank you, Patrick and Connor, for everything you've done for me, Kayla, and all the other women you are working so hard to save. Please never stop looking for them or fighting for them. I'm proof that even after fifteen years, there's still hope!"

"Aye, lass, you needn't worry 'bout that," Connor said, easing her mind. "We've no plan of stoppin' 'til we've eradicated human trafficking from Ireland. And we'll nae stop if a lead takes us ta foreign lands. It's an oath we've made."

Not able to stop herself, Tina draped her arms around Connor, and he hugged her back. "Thank you so much!"

"Come now, we've a plane ta catch."

Feeling more confident, Tina followed Kate to the elevators. Her only thoughts now were of going home to the States and making a fresh start for herself and her children. She was still young and knew she had a lifetime ahead of her. What she did with that time needed to be something Eddie would be proud of.

As she exited the elevators, Tina felt some of the weight of worry lift from her. Though the mental chains Allister had over her were still there, she knew she would be free of them soon enough. Going home with her parents would be a start.

As she walked through the last door of the prison, making her way toward the Land Rover, she took in a deep breath of fresh air. Freedom came in many forms. Today's freedom was never having to think of Allister again. She would leave all memories of him in Ireland.

Taking one last look at the prison, Tina couldn't hide her bliss. "Thank you, sweet Jesus, for freeing my soul."

Connor held the car door open for her and watched as she got in. "Oh, aye, lass. 'tis a sweet thing ta see ya so happy. Keep your focus on the man upstairs, and you'll have joy for many years ta come."

Tina couldn't stop smiling, and it felt good. Once Connor got in the driver's seat, she said, "I know it won't be easy, but just being able to make my own choices, be them good or bad, makes me happy."

"If it ever gets to be too much for you, I'm just a phone call away," Kate offered.

"Thank you. You'll never know how much that means to me."

Patrick did his usual drumroll on the dash of the Land Rover while saying, "Connor, let's get this lass to the airport."

"On it, boss."

*   *   *   *   *

Farewells never came easy for Clay and leaving Ian and Mary was tough, but saying goodbye to Emer was the hardest. He was happy when she had insisted on coming to Dublin to see him off, but knew it would be difficult for him when it was time to board the airplane.

The night before he and his sister were to leave Ireland, Kayla suggested that he should take Emer out to a nice restaurant. He argued against it because he didn't want to leave her alone. Kayla assured him she would be fine and would spend the evening with Tina and her family until he got back to the hotel. Because of her promise, he took her up on the offer.

Kate had been kind enough to make the reservations for him and even ordered a car since he still didn't know his way around Dublin. He recalled how he felt when he saw Emer walk out of her hotel room, wearing a dress that took his breath away. He hadn't wanted the night to end and was crushed that it would be the last time he'd see her.

When he saw Emer at the hotel, having breakfast with Tina and Kayla, it surprised him. That's when she told him that Kate had offered her a ride to the airport if she wanted to go. Sitting across from her now, in the airport café, Clay was happy she decided to come. Just having the extra time with her made all the difference in the world.

"Are you going to gawk at me, or will there be some dialogue between us soon?" Emer asked.

"Just gawk. I'm afraid I'll say something stupid."

"Like what?" she asked, smiling.

"Like, I'll miss you and wish I wasn't leaving. Or something stupid like, why don't you come with me?"

Emer's smile was captivating, and he loved that it was directed at him. "Well, it would be a stupid thing to say, knowing full well I can't. Besides, what would I do? Be a kept woman? I'm a doctor and a very good one at that."

"That's not true."

"What's not true?"

"The part about you being a good doctor. Mrs. Murphy would argue against that statement and probably win. And no throwing food or you'll get us kicked out of here."

"From this dump? We'd be so lucky," she grinned. "By the way, how did you get me into the international terminal without a boarding pass or passport? I didn't think that was allowed?"

"It's not. I happen to have friends in high places."

"Right, that's very true."

"Listen, I know you can't leave now, but will you think about coming to California for a visit? Let's say, next week?"

"Next week? You're being pushy and somewhat melodramatic, aren't you? I'd have to find a replacement, and that will take some time. So I'd say that next week would be quite impossible."

"Then late-night phone calls it is. There's an eight-hour difference. You'll only be a little sleep deprived," he said with a slight chuckle.

"Honestly, I quite enjoyed our little chats." Emer saw Kate and Tina coming their way, with Patrick and Connor following. She waved at them to catch their attention. "I suppose phone calls will have to do for now," she said, scooting her stool closer to Clay's so the others could sit with them.

"Hey! How did it go?" Emer asked when they sat down.

"Liberating, but very scary," Tina explained. "Allister is in the state I'd hoped to put him in when I gave him the news. It felt good to break the hold he's had over me. But talking to Brian Gallagher was a whole different story. That was tough."

"She did great with both. Now that Gallagher knows what Allister did, I'll get Allister to put Gallagher in a nice neat box for me. With each one feeding me information on the other, neither will ever get out of prison."

"That's terrific news," Clay said. "You're the best, Kate. Thanks for allowing me to stay." Then, glancing over at Patrick and Connor, he added, "And thank you both for putting up with me and for working so hard to find Kayla."

Patrick only smiled while Kate laughed, saying, "You have no idea how close I came to sending you home!"

Clay's demeanor was serious when he said, "I know, I was a bit of a pain, but thanks just the same."

"Only a bit?" Emer teased.

"Never! I don't believe it," Tina said, defending him. "You've been great, Clay. I really appreciate you and Kayla flying home with us, especially since Billy got called onto another case. That poor man, does he ever get any rest?"

"Nae much, lass," Connor answered honestly.

"Preboarding families with small children and first-class passengers for flight 192, going to Chicago O'Hare International, boarding at gate 30. Please have your boarding passes ready. Again, preboarding passengers with small children and first-class for flight 192, going to Chicago O'Hare International, boarding at gate 30."

"We need to get moving," Clay announced. He slipped off his stool and held Emer's for her as she did the same.

"Here, Tina, I almost forgot. This is for you." Kate handed her an envelope.

She eyed it with curiosity. "Thank you. But what is it?"

"Open it."

She ripped the envelope open and pulled out a check. Her eyes widened when she saw the number on it. "I'm sorry. I don't understand."

"This is just a small portion of Allister's money. The court agreed, you and the kids deserve something to get you started. Once the trial is done and the property sold, there might be more. For now, use it to get situated. You'll need it."

"I don't know what to say." Tina hugged Kate. "Thank you so much for everything. If you ever make it to Chicago, you'll always have a place to stay."

"I might take you up on that. I think I'm in need of a holiday."

"You should probably get a move on, Tina," Patrick advised.

Clay nodded in agreement, took Emer's hand, and then stepped around the women and headed for the gate. He leaned toward Emer and whispered, "I'm just going to say it—I'm going to miss you and if you don't come to visit me next week, I'm coming back here. Oh, and I wasn't kidding about the phone calls."

"FaceTime me. Or is it called skyping still?"

Clay smiled. They approached the gate, and he stopped in front of her, saying, "You're going to FaceTime me? Huh, this could be interesting."

"Keep it clean, pal!" Emer laughed.

"Always. Waking you up via FaceTime might be fun," Clay said, chuckling.

"I may not answer," Emer joked, and then in a more hushed voice, she said, "I'm going to miss you too." She grabbed a fist full of his shirt, pulled him toward her and kissed him on the lips. Just as fast, she pushed him back and without a word, made her way over to Kayla.

The kiss surprised Clay, and he watched Emer as she said good-bye to his sister and then to Tina and her family. Connor stood next to him and offered, "That one's a keeper. You'll not find a better woman ta suit ya."

"I'll check in on her, I promise," Kate added.

Never taking his eyes off Emer, he said, "Thanks, but she's not staying."

Kate and Connor both looked at him, amused, but it was Kate that said, "You're pretty sure of yourself."

"It's either that or I'm moving to Ireland," Clay said in a matter-of-fact tone.

Connor grinned and shook Clay's hand.

"Don't forget about her gutsy receptionist," Clay reminded Connor.

"Oh, you'll nae have ta worry 'bout her. I've several dates lined up already."

"Oh, brother! You men. Come here," Kate said, laughing, while motioning for Clay to give her a hug. "I'm sorry for what happened to Kayla, but I'm grateful at the same time. I hope you don't take offense to that, but we wouldn't have been able to get Gallagher without you, Kayla, or Eddie."

"I'm not sure it was worth it," Clay said when they parted. "I mean, losing Eddie and…well, I'm sure Kayla hasn't told me everything." Then, as if he'd put more thought into what she said, he offered, "You're right, of course, Tina's free and that's all Eddie ever wanted. Kayla will heal, as will Tina. So I guess this is it. Thanks again for everything, Kate."

"You're welcome. I wish I could say it was over for Kayla, but it's not. She'll have to come back for court, but she'll have plenty of time to get stronger before that happens. Take care, Clay."

Patrick and Connor stood behind Kate and Emer as they waved goodbye. Clay took one last look at them before he fell in behind his group, boarding the plane. Once he was out of sight, Kate glanced over at Emer. She could see her emotions were in a state of tug-of-war.

Kate nudged Emer with her shoulder and said, "If you're going to tell him, you'd better run."

"What?"

"The two of you are pathetic. Go on! I don't have the power to delay a plane, but I can get you out of jail."

"Out of jail? I think you're seeing something between Clay and me that isn't there."

"Seriously, Emer! Are you going to stand here and argue with me about how you don't care about Clay, or are you going to run and tell him how you really feel?"

"I—"

"Don't think. *Run*! The airline agent has stepped away from the gate, now do it!" Kate ordered, shooing her away with both hands.

"Oh, criminy," Emer said, running toward the jetway.

As she squeezed passed two passengers blocking the door, an airline agent yell for her to stop. She kept running until she collided into Clay at the corner of the jetway. He had turned around to head back toward the terminal, when Emer's arms were suddenly around his neck.

"Emer?" Her unexpected appearance surprised him.

"Miss, you can't be back here without a boarding pass!" the airline agent yelled.

Neither heard her. Emer pressed her forehead against his and whispered, "I love you." Then, without warning, she kissed him.

"Miss...excuse me...sir? She can't be back here! And, sir, you need to board the plane."

Clay heard Kate's voice saying, "I'm the director of the AHTU and this is official business."

The airline agent growled her disapproval by saying, "I have no idea what those initials mean, or how this business," the agent swirled her finger toward Clay and Emer, "could be official. But nothing can stop this plane from leaving!"

Clay lowered Emer to her feet and said, "You're such a troublemaker."

"I am not! I'm just not a rule follower, remember?"

"How could I forget." Then, gazing into her eyes, he said, "I love you too."

There was a loud commotion behind them, as three very large male airport security guards came onto the jetway. Clay and Emer turned to face the ruckus and saw Kate holding up her badge. One security officer took Kate by the arm, ignoring her badge altogether. He escorted her back into the terminal with Kate hurling threatening remarks at him about his losing his job for manhandling her the way he did.

Some passengers boarding the plane had to jump out of the way so not to be trampled on as security hauled the director back to the gate entrance.

"It might be a little longer than a week..." Emer said as one of the other guards grabbed her by the arm and dragged her off, "Though I'm sure I'll have no problem finding a replacement now!"

"If Kate can't get this straightened out," Clay shouted while laughing, "let me know, and I'll send bail money!"

Emer looked back and waved while being forced back to the terminal. The other security guard stood in front of Clay with his arms folded, saying, "Unless you want to be strip searched, I suggest you board the plane now, sir!"

Clay held up his hand and took a step back, grinning. "You do know who that woman is that you just hauled off, don't you?"

"Aye, we do. At least one of 'em. Her face has been plastered all over the telly, as has yours. We're just havin' a wee bit o' fun with her." He held out his hand to Clay and added, "Not to mention, the director's friends waitin' for her asked us to have a go at her. By the way, glad you got your sister back, Mr. Warner. Have a pleasant flight home, sir."

Clay laughed again while shaking the man's hand. "Kate's going to kill Patrick. Go easy on the doctor, would you?"

"She's a pretty one. She's your mot then?"

Clay grinned. "I don't know what that is?"

"Your girl?"

"She doesn't know it yet, but I'm going to marry her," Clay answered while smiling. "Um, listen, good luck. You're going to need it when Kate finds out you're messing with her."

"Oh, aye, but not before we have a good laugh."

Clay shook his head, grinning, and made his way toward the plane. Once on board, a concerned flight attendant greeted him and asked, "All's well, sir?"

Smiling at her, he answered, "For you and me, yes. I'm not sure about the three airport security guys though." She looked past him at the jetway and the passengers coming toward her. She shrugged her shoulders as if nothing mattered and welcomed the people boarding.

Clay found his seat next to his sister and sat down. Kayla studied him for a few seconds before asking, "What was all that noise about back there?"

"Life just got very interesting for three airport security guys," Clay answered, leaning his head back. "Oh, and Emer's going to marry me and move to Fresno."

"Really?" Kayla said, smiling. "That's a little fast. Did you ask her already?"

"Nope. But she is. She just doesn't know it yet."

"Huh. Well, just so you're aware, I'm not moving out, whether you're married or not."

Eyeing his sister, Clay leaned toward her, only inches from her face, and said, "Uh, no you're not, and you're going to come work for me." Then sitting back in his seat, he laughed. "I can't believe I'm going to have two bossy women living with me."

Kayla said nothing at first, and then in a soft voice, she whispered, "Thanks, Clay," and twisted in her seat, giving him a hug.

Surprised by her sudden change in disposition, he hugged her back and offered, "It's okay, Sis. I love you and am glad to have you and all your bossiness back in my life."

She wiped her eyes and punched him in the arm. "Okay, tell me what it is I'm going to being doing for you at your office. I get to be vice-president, right?"

"Ha, no."

"I'm not cleaning toilets."

He grinned at her. "I have a janitorial service to do that. You'll be some place where I can keep an eye on you."

"Great. Helicopter brother it is. I can handle that," she said, smiling back at him.

IRISH SLANG USED AND DEFINITIONS

AHTU: Ireland's Anti-Human Trafficking Unit
AHTTF: Anti-Human Trafficking Task Force
ARW: Army Ranger Wing
batter ya. "Beat you up."
bucket of snot. An ugly person.
chancer. Someone who takes risks.
d'yaknowwhatimeanlike. A filler and words rambled together quickly, used a lot by Dublin youth "Do you know what I mean like?"
eejit. "Idiot."
faffin'. Messing around, wasting time.
Fianogloch (Fi-a-no-glock). Meaning "Rangers."
fluthered. "Drunk."
Garda Síochána (Gar-dah Shee-oh-cahn-nah). The Irish police force for "The Guardians of Peace."
gardai. "Police officers."
Jaysus. "Jesus."
knackered. "Tired."
lashing. "Raining."
local garda. General term for local police.
mad as a box of frogs. "Crazy."
oi. "Hey."
ossified. "Drunk."
River Liffey. A large River Liffey that flows through the city of Dublin.
TVAP. Trafficking Victims Protection Act created by the US State Department to monitor and combat trafficking in persons.
yer codding me. To pull someone's leg, joking.

Dr. Doug Bennett

Dr. Doug Bennett was born in Bakersfield, California and was raised on the east side of town, where he currently lives with his wife, Angie. After a twenty-two-year battle with drugs, Doug found Jesus and was radically filled with the Holy Spirit in 2004. An electrician by trade, Doug went full time into the ministry after a word from Prophet Chris Overstreet in 2008 and an encounter with Heidi Baker in early 2009. Doug founded Magdalene Hope in April 2009 in an effort to reach out to women working in the commercial sex industry, in and around the red-light district of Bakersfield.

In 2013, MH opened Restoration Ranch Women's Shelter, located in Kern County, which is a six-bed, safe facility for women looking to escape the commercial sex industry. In 2016, Doug was nominated and awarded the Individual Humanitarian Award given out by the Bakersfield Chamber of Commerce. In 2017, MH is set to open their first coffee shop, named Rescue Grounds Coffee Company, in partnership with Dignity Health at Bakersfield Memorial Hospital. In 2018, Doug received his doctorate of divinity from Summit Bible College.

There are at least 37 million people in the world today
that were bought or sold for sex and labor.

Magdalene Hope exists to minister the love of Jesus Christ to people
whom society looks down upon. We do this by showing Christ's
unconditional love to sex trafficking victims, prostitutes, pimps,
and johns. We see every life as precious and worthy to be loved.

We believe that there is hope for restoration and healing
through Jesus. The spiritual, emotional, and physical pain
these beautiful girls have been through is more than most
of us can ever imagine. Jesus is the redeemer and can heal
each of these wounds while bringing people close to him.

At Magdalene Hope, we desire freedom for slaves.
That freedom comes through Jesus.

Also by Larissa Self
The Riley Cooper Series of Hope

Open Your Eyes Series
continues with the amazing story of **Savannah**.
Coming 2022

LARISSA SELF

Savannah

OPEN YOUR EYES SERIES BOOK TWO

ABOUT THE ATHOR

Larissa Self lived with her mother and father and two siblings in Tripoli, Libya, Lagos, Nigeria, and Aberdeen, Scotland. She returned home to the United States when she turned eighteen, enrolling in college where she received an electronics degree. She homeschooled her three youngest children over the course of thirteen years and tutored math to other homeschooled students for five years. She is the author of *An Inheritance of Hope*, *The Restoration of Hope*, and *A Beacon of Hope*. Larissa currently resides in Texas with her husband, four dogs, four cats, and the occasional scorpion that sneaks in.

CPSIA information can be obtained
at www.ICGtesting.com
Printed in the USA
BVHW090955291221
625056BV00006B/134